ALSO BY STEPHEN KING

NOVELS

Carrie

'Salem's Lot

The Shining

The Stand

The Dead Zone

Firestarter

Cujo

The Dark Tower:
The Gunslinger

Christine

Pet Sematary

Cycle of the Werewolf

The Talisman (with Peter Straub)

It

The Eyes of the Dragon

Misery

The Tommyknockers

The Dark Tower II:
The Drawing of the Three

The Dark Tower III:
The Waste Lands

The Dark Half

Needful Things

Gerald's Game

Dolores Claiborne

Insomnia

Rose Madder

Desperation

Wizard & Glass

Bag of Bones

The Girl Who Loved Tom Gordon

Hearts in Atlantis

EBOOK

Riding the Bullet

NONFICTION

Danse Macabre

On Writing

AS RICHARD BACHMAN

Rage

The Long Walk

Roadwork

The Running Man

Thinner

The Regulators

COLLECTIONS

Nightshift

Different Seasons

Skeleton Crew

Four Past Midnight

Nightmares and Dreamscapes

SCREENPLAYS

Creepshow

Cat's Eye

Silver Bullet

Maximum Overdrive

Pet Sematary

Golden Years

Sleepwalkers

Storm of the Century

Mark Geyer

STEPHEN KING

THE GREEN MILE

SCRIBNER

New York   London   Toronto   Sydney

SCRIBNER
1230 Avenue of the Americas
New York, NY 10020

First Scribner edition 2000

SCRIBNER and design are trademarks of Macmillan Library Reference USA, Inc.,
used under license by Simon & Schuster, the publisher of this work.

DESIGNED BY ERICH HOBBING

Set in Garamond No. 3

Manufactured in the United States of America

15   17   19   20   18   16

Library of Congress Cataloging-in-Publication Data is available.

ISBN-13:   978-0-7432-1089-8
ISBN-10:   0-7432-1089-1

Introduction

By Ralph Vicinanza

WEDNESDAY NIGHT . . . early September . . . the end of a long, late summer day. My assistants had just left the office when the fax machine went off. I figured it must be the *NYT* bestseller list, since publishers get the list ten days before it runs in the paper and Signet would be sending over a copy. Each week since the first monthly installment of *The Green Mile* was published in March '96 had been thrilling. But this could be it . . . a singular achievement. And there it was: six titles on the paperback bestseller list, including the last title, *Coffey on the Mile,* at #1 for that week of September 15. While any new Stephen King work of fiction does well, I hadn't really expected *The Green Mile* to be the success it turned out to be. There were serious risks involved. But there it was . . . a huge accomplishment and a new first for Stephen King.

First-time achievements have been the hallmark of Steve's career. Still, when I met Steve in 1978, I had to grapple with disappearing translation markets for his novels. While Steve's sales were growing to phenomenal levels here in the United States and even in the United Kingdom, the initial reaction to his work in translation was lackluster, and sales were diminishing. His U.S. agent at the time approached me with the idea of handling his authors in the overseas territories. Steve had voiced his concern that Doubleday, had controlled the King novels overseas, hadn't been able to build any of these markets and that sales were faltering. My strategy was fairly simple. The European hardcover was the domain of the self-appointed literati, and many of these readers would have a bias against a commercial novelist like King. Also, the very expensive hard-

7

cover (close to $35 in many European markets back in '80) would be a burden for typical King readers, most of them in their twenties. Over the course of the next few years, I resold rights to have Steve's novels reissued in handsome paperback editions that we sold at relatively inexpensive prices. We grew the markets carefully and steadily. By the time *It* was released in the mid-'80s, King was a household name throughout most of Europe. When King's German publisher released the book in a larger trade paperback edition retailing for about $20, the book sold an unprecedented 700,000 copies. Normal hardcover sales for a German best-seller were around 100,000 copies. So, obviously, the impact of this marketing was huge. This course repeated itself throughout Europe and the rest of the world, making Stephen King the first truly international megaselling author.

The origins of *The Green Mile* look very modest in retrospect. Malcolm Edwards, a British editor who has also been a friend for more than twenty years, and his family were guests of mine on Long Island in December of '94. I was showing Malcolm my collection of autographed King books when we came upon the first three annual installments of a project entitled *The Plant,* which King self-published and gave out to family and friends as Christmas gifts. Steve had abandoned the project because after *Little Shop of Horrors* was released he thought the premise was too similar. But, in his own way, Steve had started his first serial novel back then in the early '80s. Malcolm and I talked briefly about the literary tradition of novels written in installments and notably the works of Charles Dickens. I chuckled about the real estate agent who sold me this house just a few years earlier and told me she thought that the house suited me perfectly because it looked like it came right out of a Dickens novel. Well, I think more Austen than Dickens, but the coincidence was comical.

About three months later Malcolm phoned from London and suggested that I approach Steve with the idea of doing a serial novel. The idea had stayed with Malcolm and he thought that it could be commercially viable. We talked over the logistics. Malcolm's idea was to run the serial for twelve months or more with each installment costing about £1. It seemed like a gargantuan undertaking. While it could be a success, if it didn't catch on, we'd be out there with one big mess. Something about that and the timing didn't appeal to me. I told Malcolm I'd think about it and let him know.

During my more than twenty years working with Steve, people have approached me with all sorts of ideas for him—a Stephen King comic book, a horror magazine, mugs, T-shirts, you name it. Not so long ago I received a brochure from a furniture manufacturer in Europe. They explained that as the manufacturers of "designer chairs," they would be asking celebrities to allow them to use their names for a particular chair. *"The Stephen King Settee?"* I told them we don't do chairs!

Steve is a writer first and foremost and it's his name and reputation as a writer that's at stake. That's what I consider when I weigh the viability of experiments, whatever they might be. Just a couple of years before, Malcolm had come up with the idea of publishing an illustrated King short story that would have been sold as a high-priced collectors' edition. Malcolm hoped that his then rather small publishing house would publish the book and sell it alongside the new King novel for that year. The problem was that it essentially would be a short story masquerading as a novel with the ticket price of a novel or more. We decided against it. I thought the idea of a serial novel was great but the logistics needed to be worked through and the time wasn't right— based on intuition, pure and simple.

Steve finished his new novel a few months later, so I faxed him a short note asking if he'd be interested in writing a serial novel à la Dickens. I figured he'd get the note and we'd discuss it in a couple of weeks. I'd sent the letter in late September and I left New York a few days later for the Frankfurt Book Fair, the most important and largest publishing convention held annually in Frankfurt, Germany. The fair is probably the busiest time for an agent. Appointments run at half-hour intervals from the early morning well into the night, and I was just about to turn in after the first of these exhausting days, when I noticed a message under my hotel room door saying that Stephen King had called and would like to hear from me as soon as possible. It was very unusual for Steve to call me at Frankfurt. He knew how hectic those days could get.

I returned the call at once and it turned out that Steve was interested in doing a serial novel. In fact, he was very excited about the idea and he thought he had a story in mind that might work. But he wanted a better notion of how we saw the logistics.

So what would this serial look like? I figured that publishing over the course of a year or more would be drawing it out, but a shorter period with monthly installments could work very well. I thought this could happen sometime in '97. Malcolm was also at the fair and we spoke at length the next evening. We thought six to eight installments would be feasible and we thought they should run between 15,000 to 20,000 words each. I called Steve later that night and we discussed our strategy. Steve didn't want to run it for eight months and he was leaning toward four but I still thought that we needed more time to build momentum. Six made sense to both of us. He also thought that since the idea had been proposed by Malcolm, we would allow it to be published in the United Kingdom only and we would give Malcolm's company the exclusive shot at British rights.

Steve started writing and I discussed the rights situation with Malcolm. Of course, Malcolm was delighted with the prospect of publishing this project. We left Frankfurt full of anticipation of what might develop in the next few weeks. I returned to New York and awaited Malcolm's offer for what certainly seemed like the prize of his career. In the meantime Steve's enthusiasm heightened. He called and said that he thought the project was becoming too important to confine to the United Kingdom, so he asked me to offer the book to Signet for U.S. publication.

As an agent who built my company on the sale of international rights, I suggested to Steve that we seriously consider making the release of *The Green Mile* an international publishing event and offering the project to all of his major publishers throughout the world. He was not opposed to this idea. Suddenly the scope of the experiment widened and I knew I was sitting on a unique opportunity.

Days passed and I wondered why I hadn't heard from Malcolm. HarperCollinsUK, where Malcolm now worked, had never published King, and Malcolm would be delivering Steve's new book in this groundbreaking format. Unfortunately, corporate politicos were play-ing their hands and things would not turn out well for Malcolm. He finally called me on a Friday evening in late October '95. He explained there would be no offer for *The Green Mile*. HarperCollins would not participate. Malcolm was devastated.

It was possible that this would kill the project. After all, if it was such a great idea, why wouldn't Malcolm's company offer on it? I was afraid that if Steve had any doubts whatsoever, this decision would confirm and magnify them. But one of the reasons why Steve and I have worked so well together for so long is that parts of us are still boys who want to have fun despite what the "grown-ups" say. We were going to do it! We had something special and we knew it. So I offered the rights to publish the serial in the United States and the United Kingdom to Penguin, Signet's parent company. With HarperCollins no longer in play, it made sense to reverse the deal and start with Steve's U.S. publisher. The Penguin people were in a tizzy. They knew that HarperCollins had gotten a shot at this even before they were aware of it. It was the only time Stephen King had allowed that to happen during his more than fifteen-year exclusive relationship with Signet. As anxious as they were to make a deal, they didn't have a clue as to what they were buying. We had already established that there would be no hardcover. The novel was not only unfinished, but it would be published as it was being written. It was difficult for them to assess the value of this project. I made it as simple as possible so in the event of a failure, we could all pull back the rights and lick our wounds. We accepted less than the usual advance Penguin paid for a King novel, but we retained more than the usual rights; we exercised control in many areas normally reserved by the pub-lisher; and we licensed them the rights only for a short period of time. This would be an experiment in publishing and I wanted to protect my client as well as I could.

The negotiation was done, the contract drafted and the deal closed in two weeks. Publishing deals can take months to negotiate. From my first discussion with Steve during the book fair to the execution of the contract, four weeks had passed. It was early November. No one was sure how this serial format would be received by the public. We hoped it would inject a badly needed dose of adrenaline into the tired mass-market business. But no one was sure. Though Signet moved quickly to secure the rights, their uncertainty was being communicated to Steve in a variety of ways. Steve was getting nervous, and he asked that the schedule be accelerated so the first installment would be released in January. He didn't want the publisher's cold feet to lead to second-guessing.

Steve was well into the first installment and promised a December 1 delivery. Signet were now in a frenzy. They would publish in late February, early March at the latest. I had several meetings with all the people who would be involved with the project—promotion, advertising, sales, editorial. Things were rolling on a power of their own. The meetings generated excitement and enthusiasm. I had faith that this was going to work and I communicated it in the best evangelical style.

Signet felt that they were still hitting some walls. Account managers were nervous about returns. They were afraid that their mass-market accounts would buy lots of copies of the first installment as a novelty and return the unsold copies before the release of the other installments. That fear can be haunting when you consider that publishers sell mass-market books on a returnable basis. The retailer can get full credit simply by tearing off the front cover and mailing it back to the publisher; the rest of the book is thrown away. Our idea was that new readers would come to the series as the excitement grew over the months, but if accounts returned the copies of the first couple of installments before the series was completed, it just wouldn't work. In such a case, the publisher would have to reprint earlier volumes as the series caught on. It would be a publisher's nightmare, large returns and then more demand. But there could be no room for fear here. I was certain that the dynamic that followed King throughout his career would create such a groundswell of excitement that these concerns would evaporate.

The next key issue was pricing and that's one that both Steve and I were sensitive to. An important point of the serial was to sell large numbers of each installment at a relatively inexpensive price. We figured that the cost of the set should run less than what a new King novel would have cost in hardcover. The difference between the total cost and a normal paperback would be offset by this exciting new format, so we wanted the total price to fall between that of a paperback and a hardcover. Price point is an extremely difficult figure to gauge and it's an especially delicate issue to authors like King, who have a devoted readership. Initially, we thought about a $1.99 paperback, but the figures just didn't work. The cost of printing and manufacturing and shipping the books didn't make economic sense. We were being pressed into a $6.99 price per volume and neither Steve nor I liked this at all. We resisted and settled at $2.99 with the longer sixth volume at $3.99. Even then, Elaine Koster, the publisher of Signet, called to run through the figures, pointing out to me that because of Steve's high royalty and the low price point, Signet's profit margin would be so low that, if this experiment didn't work, they'd suffer large losses. I've felt it's important in business ventures for both parties to make a handsome profit and enjoy the mutual benefits of their relationship. The figures spoke for themselves, so we agreed to lower Steve's royalty on the assumption that the lower price would result in more sales, and a lesser percentage of more would exceed a greater percentage of less . . . funny how percentages work that way.

While all of this work was going on with Signet, I also had my office busy selling the international rights in *The Green Mile*. Some foreign publishers like Rolf Schmitz of Bastei in Germany got it instantly . . . others didn't get it at all. Regardless, the project moved forward on its own steam. The excitement was real and everywhere. By January '96 we were ready for a simultaneous release in the United Kingdom, Germany, France, Holland, Spain, and Italy, with the other markets joining in soon after.

The promotion and advertising for *The Green Mile* was a blitz. All the print media were covered. Steve (and the mouse, Mr. Jingles) agreed to do TV advertising spots to promote the book. The first title in the series, *The Two Dead Girls,* went on sale at the end of March . . . and within days we knew it was a hit. It zoomed to the number one position on the *New York Times* best-seller list. Sales were heavy in all locations. We were pleased with the general reaction. While some critics seem to be able to find the cloud in every blue sky, the industry was thankful for the success. Of course, we were far from home free, with five more installments to publish. Would the momentum continue? But from there on, it was about writing rather than publishing. Readers were hooked by the story. Stephen King is an absolutely brilliant writer and this was clearly evident in *The Green Mile.*

The serial format wasn't just about slicing up a novel and publishing it in pieces. Steve devoted a great deal of time and thought to the format. He delivered six separate stories, each with a satisfying ending, as well as an overall story that unifies them and brings the tale of Coffey and Edgecomb to a conclusion. Each installment works by itself but also recaps the previous work and hints at more to come. Few writers have the talent and vision to write like this *and* tackle a new format so successfully that the casual reader might not be aware that it was a challenge at all.

In the end, *The Green Mile* was an enormous success. Roughly 18 million of those little chapbooks were sold. Afterward, Plume, the trade paperback imprint of Penguin, offered the book in a single volume that sold more than 500,000 copies. And then the novel became the basis for the Frank Darabont movie, which is one of my all-time favorite movies based on Steve's work. In 1999 Pocket Books did a single-volume mass-market edition to tie in with the movie and sold over 2 million copies. The book has now been published all over the world in thirty different languages.

Malcolm Edwards left HarperCollins eventually and took a key position at Orion Books, where he published the single-volume U.K. trade paperback edition of the book. It was a huge best-seller. And here it is, *The Green Mile* in hardcover. Now that the movie will soon be released in video and DVD formats, we thought you might like to have a more permanent edition for your shelves. This is just my version of the story of how it got there.

Ralph Vicinanza
May 24, 2000

Foreword: A Letter

Dear Constant Reader,

Life is a capricious business. The story which begins in this little book exists in this form because of a chance remark made by a realtor I have never met. This happened a year ago, on Long Island. Ralph Vicinanza, a longtime friend and business associate of mine (what he does mostly is to sell foreign publishing rights for books and stories), had just rented a house there. The realtor remarked that the house "looked like something out of a story by Charles Dickens."

The remark was still on Ralph's mind when he welcomed his first houseguest, British publisher Malcolm Edwards. He repeated it to Edwards, and they began chatting about Dickens. Edwards mentioned that Dickens had published many of his novels in installments, either folded into magazines or by themselves as chapbooks (I don't know the origin of this word, meaning a smaller-than-average book, but have always loved its air of intimacy and friendliness). Some of the novels, Edwards added, were actually written and revised in the shadow of publication; Charles Dickens was one novelist apparently not afraid of a deadline.

Dickens's serialized novels were immensely popular; so popular, in fact, that one of them precipitated a tragedy in Baltimore. A large group of Dickens fans crowded onto a waterfront dock, anticipating the arrival of an English ship with copies of the final installment of *The Old Curiosity Shop* on board. According to the story, several would-be readers were jostled into the water and drowned.

I don't think either Malcolm or Ralph wanted anyone drowned, but they were curious as to what would happen if serial publication were tried again today. Neither was immediately aware that it has happened (there really is nothing new under the sun) on at least two occasions. Tom Wolfe published the first draft of his novel *Bonfire of the Vanities* serially in *Rolling Stone* magazine, and Michael McDowell (*The Amulet, Gilded Needles, The Elementals,* and the screenplay *Beetlejuice*) published a novel called *Blackwater* in paperback installments. That novel—a horror story about a Southern family with the unpleasant familial trait of turning into alligators—was not McDowell's best, but enjoyed good success for Avon Books, all the same.

. The two men further speculated about what might happen if a writer of popular fiction were to try issuing a novel in chapbook editions today—little paperbacks that might sell for a pound or two in Britain, or perhaps three dollars in America (where most paperbacks now sell for $6.99 or $7.99). Someone like Stephen King might make an interesting go of such an experiment, Malcolm said, and from there the conversation moved on to other topics.

Ralph more or less forgot the idea, but it recurred to him in the fall of 1995, following his return from the Frankfurt Book Fair, a kind of international trade show where every day is a showdown for foreign agents like Ralph. He broached the serialization/chapbook idea to me along with a number of other matters, most of which were automatic turndowns.

The chapbook idea was not an automatic turndown, though; unlike the interview in the Japanese *Playboy* or the all-expenses-paid tour of the Baltic Republics, it struck a bright spark in my imagination. I don't think that I am a modern Dickens—if such a person exists, it is probably John Irving or Salman Rushdie—but I have always loved stories told in episodes. It is a format I first encountered in *The Saturday Evening Post,* and I liked it because the end of each episode made the reader an almost equal participant with the writer—you had a whole week to try to figure out the next twist of the snake. Also, one read and experienced these stories more *intensely,* it seemed to me, because they were rationed. You couldn't gulp, even if you wanted to (and if the story was good, you did).

Best of all, in my house we often read them aloud—my brother, David, one night, myself the next, my mother taking a turn on the third, then back to my brother again. It was a rare chance to enjoy a written work as we enjoyed the movies we went to and the TV programs (*Rawhide, Bonanza, Route 66*) that we watched together; they were a family event. It wasn't until years later that I discovered Dickens's novels had been enjoyed by families of his day in much the same fashion, only their fireside agonizings over the fate of Pip and Oliver and David Copperfield went on for *years* instead of a couple of months (even the longest of the *Post* serials rarely ran much more than eight installments).

There was one other thing that I liked about the idea, an appeal that I suspect only the writer of suspense tales and spooky stories can fully appreciate: in a story which is published in installments, the writer gains an ascendancy over the reader which he or she cannot otherwise enjoy—simply put, Constant Reader, you cannot flip ahead and see how matters turn out.

I still remember walking into our living room once when I was twelve or so and seeing my mother in her favorite rocker, peeking at the end of an Agatha Christie paperback while her finger held her actual place around page 50. I was appalled, and told her so (I was twelve, remember, an age at which boys first dimly begin to realize that they know everything), suggesting that reading the end of a mystery novel before you actually get there was on a par with eating the white stuff out of the middle of Oreo cookies and then throwing the cookies themselves away. She laughed her wonderful unembarrassed laugh and said perhaps that was so, but sometimes she just couldn't resist the temptation. Giving in to temptation was a concept I could understand; I had plenty of my own, even at twelve. But here, at last, is an amusing cure for that temptation. Until the final episode arrives in bookstores, no one is going to know how *The Green Mile* turns out . . . and that may include me.

Although there was no way he could have known it, Ralph Vicinanza mentioned the idea of a novel in installments at what was, for me, the perfect psychological moment. I had been playing with a story idea on a subject I had always suspected I would get around to sooner or later:

the electric chair. "Old Sparky" has fascinated me ever since my first James Cagney movie, and the first Death Row tales I ever read (in a book called *Twenty Thousand Years in Sing Sing,* written by Warden Lewis E. Lawes) fired the darker side of my imagination. What, I wondered, would it be like to walk those last forty yards to the electric chair, knowing you were going to die there? What, for that matter, would it be like to be the man who had to strap the condemned in . . . or pull the switch? What would such a job take out of you? Even creepier, what might it add?

I had tried these basic ideas, always tentatively, on a number of different frameworks over the last twenty or thirty years. I had written one successful novella set in prison (*Rita Hayworth and Shawshank Redemption*), and had sort of come to the conclusion that that was probably it for me, when this take on the idea came along There were lots of things I liked about it, but nothing more than the narrator's essentially decent voice; low-key, honest, perhaps a little wide-eyed, he is a Stephen King narrator if ever there was one. So I got to work, but in a tentative, stop-and-start way. Most of the second chapter was written during a rain delay at Fenway Park!

When Ralph called, I had filled a notebook with scribbled pages of *The Green Mile,* and realized I was building a novel when I should have been spending my time clearing my desk for revisions on a book already written (*Desperation*—you'll see it soon, Constant Reader). At the point I had come to on *Mile,* there are usually just two choices: put it away (probably never to be picked up again) or cast everything else aside and chase.

Ralph suggested a possible third alternative, a story that could be written the same way it would be read—in installments. And I liked the high-wire aspect of it, too: fall down on the job, fail to carry through, and all at once about a million readers are howling for your blood. No one knows this any better than me, unless it's my secretary, Juliann Eugley; we get dozens of angry letters each week, demanding the next book in the *Dark Tower* cycle (patience, followers of Roland; another year or so and your wait will end, I promise). One of these contained a Polaroid of a teddy-bear in chains, with a message cut out of newspaper headlines and magazine covers: RELEASE THE NEXT *DARK TOWER* BOOK AT ONCE OR

THE BEAR DIES, it said. I put it up in my office to remind myself both of my responsibility and of how wonderful it is to have people actually care—a little—about the creatures of one's imagination.

In any case, I've decided to publish *The Green Mile* in a series of small paperbacks, in the nineteenth-century manner, and I hope you'll write and tell me (a) if you liked the story, and (b) if you liked the seldom-used but rather amusing delivery system. It has certainly energized the writing of the story, although at this moment (a rainy evening in October of 1995) it is still far from done, even in rough draft, and the outcome remains in some doubt. That is part of the excitement of the whole thing, though—at this point I'm driving through thick fog with the pedal all the way to the metal.

Most of all, I want to say that if you have even half as much fun reading this as I did writing it, we'll both be well off. Enjoy . . . and why not read this aloud, with a friend? If nothing else, it will shorten the time until the next installment appears on your newsstand or in your local bookstore.

In the meantime, take care, and be good to one another.

—Stephen King

PART ONE

THE TWO DEAD GIRLS

1

THIS HAPPENED in 1932, when the state penitentiary was still at Cold Mountain. And the electric chair was there, too, of course.

The inmates made jokes about the chair, the way people always make jokes about things that frighten them but can't be gotten away from. They called it Old Sparky, or the Big Juicy. They made cracks about the power bill, and how Warden Moores would cook his Thanksgiving dinner that fall, with his wife, Melinda, too sick to cook.

But for the ones who actually had to sit down in that chair, the humor went out of the situation in a hurry. I presided over seventy-eight executions during my time at Cold Mountain (that's one figure I've never been confused about; I'll remember it on my deathbed), and I think that, for most of those men, the truth of what was happening to them finally hit all the way home when their ankles were being clamped to the stout oak of "Old Sparky's" legs. The realization came then (you would see it rising in their eyes, a kind of cold dismay) that their own legs had finished their careers. The blood still ran in them, the muscles were still strong, but they were finished, all the same; they were never going to walk another country mile or dance with a girl at a barn-raising. Old Sparky's clients came to a knowledge of their deaths from the ankles up. There was a black silk bag that went over their heads after they had finished their rambling and mostly disjointed last remarks. It was supposed to be for them, but I always thought it was really for us, to keep us from seeing the awful tide of dismay in their eyes as they realized they were going to die with their knees bent.

There was no death row at Cold Mountain, only E Block, set apart from the other four and about a quarter their size, brick instead of wood, with a horrible bare metal roof that glared in the summer sun like a delirious eyeball. Six cells inside, three on each side of a wide center aisle, each almost twice as big as the cells in the other four blocks. Singles, too. Great accommodations for a prison (especially in the thirties), but the inmates would have traded for cells in any of the other four. Believe me, they would have traded.

There was never a time during my years as block superintendent when all six cells were occupied at one time—thank God for small favors. Four was the most, mixed black and white (at Cold Mountain, there was no segregation among the walking dead), and that was a little piece of hell. One was a woman, Beverly McCall. She was black as the ace of spades and as beautiful as the sin you never had nerve enough to commit. She put up with six years of her husband beating her, but wouldn't put up with his creeping around for a single day. On the evening after she found out he was cheating, she stood waiting for the unfortunate Lester McCall, known to his pals (and, presumably, to his extremely short-term mistress) as Cutter, at the top of the stairs leading to the apartment over his barber shop. She waited until he got his overcoat half off, then dropped his cheating guts onto his tu-tone shoes. Used one of Cutter's own razors to do it. Two nights before she was due to sit in Old Sparky, she called me to her cell and said she had been visited by her African spirit-father in a dream. He told her to discard her slave-name and to die under her free name, Matuomi. That was her request, that her death-warrant should be read under the name of Beverly Matuomi. I guess her spirit-father didn't give her any first name, or one she could make out, anyhow. I said yes, okay, fine. One thing those years serving as the bull-goose screw taught me was never to refuse the condemned unless I absolutely had to. In the case of Beverly Matuomi, it made no difference, anyway. The governor called the next day around three in the afternoon, commuting her sentence to life in the Grassy Valley Penal Facility for Women—all penal and no penis, we used to say back then. I was glad to see Bev's round ass going left instead of right when she got to the duty desk, let me tell you.

Thirty-five years or so later—had to be at least thirty-five—I saw that name on the obituary page of the paper, under a picture of a skinny-faced black lady with a cloud of white hair and glasses with rhinestones at the corners. It was Beverly. She'd spent the last ten years of her life a free woman, the obituary said, and had rescued the small-town library of Raines Falls pretty much single-handed. She had also taught Sunday school and had been much loved in that little backwater. LIBRARIAN DIES OF HEART FAILURE, the headline said, and below that, in smaller type, almost as an afterthought: *Served Over Two Decades in Prison for Murder.* Only the eyes, wide and blazing behind the glasses with the rhinestones at the corners, were the same. They were the eyes of a woman who even at seventy-whatever would not hesitate to pluck a safety razor from its blue jar of disinfectant, if the urge seemed pressing. You know murderers, even if they finish up as old lady librarians in dozey little towns. At least you do if you've spent as much time minding murderers as I did. There was only one time I ever had a question about the nature of my job. That, I reckon, is why I'm writing this.

The wide corridor up the center of E Block was floored with linoleum the color of tired old limes, and so what was called the Last Mile at other prisons was called the Green Mile at Cold Mountain. It ran, I guess, sixty long paces from south to north, bottom to top. At the bottom was the restraint room. At the top end was a T-junction. A left turn meant life—if you called what went on in the sunbaked exercise yard life, and many did; many lived it for years, with no apparent ill effects. Thieves and arsonists and sex criminals, all talking their talk and walking their walk and making their little deals.

A right turn, though—that was different. First you went into my office (where the carpet was also green, a thing I kept meaning to change and not getting around to), and crossed in front of my desk, which was flanked by the American flag on the left and the state flag on the right. On the far side were two doors. One led into the small W.C. that I and the E Block guards (sometimes even Warden Moores) used; the other opened on a kind of storage shed. This was where you ended up when you walked the Green Mile.

It was a small door—I had to duck my head when I went through, and John Coffey actually had to sit and scoot. You came out on a little landing, then went down three cement steps to a board floor. It was a miserable room without heat and with a metal roof, just like the one on the block to which it was an adjunct. It was cold enough in there to see your breath during the winter, and stifling in the summer. At the execution of Elmer Manfred—in July or August of '30, that one was, I believe—we had nine witnesses pass out.

On the left side of the storage shed—again—there was life. Tools (all locked down in frames crisscrossed with chains, as if they were carbine rifles instead of spades and pickaxes), dry goods, sacks of seeds for spring planting in the prison gardens, boxes of toilet paper, pallets cross-loaded with blanks for the prison plate-shop . . . even bags of lime for marking out the baseball diamond and the football gridiron—the cons played in what was known as The Pasture, and fall afternoons were greatly looked forward to at Cold Mountain.

On the right—once again—death. Old Sparky his ownself, sitting up on a plank platform at the southeast corner of the storeroom, stout oak legs, broad oak arms that had absorbed the terrorized sweat of scores of men in the last few minutes of their lives, and the metal cap, usually hung jauntily on the back of the chair, like some robot kid's beanie in a Buck Rogers comic-strip. A cord ran from it and through a gasket-circled hole in the cinderblock wall behind the chair. Off to one side was a galvanized tin bucket. If you looked inside it, you would see a circle of sponge, cut just right to fit the metal cap. Before executions, it was soaked in brine to better conduct the charge of direct-current electricity that ran through the wire, through the sponge, and into the condemned man's brain.

2

1932 WAS THE YEAR of John Coffey. The details would be in the papers, still there for anyone who cared enough to look them out—someone with more energy than one very old man whittling away the end of his life in a Georgia nursing home. That was a hot fall, I remember that; very hot, indeed. October almost like August, and the warden's wife, Melinda, up in the hospital at Indianola for a spell. It was the fall I had the worst urinary infection of my life, not bad enough to put me in the hospital myself, but almost bad enough for me to wish I was dead every time I took a leak. It was the fall of Delacroix, the little half-bald Frenchman with the mouse, the one that came in the summer and did that cute trick with the spool. Mostly, though, it was the fall that John Coffey came to E Block, sentenced to death for the rape-murder of the Detterick twins.

There were four or five guards on the block each shift, but a lot of them were floaters. Dean Stanton, Harry Terwilliger, and Brutus Howell (the men called him "Brutal," but it was a joke, he wouldn't hurt a fly unless he had to, in spite of his size) are all dead now, and so is Percy Wetmore, who really *was* brutal . . . not to mention stupid. Percy had no business on E Block, where an ugly nature was useless and sometimes dangerous, but he was related to the governor by marriage, and so he stayed.

It was Percy Wetmore who ushered Coffey onto the block, with the supposedly traditional cry of "Dead man walking! Dead man walking here!"

It was still as hot as the hinges of hell, October or not. The door to the exercise yard opened, letting in a flood of brilliant light and the biggest man I've ever seen, except for some of the basketball fellows they have on the TV down in the "Resource Room" of this home for wayward droolers I've finished up in. He wore chains on his arms and across his water-barrel of a chest; he wore legirons on his ankles and shuffled a chain between them that sounded like cascading coins as it ran along the lime-colored corridor between the cells. Percy Wetmore was on one side of him, skinny little Harry Terwilliger was on the other, and they looked like children walking along with a captured bear. Even Brutus Howell looked like a kid next to Coffey, and Brutal was over six feet tall and broad as well, a football tackle who had gone on to play at LSU until he flunked out and came back home to the ridges.

John Coffey was black, like most of the men who came to stay for awhile in E Block before dying in Old Sparky's lap, and he stood six feet, eight inches tall. He wasn't all willowy like the TV basketball fellows, though—he was broad in the shoulders and deep through the chest, laced over with muscle in every direction. They'd put him in the biggest denims they could find in Stores, and still the cuffs of the pants rode halfway up on his bunched and scarred calves. The shirt was open to below his chest, and the sleeves stopped somewhere on his forearms. He was holding his cap in one huge hand, which was just as well; perched on his bald mahogany ball of a head, it would have looked like the kind of cap an organ-grinder's monkey wears, only blue instead of red. He looked like he could have snapped the chains that held him as easily as you might snap the ribbons on a Christmas present, but when you looked in his face, you knew he wasn't going to do anything like that. It wasn't dull—although that was what Percy thought, it wasn't long before Percy was calling him the ijit—but *lost*. He kept looking around as if to make out where he was. Maybe even *who* he was. My first thought was that he looked like a black Samson . . . only after Delilah had shaved him smooth as her faithless little hand and taken all the fun out of him.

"Dead man walking!" Percy trumpeted, hauling on that bear of a man's wristcuff, as if he really believed he could move him if Coffey decided he didn't want to move anymore on his own. Harry didn't say anything, but he looked embarrassed. "Dead man—"

"That'll be enough of that," I said. I was in what was going to be Coffey's cell, sitting on his bunk. I'd known he was coming, of course, was there to welcome him and take charge of him, but had no idea of the man's pure size until I saw him. Percy gave me a look that said we all knew I was an asshole (except for the big dummy, of course, who only knew how to rape and murder little girls), but he didn't say anything.

The three of them stopped outside the cell door, which was standing open on its track. I nodded to Harry, who said: "Are you sure you want to be in there with him, boss?" I didn't often hear Harry Terwilliger sound nervous—he'd been right there by my side during the riots of six or seven years before and had never wavered, even when the rumors that some of them had guns began to circulate—but he sounded nervous then.

"Am I going to have any trouble with you, big boy?" I asked, sitting there on the bunk and trying not to look or sound as miserable as I felt—that urinary infection I mentioned earlier wasn't as bad as it eventually got, but it was no day at the beach, let me tell you.

Coffey shook his head slowly—once to the left, once to the right, then back to dead center. Once his eyes found me, they never left me.

Harry had a clipboard with Coffey's forms on it in one hand. "Give it to him," I said to Harry. "Put it in his hand."

Harry did. The big mutt took it like a sleepwalker.

"Now bring it to me, big boy," I said, and Coffey did, his chains jingling and rattling. He had to duck his head just to enter the cell.

I looked up and down mostly to register his height as a fact and not an optical illusion. It was real: six feet, eight inches. His weight was given as two-eighty, but I think that was only an estimate; he had to have been three hundred and twenty, maybe as much as three hundred and fifty pounds. Under the space for scars and identifying marks, one word had been blocked out in the laborious printing of Magnusson, the old trusty in Registration: *Numerous.*

I looked up. Coffey had shuffled a bit to one side and I could see Harry standing across the corridor in front of Delacroix's cell—he was our only other prisoner in E Block when Coffey came in. Del was a slight, balding man with the worried face of an accountant who knows his embezzlement will soon be discovered. His tame mouse was sitting on his shoulder.

Percy Wetmore was leaning in the doorway of the cell which had just become John Coffey's. He had taken his hickory baton out of the custom-made holster he carried it in, and was tapping it against one palm the way a man does when he has a toy he wants to use. And all at once I couldn't stand to have him there. Maybe it was the unseasonable heat, maybe it was the urinary infection heating up my groin and making the itch of my flannel underwear all but unbearable, maybe it was knowing that the state had sent me a black man next door to an idiot to execute, and Percy clearly wanted to hand-tool him a little first. Probably it was all those things. Whatever it was, I stopped caring about his political connections for a little while.

"Percy," I said. "They're moving house over in the infirmary."

"Bill Dodge is in charge of that detail—"

"I know he is," I said. "Go and help him."

"That isn't my job," Percy said. "This big lugoon is my job." "Lugoon" was Percy's joke name for the big ones—a combination of *lug* and *goon*. He resented the big ones. He wasn't skinny, like Harry Terwilliger, but he was short. A banty-rooster sort of guy, the kind that likes to pick fights, especially when the odds are all their way. And vain about his hair. Could hardly keep his hands off it.

"Then your job is done," I said. "Get over to the infirmary."

His lower lip pooched out. Bill Dodge and his men were moving boxes and stacks of sheets, even the beds; the whole infirmary was going to a new frame building over on the west side of the prison. Hot work, heavy lifting. Percy Wetmore wanted no part of either.

"They got all the men they need," he said.

"Then get over there and straw-boss," I said, raising my voice. I saw Harry wince and paid no attention. If the governor ordered Warden Moores to fire me for ruffling the wrong set of feathers, who was Hal Moores going to put in my place? Percy? It was a joke. "I really don't care what you do, Percy, as long as you get out of here for awhile."

For a moment I thought he was going to stick and there'd be real trouble, with Coffey standing there the whole time like the world's biggest stopped clock. Then Percy rammed his billy back into its hand-tooled holster—foolish damned vanitorious thing—and went stalking up the corridor. I don't remember which guard was sitting at the duty desk that day—one of the floaters, I guess—but Percy must not have liked the way he looked, because he growled, "You wipe that smirk off your shitepoke face or I'll wipe it off for you" as he went by. There was a rattle of keys, a momentary blast of hot sunlight from the exercise yard, and then Percy Wetmore was gone, at least for the time being. Delacroix's mouse ran back and forth from one of the little Frenchman's shoulders to the other, his filament whiskers twitching.

"Be still, Mr. Jingles," Delacroix said, and the mouse stopped on his left shoulder just as if he had understood. "Just be so still and so quiet." In Delacroix's lilting Cajun accent, *quiet* came out sounding exotic and foreign—*kwaht*.

"You go lie down, Del," I said curtly. "Take you a rest. This is none of your business, either."

He did as I said. He had raped a young girl and killed her, and had then dropped her body behind the apartment house where she lived, doused it with coal-oil, and then set it on fire, hoping in some muddled way to dispose of the evidence of his crime. The fire had spread to the building itself, had engulfed it, and six more people had died, two of them children. It was the only crime he had in him, and now he was just a mild-mannered man with a worried face, a bald pate, and long hair straggling over the back of his shirt-collar. He would sit down with Old Sparky in a little while, and Old Sparky would make an end to him . . . but whatever it was that had done that awful thing was already gone, and now he lay on his bunk, letting his little companion run squeaking over his hands. In a way, that was the worst; Old Sparky never burned what was inside them, and the drugs they inject them with today don't put it to sleep. It vacates, jumps to someone else, and leaves us to kill husks that aren't really alive anyway.

I turned my attention to the giant.

"If I let Harry take those chains off you, are you going to be nice?"

He nodded. It was like his head-shake: down, up, back to center. His strange eyes looked at me. There was a kind of peace in them, but not a kind I was sure I could trust. I crooked a finger to Harry, who came in and unlocked the chains. He showed no fear now, even when he knelt between Coffey's treetrunk legs to unlock the ankle irons, and that eased me some. It was Percy who had made Harry nervous, and I trusted Harry's instincts. I trusted the instincts of all my day-to-day E Block men, except for Percy.

I have a little set speech I make to men new on the block, but I hesitated with Coffey, because he seemed so abnormal, and not just in his size.

When Harry stood back (Coffey had remained motionless during the entire unlocking ceremony, as placid as a Percheron), I looked up at my new charge, tapping on the clipboard with my thumb, and said: "Can you talk, big boy?"

"Yes, sir, boss, I can talk," he said. His voice was a deep and quiet rumble. It made me think of a freshly tuned tractor engine. He had no real Southern drawl—he said *I*, not *Ah*—but there was a kind of Southern construction to his speech that I noticed later. As if he was *from* the South, but not *of* it. He didn't sound illiterate, but he didn't sound educated. In his speech as in so many other things, he was a mystery. Mostly it was his eyes that troubled me—a kind of peaceful absence in them, as if he were floating far, far away.

"Your name is John Coffey."

"Yes, sir, boss, like the drink, only not spelled the same way."

"So you can spell, can you? Read and write?"

"Just my name, boss," said he, serenely.

I sighed, then gave him a short version of my set speech. I'd already decided he wasn't going to be any trouble. In that I was both right and wrong.

"My name is Paul Edgecombe," I said. "I'm the E Block super—the head screw. You want something from me, ask for me by name. If I'm not here, ask this other man—his name is Harry Terwilliger. Or you ask for Mr. Stanton or Mr. Howell. Do you understand that?"

Coffey nodded.

"Just don't expect to get what you want unless we decide it's what you need—this isn't a hotel. Still with me?"

He nodded again.

"This is a quiet place, big boy—not like the rest of the prison. It's just you and Delacroix over there. You won't work; mostly you'll just sit. Give you a chance to think things over." Too much time for most of them, but I didn't say that. "Sometimes we play the radio, if all's in order. You like the radio?"

He nodded, but doubtfully, as if he wasn't sure what the radio was. I later found out that was true, in a way; Coffey knew things when he encountered them again, but in between he forgot. He knew the characters on *Our Gal Sunday,* but had only the haziest memory of what they'd been up to the last time.

"If you behave, you'll eat on time, you'll never see the solitary cell down at the far end, or have to wear one of those canvas coats that buttons up the back. You'll have two hours in the yard afternoons from four until six, except on Saturdays when the rest of the prison population has their flag football games. You'll have your visitors on Sunday afternoons, if you have someone who wants to visit you. Do you, Coffey?"

He shook his head. "Got none, boss," he said.

"Well, your lawyer, then."

"I believe I've seen the back end of him," he said. "He was give to me on loan. Don't believe he could find his way up here in the mountains."

I looked at him closely to see if he might be trying a little joke, but he didn't seem to be. And I really hadn't expected any different. Appeals weren't for the likes of John Coffey, not back then; they had their day in court and then the world forgot them until they saw a squib in the paper saying a certain fellow had taken a little electricity along about midnight. But a man with a wife, children, or friends to look forward to on Sunday afternoons was easier to control, if control looked to be a problem. Here it didn't, and that was good. Because he was so damned big.

I shifted a little on the bunk, then decided I might feel a little more comfortable in my nether parts if I stood up, and so I did. He backed away from me respectfully, and clasped his hands in front of him.

"Your time here can be easy or hard, big boy, it all depends on you. I'm here to say you might as well make it easy on all of us, because it comes to the same in the end. We'll treat you as right as you deserve. Do you have any questions?"

"Do you leave a light on after bedtime?" he asked right away, as if he had only been waiting for the chance.

I blinked at him. I had been asked a lot of strange questions by new-comers to E Block—once about the size of my wife's tits—but never that one.

Coffey was smiling a trifle uneasily, as if he knew we would think him foolish but couldn't help himself. "Because I get a little scared in the dark sometimes," he said. "If it's a strange place."

I looked at him—the pure size of him—and felt strangely touched. They did touch you, you know; you didn't see them at their worst, hammering out their horrors like demons at a forge.

"Yes, it's pretty bright in here all night long," I said. "Half the lights along the Mile burn from nine until five every morning." Then I real-ized he wouldn't have any idea of what I was talking about—he didn't know the Green Mile from Mississippi mud—and so I pointed. "In the corridor."

He nodded, relieved. I'm not sure he knew what a corridor was, either, but he could see the 200-watt bulbs in their wire cages.

I did something I'd never done to a prisoner before, then—I offered him my hand. Even now I don't know why. Him asking about the lights, maybe. It made Harry Terwilliger blink, I can tell you that. Cof-fey took my hand with surprising gentleness, my hand all but disap-pearing into his, and that was all of it. I had another moth in my killing bottle. We were done.

I stepped out of the cell. Harry pulled the door shut on its track and ran both locks. Coffey stood where he was a moment or two longer, as if he didn't know what to do next, and then he sat down on his bunk, clasped his giant's hands between his knees, and lowered his head like a man who grieves or prays. He said something then in his strange, almost-Southern voice. I heard it with perfect clarity, and although I didn't know much about what he'd done then—you don't need to know about what a man's done in order to feed him and groom him until it's time for him to pay off what he owes—it still gave me a chill.

"I couldn't help it, boss," he said. "I tried to take it back, but it was too late."

3

"YOU'RE GOING to have you some trouble with Percy," Harry said as we walked back up the hall and into my office. Dean Stanton, sort of my third in command—we didn't actually have such things, a situation Percy Wetmore would have fixed up in a flash—was sitting behind my desk, updating the files, a job I never seemed to get around to. He barely looked up as we came in, just gave his little glasses a shove with the ball of his thumb and dived back into his paperwork.

"I been having trouble with that peckerwood since the day he came here," I said, gingerly, pulling my pants away from my crotch and wincing. "Did you hear what he was shouting when he brought that big galoot down?"

"Couldn't very well not," Harry said. "I was there, you know."

"I was in the john and heard it just fine," Dean said. He drew a sheet of paper to him, held it up into the light so I could see there was a coffee-ring as well as typing on it, and then tossed it into the waste basket. " 'Dead man walking.' Must have read that in one of those magazines he likes so much."

And he probably had. Percy Wetmore was a great reader of *Argosy* and *Stag* and *Men's Adventure.* There was a prison tale in every issue, it seemed, and Percy read them avidly, like a man doing research. It was like he was trying to find out how to act, and thought the information was in those magazines. He'd come just after we did Anthony Ray, the hatchet-killer—and he hadn't actually participated in an execution yet, although he'd witnessed one from the switch-room.

"He knows people," Harry said. "He's connected. You'll have to answer for sending him off the block, and you'll have to answer even harder for expecting him to do some real work."

"I don't expect it," I said, and I didn't . . . but I had hopes. Bill Dodge wasn't the sort to let a man just stand around and do the heavy looking-on. "I'm more interested in the big boy, for the time being. Are we going to have trouble with him?"

Harry shook his head with decision.

"He was quiet as a lamb at court down there in Trapingus County," Dean said. He took his little rimless glasses off and began to polish them on his vest. "Of course they had more chains on him than Scrooge saw on Marley's ghost, but he could have kicked up dickens if he'd wanted. That's a pun, son."

"I know," I said, although I didn't. I just hate letting Dean Stanton get the better of me.

"Big one, ain't he?" Dean said.

"He is," I agreed. "Monstrous big."

"Probably have to crank Old Sparky up to Super Bake to fry his ass."

"Don't worry about Old Sparky," I said absently. "He makes the big 'uns little."

Dean pinched the sides of his nose, where there were a couple of angry red patches from his glasses, and nodded. "Yep," he said. "Some truth to that, all right."

I asked, "Do either of you know where he came from before he showed up in . . . Tefton? It was Tefton, wasn't it?"

"Yep," Dean said. "Tefton, down in Trapingus County. Before he showed up there and did what he did, no one seems to know. He just drifted around, I guess. You might be able to find out a little more from the newspapers in the prison library, if you're really interested. They probably won't get around to moving those until next week." He grinned. "You might have to listen to your little buddy bitching and moaning upstairs, though."

"I might just go have a peek, anyway," I said, and later on that afternoon I did.

The prison library was in back of the building that was going to become the prison auto shop—at least that was the plan. More pork in someone's pocket was what I thought, but the Depression was on, and I kept my opinions to myself—the way I should have kept my mouth shut about Percy, but sometimes a man just can't keep it clapped tight. A man's mouth gets him in more trouble than his pecker ever could, most of the time. And the auto shop never happened, anyway—the next spring, the prison moved sixty miles down the road to Brighton. More backroom deals, I reckon. More barrels of pork. Wasn't nothing to me.

Administration had gone to a new building on the east side of the yard; the infirmary was being moved (whose country-bumpkin idea it had been to put an infirmary on the second floor in the first place was just another of life's mysteries); the library was still partly stocked—not that it ever had much in it—and standing empty. The old building was a hot clapboard box kind of shouldered in between A and B Blocks. Their bathrooms backed up on it and the whole building was always swimming with this vague pissy smell, which was probably the only good reason for the move. The library was L-shaped, and not much bigger than my office. I looked for a fan, but they were all gone. It must have been a hundred degrees in there, and I could feel that hot throb in my groin when I sat down. Sort of like an infected tooth. I know that's absurd, considering the region we're talking about here, but it's the only thing I could compare it to. It got a lot worse during and just after taking a leak, which I had done just before walking over.

There was one other fellow there after all—a scrawny old trusty named Gibbons dozing away in the corner with a Wild West novel in his lap and his hat pulled down over his eyes. The heat wasn't bothering him, nor were the grunts, thumps, and occasional curses from the infirmary upstairs (where it had to be at least ten degrees hotter, and I hoped Percy Wetmore was enjoying it). I didn't bother him, either, but went around to the short side of the L, where the newspapers were kept. I thought they might be gone along with the fans, in spite of what Dean had said. They weren't, though, and the business about the Detterick twins was easily enough looked out; it had been front-page news from the commission of the crime in June right through the trial in late August and September.

Soon I had forgotten the heat and the thumps from upstairs and old Gibbons's wheezy snores. The thought of those little nine-year-old girls—their fluffy heads of blonde hair and their engaging Bobbsey Twins smiles—in connection with Coffey's hulking darkness was unpleasant but impossible to ignore. Given his size, it was easy to imagine him actually eating them, like a giant in a fairy tale. What he *had* done was even worse, and it was a lucky thing for him that he hadn't just been lynched right there on the riverbank. If, that was, you considered waiting to walk the Green Mile and sit in Old Sparky's lap lucky.

4

KING COTTON had been deposed in the South seventy years before all these things happened and would never be king again, but in those years of the thirties it had a little revival. There were no more cotton plantations, but there were forty or fifty prosperous cotton farms in the southern part of our state. Klaus Detterick owned one of them. By the standards of the nineteen-fifties he would have been considered only a rung above shirttail poor, but by those of the thirties he was considered well-to-do because he actually paid his store bill in cash at the end of most months, and he could meet the bank president's eyes if they happened to pass on the street. The farmhouse was clean and commodious. In addition to the cotton, there were the other two *c*'s: chickens and a few cows. He and his wife had three children: Howard, who was twelve or thereabouts, and the twin girls, Cora and Kathe.

On a warm night in June of that year, the girls asked for and were given permission to sleep on the screen-enclosed side porch, which ran the length of the house. This was a great treat for them. Their mother kissed them goodnight just shy of nine, when the last light had gone out of the sky. It was the final time she saw either of them until they were in their coffins and the undertaker had repaired the worst of the damage.

Country families went to bed early in those days—"soon as 'twas dark under the table," my own mother sometimes said—and slept soundly. Certainly Klaus, Marjorie, and Howie Detterick did on the night the twins were taken. Klaus would almost certainly have been wakened by

40

Bowser, the family's big old half-breed collie, if he had barked, but Bowser didn't. Not that night, not ever again.

Klaus was up at first light to do the milking. The porch was on the side of the house away from the barn, and Klaus never thought to look in on the girls. Bowser's failure to join him was no cause for alarm, either. The dog held the cows and the chickens alike in great disdain, and usually hid in his doghouse behind the barn when the chores were being performed, unless called . . . and called energetically, at that.

Marjorie came downstairs fifteen minutes or so after her husband had pulled on his boots in the mudroom and tromped out to the barn. She started the coffee, then put bacon on to fry. The combined smells brought Howie down from his room under the eaves, but not the girls from the porch. She sent Howie out to fetch them as she cracked eggs into the bacon grease. Klaus would want the girls out to get fresh ones as soon as breakfast was over. Except no breakfast was eaten in the Detterick house that morning. Howie came back from the porch, white around the gills and with his formerly sleep-puffy eyes now wide open.

"They're gone," he said.

Marjorie went out onto the porch, at first more annoyed than alarmed. She said later that she had supposed, if she had supposed anything, that the girls had decided to take a walk and pick flowers by the dawn's early light. That or some similar green-girl foolishness. One look, and she understood why Howie had been white.

She screamed for Klaus—*shrieked* for him—and Klaus came on the dead run, his workboots whitened by the half-full pail of milk he had spilled on them. What he found on the porch would have jellied the legs of the most courageous parent. The blankets in which the girls would have bundled themselves as the night drew on and grew colder had been cast into one corner. The screen door had been yanked off its upper hinge and hung drunkenly out into the dooryard. And on the boards of both the porch and the steps beyond the mutilated screen door, there were spatters of blood.

Marjorie begged her husband not to go hunting after the girls alone, and not to take their son if he felt he had to go after them, but she could have saved her breath. He took the shotgun he kept mounted in

the mudroom high out of the reach of little hands, and gave Howie the
.22 they had been saving for his birthday in July. Then they went, neither of them paying the slightest attention to the shrieking, weeping
woman who wanted to know what they would do if they met a gang of
wandering hobos or a bunch of bad niggers escaped from the county
farm over in Laduc. In this I think the men were right, you know. The
blood was no longer runny, but it was only tacky yet, and still closer to
true red than the maroon that comes when blood has well dried. The
abduction hadn't happened too long ago. Klaus must have reasoned
that there was still a chance for his girls, and he meant to take it.

Neither one of them could track worth a damn—they were gather-
ers, not hunters, men who went into the woods after coon and deer in
their seasons not because they much wanted to, but because it was an
expected thing. And the dooryard around the house was a blighted
patch of dirt with tracks all overlaid in a meaningless tangle. They
went around the barn, and saw almost at once why Bowser, a bad biter
but a good barker, hadn't sounded the alarm. He lay half in and half
out of a doghouse which had been built of leftover barnboards (there
was a signboard with the word *Bowser* neatly printed on it over the
curved hole in the front—I saw a photograph of it in one of the papers),
his head turned most of the way around on his neck. It would have
taken a man of enormous power to have done that to such a big animal,
the prosecutor later told John Coffey's jury . . . and then he had looked
long and meaningfully at the hulking defendant, sitting behind the
defense table with his eyes cast down and wearing a brand-new pair
of state-bought bib overalls that looked like damnation in and of themselves. Beside the dog, Klaus and Howie found a scrap of cooked link
sausage. The theory—a sound one, I have no doubt—was that Coffey
had first charmed the dog with treats, and then, as Bowser began to eat
the last one, had reached out his hands and broken its neck with one
mighty snap of his wrists.

Beyond the barn was Detterick's north pasture, where no cows
would graze that day. It was drenched with morning dew, and leading
off through it, cutting on a diagonal to the northwest and plain as day,
was the beaten track of a man's passage.

Even in his state of near-hysteria, Klaus Detterick hesitated at first to follow it. It wasn't fear of the man or men who had taken his daughters; it was fear of following the abductor's backtrail . . . of going off in exactly the wrong direction at a time when every second might count.

Howie solved that dilemma by plucking a shred of yellow cotton cloth from a bush growing just beyond the edge of the dooryard. Klaus was shown this same scrap of cloth as he sat on the witness stand, and began to weep as he identified it as a piece of his daughter Kathe's sleeping-shorts. Twenty yards beyond it, hanging from the jutting finger of a juniper shrub, they found a piece of faded green cloth that matched the nightie Cora had been wearing when she kissed her ma and pa goodnight.

The Dettericks, father and son, set off at a near-run with their guns held in front of them, as soldiers do when crossing contested ground under heavy fire. If I wonder at anything that happened that day, it is that the boy, chasing desperately after his father (and often in danger of being left behind completely), never fell and put a bullet in Klaus Detterick's back.

The farmhouse was on the exchange—another sign to the neighbors that the Dettericks were prospering, at least moderately, in disastrous times—and Marjorie used Central to call as many of her neighbors that were also on the exchange as she could, telling them of the disaster which had fallen like a lightning-stroke out of a clear sky, knowing that each call would produce overlapping ripples, like pebbles tossed rapidly into a stilly pond. Then she lifted the handset one last time, and spoke those words that were almost a trademark of the early telephone systems of that time, at least in the rural South: "Hello, Central, are you on the line?"

Central was, but for a moment could say nothing; that worthy woman was all agog. At last she managed, "Yes, ma'am, Mrs. Detterick, I sure am, oh dear sweet blessed Jesus, I'm a-prayin right now that your little girls are all right—"

"Yes, thank you," Marjorie said. "But you tell the Lord to wait long enough for you to put me through to the high sheriff's office down Tefton, all right?"

The Trapingus County high sheriff was a whiskey-nosed old boy with a gut like a washtub and a head of white hair so fine it looked like pipe-cleaner fuzz. I knew him well; he'd been up to Cold Mountain plenty of times to see what he called "his boys" off into the great beyond. Execution witnesses sat in the same folding chairs you've probably sat in yourself a time or two, at funerals or church suppers or Grange bingo (in fact, we borrowed ours from the Mystic Tie No. 44 Grange back in those days), and every time Sheriff Homer Cribus sat down in one, I waited for the dry crack that would signal collapse. I dreaded that day and hoped for it, both at the same time, but it was a day that never came. Not long after—couldn't have been more than one summer after the Detterick girls were abducted—he had a heart attack in his office, apparently while screwing a seventeen-year-old black girl named Daphne Shurtleff. There was a lot of talk about that, with him always sporting his wife and six boys around so prominent come election time—those were the days when, if you wanted to run for something, the saying used to be "Be Baptist or be gone." But people love a hypocrite, you know—they recognize one of their own, and it always feels so good when someone gets caught with his pants down and his dick up and it isn't you.

Besides being a hypocrite, he was incompetent, the kind of fellow who'd get himself photographed petting some lady's cat when it was someone else—Deputy Rob McGee, for instance—who'd actually risked a broken collarbone by going up the tree where Mistress Pussycat was and bringing her down.

McGee listened to Marjorie Detterick babble for maybe two minutes, then cut her off with four or five questions—quick and curt, like a trained fighter's flicking little jabs to the face, the kind of punches that are so small and so hard that the blood comes before the sting. When he had answers to these, he said: "I'll call Bobo Marchant. He's got dogs. You stay put, Miz Detterick. If your man and your boy come back, make them stay put, too. Try, anyway."

Her man and her boy had, meanwhile, followed the track of the abductor three miles to the northwest, but when his trail ran out of open fields and into piney woods, they lost it. They were farmers, not hunters, as I have said, and by then they knew it was an animal they were after. Along the way they had found the yellow top that matched Kathe's shorts, and another piece of Cora's nightie. Both items were drenched with blood, and neither Klaus nor Howie was in as much of a hurry as they had been at the start; a certain cold certainty must have been filtering into their hot hopes by then, working its way downward the way cold water does, sinking because it is heavier.

They cast into the woods, looking for signs, found none, cast in a second place with similar lack of result, then in a third. This time they found a fantail of blood splashed across the needles of a loblolly pine. They went in the direction it seemed to point for a little way, then began the casting-about process again. It was by then nine o'clock in the morning, and from behind them they began to hear shouting men and baying dogs. Rob McGee had put together a jackleg posse in the time it would have taken Sheriff Cribus to finish his first brandy-sweetened cup of coffee, and by quarter past the hour they reached Klaus and Howie Detterick, the two of them stumbling desperately around on the edge of the woods. Soon the men were moving again, with Bobo's dogs leading the way. McGee let Klaus and Howie go on with them— they wouldn't have gone back if he'd ordered them, no matter how much they dreaded the outcome, and McGee must have seen that—but he made them unload their weapons. The others had done the same, McGee said; it was safer. What he didn't tell them (nor did anyone else) was that the Dettericks were the only ones who had been asked to turn their loads over to the deputy. Half-distracted and wanting only to go through to the end of the nightmare and be done with it, they did as he asked. When Rob McGee got the Dettericks to unload their guns and give him their loads, he probably saved John Coffey's miserable excuse for a life.

The baying, yawping dogs pulled them through two miles of scrub pine, always on that same rough northwest heading. Then they came out on the edge of the Trapingus River, which is wide and slow at that point, running southeast through low, wooded hills where families named Cray and Robinette and Duplissey still made their own mandolins and often spat out their own rotted teeth as they plowed; deep countryside where men were apt to handle snakes on Sunday morning and lie down in carnal embrace with their daughters on Sunday night. I knew their families; most of them had sent Sparky a meal from time to time. On the far side of the river, the members of the posse could see the June sun glinting off the steel rails of a Great Southern branch line. About a mile downstream to their right, a trestle crossed toward the coal-fields of West Green.

Here they found a wide trampled patch in the grass and low bushes, a patch so bloody that many of the men had to sprint back into the woods and relieve themselves of their breakfasts. They also found the rest of Cora's nightgown lying in this bloody patch, and Howie, who had held up admirably until then, reeled back against his father and nearly fainted.

And it was here that Bobo Marchant's dogs had their first and only disagreement of the day. There were six in all, two bloodhounds, two bluetick hounds, and a couple of those terrierlike mongrels border Southerners call coon hounds. The coonies wanted to go northwest, upstream along the Trapingus; the rest wanted to go in the other direction, southeast. They got all tangled in their leads, and although the papers said nothing about this part, I could imagine the horrible curses Bobo must have rained down on them as he used his hands—surely the most educated part of him—to get them straightened around again. I have known a few hound-dog men in my time, and it's been my experience that, as a class, they run remarkably true to type.

Bobo shortleashed them into a pack, then ran Cora Detterick's torn nightgown under their noses, to kind of remind them what they were doing out on a day when the temperature would be in the mid-nineties by noon and the noseeums were already circling the heads of the possemen in clouds. The coonies took another sniff, decided to vote the straight ticket, and off they all went downstream, in full cry.

It wasn't but ten minutes later when the men stopped, realizing they could hear more than just the dogs. It was a howling rather than a baying, and a sound no dog had ever made, not even in its dying extremities. It was a sound none of them had ever heard *anything* make, but they knew right away, all of them, that it was a man. So they said, and

I believed them. I think I would have recognized it, too. I have heard men scream just that way, I think, on their way to the electric chair. Not a lot—most button themselves up and go either quiet or joking, like it was the class picnic—but a few. Usually the ones who believe in hell as a real place, and know it is waiting for them at the end of the Green Mile.

Bobo shortleashed his dogs again. They were valuable, and he had no intention of losing them to the psychopath howling and gibbering just down yonder. The other men reloaded their guns and snapped them closed. That howling had chilled them all, and made the sweat under their arms and running down their backs feel like icewater. When men take a chill like that, they need a leader if they are to go on, and Deputy McGee led them. He got out in front and walked briskly (I bet he didn't *feel* very brisk right then, though) to a stand of alders that jutted out of the woods on the right, with the rest of them trundling along nervously about five paces behind. He paused just once, and that was to motion the biggest man among them—Sam Hollis—to keep near Klaus Detterick.

On the other side of the alders there was more open ground stretching back to the woods on the right. On the left was the long, gentle slope of the riverbank. They all stopped where they were, thunderstruck. I think they would have given a good deal to unsee what was before them, and none of them would ever forget it—it was the sort of nightmare, bald and almost smoking in the sun, that lies beyond the drapes and furnishings of good and ordinary lives—church suppers, walks along country lanes, honest work, love-kisses in bed. There is a skull in every man, and I tell you there is a skull in the lives of all men. They saw it that day, those men—they saw what sometimes grins behind the smile.

Sitting on the riverbank in a faded, bloodstained jumper was the biggest man any of them had ever seen—John Coffey. His enormous, splay-toed feet were bare. On his head he wore a faded red bandanna, the way a country woman would wear a kerchief into church. Gnats circled him in a black cloud. Curled in each arm was the body of a naked girl. Their blonde hair, once curly and light as milkweed fluff, was now matted to their heads and streaked red. The man holding them sat bawling up at the sky like a moonstruck calf, his dark brown cheeks slicked with tears, his face twisted in a monstrous cramp of grief. He drew breath in hitches, his chest rising until the snaps holding the straps of his jumper were strained, and then let that vast catch of air out in another of those howls. So often you read in the paper that "the killer showed no remorse," but that wasn't the case here. John Coffey was torn open by what he had done . . . but he would live. The girls would not. They had been torn open in a more fundamental way.

No one seemed to know how long they stood there, looking at the howling man who was, in his turn, looking across the great still plate of the river at a train on the other side, storming down the tracks toward the trestle that crossed the river. It seemed they looked for an hour or for forever, and yet the train got no farther along, it seemed to storm only in one place, like a child doing a tantrum, and the sun did not go behind a cloud, and the sight was not blotted from their eyes. It was there before them, as real as a dogbite. The black man rocked back and forth; Cora and Kathe rocked with him like dolls in the arms of a giant. The bloodstained muscles in the man's huge, bare arms flexed and relaxed, flexed and relaxed, flexed and relaxed.

It was Klaus Detterick who broke the tableau. Screaming, he flung himself at the monster who had raped and killed his daughters. Sam Hollis knew his job and tried to do it, but couldn't. He was six inches taller than Klaus and outweighed him by at least seventy pounds, but Klaus seemed to almost shrug his encircling arms off. Klaus flew across the intervening open ground and launched a flying kick at Coffey's head. His workboot, caked with spilled milk that had already soured in the heat, scored a direct hit on Coffey's left temple, but Coffey seemed not to feel it at all. He only sat there, keening and rocking and looking out across the river; the way I imagine it, he could almost have been a picture out of some piney woods Pentecostal sermon, the faithful follower of the Cross looking out toward Goshen Land . . . if not for the corpses, that was.

It took four men to haul the hysterical farmer off John Coffey, and he fetched Coffey I don't know how many good licks before they finally did. It didn't seem to matter to Coffey, one way or the other; he just went on looking out across the river and keening. As for Detterick, all the fight went out of him when he was finally pulled off—as if some strange galvanizing current had been running through the huge black man (I still have a tendency to think in electrical metaphors; you'll have to pardon me), and when Detterick's contact with that power source was finally broken, he went as limp as a man flung back from a live wire. He knelt wide-legged on the riverbank with his hands to his face, sobbing. Howie joined him and they hugged each other forehead to forehead.

Two men watched them while the rest formed a rifle-toting ring around the rocking, wailing black man. He still seemed not to realize that anyone but him was there. McGee stepped forward, shifted uncertainly from foot to foot for a bit, then hunkered.

"Mister," he said in a quiet voice, and Coffey hushed at once. McGee looked at eyes that were bloodshot from crying. And still they streamed, as if someone had left a faucet on inside him. Those eyes wept, and yet were somehow untouched . . . distant and serene. I thought them the strangest eyes I had ever seen in my life, and McGee felt much the same. "Like the eyes of an animal that never saw a man before," he told a reporter named Hammersmith just before the trial.

"Mister, do you hear me?" McGee asked.

Slowly, Coffey nodded his head. Still he curled his arms around his unspeakable dolls, their chins down on their chests so their faces could not be clearly seen, one of the few mercies God saw fit to bestow that day.

"Do you have a name?" McGee asked.

"John Coffey," he said in a thick and tear-clotted voice. "Coffey like the drink, only not spelled the same way."

McGee nodded, then pointed a thumb at the chest pocket of Coffey's jumper, which was bulging. It looked to McGee like it might have been a gun—not that a man Coffey's size would need a gun to do some major damage, if he decided to go off. "What's that in there, John Coffey? Is that maybe a heater? A pistol?"

"Nosir," Coffey said in his thick voice, and those strange eyes—welling tears and agonized on top, distant and weirdly serene underneath, as if the true John Coffey was somewhere else, looking out on some other landscape where murdered little girls were nothing to get all worked up about—never left Deputy McGee's. "That's just a little lunch I have."

"Oh, now, a little lunch, is that right?" McGee asked, and Coffey nodded and said yessir with his eyes running and clear snot-runners hanging out of his nose. "And where did the likes of you get a little lunch, John Coffey?" Forcing himself to be calm, although he could smell the girls by then, and could see the flies lighting and sampling the places on them that were wet. It was their hair that was the worst, he said later . . . and this wasn't in any newspaper story; it was considered too grisly for family reading. No, this I got from the reporter who wrote the story, Mr. Hammersmith. I looked him up later on, because later on John Coffey became sort of an obsession with me. McGee told this Hammersmith that their blonde hair wasn't blonde anymore. It was auburn. Blood had run down their cheeks out of it like it was a bad dye-job, and you didn't have to be a doctor to see that their fragile skulls had been dashed together with the force of those mighty arms. Probably they had been crying. Probably he had wanted to make them stop. If the girls had been lucky, this had happened before the rapes.

Looking at that made it hard for a man to think, even a man as determined to do his job as Deputy McGee was. Bad thinking could cause mistakes, maybe more bloodshed. McGee drew him in a deep breath and calmed himself. Tried, anyway.

"Wellsir, I don't exactly remember, be dog if I do," Coffey said in his tear-choked voice, "but it's a little lunch, all right, sammidges and I think a swee' pickle."

"I might just have a look for myself, it's all the same to you," McGee said. "Don't you move now, John Coffey. Don't do it, boy, because there are enough guns aimed at you to make you disappear from the waist up should you so much as twitch a finger."

Coffey looked out across the river and didn't move as McGee gently reached into the chest pocket of those biballs and pulled out something wrapped in newspaper and tied with a hank of butcher's twine. McGee snapped the string and opened the paper, although he was pretty sure it was just what Coffey said it was, a little lunch. There was a bacon-tomato sandwich and a jelly fold-over. There was also a pickle, wrapped in its own piece of a funny page John Coffey would never be able to puzzle out. There were no sausages. Bowser had gotten the sausages out of John Coffey's little lunch.

McGee handed the lunch back over his shoulder to one of the other men without taking his eyes off Coffey. Hunkered down like that, he was too close to want to let his attention stray for even a second. The lunch, wrapped up again and tied for good measure, finally ended up with Bobo Marchant, who put it in his knapsack, where he kept treats for his dogs (and a few fishing lures, I shouldn't wonder). It wasn't introduced into evidence at the trial—justice in this part of the world is swift, but not as swift as a bacon-tomato sandwich goes over—though photographs of it were.

"What happened here, John Coffey?" McGee asked in his low, earnest voice. "You want to tell me that?"

And Coffey said to McGee and the others almost exactly the same thing he said to me; they were also the last words the prosecutor said to the jury at Coffey's trial. "I couldn't help it," John Coffey said, holding the murdered, violated girls naked in his arms. The tears began to pour down his cheeks again. "I tried to take it back, but it was too late."

"Boy, you are under arrest for murder," McGee said, and then he spit in John Coffey's face.

The jury was out forty-five minutes. Just about time enough to eat a little lunch of their own. I wonder they had any stomach for it.

5

I THINK YOU KNOW I didn't find all that out during one hot October afternoon in the soon-to-be-defunct prison library, from one set of old newspapers stacked in a pair of Pomona orange crates, but I learned enough to make it hard for me to sleep that night. When my wife got up at two in the morning and found me sitting in the kitchen, drinking buttermilk and smoking home-rolled Bugler, she asked me what was wrong and I lied to her for one of the few times in the long course of our marriage. I said I'd had another run-in with Percy Wetmore. I had, of course, but that wasn't the reason she'd found me sitting up late. I was usually able to leave Percy at the office.

"Well, forget that rotten apple and come on back to bed," she said. "I've got something that'll help you sleep, and you can have all you want."

"That sounds good, but I think we'd better not," I said. "I've got a little something wrong with my waterworks, and wouldn't want to pass it on to you."

She raised an eyebrow. "Waterworks, huh," she said. "I guess you must have taken up with the wrong streetcorner girl the last time you were in Baton Rouge." I've never been in Baton Rouge and never so much as touched a streetcorner girl, and we both knew it.

"It's just a plain old urinary infection," I said. "My mother used to say boys got them from taking a leak when the north wind was blowing."

"Your mother also used to stay in all day if she spilled the salt," my wife said. "Dr. Sadler—"

"No, sir," I said, raising my hand. "He'll want me to take sulfa, and I'll be throwing up in every corner of my office by the end of the week. It'll run its course, but in the meantime, I guess we best stay out of the playground."

She kissed my forehead right over my left eyebrow, which always gives me the prickles . . . as Janice well knew. "Poor baby. As if that awful Percy Wetmore wasn't enough. Come to bed soon."

I did, but before I did, I stepped out onto the back porch to empty out (and checked the wind direction with a wet thumb before I did— what our parents tell us when we are small seldom goes ignored, no matter how foolish it may be). Peeing outdoors is one joy of country living the poets never quite got around to, but it was no joy that night; the water coming out of me burned like a line of lit coal-oil. Yet I thought it had been a little worse that afternoon, and *knew* it had been worse the two or three days before. I had hopes that maybe I had started to mend. Never was a hope more ill-founded. No one had told me that sometimes a bug that gets up inside there, where it's warm and wet, can take a day or two off to rest before coming on strong again. I would have been surprised to know it. I would have been even more surprised to know that, in another fifteen or twenty years, there would be pills you could take that would smack that sort of infection out of your system in record time . . . and while those pills might make you feel a little sick at your stomach or loose in your bowels, they almost never made you vomit the way Dr. Sadler's sulfa pills did. Back in '32, there wasn't much you could do but wait, and try to ignore that feeling that someone had spilled coal-oil inside your works and then touched a match to it.

I finished my butt, went into the bedroom, and finally got to sleep. I dreamed of girls with shy smiles and blood in their hair.

6

THE NEXT MORNING there was a pink memo slip on my desk, asking me to stop by the warden's office as soon as I could. I knew what that was about—there were unwritten but very important rules to the game, and I had stopped playing by them for awhile yesterday—and so I put it off as long as possible. Like going to the doctor about my waterworks problem, I suppose. I've always thought this "get-it-over-with" business was overrated.

Anyway, I didn't hurry to Warden Moores's office. I stripped off my wool uniform coat instead, hung it over the back of my chair, and turned on the fan in the corner—it was another hot one. Then I sat down and went over Brutus Howell's night-sheet. There was nothing there to get alarmed about. Delacroix had wept briefly after turning in—he did most nights, and more for himself than for the folks he had roasted alive, I am quite sure—and then had taken Mr. Jingles, the mouse, out of the cigar box he slept in. That had calmed Del, and he had slept like a baby the rest of the night. Mr. Jingles had most likely spent it on Delacroix's stomach, with his tail curled over his paws, eyes unblinking. It was as if God had decided Delacroix needed a guardian angel, but had decreed in His wisdom that only a mouse would do for a rat like our homicidal friend from Louisiana. Not all *that* was in Brutal's report, of course, but I had done enough night watches myself to fill in the stuff between the lines. There was a brief note about Coffey: "Laid awake, mostly quiet, may have cried some. I tried to get some talk started, but after a few grunted replies from Coffey, gave up. Paul or Harry may have better luck."

"Getting the talk started" was at the center of our job, really. I didn't know it then, but looking back from the vantage point of this strange old age (I think all old ages seem strange to the folk who must endure them), I understand that it was, and why I didn't see it then—it was too big, as central to our work as our respiration was to our lives. It wasn't important that the floaters be good at "getting the talk started," but it was vital for me and Harry and Brutal and Dean . . . and it was one reason why Percy Wetmore was such a disaster. The inmates hated him, the guards hated him . . . everyone hated him, presumably, except for his political connections, Percy himself, and maybe (but only maybe) his mother. He was like a dose of white arsenic sprinkled into a wedding cake, and I think I knew he spelled disaster from the start. He was an accident waiting to happen. As for the rest of us, we would have scoffed at the idea that we functioned most usefully not as the guards of the condemned but as their psychiatrists—part of me still wants to scoff at that idea today—but we knew about getting the talk started . . . and without the talk, men facing Old Sparky had a nasty habit of going insane.

I made a note at the bottom of Brutal's report to talk to John Coffey—to try, at least—and then passed on to a note from Curtis Anderson, the warden's chief assistant. It said that he, Anderson, expected a DOE order for Edward Delacrois (Anderson's misspelling; the man's name was actually Eduard Delacroix) very soon. DOE stood for date of execution, and according to the note, Curtis had been told on good authority that the little Frenchman would take the walk shortly before Halloween—October 27th was his best guess, and Curtis Anderson's guesses were very informed. But before then we could expect a new resident, name of William Wharton. "He's what you like to call 'a problem child,' " Curtis had written in his back-slanting and somehow prissy script. "Crazy-wild and proud of it. Has rambled all over the state for the last year or so, and has hit the big time at last. Killed three people in a holdup, one a pregnant woman, killed a fourth in the getaway. State Patrolman. All he missed was a nun and a blind man." I smiled a little at that. "Wharton is 19 years old, has *Billy the Kid* tattooed on upper l. forearm. You will have to slap his nose a time or two, I guarantee you that, but be careful when you do it. <u>This man just doesn't care.</u>" He had underlined this last sentiment twice, then finished: "Also, he may be a hang-arounder. He's working appeals, and there's the fact that he is a minor."

A crazy kid, working appeals, apt to be around for awhile. Oh, that all sounded just fine. Suddenly the day seemed hotter than ever, and I could no longer put off seeing Warden Moores.

I worked for three wardens during my years as a Cold Mountain guard; Hal Moores was the last and best of them. In a walk. Honest, straightforward, lacking even Curtis Anderson's rudimentary wit, but equipped with just enough political savvy to keep his job during those grim years . . . and enough integrity to keep from getting seduced by the game. He would not rise any higher, but that seemed all right with him. He was fifty-eight or -nine back then, with a deeply lined bloodhound face that Bobo Marchant probably would have felt right at home with. He had white hair and his hands shook with some sort of palsy, but he was strong. The year before, when a prisoner had rushed him in the exercise yard with a shank whittled out of a crate-slat, Moores had stood his ground, grabbed the skatehound's wrist, and had twisted it so hard that the snapping bones had sounded like dry twigs burning in a hot fire. The skatehound, all his grievances forgotten, had gone down on his knees in the dirt and begun screaming for his mother. "I'm not her," Moores said in his cultured Southern voice, "but if I was, I'd raise up my skirts and piss on you from the loins that gave you birth."

When I came into his office, he started to get up and I waved him back down. I took the seat across the desk from him, and began by asking about his wife . . . except in our part of the world, that's not how you do it. "How's that pretty gal of yours?" is what I asked, as if Melinda had seen only seventeen summers instead of sixty-two or -three. My concern was genuine—she was a woman I could have loved and married myself, if the lines of our lives had coincided—but I didn't mind diverting him a little from his main business, either.

He sighed deeply. "Not so well, Paul. Not so well at all."

"More headaches?"

"Only one this week, but it was the worst yet—put her flat on her back for most of the day before yesterday. And now she's developed this weakness in her right hand—" He raised his own liverspotted right hand. We both watched it tremble above his blotter for a moment or two, and then he lowered it again. I could tell he would have given just about anything not to be telling me what he was telling me, and I would have given just about anything not to be hearing it. Melinda's headaches had started in the spring, and all that summer her doctor had been saying they were "nervous-tension migraines," perhaps caused by the stress of Hal's coming retirement. Except that neither of them could *wait* for his retirement, and my own wife had told me that migraine is not a disease of the old but the young; by the time its sufferers reached Melinda Moores's age, they were usually getting better, not worse. And now this weakness of the hand. It didn't sound like nervous tension to me; it sounded like a damned stroke.

"Dr. Haverstrom wants her to go in hospital up to Indianola," Moores said. "Have some tests. Head X-rays, he means. Who knows what else. She is scared to death." He paused, then added, "Truth to tell, so am I."

"Yeah, but you see she does it," I said. "Don't wait. If it turns out to be something they can see with an X-ray, it may turn out to be something they can fix."

"Yes," he agreed, and then, for just a moment—the only one during that part of our interview, as I recall—our eyes met and locked. There was the sort of nakedly perfect understanding between us that needs no words. It could be a stroke, yes. It could also be a cancer growing in her brain, and if it was that, the chances that the doctors at Indianola could do anything about it were slim going on none. This was '32, remember, when even something as relatively simple as a urinary infection was either sulfa and stink or suffer and wait.

"I thank you for your concern, Paul. Now let's talk about Percy Wetmore."

I groaned and covered my eyes.

"I had a call from the state capital this morning," the warden said evenly. "It was quite an angry call, as I'm sure you can imagine. Paul, the governor is so married he's almost not there, if you take my meaning. And his wife has a brother who has one child. That child is Percy

Wetmore. Percy called his dad last night, and Percy's dad called Percy's aunt. Do I have to trace the rest of this out for you?"

"No," I said. "Percy squealed. Just like the schoolroom sissy telling teacher he saw Jack and Jill smooching in the cloakroom."

"Yep," Moores agreed, "that's about the size of it."

"You know what happened between Percy and Delacroix when Delacroix came in?" I asked. "Percy and his damned hickory billy-club?"

"Yes, but—"

"And you know how he runs it along the bars sometimes, just for the pure hell of it. He's mean, and he's stupid, and I don't know how much longer I can take him. That's the truth."

We'd known each other five years. That can be a long time for men who get on well, especially when part of the job is trading life for death. What I'm saying is that he understood what I meant. Not that I would quit; not with the Depression walking around outside the prison walls like a dangerous criminal, one that couldn't be caged as our charges were. Better men than me were out on the roads or riding the rods. I was lucky and knew it—children grown and the mortgage, that two-hundred-pound block of marble, had been off my chest for the last two years. But a man's got to eat, and his wife has to eat, too. Also, we were used to sending our daughter and son-in-law twenty bucks whenever we could afford it (and sometimes when we couldn't, if Jane's letters sounded particularly desperate). He was an out-of-work high-school teacher, and if that didn't qualify for desperate back in those days, then the word had no meaning. So no, you didn't walk off a steady-paycheck job like mine . . . not in cold blood, that was. But my blood *wasn't* cold that fall. The temperatures outside were unseasonable, and the infection crawling around inside me had turned the thermostat up even more. And when a man's in that kind of situation, why, sometimes his fist flies out pretty much of its own accord. And if you slug a connected man like Percy Wetmore once, you might as well just go right on slugging, because there's no going back.

"Stick with it," Moores said quietly. "That's what I called you in here to say. I have it on good authority—the person who called me this morning, in fact—that Percy has an application in at Briar, and that his application will be accepted."

"Briar," I said. That was Briar Ridge, one of two state-run hospitals. "What's this kid doing? Touring state facilities?"

"It's an administration job. Better pay, and papers to push instead of hospital beds in the heat of the day." He gave me a slanted grin. "You know, Paul, you might be shed of him already if you hadn't put him in the switch-room with Van Hay when The Chief walked."

For a moment what he said seemed so peculiar I didn't have a clue what he was getting at. Maybe I didn't *want* to have a clue.

"Where else would I put him?" I asked. "Christ, he hardly knows what he's doing on the block! To make him part of the active execution team—" I didn't finish. Couldn't finish. The potential for screw-ups seemed endless.

"Nevertheless, you'd do well to put him out for Delacroix. If you want to get rid of him, that is."

I looked at him with my jaw hung. At last I was able to get it up where it belonged so I could talk. "What are you saying? That he wants to experience one right up close where he can smell the guy's nuts cooking?"

Moores shrugged. His eyes, so soft when he had been speaking about his wife, now looked flinty. "Delacroix's nuts are going to cook whether Wetmore's on the team or not," he said. "Correct?"

"Yes, but he could screw up. In fact, Hal, he's almost *bound* to screw up. And in front of thirty or so witnesses . . . reporters all the way up from Louisiana . . ."

"You and Brutus Howell will make sure he doesn't," Moores said. "And if he does anyway, it goes on his record, and it'll still be there long after his statehouse connections are gone. You understand?"

I did. It made me feel sick and scared, but I did.

"He may want to stay for Coffey, but if we're lucky, he'll get all he needs from Delacroix. You just make sure you put him out for that one."

I had planned to stick Percy in the switch-room again, then down in the tunnel, riding shotgun on the gurney that would take Delacroix to the meatwagon parked across the road from the prison, but I tossed all those plans back over my shoulder without so much as a second look. I nodded. I had the sense to know it was a gamble I was taking, but I didn't care. If it would get rid of Percy Wetmore, I'd tweak the devil's nose. He could take part in his execution, clamp on the cap, and then look through the grille and tell Van Hay to roll on two; he could watch the little Frenchman ride the lightning that he, Percy Wetmore, had let out of the bottle. Let him have his nasty little thrill, if that's what state-sanctioned murder was to him. Let him go on to Briar Ridge, where he would have his own office and a fan to cool it. And if his uncle by marriage was voted out of office in the next election and he had to find out what work was like in the tough old sunbaked world where not all the bad guys were locked behind bars and sometimes you got your own head whipped, so much the better.

"All right," I said, standing up. "I'll put him out front for Delacroix. And in the meantime, I'll keep the peace."

"Good," he said, and stood up himself. "By the way, how's that problem of yours?" He pointed delicately in the direction of my groin.

"Seems a little better."

"Well, that's fine." He saw me to the door. "What about Coffey, by the way? Is he going to be a problem?"

"I don't think so," I said. "So far he's been as quiet as a dead rooster. He's strange—strange *eyes*—but quiet. We'll keep tabs on him, though. Don't worry about that."

"You know what he did, of course."

"Sure."

He was seeing me through to the outer office by then, where old Miss Hannah sat bashing away at her Underwood as she had ever since the last ice age had ended, it seemed. I was happy to go. All in all, I felt as if I'd gotten off easy. And it was nice to know there was a chance of surviving Percy, after all.

"You send Melinda a whole basket of my love," I said. "And don't go buying you an extra crate of trouble, either. It'll probably turn out to be nothing but migraine, after all."

"You bet," he said, and below his sick eyes, his lips smiled. The combination was damned near ghoulish.

As for me, I went back to E Block to start another day. There was paperwork to be read and written, there were floors to be mopped, there were meals to be served, a duty roster to be made out for the following week, there were a hundred details to be seen to. But mostly there was waiting—in prison there's always plenty of that, so much it never gets done. Waiting for Eduard Delacroix to walk the Green Mile, waiting for William Wharton to arrive with his curled lip and Billy the Kid tattoo, and, most of all, waiting for Percy Wetmore to be gone out of my life.

7

DELACROIX'S MOUSE was one of God's mysteries. I never saw one in E Block before that summer, and never saw one after that fall, when Delacroix passed from our company on a hot and thundery night in October—passed from it in a manner so unspeakable I can barely bring myself to recall it. Delacroix claimed that he trained that mouse, which started its life among us as Steamboat Willy, but I really think it was the other way around. Dean Stanton felt the same way, and so did Brutal. Both of them were there the night the mouse put in its first appearance, and as Brutal said, "The thing 'us half-tame already, and twice as smart as that Cajun what thought he owned it."

Dean and I were in my office, going over the record-box for the last year, getting ready to write follow-up letters to witnesses of five executions, and to write follow-ups to follow-ups in another six stretching all the way back to '29. Basically, we wanted to know just one thing: were they pleased with the service? I know it sounds grotesque, but it was an important consideration. As taxpayers they were our customers, but very special ones. A man or a woman who will turn out at midnight to watch a man die has got a special, pressing reason to be there, a special need, and if execution is a proper punishment, then that need ought to be satisfied. They've had a nightmare. The purpose of the execution is to show them that the nightmare is over. Maybe it even works that way. Sometimes.

"Hey!" Brutal called from outside the door, where he was manning the desk at the head of the hall. "Hey, you two! Get out here!"

Dean and I gazed at each other with identical expressions of alarm, thinking that something had happened to either the Indian from Oklahoma (his name was Arlen Bitterbuck, but we called him The Chief . . . or, in Harry Terwilliger's case, Chief Goat Cheese, because that was what Harry claimed Bitterbuck smelled like), or the fellow we called The President. But then Brutal started to laugh, and we hurried to see what was happening. Laughing in E Block sounded almost as wrong as laughing in church.

Old Toot-Toot, the trusty who ran the food-wagon in those days, had been by with his holy-rolling cartful of goodies, and Brutal had stocked up for a long night—three sandwiches, two pops, and a couple of Moon Pies. Also a side of potato salad Toot had undoubtedly filched from the prison kitchen, which was supposed to be off-limits to him. Brutal had the logbook open in front of him, and for a wonder he hadn't spilled anything on it yet. Of course, he was just getting started.

"What?" Dean asked. "What is it?"

"State legislature must have opened the purse-strings enough to hire another screw this year after all," Brutal said, still laughing. "Lookie yonder."

He pointed and we saw the mouse. I started to laugh, too, and Dean joined in. You really couldn't help it, because a guard doing quarter-hour check rounds was just what that mouse looked like: a tiny, furry guard making sure no one was trying to escape or commit suicide. It would trot a little way toward us along the Green Mile, then turn its head from side to side, as if checking the cells. Then it would make another forward spurt. The fact that we could hear both of our current inmates snoring away in spite of the yelling and the laughter somehow made it even funnier.

It was a perfectly ordinary brown mouse, except for the way it seemed to be checking into the cells. It even went into one or two of them, skipping nimbly in between the lower bars in a way I imagine many of our inmates, past and present, would envy. Except it was *out* that the cons would always be wanting to skip, of course.

The mouse didn't go into either of the occupied cells; only the empties. And finally it had worked its way almost up to where we were.

I kept expecting it to turn back, but it didn't. It showed no fear of us at all.

"It ain't normal for a mouse to come up on people that way," Dean said, a little nervously. "Maybe it's rabid."

"Oh, my Christ," Brutal said through a mouthful of corned-beef sandwich. "The big mouse expert. The Mouse Man. You see it foamin at the mouth, Mouse Man?"

"I can't see its mouth at all," Dean said, and that made us all laugh again. I couldn't see its mouth, either, but I could see the dark little drops that were its eyes, and they didn't look crazy or rabid to me. They looked interested and intelligent. I've put men to death—men with supposedly immortal souls—that looked dumber than that mouse.

It scurried up the Green Mile to a spot that was less than three feet from the duty desk . . . which wasn't something fancy, like you might be imagining, but only the sort of desk the teachers used to sit behind up at the district high school. And there it did stop, curling its tail around its paws as prim as an old lady settling her skirts.

I stopped laughing all at once, suddenly feeling cold through my flesh all the way to the bones. I want to say I don't know why I felt that way—no one likes to come out with something that's going to make them look or sound ridiculous—but of course I do, and if I can tell the truth about the rest, I guess I can tell the truth about this. For a moment I imagined myself to be that mouse, not a guard at all but just another convicted criminal there on the Green Mile, convicted and condemned but still managing to look bravely up at a desk that must have seemed miles high to it (as the judgment seat of God will no doubt someday seem to us), and at the heavy-voiced, blue-coated giants who sat behind it. Giants that shot its kind with BB guns, or swatted them with brooms, or set traps on them, traps that broke their backs while they crept cautiously over the word VICTOR to nibble at the cheese on the little copper plate.

There was no broom by the duty desk, but there was a rolling mop-bucket with the mop still in the wringer; I'd taken my turn at swabbing the green lino and all six of the cells shortly before sitting down to the record-box with Dean. I saw that Dean meant to grab the mop and take a swing with it. I touched his wrist just as his fingers touched the slender wooden handle. "Leave it be," I said.

He shrugged and drew his hand back. I had a feeling he didn't want to swat it any more than I did.

Brutal tore a corner off his corned-beef sandwich and held it out over the front of the desk, tweezed delicately between two fingers. The mouse seemed to look up with an even livelier interest, as if it knew exactly what it was. Probably did; I could see its whiskers twitch as its nose wriggled.

"Aw, Brutal, no!" Dean exclaimed, then looked at me. "Don't let him do that, Paul! If he's gonna feed the damn thing, we might as well put out the welcome mat for anything on four legs."

"I just want to see what he'll do," Brutal said. "In the interests of science, like." He looked at me—I was the boss, even in such minor detours from routine as this. I thought about it and shrugged like it didn't matter much, one way or another. The truth was, I kind of wanted to see what he'd do, too.

Well, he ate it—of course. There was a Depression on, after all. But the *way* he ate it fascinated us all. He approached the fragment of sandwich, sniffed his way around it, and then he sat up in front of it like a dog doing a trick, grabbed it, and pulled the bread apart to get at the meat. He did it as deliberately and knowingly as a man tucking into a good roast-beef dinner in his favorite restaurant. I never saw an animal eat like that, not even a well-trained house dog. And all the while he was eating, his eyes never left us.

"Either one smart mouse or hungry as hell," a new voice said. It was Bitterbuck. He had awakened and now stood at the bars of his cell, naked except for a pair of saggy-seated boxer shorts. A home-rolled cigarette poked out from between the second and third knuckles of his right hand, and his iron-gray hair lay over his shoulders—once probably muscular but now beginning to soften—in a pair of braids.

"You got any Injun wisdom about micies, Chief?" Brutal asked, watching the mouse eat. We were all pretty fetched by the neat way it held the bit of corned beef in its forepaws, occasionally turning it or glancing at it, as if in admiration and appreciation.

"Naw," Bitterbuck said. "Knowed a brave once had a pair of what he claimed were mouse-skin gloves, but I didn't believe it." Then he laughed, as if the whole thing was a joke, and left the bars. We heard the bunk creak as he lay down again.

That seemed to be the mouse's signal to go. It finished up what it was holding, sniffed at what was left (mostly bread with yellow mustard soaking into it), and then looked back at us, as if it wanted to remember our faces if we met again. Then it turned and scurried off the way it had come, not pausing to do any cell-checks this time. Its hurry made me think of the White Rabbit in *Alice's Adventures in Wonderland,* and I smiled. It didn't pause at the door to the restraint room, but disappeared beneath it. The restraint room had soft walls, for people whose brains had softened a little. We kept cleaning equipment stored in there when we didn't need the room for its created purpose, and a few books (most were westerns by Clarence Mulford, but one—loaned out only on special occasions—featured a profusely illustrated tale in which Popeye, Bluto, and even Wimpy the hamburger fiend took turns shtupping Olive Oyl). There were craft items as well, including the crayons Delacroix later put to some good use. Not that he was our problem yet; this was earlier, remember. Also in the restraint room was the jacket no one wanted to wear—white, made of double-sewn canvas, and with the buttons and snaps and buckles going up the back. We all knew how to zip a problem child into that jacket lickety-larrup. They didn't get violent often, our lost boys, but when they did, brother, you didn't wait around for the situation to improve on its own.

Brutal reached into the desk drawer above the kneehole and brought out the big leather-bound book with the word VISITORS stamped on the front in gold leaf. Ordinarily, that book stayed in the drawer from one month to the next. When a prisoner had visitors—unless it was a lawyer or a minister—he went over to the room off the messhall that was kept special for that purpose. The Arcade, we called it. I don't know why.

"Just what in the Gorry do you think *you're* doing?" Dean Stanton asked, peering over the tops of his spectacles as Brutal opened the book and paged grandly past years of visitors to men now dead.

"Obeyin Regulation 19," Brutal said, finding the current page. He took the pencil and licked the tip—a disagreeable habit of which he could not be broken—and prepared to write. Regulation 19 stated simply: "Each visitor to E Block shall show a yellow Administration pass and shall be recorded *without fail.*"

"He's gone nuts," Dean said to me.

"He didn't show us his pass, but I'm gonna let it go this time," Brutal said. He gave the tip of his pencil an extra lick for good luck, then filled in 9:49 p.m. under the column headed TIME ON BLOCK.

"Sure, why not, the big bosses probably make exceptions for mice," I said.

"Course they do," Brutal agreed. "Lack of pockets." He turned to look at the wall-clock behind the desk, then printed 10:01 in the column headed TIME OFF BLOCK. The longer space between these two numbers was headed NAME OF VISITOR. After a moment's hard thought—probably to muster his limited spelling skills, as I'm sure the idea was in his head already—Brutus Howell carefully wrote STEAMBOAT WILLY, which was what most people called Mickey Mouse back in those days. It was because of that first talkie cartoon, where he rolled his eyes and bumped his hips around and pulled the whistle cord in the pilothouse of the steamboat.

"There," Brutal said, slamming the book closed and returning it to its drawer, "all done and buttoned up."

I laughed, but Dean, who couldn't help being serious about things even when he saw the joke, was frowning and polishing his glasses furiously. "You'll be in trouble if someone sees that." He hesitated and added, "The wrong someone." He hesitated again, looking nearsightedly around almost as if he expected to see that the walls had grown ears, before finishing: "Someone like Percy Kiss-My-Ass-and-Go-to-Heaven Wetmore."

"Huh," Brutal said. "The day Percy Wetmore sits his narrow shanks down here at this desk will be the day I resign."

"You won't have to," Dean said. "They'll fire you for making jokes in the visitors' book if Percy puts the right word in the right ear. And he can. You know he can."

Brutal glowered but said nothing. I reckoned that later on that night he would erase what he had written. And if he didn't, I would.

The next night, after getting first Bitterbuck and then The President over to D Block, where we showered our group after the regular cons were locked down, Brutal asked me if we shouldn't have a look for Steamboat Willy down there in the restraint room.

"I guess we ought to," I said. We'd had a good laugh over that mouse the night before, but I knew that if Brutal and I found it down there in the restraint room—particularly if we found it had gnawed itself the beginnings of a nest in one of the padded walls—we would kill it. Better to kill the scout, no matter how amusing it might be, than have to live with the pilgrims. And, I shouldn't have to tell you, neither of us was very squeamish about a little mouse-murder. Killing rats was what the state paid us for, after all.

But we didn't find Steamboat Willy—later to be known as Mr. Jingles—that night, not nested in the soft walls, or behind any of the collected junk we hauled out into the corridor. There was a great deal of junk, too, more than I would have expected, because we hadn't had to use the restraint room in a long time. That would change with the advent of William Wharton, but of course we didn't know that at the time. Lucky us.

"Where'd it go?" Brutal asked at last, wiping sweat off the back of his neck with a big blue bandanna. "No hole, no crack . . . there's that, but—" He pointed to the drain in the floor. Below the grate, which the mouse could have gotten through, was a fine steel mesh that not even a fly would have passed. "How'd it get in? How'd it get out?"

"I don't know," I said.

"He *did* come in here, didn't he? I mean, the three of us saw him."

"Yep, right under the door. He had to squeeze a little, but he made it."

"Gosh," Brutal said—a word that sounded strange, coming from a man that big. "It's a good thing the cons can't make themselves small like that, isn't it?"

"You bet," I said, running my eye over the canvas walls one last time, looking for a hole, a crack, anything. There was nothing. "Come on. Let's go."

Steamboat Willy showed up again three nights later, when Harry Terwilliger was on the duty desk. Percy was also on, and chased the mouse back down the Green Mile with the same mop Dean had been thinking of using. The rodent avoided Percy easily, slipping through the crack beneath the restraint-room door a hands-down winner. Cursing at the top of his voice, Percy unlocked the door and hauled all that shit out again. It was funny and scary at the same time, Harry said. Percy was vowing he'd catch the goddam mouse and tear its diseased little head right off, but he didn't, of course. Sweaty and disheveled, the shirttail of his uniform hanging out in the back, he returned to the duty desk half an hour later, brushing his hair out of his eyes and telling Harry (who had sat serenely reading through most of the ruckus) that he was going to put a strip of insulation on the bottom of the door down there; *that* would solve the vermin problem, he declared.

"Whatever you think is best, Percy," Harry said, turning a page of the oat opera he was reading. He thought Percy would forget about blocking the crack at the bottom of that door, and he was right.

8

Late that winter, long after these events were over, Brutal came to me one night when it was just the two of us, E Block temporarily empty and all the other guards temporarily reassigned. Percy had gone on to Briar Ridge.

"Come here," Brutal said in a funny, squeezed voice that made me look around at him sharply. I had just come in out of a cold and sleety night, and had been brushing off the shoulders of my coat prior to hanging it up.

"Is something wrong?" I asked.

"No," he said, "but I found out where Mr. Jingles was staying. When he first came, I mean, before Delacroix took him over. Do you want to see?"

Of course I did. I followed him down the Green Mile to the restraint room. All the stuff we kept stored there was out in the hall; Brutal had apparently taken advantage of the lull in customer traffic to do some cleaning up. The door was open, and I saw our mop-bucket inside. The floor, that same sick lime shade as the Green Mile itself, was drying in streaks. Standing in the middle of the floor was a stepladder, the one that was usually kept in the storage room, which also happened to serve as the final stop for the state's condemned. There was a shelf jutting out from the back of the ladder near the top, the sort of thing a workman would use to hold his toolkit or a painter the bucket he was working out of. There was a flashlight on it. Brutal handed it to me.

"Get on up there. You're shorter than me, so you'll have to go pretty near all the way, but I'll hold your legs."

"I'm ticklish down there," I said, starting up. "Especially my knees."

"I'll mind that."

"Good," I said, "because a broken hip's too high a price to pay in order to discover the origins of a single mouse."

"Huh?"

"Never mind." My head was up by the caged light in the center of the ceiling by then, and I could feel the ladder wiggling a little under my weight. Outside, I could hear the winter wind moaning. "Just hold on to me."

"I got you, don't worry." He gripped my calves firmly, and I went up one more step. Now the top of my head was less than a foot from the ceiling, and I could see the cobwebs a few enterprising spiders had spun in the crotches where the roof beams came together. I shone the light around but didn't see anything worth the risk of being up here.

"No," Brutal said. "You're looking too far away, Paul. Look to your left, where those two beams come together. You see them? One's a little discolored."

"I see."

"Shine the light on the join."

I did, and saw what he wanted me to see almost right away. The beams had been pegged together with dowels, half a dozen of them, and one was gone, leaving a black, circular hole the size of a quarter. I looked at it, then looked doubtfully back over my shoulder at Brutal. "It was a small mouse," I said, "but that small? Man, I don't think so."

"But that's where he went," Brutal said. "I'm just as sure as houses."

"I don't see how you can be."

"Lean closer—don't worry, I got you—and take a whiff."

I did as he asked, groping with my left hand for one of the other beams, and feeling a little better when I had hold of it. The wind outside gusted again; air puffed out of that hole and into my face. I could smell the keen breath of a winter night in the border South . . . and something else, as well.

The smell of peppermint.

Don't let nothing happen to Mr. Jingles, I could hear Delacroix saying in a voice that wouldn't stay steady. I could hear that, and I could feel the warmth of Mr. Jingles as the Frenchman handed it to me, just a mouse, smarter than most of the species, no doubt, but still just a mouse for a' that and a' that. *Don't let that bad 'un hurt my mouse,* he'd said, and I had promised, as I always promised them at the end, when walking the Green Mile was no longer a myth or a hypothesis but something they really had to do. Mail this letter to my brother, who I haven't seen for twenty years? I promise. Say fifteen Hail Marys for my soul? I promise. Let me die under my spirit-name and see that it goes on my tombstone? I promise. It was the way you got them to go and be good about it, the way you saw them into the chair sitting at the end of the Green Mile with their sanity intact. I couldn't keep all of those promises, of course, but I kept the one I made to Delacroix. As for the Frenchman himself, there had been hell to pay. The bad 'un had hurt Delacroix, hurt him plenty. Oh, I know what he did, all right, but no one deserved what happened to Eduard Delacroix when he fell into Old Sparky's savage embrace.

A smell of peppermint.

And something else. Something back inside that hole.

I took a pen out of my breast pocket with my right hand, still holding onto the beam with my left, not worried anymore about Brutal inadvertently tickling my sensitive knees. I unscrewed the pen's cap one-handed, then poked the nib in and teased something out. It was a tiny splinter of wood which had been tinted a bright yellow, and I heard Delacroix's voice again, so clearly this time that his ghost might have been lurking in that room with us—the one where William Wharton spent so much of his time.

Hey, you guys! the voice said this time—the laughing, amazed voice of a man who has forgotten, at least for a little while, where he is and what awaits him. *Come and see what Mr. Jingles can do!*

"Christ," I whispered. I felt as if the wind had been knocked out of me.

"You found another one, didn't you?" Brutal asked. "I found three or four."

I came down and shone the light on his big, outstretched palm. Several splinters of wood were scattered there, like jackstraws for elves. Two were yellow, like the one I had found. One was green and one was red. They hadn't been painted but colored, with wax Crayola crayons.

"Oh, boy," I said in a low, shaky voice. "Oh, hey. It's pieces of that spool, isn't it? But why? Why up there?"

"When I was a kid I wasn't big like I am now," Brutal said. "I got most of my growth between fifteen and seventeen. Until then I was a shrimp. And when I went off to school the first time, I felt as small as . . . why, as small as a mouse, I guess you'd say. I was scared to death. So you know what I did?"

I shook my head. Outside, the wind gusted again. In the angles formed by the beams, cobwebs shook in feathery drafts, like rotted lace. Never had I been in a place that felt so nakedly haunted, and it was right then, as we stood there looking down at the splintered remains of the spool which had caused so much trouble, that my head began to know what my heart had understood ever since John Coffey had walked the Green Mile: I couldn't do this job much longer. Depression or no Depression, I couldn't watch many more men walk through my office to their deaths. Even one more might be too many.

"I asked my mother for one of her hankies," Brutal said. "So when I felt weepy and small, I could sneak it out and smell her perfume and not feel so bad."

"You think—what?—that mouse chewed off some of that colored spool to remember Delacroix by? That a *mouse*—"

He looked up. I thought for a moment I saw tears in his eyes, but I guess I was probably wrong about that. "I ain't saying nothing, Paul. But I found them up there, and I smelled peppermint, same as you— you know you did. And I can't do this no more. I *won't* do this no more. Seeing one more man in that chair'd just about kill me. I'm going to put in for a transfer to Boys' Correctional on Monday. If I get it before the next one, that's fine. If I don't, I'll resign and go back to farming."

"What did you ever farm, besides rocks?"

"It don't matter."

"I know it doesn't," I said. "I think I'll put in with you."

73

He looked at me close, making sure I wasn't just having some sport with him, then nodded as if it was a settled thing. The wind gusted again, strong enough this time to make the beams creak and settle, and we both looked around uneasily at the padded walls. I think for a moment we could hear William Wharton—not Billy the Kid, not him, he had been "Wild Bill" to us from his first day on the block—screaming and laughing, telling us we were going to be damned glad to be rid of him, telling us we would never forget him. About those things he was right.

As for what Brutal and I agreed on that night in the restraint room, it turned out just that way. It was almost as if we had taken a solemn oath on those tiny bits of colored wood. Neither of us ever took part in another execution. John Coffey was the last.

PART TWO

—

THE MOUSE
ON THE MILE

1

THE NURSING HOME where I am crossing my last bunch of t's and dotting my last mess of i's is called Georgia Pines. It's about sixty miles from Atlanta and about two hundred light-years from life as most people—people under the age of eighty, let's say—live it. You who are reading this want to be careful that there isn't a place like it waiting in your future. It's not a cruel place, not for the most part; there's cable TV, the food's good (although there's damned little a man can chew), but in its way, it's as much of a killing bottle as E Block at Cold Mountain ever was.

There's even a fellow here who reminds me a little of Percy Wetmore, who got his job on the Green Mile because he was related to the governor of the state. I doubt if this fellow is related to anyone important, even though he acts that way. Brad Dolan, his name is. He's always combing his hair, like Percy was, and he's always got something to read stuffed into his back pocket. With Percy it was magazines like *Argosy* and *Men's Adventure*; with Brad it's these little paperbacks called *Gross Jokes* and *Sick Jokes*. He's always asking people why the Frenchman crossed the road or how many Polacks it takes to screw in a lightbulb or how many pallbearers there are at a Harlem funeral. Like Percy, Brad is a dimwit who thinks nothing is funny unless it's mean.

Something Brad said the other day struck me as actually smart, but I don't give him a lot of credit for it; even a stopped clock is right twice a day, the proverb has it. "You're just lucky you don't have that Alzheimer's disease, Paulie," was what he said. I hate him calling me that,

Paulie, but he goes on doing it, anyway; I've given up asking him to quit. There are other sayings—not quite proverbs—that apply to Brad Dolan: "You can lead a horse to water but you can't make him drink" is one; "You can dress him up but you can't take him out" is another. In his thickheadedness he is also like Percy.

When he made his comment about Alzheimer's, he was mopping the floor of the solarium, where I had been going over the pages I have already written. There's a great lot of them, and I think there's apt to be a great lot more before I am through. "That Alzheimer's, do you know what it really is?"

"No," I said, "but I'm sure you'll tell me, Brad."

"It's AIDS for old people," he said, and then burst out laughing, hucka-hucka-hucka-*huck*!, just like he does over those idiotic jokes of his.

I didn't laugh, though, because what he said struck a nerve somewhere. Not that I have Alzheimer's; although there's plenty of it on view here at beautiful Georgia Pines, I myself just suffer the standard old-guy memory problems. Those problems seem to have more to do with *when* than *what*. Looking over what I have written so far, it occurs to me that I *remember* everything that happened back in '32; it's the order of events that sometimes gets confused in my head. Yet, if I'm careful, I think I can keep even that sorted out. More or less.

John Coffey came to E Block and the Green Mile in October of that year, condemned for the murder of the nine-year-old Detterick twins. That's my major landmark, and if I keep it in view, I should do just fine. William "Wild Bill" Wharton came after Coffey; Delacroix came before. So did the mouse, the one Brutus Howell—Brutal, to his friends—called Steamboat Willy and Delacroix ended up calling Mr. Jingles.

Whatever you called him, the mouse came first, even before Del—it was still summer when he showed up, and we had two other prisoners on the Green Mile: The Chief, Arlen Bitterbuck; and The Pres, Arthur Flanders.

That mouse. That goddam mouse. Delacroix loved it, but Percy Wetmore sure didn't.

Percy hated it from the first.

2

THE MOUSE came back just about three days after Percy had chased it down the Green Mile that first time. Dean Stanton and Bill Dodge were talking politics . . . which meant, in those days, they were talking Roosevelt and Hoover—Herbert, not J. Edgar. They were eating Ritz crackers from a box Dean had purchased from old Toot-Toot an hour or so before. Percy was standing in the office doorway, practicing quick draws with the baton he loved so much, as he listened. He'd pull it out of that ridiculous hand-tooled holster he'd gotten somewhere, then twirl it (or try to; most times he would have dropped it if not for the rawhide loop he kept on his wrist), then re-holster it. I was off that night, but got the full report from Dean the following evening.

The mouse came up the Green Mile just as it had before, hopping along, then stopping and seeming to check the empty cells. After a bit of that it would hop on, undiscouraged, as if it had known all along it would be a long search, and it was up to that.

The President was awake this time, standing at his cell door. That guy was a piece of work, managing to look natty even in his prison blues. We knew just by the way he looked that he wasn't made for Old Sparky, and we were right—less than a week after Percy's second run at that mouse, The Pres's sentence was commuted to life and he joined the general population.

"Say!" he called. "There's a mouse in here! What kind of a joint are you guys running, anyway?" He was kind of laughing, but Dean said he also sounded kind of outraged, as if even a murder rap hadn't been quite

79

enough to knock the Kiwanis out of his soul. He had been the regional head of an outfit called Mid-South Realty Associates, and had thought himself smart enough to be able to get away with pushing his half-senile father out a third-story window and collect on a double-indemnity whole-life policy. On that he had been wrong, but maybe not by much.

"Shut up, you lugoon," Percy said, but that was pretty much automatic. He had his eye on the mouse. He had re-holstered his baton and taken out one of his magazines, but now he tossed the magazine on the duty desk and pulled the baton out of its holster again. He began tapping it casually against the knuckles of his left hand.

"Son of a bitch," Bill Dodge said. "I've never seen a mouse in here before."

"Aw, he's sort of cute," Dean said. "And not afraid at all."

"How do you know?"

"He was in the other night. Percy saw him, too. Brutal calls him Steamboat Willy."

Percy kind of sneered at that, but for the time being said nothing. He was tapping the baton faster now on the back of his hand.

"Watch this," Dean said. "He came all the way up to the desk before. I want to see if he'll do it again."

It did, skirting wide of The Pres on its way, as if it didn't like the way our resident parricide smelled. It checked two of the empty cells, even ran up onto one of the bare, unmattressed cots for a sniff, then came back to the Green Mile. And Percy standing there the whole time, tapping and tapping, not talking for a change, wanting to make it sorry for coming back. Wanting to teach it a lesson.

"Good thing you guys don't have to put him in Sparky," Bill said, interested in spite of himself. "You'd have a hell of a time getting the clamps and the cap on."

Percy said nothing still, but he very slowly gripped the baton between his fingers, the way a man would hold a good cigar.

The mouse stopped where it had before, no more than three feet from the duty desk, looking up at Dean like a prisoner before the bar. It glanced up at Bill for a moment, then switched its attention back to Dean. Percy it hardly seemed to notice at all.

"He's a brave little barstid, I got to give him that," Bill said. He raised his voice a little. "Hey! Hey! Steamboat Willy!"

The mouse flinched a little and fluttered its ears, but it didn't run, or even show any signs of wanting to.

"Now watch this," Dean said, remembering how Brutal had fed it some of his corned-beef sandwich. "I don't know if he'll do it again, but—"

He broke off a piece of Ritz cracker and dropped it in front of the mouse. It just looked with its sharp black eyes at the orangey fragment for a second or two, its filament-fine whiskers twitching as it sniffed. Then it reached out, took the cracker in its paws, sat up, and began to eat.

"Well, I'll be shucked and boiled!" Bill exclaimed. "Eats as neat as a parson on parish house Saturday night!"

"Looks more like a nigger eating watermelon to me," Percy remarked, but neither guard paid him any mind. Neither did The Chief or The Pres, for that matter. The mouse finished the cracker but continued to sit, seemingly balanced on the talented coil of its tail, looking up at the giants in blue.

"Lemme try," Bill said. He broke off another piece of cracker, leaned over the front of the desk, and dropped it carefully. The mouse sniffed but did not touch.

"Huh," Bill said. "Must be full."

"Nah," Dean said, "he knows you're a floater, that's all."

"Floater, am I? I like that! I'm here almost as much as Harry Terwilliger! Maybe more!"

"Simmer down, old-timer, simmer down," Dean said, grinning. "But watch and see if I'm not right." He bombed another piece of cracker over the side. Sure enough, the mouse picked that one up and began to eat again, still ignoring Bill Dodge's contribution completely. But before it had done more than take a preliminary nibble or two, Percy threw his baton at it, launching it like a spear.

The mouse was a small target, and give the devil his due—it was a wickedly good shot, and might have taken "Willy's" head clean off, if its reflexes hadn't been as sharp as shards of broken glass. It ducked—yes, just as a human being would have—and dropped the chunk of cracker. The heavy hickory baton passed over its head and spine close enough so its fur ruffled (that's what Dean said, anyway, and so I pass it on, although I'm not sure I really believe it), then hit the green linoleum and bounced against the bars of an empty cell. The mouse didn't wait to see if it was a mistake; apparently remembering a pressing engagement elsewhere, it turned and was off down the corridor toward the restraint room in a flash.

Percy roared with frustration—he knew how close he had come—and chased after it again. Bill Dodge grabbed at his arm, probably out of simple instinct, but Percy pulled away from him. Still, Dean said, it was probably that grab which saved Steamboat Willy's life, and it was still a near thing. Percy wanted not just to kill the mouse but to *squash* it, so he ran in big, comical leaps, like a deer, stamping down with his heavy black workshoes. The mouse barely avoided Percy's last two jumps, first zigging and then zagging. It went under the door with a final flick of its long pink tail, and so long, stranger—it was gone.

"*Fuck!*" Percy said, and slammed the flat of his hand against the door. Then he began to sort through his keys, meaning to go into the restraint room and continue the chase.

Dean came down the corridor after him, deliberately walking slow in order to get his emotions under control. Part of him wanted to laugh at Percy, he told me, but part of him wanted to grab the man, whirl him around, pin him against the restraint-room door, and whale the living daylights out of him. Most of it, of course, was just being startled; our job on E Block was to keep rumpus to a minimum, and rumpus was practically Percy Wetmore's middle name. Working with him was sort of like trying to defuse a bomb with somebody standing behind you and every now and then clashing a pair of cymbals together. In a word, upsetting. Dean said he could see that upset in Arlen Bitterbuck's eyes . . . even in The President's eyes, although that gentleman was usually as cool as the storied cucumber.

And there was something else, as well. In some part of his mind, Dean had already begun to accept the mouse as—well, maybe not as a friend, but as a part of life on the block. That made what Percy had done and what he was trying to do not right. Not even if it was a mouse he was trying to do it to. And the fact that Percy would never understand how come it wasn't right was pretty much the perfect example of why he was all wrong for the job he thought he was doing.

By the time Dean reached the end of the corridor, he had gotten himself under control again, and knew how he wanted to handle the matter. The one thing Percy absolutely couldn't stand was to look foolish, and we all knew it.

"Coises, foiled again," he said, grinning a little, kidding Percy along.

Percy gave him an ugly look and flicked his hair off his brow. "Watch your mouth, Four-Eyes. I'm riled. Don't make it worse."

"So it's moving day again, is it?" Dean said, not quite laughing . . . but laughing with his eyes. "Well, when you get everything out this time, would you mind mopping the floor?"

Percy looked at the door. Looked at his keys. Thought about another long, hot, fruitless rummage in the room with the soft walls while they all stood around and watched him . . . The Chief and The Pres, too.

"I'll be damned if I understand what's so funny," he said. "We don't need mice in the cellblock—we got enough vermin in here already, without adding mice."

"Whatever you say, Percy," Dean said, holding up his hands. He had a moment right there, he told me the next night, when he believed Percy might just take after him.

Bill Dodge strolled up then and smoothed it over. "Think you dropped this," he said, and handed Percy his baton. "An inch lower, you woulda broken the little barstid's back."

Percy's chest expanded at that. "Yeah, it wasn't a bad shot," he said, carefully re-seating his head-knocker in its foolish holster. "I used to be a pitcher in high school. Threw two no-hitters."

"Is that right, now?" Bill said, and the respectful tone of voice (although he winked at Dean when Percy turned away) was enough to finish defusing the situation.

"Yep," Percy said. "Threw one down in Knoxville. Those city boys didn't know what hit em. Walked two. Could have had a perfect game if the ump hadn't been such a lugoon."

Dean could have left it at that, but he had seniority on Percy, and part of a senior's job is to instruct, and at that time—before Coffey, before Delacroix—he still thought Percy might be teachable. So he reached out and grasped the younger man's wrist. "You want to think about what you was doing just now," Dean said. His intention, he said later, was to sound serious but not disapproving. Not *too* disapproving, anyway.

Except with Percy, that didn't work. He might not learn . . . but we would eventually.

"Say, Four-Eyes, I know what I was doing—trying to get that mouse! What're you, blind?"

"You also scared the cheese out of Bill, out of me, and out of them," Dean said, pointing in the direction of Bitterbuck and Flanders.

"So what?" Percy asked, drawing himself up. "They ain't in cradle-school, in case you didn't notice. Although you guys treat them that way half the time."

"Well, *I* don't like to be scared," Bill rumbled, "and I work here, Wetmore, in case you didn't notice. *I* ain't one of your lugoons."

Percy gave him a look that was narrow-eyed and a touch uncertain.

"And we don't scare them any more than we have to, because they're under a lot of strain," Dean said. He was still keeping his voice low. "Men that are under a lot of strain can snap. Hurt themselves. Hurt others. Sometimes get folks like us in trouble, too."

Percy's mouth twitched at that. "In trouble" was an idea that had power over him. Making trouble was okay. Getting into it was not.

"Our job is talking, not yelling," Dean said. "A man who is yelling at prisoners is a man who has lost control."

Percy knew who had written that scripture—me. The boss. There was no love lost between Percy Wetmore and Paul Edgecombe, and this was still summer, remember—long before the real festivities started.

"You'll do better," Dean said, "if you think of this place as like an intensive-care ward in a hospital. It's best to be quiet—"

"I think of it as a bucket of piss to drown rats in," Percy said, "and that's all. Now let me go."

He tore free of Dean's hand, stepped between him and Bill, and stalked up the corridor with his head down. He walked a little too close to The President's side—close enough so that Flanders could have reached out, grabbed him, and maybe headwhipped him with his own prized hickory baton, had Flanders been that sort of man. He wasn't, of course, but The Chief perhaps was. The Chief, if given a chance, might have administered such a beating just to teach Percy a lesson. What Dean said to me on that subject when he told me this story the following night has stuck with me ever since, because it turned out to be a kind of prophecy. "Wetmore don't understand that he hasn't got any power over them," Dean said. "That nothing he does can really make things worse for them, that they can only be electrocuted once. Until he gets his head around that, he's going to be a danger to himself and to everyone else down here."

Percy went into my office and slammed the door behind him.

"My, my," Bill Dodge said. "Ain't he the swollen and badly infected testicle."

"You don't know the half of it," Dean said.

"Oh, look on the bright side," Bill said. He was always telling people to look on the bright side; it got so you wanted to punch his nose every time it came out of his mouth. "Your trick mouse got away, at least."

"Yeah, but we won't see him no more," Dean said. "I imagine this time goddam Percy Wetmore's scared him off for good."

3

THAT WAS LOGICAL but wrong. The mouse was back the very next evening, which just happened to be the first of Percy Wetmore's two nights off before he slid over to the graveyard shift.

Steamboat Willy showed up around seven o'clock. I was there to see his reappearance; so was Dean. Harry Terwilliger, too. Harry was on the desk. I was technically on days, but had stuck around to spend an extra hour with The Chief, whose time was getting close by then. Bitterbuck was stoical on the outside, in the tradition of his tribe, but I could see his fear of the end growing inside him like a poison flower. So we talked. You could talk to them in the daytime but it wasn't so good, with the shouts and conversation (not to mention the occasional fistfight) coming from the exercise yard, the chonk-chonk-chonk of the stamping machines in the plate-shop, the occasional yell of a guard for someone to put down that pick or grab up that hoe or just to get your ass over here, Harvey. After four it got a little better, and after six it got better still. Six to eight was the optimum time. After that you could see the long thoughts starting to steal over their minds again—in their eyes you could see it, like afternoon shadows—and it was best to stop. They still heard what you were saying, but it no longer made sense to them. Past eight they were getting ready for the watches of the night and imagining how the cap would feel when it was clamped to the tops of their heads, and how the air would smell inside the black bag which had been rolled down over their sweaty faces.

But I got The Chief at a good time. He told me about his first wife, and how they had built a lodge together up in Montana. Those had been the happiest days of his life, he said. The water was so pure and so cold that it felt like your mouth was cut every time you drank.

"Hey, Mr. Edgecombe," he said. "You think, if a man he sincerely repent of what he done wrong, he might get to go back to the time that was happiest for him and live there forever? Could that be what heaven is like?"

"I've just about believed that very thing," I said, which was a lie I didn't regret in the least. I had learned of matters eternal at my mother's pretty knee, and what I believed is what the Good Book says about murderers: that there is no eternal life in them. I think they go straight to hell, where they burn in torment until God finally gives Gabriel the nod to blow the Judgment Trump. When he does, they'll wink out . . . and probably glad to go they will be. But I never gave a hint of such beliefs to Bitterbuck, or to any of them. I think in their hearts they knew it. Where is your brother, his blood crieth to me from the ground, God said to Cain, and I doubt if the words were much of a surprise to that particular problem-child; I bet he heard Abel's blood whining out of the earth at him with each step he took.

The Chief was smiling when I left, perhaps thinking about his lodge in Montana and his wife lying bare-breasted in the light of the fire. He would be walking in a warmer fire soon, I had no doubt.

I went back up the corridor, and Dean told me about his set-to with Percy the previous night. I think he'd waited around just so he could, and I listened carefully. I always listened carefully when the subject was Percy, because I agreed with Dean a hundred percent—I thought Percy was the sort of man who could cause a lot of trouble, as much for the rest of us as for himself.

As Dean was finishing, old Toot-Toot came by with his red snack-wagon, which was covered with hand-lettered Bible quotes ("REPENT for the LORD shall judge his people," Deut. 32:36, "And surely your BLOOD of your lives will I require," Gen. 9:5, and similar cheery, uplifting sentiments), and sold us some sandwiches and pops. Dean was hunting for change in his pocket and saying that we wouldn't see Steamboat

Willy anymore, that goddam Percy Wetmore had scared him off for good, when old Toot-Toot said, "What's that'ere, then?"

We looked, and here came the mouse of the hour his ownself, hopping up the middle of the Green Mile. He'd come a little way, then stop, look around with his bright little oildrop eyes, then come on again.

"Hey, mouse!" The Chief said, and the mouse stopped and looked at him, whiskers twitching. I tell you, it was exactly as if the damned thing knew it had been called. "You some kind of spirit guide?" Bitterbuck tossed the mouse a little morsel of cheese from his supper. It landed right in front of the mouse, but Steamboat Willy hardly even glanced at it, just came on his way again, up the Green Mile, looking in empty cells.

"Boss Edgecombe!" The President called. "Do you think that little bastard knows Wetmore isn't here? I do, by God!"

I felt about the same . . . but I wasn't going to say so out loud.

Harry came out into the hall, hitching up his pants the way he always did after he'd spent a refreshing few minutes in the can, and stood there with his eyes wide. Toot-Toot was also staring, a sunken grin doing unpleasant things to the soft and toothless lower half of his face.

The mouse stopped in what was becoming its usual spot, curled its tail around its paws, and looked at us. Again I was reminded of pictures I had seen of judges passing sentence on hapless prisoners . . . yet, had there ever been a prisoner as small and unafraid as this one? Not that it really was a prisoner, of course; it could come and go pretty much as it pleased. Yet the idea would not leave my mind, and it again occurred to me that most of us would feel that small when approaching God's judgment seat after our lives were over, but very few of us would be able to look so unafraid.

"Well, I swear," Old Toot-Toot said. "There he sits, big as Billy-Be-Frigged."

"You ain't seen nothing yet, Toot," Harry said. "Watch this." He reached into his breast pocket and came out with a slice of cinnamon apple wrapped in waxed paper. He broke off the end and tossed it on the floor. It was dry and hard and I thought it would bounce right past the mouse, but it reached out one paw, as carelessly as a man swatting at a fly to pass the time, and batted it flat. We all laughed in admiration and surprise, an outburst of sound that should have sent the mouse skittering, but it barely twitched. It picked up the piece of dried apple in its paws, gave it a couple of licks, then dropped it and looked up at us as if to say, Not bad, what else do you have?

Toot-Toot opened his cart, took out a sandwich, unwrapped it, and tore off a scrap of bologna.

"Don't bother," Dean said.

"What do you mean?" Toot-Toot asked. "Ain't a mouse alive'd pass up bologna if he could get it. You a crazy guy!"

But I knew Dean was right, and I could see by Harry's face that he knew it, too. There were floaters and there were regulars. Somehow, that mouse seemed to know the difference. Nuts, but true.

Old Toot-Toot tossed the scrap of bologna down, and sure enough, the mouse wouldn't have a thing to do with it; sniffed it once and then backed off a pace.

"I'll be a goddamned son of a bitch," Old Toot-Toot said, sounding offended.

I held out my hand. "Give it to me."

"What—same sammitch?"

"Same one. I'll pay for it."

Toot-Toot handed it over. I lifted the top slice of bread, tore off another sliver of meat, and dropped it over the front of the duty desk. The mouse came forward at once, picked it up in its paws, and began to eat. The bologna was gone before you could say Jack Robinson.

"I'll be *goddamned*!" Toot-Toot cried. "Bloody hell! Gimme dat!"

He snatched back the sandwich, tore off a much larger piece of meat—not a scrap this time but a flap—and dropped it so close to the mouse that Steamboat Willy almost ended up wearing it for a hat. It drew back again, sniffed (surely no mouse ever hit such a jackpot during the Depression—not in *our* state, at least), and then looked up at us.

"Go on, eat it!" Toot-Toot said, sounding more offended than ever. "What's wrong witchoo?"

Dean took the sandwich and dropped a piece of meat—by then it was like some strange communion service. The mouse picked it up at once and bolted it down. Then it turned and went back down the corridor to the restraint room, pausing along the way to peer into a couple of empty cells and to take a brief investigatory tour of a third. Once again the idea that it was looking for someone occurred to me, and this time I dismissed the thought more slowly.

"I'm not going to talk about this," Harry said. He sounded as if he was half-joking, half-not. "First of all, nobody'd care. Second, they wouldn't believe me if they did."

"He only ate from you fellas," Toot-Toot said. He shook his head in disbelief, then bent laboriously over, picked up what the mouse had disdained, and popped it into his own toothless maw, where he began the job of gumming it into submission. "Now why he do dat?"

"I've got a better one," Harry said. "How'd he know Percy was off?"

"He didn't," I said. "It was just coincidence, that mouse showing up tonight."

Except that got harder and harder to believe as the days went by and the mouse showed up only when Percy was off, on another shift, or in another part of the prison. We—Harry, Dean, Brutal, and me—decided that it must know Percy's voice, or his smell. We carefully avoided too much discussion about the mouse itself—*himself*. That, we seemed to have decided without saying a word, might go a long way toward spoiling something that was special . . . and beautiful, by virtue of its strangeness and delicacy. Willy had chosen us, after all, in some way I do not understand, even now. Maybe Harry came closest when he said it would do no good to tell other people, not just because they wouldn't believe but because they wouldn't care.

4

THEN IT WAS TIME for the execution of Arlen Bitterbuck, in reality no chief but first elder of his tribe on the Washita Reservation, and a member of the Cherokee Council as well. He had killed a man while drunk—while both of them were drunk, in fact. The Chief had crushed the man's head with a cement block. At issue had been a pair of boots. So, on July seventeenth of that rainy summer, *my* council of elders intended for his life to end.

Visiting hours for most Cold Mountain prisoners were as rigid as steel beams, but that didn't hold for our boys on E Block. So, on the sixteenth, Bitterbuck was allowed over to the long room adjacent to the cafeteria—the Arcade. It was divided straight down the middle by mesh interwoven with strands of barbed wire. Here The Chief would visit with his second wife and those of his children who would still treat with him. It was time for the good-byes.

He was taken over there by Bill Dodge and two other floaters. The rest of us had work to do—one hour to cram in at least two rehearsals. Three if we could manage it.

Percy didn't make much protest over being put in the switch room with Jack Van Hay for the Bitterbuck electrocution; he was too green to know if he was being given a good spot or a bad one. What he did know was that he had a rectangular mesh window to look through, and although he probably didn't care to be looking at the back of the chair instead of the front, he would still be close enough to see the sparks flying.

Right outside that window was a black wall telephone with no crank or dial on it. That phone could only ring in, and only from one place: the governor's office. I've seen lots of jailhouse movies over the years where the official phone rings just as they're getting ready to pull the switch on some poor innocent sap, but ours never rang during all my years on E Block, never once. In the movies, salvation is cheap. So is innocence. You pay a quarter, and a quarter's worth is just what you get. Real life costs more, and most of the answers are different.

We had a tailor's dummy down in the tunnel for the run to the meatwagon, and we had Old Toot-Toot for the rest. Over the years, Toot had somehow become the traditional stand-in for the condemned, as time-honored in his way as the goose you sit down to on Christmas, whether you like goose or not. Most of the other screws liked him, were amused by his funny accent—also French, but Canadian rather than Cajun, and softened into its own thing by his years of incarceration in the South. Even Brutal got a kick out of Old Toot. Not me, though. I thought he was, in his way, an older and dimmer version of Percy Wetmore, a man too squeamish to kill and cook his own meat but who did, all the same, just *love* the smell of a barbecue.

We were all there for the rehearsal, just as we would all be there for the main event. Brutus Howell had been "put out," as we said, which meant that he would place the cap, monitor the governor's phone-line, summon the doctor from his place by the wall if he was needed, and give the actual order to roll on two when the time came. If it went well, there would be no credit for anyone. If it didn't go well, Brutal would be blamed by the witnesses and I would be blamed by the warden. Neither of us complained about this; it wouldn't have done any good. The world turns, that's all. You can hold on and turn with it, or stand up to protest and be spun right off.

Dean, Harry Terwilliger, and I walked down to The Chief's cell for the first rehearsal not three minutes after Bill and his troops had escorted Bitterbuck off the block and over to the Arcade. The cell door was open, and Old Toot-Toot sat on The Chief's bunk, his wispy white hair flying.

"There come-stains all over dis sheet," Toot-Toot remarked. "He mus' be tryin to get rid of it before you fellas boil it off." And he cackled.

"Shut up, Toot," Dean said. "Let's play this serious."

"Okay," Toot-Toot said, immediately composing his face into an expression of thunderous gravity. But his eyes twinkled. Old Toot never looked so alive as when he was playing dead.

I stepped forward. "Arlen Bitterbuck, as an officer of the court and of the state of blah-blah, I have a warrant for blah-blah, such execution to be carried out at twelve-oh-one on blah-blah, will you step forward?"

Toot got off the bunk. "I'm steppin forward, I'm steppin forward, I'm steppin forward," he said.

"Turn around," Dean said, and when Toot-Toot turned, Dean examined the dandruffy top of his head. The crown of The Chief's head would be shaved tomorrow night, and Dean's check then would be to make sure he didn't need a touch-up. Stubble could impede conduction, make things harder. Everything we were doing today was about making things easier.

"All right, Arlen, let's go," I said to Toot-Toot, and away we went.

"I'm walkin down the corridor, I'm walkin down the corridor, I'm walkin down the corridor," Toot said. I flanked him on the left, Dean on the right. Harry was directly behind him. At the head of the corridor we turned right, away from life as it was lived in the exercise yard and toward death as it was died in the storage room. We went into my office, and Toot dropped to his knees without having to be asked. He knew the script, all right, probably better than any of us. God knew he'd been there longer than any of us.

"I'm prayin, I'm prayin, I'm prayin," Toot-Toot said, holding his gnarled hands up. They looked like that famous engraving, you probably know the one I mean. "The Lord is my shepherd, so on n so forth."

"Who's Bitterbuck got?" Harry asked. "We're not going to have some Cherokee medicine man in here shaking his dick, are we?"

"Actually—"

"Still prayin, still prayin, still gettin right with Jesus," Toot overrode me.

"Shut up, you old gink," Dean said.

"I'm prayin!"

"Then pray to yourself."

"What's keepin you guys?" Brutal hollered in from the storage room. That had also been emptied for our use. We were in the killing zone again, all right; it was a thing you could almost smell.

"Hold your friggin water!" Harry yelled back. "Don't be so goddam impatient!"

"Prayin," Toot said, grinning his unpleasant sunken grin. "Prayin for patience, just a little goddam patience."

"Actually, Bitterbuck's a Christian—he says," I told them, "and he's perfectly happy with the Baptist guy who came for Tillman Clark. Schuster, his name is. I like him, too. He's fast, and he doesn't get them all worked up. On your feet, Toot. You prayed enough for one day."

"Walkin," Toot said. "Walkin again, walkin again, yes sir, walkin on the Green Mile."

Short as he was, he still had to duck a little to get through the door on the far side of the office. The rest of us had to duck even more. This was a vulnerable time with a real prisoner, and when I looked across to the platform where Old Sparky stood and saw Brutal with his gun drawn, I nodded with satisfaction. Just right.

Toot-Toot went down the steps and stopped. The folding wooden chairs, about forty of them, were already in place. Bitterbuck would cross to the platform on an angle that would keep him safely away from the seated spectators, and half a dozen guards would be added for insurance. Bill Dodge would be in charge of those. We had never had a witness menaced by a condemned prisoner in spite of what was, admittedly, a raw set-up . . . and that was how I meant to keep it.

"Ready, boys?" Toot asked when we were back in our original formation at the foot of the stairs leading down from my office. I nodded, and we walked to the platform. What we looked like more than anything, I often thought, was a color-guard that had forgotten its flag.

"What am *I* supposed to do?" Percy called from behind the wire mesh between the storage room and the switch room.

"Watch and learn," I called back.

"And keep yer hands off yer wiener," Harry muttered. Toot-Toot heard him, though, and cackled.

We escorted him up onto the platform and Toot turned around on his own—the old vet in action. "Sittin down," he said, "sittin down, sittin down, takin a seat in Old Sparky's lap."

I dropped to my right knee before his right leg. Dean dropped to his left knee before his left leg. It was at this point we ourselves would be most vulnerable to physical attack, should the condemned man go berserk . . . which, every now and then, they did. We both turned the cocked knee slightly inward, to protect the crotch area. We dropped our chins to protect our throats. And, of course, we moved to secure the ankles and neutralize the danger as fast as we could. The Chief would be wearing slippers when he took his final promenade, but "it could have been worse" isn't much comfort to a man with a ruptured larynx. Or writhing on the floor with his balls swelling up to the size of Mason jars, for that matter, while forty or so spectators—many of them gentlemen of the press—sit in those Grange-hall chairs, watching the whole thing.

We clamped Toot-Toot's ankles. The clamp on Dean's side was slightly bigger, because it carried the juice. When Bitterbuck sat down tomorrow night, he would do so with a shaved left calf. Indians have very little body-hair as a rule, but we would take no chances.

While we were clamping Toot-Toot's ankles, Brutal secured his right wrist. Harry stepped smoothly forward and clamped the left. When they were done, Harry nodded to Brutal, and Brutal called back to Van Hay: "Roll on one!"

I heard Percy asking Jack Van Hay what that meant (it was hard to believe how little he knew, how little he'd picked up during his time on E Block) and Van Hay's murmur of explanation. Today *Roll on one* meant nothing, but when he heard Brutal say it tomorrow night, Van Hay would turn the knob that goosed the prison generator behind B Block. The witnesses would hear the genny as a steady low humming, and the lights all over the prison would brighten. In the other cellblocks, prisoners would observe those overbright lights and think it had happened, the execution was over, when in fact it was just beginning.

Brutal stepped around the chair so that Toot could see him. "Arlen Bitterbuck, you have been condemned to die in the electric chair, sentence passed by a jury of your peers and imposed by a judge in good standing in this state. God save the people of this state. Do you have anything to say before sentence is carried out?"

"Yeah," Toot said, eyes gleaming, lips bunched in a toothless happy grin. "I want a fried chicken dinner with gravy on the taters, I want to shit in your hat, and I got to have Mae West sit on my face, because I am one horny motherfucker."

Brutal tried to hold onto his stern expression, but it was impossible. He threw back his head and began laughing. Dean collapsed onto the edge of the platform like he'd been gutshot, head down between his knees, howling like a coyote, with one hand clapped to his brow as if to keep his brains in there where they belonged. Harry was knocking his own head against the wall and going *huh-huh-huh* as if he had a glob of food stuck in his throat. Even Jack Van Hay, a man not known for his sense of humor, was laughing. I felt like it myself, of course I did, but controlled it somehow. Tomorrow night it was going to be for real, and a man would die there where Toot-Toot was sitting.

"Shut up, Brutal," I said. "You too, Dean. Harry. And Toot, the next remark like that to come out of your mouth will be your last. I'll have Van Hay roll on two for real."

Toot gave me a grin as if to say that was a good 'un, Boss Edge-combe, a real good 'un. It faltered into a narrow, puzzled look when he saw I wasn't answering it. "What's wrong witchoo?" he asked.

"It's not funny," I said. "That's what's wrong with me, and if you're not smart enough to get it, you better just keep your gob shut." Except it *was* funny, in its way, and I suppose that was what had really made me mad.

I looked around, saw Brutal staring at me, still grinning a little.

"Shit," I said, "I'm getting too old for this job."

"Nah," Brutal said. "You're in your prime, Paul." But I wasn't, neither was he, not as far as this goddam job went, and both of us knew it. Still, the important thing was that the laughing fit had passed. That was good, because the last thing I wanted was somebody remembering Toot's smart-aleck remark tomorrow night and getting going again. You'd say such a thing would be impossible, a guard laughing his ass off as he escorted a condemned man past the witnesses to the electric chair, but when men are under stress, *anything* can happen. And a thing like that, people would have talked about it for twenty years.

"Are you going to be quiet, Toot?" I asked.

"Yes," he said, his averted face that of the world's oldest, poutiest child.

I nodded to Brutal that he should get on with the rehearsal. He took the mask from the brass hook on the back of the chair and rolled it down over Toot-Toot's head, pulling it snug under his chin, which opened the hole at the top to its widest diameter. Then Brutal leaned over, picked the wet circle of sponge out of the bucket, pressed one finger against it, then licked the tip of the finger. That done, he put the sponge back in the bucket. Tomorrow he wouldn't. Tomorrow he would tuck it into the cap perched on the back of the chair. Not today, though; there was no need to get Toot's old head wet.

The cap was steel, and with the straps dangling down on either side, it looked sort of like a doughboy's helmet. Brutal put it on Old Toot-Toot's head, snugging it down over the hole in the black head-covering.

"Gettin the cap, gettin the cap, gettin the cap," Toot said, and now his voice sounded squeezed as well as muffled. The straps held his jaw almost closed, and I suspected Brutal had snugged it down a little tighter than he strictly had to for purposes of rehearsal. He stepped back, faced the empty seats, and said: "Arlen Bitterbuck, electricity shall now be passed through your body until you are dead, in accordance with state law. May God have mercy on your soul."

Brutal turned to the mesh-covered rectangle. "Roll on two."

Old Toot, perhaps trying to recapture his earlier flare of comic genius, began to buck and flail in the chair, as Old Sparky's actual customers almost never did. "Now I'm fryin!" he cried. "Fryin! Fryyyin! *Geeeaah!* I'm a done tom turkey!"

Harry and Dean, I saw, were not watching this at all. They had turned away from Sparky and were looking across the empty storage room at the door leading back into my office. "Well, I'll be goddamned," Harry said. "One of the witnesses came a day early."

Sitting in the doorway with its tail curled neatly around its paws, watching with its beady black oilspot eyes, was the mouse.

5

THE EXECUTION went well—if there was ever such a thing as "a good one" (a proposition I strongly doubt), then the execution of Arlen Bitterbuck, council elder of the Washita Cherokee, was it. He got his braids wrong—his hands were shaking too badly to make a good job of it—and his eldest daughter, a woman of thirty-odd, was allowed to plait them nice and even. She wanted to weave feathers in at the tips, the pinfeathers of a hawk, his bird, but I couldn't allow it. They might catch fire and burn. I didn't tell her that, of course, just said it was against regulations. She made no protest, only bowed her head and put her hands to her temples to show her disappointment and her disapproval. She conducted herself with great dignity, that woman, and by doing so practically guaranteed that her father would do the same.

The Chief left his cell with no protest or holding back when the time came. Sometimes we had to pry their fingers off the bars—I broke one or two in my time and have never forgotten the muffled snapping sound—but The Chief wasn't one of those, thank God. He walked strong up the Green Mile to my office, and there he dropped to his knees to pray with Brother Schuster, who had driven down from the Heavenly Light Baptist Church in his flivver. Schuster gave The Chief a few psalms, and The Chief started to cry when Schuster got to the one about lying down beside the still waters. It wasn't bad, though, no hysteria, nothing like that. I had an idea he was thinking about still water so pure and so cold it felt like it was cutting your mouth every time you drank some.

Actually, I like to see them cry a little. It's when they don't that I get worried.

A lot of men can't get up from their knees again without help, but The Chief did okay in that department. He swayed a little at first, like he was light-headed, and Dean put out a hand to steady him, but Bitterbuck had already found his balance again on his own, so out we went.

Almost all the chairs were occupied, with the people in them murmuring quietly among themselves, like folks do when they're waiting for a wedding or a funeral to get started. That was the only time Bitterbuck faltered. I don't know if it was any one person in particular that bothered him, or all of them together, but I could hear a low moaning start up in his throat, and all at once the arm I was holding had a drag in it that hadn't been there before. Out of the corner of my eye I could see Harry Terwilliger moving up to cut off The Chief's retreat if Bitterbuck all at once decided he wanted to go hard.

I tightened my grip on his elbow and tapped the inside of his arm with one finger. "Steady, Chief," I said out of the corner of my mouth, not moving my lips. "The only thing most of these people will remember about you is how you go out, so give them something good—show them how a Washita does it."

He glanced at me sideways and gave a little nod. Then he took one of the braids his daughter had made and kissed it. I looked to Brutal, standing at parade rest behind the chair, resplendent in his best blue uniform, all the buttons on the tunic polished and gleaming, his hat sitting square-john perfect on his big head. I gave him a little nod and he shot it right back, stepping forward to help Bitterbuck mount the platform if he needed help. Turned out he didn't.

It was less than a minute from the time Bitterbuck sat down in the chair to the moment when Brutal called "Roll on two!" softly back over his shoulder. The lights dimmed down again, but only a little; you wouldn't have noticed it if you hadn't been looking for it. That meant Van Hay had pulled the switch some wit had labeled MABEL'S HAIR DRIER. There was a low humming from the cap, and Bitterbuck surged forward against the clamps and the restraining belt across his chest. Over against the wall, the prison doctor watched expressionlessly, lips thinned down until his mouth looked like a single white stitch. There was no flopping and flailing, such as Old Toot-Toot had done at rehearsal, only that powerful forward surge, as a man may surge forward from the hips while in the grip of a powerful orgasm. The Chief's blue shirt pulled tight at the buttons, creating little strained smiles of flesh between them.

And there was a smell. Not bad in itself, but unpleasant in its associations. I've never been able to go down in the cellar at my granddaughter's house when they bring me there, although that's where their little boy has his Lionel set-up, which he would dearly love to share with his great-grampa. I don't mind the trains, as I'm sure you can guess—it's the transformer I can't abide. The way it hums. And the way, when it gets hot, it *smells*. Even after all these years, that smell reminds me of Cold Mountain.

Van Hay gave him thirty seconds, then turned the juice off. The doctor stepped forward from his place and listened with his stethoscope. There was no talk from the witnesses now. The doctor straightened up and looked through the mesh. "Disorganized," he said, and made a twirling, cranking gesture with one finger. He had heard a few random heartbeats from Bitterbuck's chest, probably as meaningless as the final jitters of a decapitated chicken, but it was better not to take chances. You didn't want him suddenly sitting up on the gurney when you had him halfway through the tunnel, bawling that he felt like he was on fire.

Van Hay rolled on three and The Chief surged forward again, twisting a little from side to side in the grip of the current. When doc listened this time, he nodded. It was over. We had once again succeeded in destroying what we could not create. Some of the folks in the audience had begun talking in those low voices again; most sat with their heads down, looking at the floor, as if stunned. Or ashamed.

Harry and Dean came up with the stretcher. It was actually Percy's job to take one end, but he didn't know and no one had bothered to tell him. The Chief, still wearing the black silk hood, was loaded onto it by Brutal and me, and we whisked him through the door which led to the tunnel as fast as we could manage it without actually running. Smoke—too much of it—was rising from the hole in the top of the mask, and there was a horrible stench.

"Aw, man!" Percy cried, his voice wavering. "What's that smell?"

"Just get out of my way and stay out of it," Brutal said, shoving past him to get to the wall where there was a mounted fire extinguisher. It was one of the old chemical kind that you had to pump. Dean, meanwhile, had stripped off the hood. It wasn't as bad as it could have been; Bitterbuck's left braid was smouldering like a pile of wet leaves.

"Never mind that thing," I told Brutal. I didn't want to have to clean a load of chemical slime off the dead man's face before putting him in the back of the meatwagon. I slapped at The Chief's head (Percy staring at me, wide-eyed, the whole time) until the smoke quit rising. Then we carried the body down the twelve wooden steps to the tunnel. Here it was as chilly and dank as a dungeon, with the hollow plink-plink sound of dripping water. Hanging lights with crude tin shades—they were made in the prison machine-shop—showed a brick tube that ran thirty feet under the highway. The top was curved and wet. It made me feel like a character in an Edgar Allan Poe story every time I used it.

There was a gurney waiting. We loaded Bitterbuck's body onto it, and I made a final check to make sure his hair was out. That one braid was pretty well charred, and I was sorry to see that the cunning little bow on that side of his head was now nothing but a blackened lump.

Percy slapped the dead man's cheek. The flat smacking sound of his hand made us all jump. Percy looked around at us with a cocky smile on his mouth, eyes glittering. Then he looked back at Bitterbuck again. "Adiós, Chief," he said. "Hope hell's hot enough for you."

"Don't do that," Brutal said, his voice hollow and declamatory in the dripping tunnel. "He's paid what he owed. He's square with the house again. You keep your hands off him."

"Aw, blow it out," Percy said, but he stepped back uneasily when Brutal moved toward him, shadow rising behind him like the shadow of that ape in the story about the Rue Morgue. But instead of grabbing at Percy, Brutal grabbed hold of the gurney and began pushing Arlen Bitterbuck slowly toward the far end of the tunnel, where his last ride was waiting, parked on the soft shoulder of the highway. The gurney's hard rubber wheels moaned on the boards; its shadow rode the bulging brick wall, waxing and waning; Dean and Harry grasped the sheet at the foot and pulled it up over The Chief's face, which had already begun to take on the waxy, characterless cast of all dead faces, the innocent as well as the guilty.

6

WHEN I WAS EIGHTEEN, my Uncle Paul—the man I was named for—died of a heart attack. My mother and dad took me to Chicago with them to attend his funeral and visit relatives from my father's side of the family, many of whom I had never met. We were gone almost a month. In some ways that was a good trip, a necessary and exciting trip, but in another way it was horrible. I was deeply in love, you see, with the young woman who was to become my wife two weeks after my nineteenth birthday. One night when my longing for her was like a fire burning out of control in my heart and my head (oh yes, all right, and in my balls, as well), I wrote her a letter that just seemed to go on and on—I poured out my whole heart in it, never looking back to see what I'd said because I was afraid cowardice would make me stop. I didn't stop, and when a voice in my head clamored that it would be madness to mail such a letter, that I would be giving her my naked heart to hold in her hand, I ignored it with a child's breathless disregard of the consequences. I often wondered if Janice kept that letter, but never quite got up enough courage to ask. All I know for sure is that I did not find it when I went through her things after the funeral, and of course that by itself means nothing. I suppose I never asked because I was afraid of discovering that burning epistle meant less to her than it did to me.

It was four pages long. I thought I would never write anything longer in my life, and now look at this. All this, and the end still not in sight. If I'd known the story was going to go on this long, I might never have started. What I didn't realize was how many doors the act of writing unlocks, as if my Dad's old fountain pen wasn't really a pen at all, but some strange variety of skeleton key. The mouse is probably the best example of what I'm talking about—Steamboat Willy, Mr. Jingles, the mouse on the Mile. Until I started to write, I never realized how important he (yes, *he*) was. The way he seemed to be looking for Delacroix before Delacroix arrived, for instance—I don't think that ever occurred to me, not to my conscious mind, anyway, until I began to write and remember.

I guess what I'm saying is that I didn't realize how far back I'd have to go in order to tell you about John Coffey, or how long I'd have to leave him there in his cell, a man so huge his feet didn't just stick off the end of his bunk but hung down all the way to the floor. I don't want you to forget him, all right? I want you to see him there, looking up at the ceiling of his cell, weeping his silent tears, or putting his arms over his face. I want you to hear him, his sighs that trembled like sobs, his occasional watery groan. These weren't the sounds of agony and regret we sometimes heard on E Block, sharp cries with splinters of remorse in them; like his wet eyes, they were somehow removed from the pain we were used to dealing with. In a way—I know how crazy this will sound, of course I do, but there is no sense in writing something as long as this if you can't say what feels true to your heart—in a way it was as if it was sorrow for the whole world he felt, something too big ever to be completely eased. Sometimes I sat and talked to him, as I did with all of them—talking was our biggest, most important job, as I believe I have said—and I tried to comfort him. I don't feel that I ever did, and part of my heart was glad he was suffering, you know. Felt he *deserved* to suffer. I even thought sometimes of calling the governor (or getting Percy to do it—hell, he was Percy's damn uncle, not mine) and asking for a stay of execution. *We shouldn't burn him yet,* I'd say. *It's still hurting him too much, biting into him too much, twisting in his guts like a nice sharp stick. Give him another ninety days, your honor, sir. Let him go on doing to himself what we can't do to him.*

It's that John Coffey I'd have you keep to one side of your mind while I finish catching up to where I started—that John Coffey lying on his bunk, that John Coffey who was afraid of the dark perhaps with

good reason, for in the dark might not two shapes with blonde curls—
no longer little girls but avenging harpies—be waiting for him? That
John Coffey whose eyes were always streaming tears, like blood from a
wound that can never heal.

7

So The Chief burned and The President walked—as far as C Block, anyway, which was home to most of Cold Mountain's hundred and fifty lifers. Life for The Pres turned out to be twelve years. He was drowned in the prison laundry in 1944. Not the Cold Mountain prison laundry; Cold Mountain closed in 1933. I don't suppose it mattered much to the inmates—walls is walls, as the cons say, and Old Sparky was every bit as lethal in his own little stone death chamber, I reckon, as he'd ever been in the storage room at Cold Mountain.

As for The Pres, someone shoved him face-first into a vat of dry-cleaning fluid and held him there. When the guards pulled him out again, his face was almost entirely gone. They had to ID him by his fingerprints. On the whole, he might have been better off with Old Sparky . . . but then he never would have had those extra twelve years, would he? I doubt he thought much about them, though, in the last minute or so of his life, when his lungs were trying to learn how to breathe Hexlite and lye cleanser.

They never caught whoever did for him. By then I was out of the corrections line of work, but Harry Terwilliger wrote and told me. "He got commuted mostly because he was white," Harry wrote, "but he got it in the end, just the same. I just think of it as a long stay of execution that finally ran out."

There was a quiet time for us in E Block, once The Pres was gone. Harry and Dean were temporarily reassigned, and it was just me, Brutal, and Percy on the Green Mile for a little bit. Which actually meant just me and Brutal, because Percy kept pretty much to himself. I tell you, that young man was a genius at finding things not to do. And every so often (but only when Percy wasn't around), the other guys would show up to have what Harry liked to call "a good gab." On many of these occasions the mouse would also show up. We'd feed him and he'd sit there eating, just as solemn as Solomon, watching us with his bright little oilspot eyes.

That was a good few weeks, calm and easy even with Percy's more than occasional carping. But all good things come to an end, and on a rainy Monday in late July—have I told you how rainy and dank that summer was?—I found myself sitting on the bunk of an open cell and waiting for Eduard Delacroix.

He came with an unexpected bang. The door leading into the exercise yard slammed open, letting in a flood of light, there was a confused rattle of chains, a frightened voice babbling away in a mixture of English and Cajun French (a patois the cons at Cold Mountain used to call *da bayou*), and Brutal hollering, "Hey! Quit it! For Chrissakes! Quit it, Percy!"

I had been half-dozing on what was to become Delacroix's bunk, but I was up in a hurry, my heart slugging away hard in my chest. Noise of that kind on E Block almost never happened until Percy came; he brought it along with him like a bad smell.

"Come on, you fuckin French-fried faggot!" Percy yelled, ignoring Brutal completely. And here he came, dragging a guy not much bigger than a bowling pin by one arm. In his other hand, Percy had his baton. His teeth were bared in a strained grimace, and his face was bright red. Yet he did not look entirely unhappy. Delacroix was trying to keep up with him, but he had the leg-irons on, and no matter how fast he shuffled his feet, Percy pulled him along faster. I sprang out of the cell just in time to catch him as he fell, and that was how Del and I were introduced.

Percy rounded on him, baton raised, and I held him back with one arm. Brutal came puffing up to us, looking as shocked and nonplussed by all this as I felt.

"Don't let him hit me no mo, *m'sieu*," Delacroix babbled. *"S'il vous plaît, s'il vous plaît!"*

"Let me at im, let me at im!" Percy cried, lunging forward. He began to hit at Delacroix's shoulders with his baton. Delacroix held his arms up, screaming, and the stick went whap-whap-whap against the sleeves of his blue prison shirt. I saw him that night with the shirt off, and that boy had bruises from Christmas to Easter. Seeing them made me feel bad. He was a murderer, and nobody's darling, but that's not the way we did things on E Block. Not until Percy came, anyhow.

"Whoa! Whoa!" I roared. "Quit that! What's it all about, anyway?" I was trying to get my body in between Delacroix's and Percy's, but it wasn't working very well. Percy's club continued to flail away, now on one side of me and now on the other. Sooner or later he was going to bring one down on *me* instead of on his intended target, and then there was going to be a brawl right here in this corridor, no matter who his relations were. I wouldn't be able to help myself, and Brutal was apt to join in. In some ways, you know, I wish we'd done it. It might have changed some of the things that happened later on.

"Fucking faggot! I'll teach you to keep your hands off me, you lousy bum-puncher!"

Whap! Whap! Whap! And now Delacroix was bleeding from one ear and screaming. I gave up trying to shield him, grabbed him by one shoulder, and hurled him into his cell, where he went sprawling on the bunk. Percy darted around me and gave him a final hard whap on the butt—one to go on, you could say. Then Brutal grabbed him— Percy, I mean—by the shoulders and hauled him across the corridor.

I grabbed the cell door and ran it shut on its tracks. Then I turned to Percy, my shock and bewilderment at war with pure fury. Percy had been around about several months at that point, long enough for all of us to decide we didn't like him very much, but that was the first time I fully understood how out of control he was.

He stood watching me, not entirely without fear—he was a coward at heart, I never had any doubt of that—but still confident that his connections would protect him. In that he was correct. I suspect there are people who wouldn't understand why that was, even after all I've said, but they would be people who only know the phrase *Great Depression* from the history books. If you were there, it was a lot more than a phrase in a book, and if you had a steady job, brother, you'd do almost anything to keep it.

The color was fading out of Percy's face a little by then, but his cheeks were still flushed, and his hair, which was usually swept back and gleaming with brilliantine, had tumbled over his forehead.

"What in the Christ was *that* all about?" I asked. "I have never—I have *never*!—had a prisoner beaten onto my block before!"

"Little fag bastard tried to cop my joint when I pulled him out of the van," Percy said. "He had it coming, and I'd do it again."

I looked at him, too flabbergasted for words. I couldn't imagine the most predatory homosexual on God's green earth doing what Percy had just described. Preparing to move into a crossbar apartment on the Green Mile did not, as a rule, put even the most deviant of prisoners in a sexy mood.

I looked back at Delacroix, cowering on his bunk with his arms still up to protect his face. There were cuffs on his wrists and a chain running between his ankles. Then I turned to Percy. "Get out of here," I said. "I'll want to talk to you later."

"Is this going to be in your report?" he demanded truculently. "Because if it is, I can make a report of my own, you know."

I didn't want to make a report; I only wanted him out of my sight. I told him so.

"The matter's closed," I finished. I saw Brutal looking at me disapprovingly, but ignored it. "Go on, get out of here. Go over to Admin and tell them you're supposed to read letters and help in the package room."

"Sure." He had his composure back, or the crack-headed arrogance that served him as composure. He brushed his hair back from his forehead with his hands—soft and white and small, the hands of a girl in her early teens, you would have thought—and then approached the cell. Delacroix saw him, and he cringed back even farther on his bunk, gibbering in a mixture of English and stewpot French.

"I ain't done with you, Pierre," he said, then jumped as one of Brutal's huge hands fell on his shoulder.

"Yes you are," Brutal said. "Now go on. Get in the breeze."

"You don't scare me, you know," Percy said. "Not a bit." His eyes shifted to me. "Either of you." But we did. You could see that in his eyes as clear as day, and it made him even more dangerous. A guy like Percy doesn't even know himself what he means to do from minute to minute and second to second.

What he did right then was turn away from us and go walking up the corridor in long, arrogant strides. He had shown the world what happened when scrawny, half-bald little Frenchmen tried to cop his joint, by God, and he was leaving the field a victor.

I went through my set speech, all about how we had the radio— *Make Believe Ballroom* and *Our Gal Sunday*, and how we'd treat him jake if he did the same for us. That little homily was not what you'd call one of my great successes. He cried all the way through it, sitting huddled up at the foot of his bunk, as far from me as he could get without actually fading into the corner. He cringed every time I moved, and I don't think he heard one word in six. Probably just as well. I don't think that particular homily made a whole lot of sense, anyway.

Fifteen minutes later I was back at the desk, where a shaken-looking Brutus Howell was sitting and licking the tip of the pencil we kept with the visitors' book. "Will you stop that before you poison yourself, for God's sake?" I asked.

"Christ almighty Jesus," he said, putting the pencil down. "I *never* want to have another hooraw like that with a prisoner coming on the block."

"My Daddy always used to say things come in threes," I said.

"Well, I hope your Daddy was full of shit on that subject," Brutal said, but of course he wasn't. There was a squall when John Coffey came in, and a full-blown storm when "Wild Bill" joined us—it's funny, but things really *do* seem to come in threes. The story of our introduction to Wild Bill, how he came onto the Mile trying to commit murder, is something I'll get to shortly; fair warning.

"What's this about Delacroix copping his joint?" I asked.

Brutal snorted. "He was ankle-chained and ole Percy was just pulling him too fast, that's all. He stumbled and started to fall as he got out of the stagecoach. He put his hands out same as anyone would when they start to fall, and one of them brushed the front of Percy's pants. It was a complete accident."

"Did Percy know that, do you think?" I asked. "Was he maybe using it as an excuse just because he felt like whaling on Delacroix a little bit? Showing him who bosses the shooting match around here?"

Brutal nodded slowly. "Yeah. I think that was probably it."

"We have to watch him, then," I said, and ran my hands through my hair. As if the job wasn't hard enough. "God, I hate this. I hate *him*."

"Me, too. And you want to know something else, Paul? I don't understand him. He's got connections, I understand *that*, all right, but why would he use them to get a job on the Green fucking Mile? *Any-where* in the state pen, for that matter? Why not as a page in the state senate, or the guy who makes the lieutenant governor's appointments? Surely his people could've gotten him something better if he'd asked them, so why *here*?"

I shook my head. I didn't know. There were a lot of things I didn't know then. I suppose I was naive.

8

AFTER THAT, things went back to normal again . . . for awhile, at least. Down in the county seat, the state was preparing to bring John Coffey to trial, and Trapingus County Sheriff Homer Cribus was pooh-poohing the idea that a lynch-mob might hurry justice along a little bit. None of that mattered to us; on E Block, no one paid much attention to the news. Life on the Green Mile was, in a way, like life in a soundproof room. From time to time you heard mutterings that were probably explosions in the outside world, but that was about all. They wouldn't hurry with John Coffey; they'd want to make damned sure of him.

On a couple of occasions Percy got to ragging Delacroix, and the second time I pulled him aside and told him to come up to my office. It wasn't my first interview with Percy on the subject of his behavior, and it wouldn't be the last, but it was prompted by what was probably the clearest understanding of what he was. He had the heart of a cruel boy who goes to the zoo not so he can study the animals but so he can throw stones at them in their cages.

"You stay away from him, now, you hear?" I said. "Unless I give you a specific order, just stay the hell away from him."

Percy combed his hair back, then patted at it with his sweet little hands. That boy just loved touching his hair. "I wasn't doing nothing to him," he said. "Only asking how it felt to know you had burned up some babies, is all." Percy gave me a round-eyed, innocent stare.

"You quit with it, or there'll be a report," I said.

He laughed. "Make any report you want," he said. "Then I'll turn around and make my own. Just like I told you when he came in. We'll see who comes off the best."

I leaned forward, hands folded on my desk, and spoke in a tone I hoped would sound like a friend being confidential. "Brutus Howell doesn't like you much," I said. "And when Brutal doesn't like someone, he's been known to make his own report. He isn't much shakes with a pen, and he can't quit from licking that pencil, so he's apt to report with his fists. If you know what I mean."

Percy's complacent little smile faltered. "What are you trying to say?"

"I'm not *trying* to say anything. I *have* said it. And if you tell any of your . . . friends . . . about this discussion, I'll say you made the whole thing up." I looked at him all wide-eyed and earnest. "Besides, I'm trying to be your friend, Percy. A word to the wise is sufficient, they say. And why would you want to get into it with Delacroix in the first place? He's not worth it."

And for awhile that worked. There was peace. A couple of times I was even able to send Percy with Dean or Harry when Delacroix's time to shower had rolled around. We had the radio at night, Delacroix began to relax a little into the scant routine of E Block, and there was peace.

Then, one night, I heard him laughing.

Harry Terwilliger was on the desk, and soon he was laughing, too. I got up and went on down to Delacroix's cell to see what he possibly had to laugh about.

"Look, Cap'n!" he said when he saw me. "I done tame me a mouse!"

It was Steamboat Willy. He was in Delacroix's cell. More: he was sitting on Delacroix's shoulder and looking calmly out through the bars at us with his little oildrop eyes. His tail was curled around his paws, and he looked completely at peace. As for Delacroix—friend, you wouldn't have known it was the same man who'd sat cringing and shuddering at the foot of his bunk not a week before. He looked like my daughter used to on Christmas morning, when she came down the stairs and saw the presents.

"Watch dis!" Delacroix said. The mouse was sitting on his right shoulder. Delacroix stretched out his left arm. The mouse scampered up to the top of Delacroix's head, using the man's hair (which was thick enough in back, at least) to climb up. Then he scampered down the other side, Delacroix giggling as his tail tickled the side of his neck. The mouse ran all the way down his arm to his wrist, then turned, scampered back up to Delacroix's left shoulder, and curled his tail around his feet again.

"I'll be damned," Harry said.

"I train him to do that," Delacroix said proudly. I thought, *In a pig's ass you did,* but kept my mouth shut. "His name is Mr. Jingles."

"Nah," Harry said goodnaturedly. "It's Steamboat Willy, like in the pitcher-show. Boss Howell named him."

"It's Mr. Jingles," Delacroix said. On any other subject he would have told you that shit was Shinola, if you wanted him to, but on the subject of the mouse's name he was perfectly adamant. "He whisper it in my ear. Cap'n, can I have a box for him? Can I have a box for my mous', so he can sleep in here wit me?" His voice began to fall into wheedling tones I had heard a thousand times before. "I put him under my bunk and he never be a scrid of trouble, not one."

"Your English gets a hell of a lot better when you want something," I said, stalling for time.

"Oh-oh," Harry murmured, nudging me. "Here comes trouble."

But Percy didn't look like trouble to me, not that night. He wasn't running his hands through his hair or fiddling with that baton of his, and the top button of his uniform shirt was actually undone. It was the first time I'd seen him that way, and it was amazing, what a change a little thing like that could make. Mostly, though, what struck me was the expression on his face. There was a calmness there. Not serenity— I don't think Percy Wetmore had a serene bone in his body—but the look of a man who has discovered he can wait for the things he wants. It was quite a change from the young man I'd had to threaten with Brutus Howell's fists only a few days before.

Delacroix didn't see the change, though; he cringed against the wall of his cell, drawing his knees up to his chest. His eyes seemed to grow until they were taking up half his face. The mouse scampered up on his bald pate and sat there. I don't know if he remembered that he also had reason to distrust Percy, but it certainly looked as if he did. Probably it was just smelling the little Frenchman's fear, and reacting off that.

"Well, well," Percy said. "Looks like you found yourself a friend, Eddie."

Delacroix tried to reply—some hollow defiance about what would happen to Percy if Percy hurt his new pal would have been my guess— but nothing came out. His lower lip trembled a little, but that was all. On top of his head, Mr. Jingles wasn't trembling. He sat perfectly still with his back feet in Delacroix's hair and his front ones splayed on Delacroix's bald skull, looking at Percy, seeming to size him up. The way you'd size up an old enemy.

Percy looked at me. "Isn't that the same one I chased? The one that lives in the restraint room?"

I nodded. I had an idea Percy hadn't seen the newly named Mr. Jingles since that last chase, and he showed no signs of wanting to chase it now.

"Yes, that's the one," I said. "Only Delacroix there says his name is Mr. Jingles, not Steamboat Willy. Says the mouse whispered it in his ear."

"Is that so," Percy said. "Wonders never cease, do they?" I half-expected him to pull out his baton and start tapping it against the bars, just to show Delacroix who was boss, but he only stood there with his hands on his hips, looking in.

And for no reason I could have told you in words, I said: "Delacroix there was just asking for a box, Percy. He thinks that mouse will sleep in it, I guess. That he can keep it for a pet." I loaded my voice with skepticism, and sensed more than saw Harry looking at me in surprise. "What do you think about that?"

"I think it'll probably shit up his nose some night while he's sleeping and then run away," Percy said evenly, "but I guess that's the French boy's lookout. I seen a pretty nice cigar box on Toot-Toot's cart the other night. I don't know if he'd give it away, though. Probably want a nickel for it, maybe even a dime."

Now I did risk a glance at Harry, and saw his mouth hanging open. This wasn't quite like the change in Ebenezer Scrooge on Christmas morning, after the ghosts had had their way with him, but it was damned close.

Percy leaned closer to Delacroix, putting his face between the bars. Delacroix shrank back even farther. I swear to God that he would have melted into that wall if he'd been able.

"You got a nickel or maybe as much as a dime to pay for a cigar box, you lugoon?" he asked.

"I got four pennies," Delacroix said. "I give them for a box, if it a good one, *s'il est bon.*"

"I'll tell you what," Percy said. "If that toothless old whoremaster will sell you that Corona box for four cents, I'll sneak some cotton batting out of the dispensary to line it with. We'll make us a regular Mousie Hilton, before we're through." He shifted his eyes to me. "I'm supposed to write a switch-room report about Bitterbuck," he said. "Is there some pens in your office, Paul?"

"Yes, indeed," I said. "Forms, too. Lefthand top drawer."

"Well, that's aces," he said, and went swaggering off.

Harry and I looked at each other. "Is he sick, do you think?" Harry asked. "Maybe went to his doctor and found out he's only got three months to live?"

I told him I didn't have the slightest idea what was up. It was the truth then, and for awhile after, but I found out in time. And a few years later, I had an interesting supper-table conversation with Hal Moores. By then we could talk freely, what with him being retired and me being at the Boys' Correctional. It was one of those meals where you drink too much and eat too little, and tongues get loosened. Hal told me that Percy had been in to complain about me and about life on the Mile in general. This was just after Delacroix came on the block, and Brutal and I had kept Percy from beating him half to death. What had griped Percy the most was me telling him to get out of my sight. He didn't think a man who was related to the governor should have to put up with talk like that.

Well, Moores told me, he had stood Percy off for as long as he could, and when it became clear to him that Percy was going to try pulling some strings to get me reprimanded and moved to another part of the prison at the very least, he, Moores, had pulled Percy into his office and told him that if he quit rocking the boat, Moores would make sure that Percy was out front for Delacroix's execution. That he would, in fact, be placed right beside the chair. I would be in charge, as always, but the witnesses wouldn't know that; to them it would look as if Mr. Percy Wetmore was boss of the cotillion. Moores wasn't promising any more than what we'd already discussed and I'd gone along with, but Percy didn't know that. He agreed to leave off his threats to have me reassigned, and the atmosphere on E Block sweetened. He had even agreed that Delacroix could keep Percy's old nemesis as a pet. It's amazing how some men can change, given the right incentive; in Percy's case, all Warden Moores had to offer was the chance to take a bald little Frenchman's life.

9

TOOT-TOOT FELT that four cents was far too little for a prime Corona cigar box, and in that he was probably right—cigar boxes were highly prized objects in prison. A thousand different small items could be stored in them, the smell was pleasant, and there was something about them that reminded our customers of what it was like to be free men. Because cigarettes were permitted in prison but cigars were not, I imagine.

Dean Stanton, who was back on the block by then, added a penny to the pot, and I kicked one in, as well. When Toot still proved reluctant, Brutal went to work on him, first telling him he ought to be ashamed of himself for behaving like such a cheapskate, then promising him that he, Brutus Howell, would personally put that Corona box back in Toot's hands the day after Delacroix's execution. "Six cents might or might not be enough if you was speaking about *selling* that cigar box, we could have a good old barber-shop argument about that," Brutal said, "but you have to admit it's a great price for *renting* one. He's gonna walk the Mile in a month, six weeks at the very outside. Why, that box'll be back on the shelf under your cart almost before you know it's gone."

"He could get a soft-hearted judge to give im a stay and still be here to sing 'Should old acquaintance be forgot,' " Toot said, but he knew better and Brutal knew he did. Old Toot-Toot had been pushing that damned Bible-quoting cart of his around Cold Mountain since Pony Express days, practically, and he had plenty of sources . . . better than ours, I thought then. He knew Delacroix was fresh out of soft-hearted judges. All he had left to hope for was the governor, who as a rule didn't issue clemency to folks who had baked half a dozen of his constituents.

"Even if he don't get a stay, that mouse'd be shitting in that box until October, maybe even Thanksgiving," Toot argued, but Brutal could see he was weakening. "Who gonna buy a cigar box some mouse been using for a toilet?"

"Oh jeez-Louise," Brutal said. "That's the numbest thing I've ever heard you say, Toot. I mean, that takes the cake. First, Delacroix will keep the box clean enough to eat a church dinner out of—the way he loves that mouse, he'd lick it clean if that's what it took."

"Easy on dat stuff," Toot said, wrinkling his nose.

"Second," Brutal went on, "mouse-shit is no big deal, anyway. It's just hard little pellets, looks like birdshot. Shake it right out. Nothing to it."

Old Toot knew better than to carry his protest any further; he'd been on the yard long enough to understand when he could afford to face into the breeze and when he'd do better to bend in the hurricane. This wasn't exactly a hurricane, but we bluesuits liked the mouse, and we liked the idea of Delacroix having the mouse, and that meant it was at least a gale. So Delacroix got his box, and Percy was as good as his word—two days later the bottom was lined with soft pads of cotton batting from the dispensary. Percy handed them over himself, and I could see the fear in Delacroix's eyes as he reached out through the bars to take them. He was afraid Percy would grab his hand and break his fingers. I was a little afraid of it, too, but no such thing happened. That was the closest I ever came to liking Percy, but even then it was hard to mistake the look of cool amusement in his eyes. Delacroix had a pet; Percy had one, too. Delacroix would keep his, petting it and loving it as long as he could; Percy would wait patiently (as patiently as a man like him could, anyway), and then burn his alive.

"Mousie Hilton, open for business," Harry said. "The only question is, will the little bugger use it?"

That question was answered as soon as Delacroix caught Mr. Jingles up in one hand and lowered him gently into the box. The mouse snuggled into the white cotton as if it were Aunt Bea's comforter, and that was his home from then until . . . well, I'll get to the end of Mr. Jingles's story in good time.

Old Toot-Toot's worries that the cigar box would fill up with mouse-shit proved to be entirely groundless. I never saw a single turd in there, and Delacroix said he never did, either . . . anywhere in his cell, for that matter. Much later, around the time Brutal showed me the hole in the beam and we found the colored splinters, I moved a chair out of the restraint room's east corner and found a little pile of mouse turds back there. He had always gone back to the same place to do his business, seemingly, and as far from us as he could get. Here's another thing: I never saw him peeing, and usually mice can hardly turn the faucet off for two minutes at a time, especially while they're eating. I told you, the damned thing was one of God's mysteries.

A week or so after Mr. Jingles had settled into the cigar box, Delacroix called me and Brutal down to his cell to see something. He did that so much it was annoying—if Mr. Jingles so much as rolled over on his back with his paws in the air, it was the cutest thing on God's earth, as far as that half-pint Cajun was concerned—but this time what he was up to really was sort of amusing.

Delacroix had been pretty much forgotten by the world following his conviction, but he had one relation—an old maiden aunt, I believe—who wrote him once a week. She had also sent him an enormous bag of peppermint candies, the sort which are marketed under the name Canada Mints these days. They looked like big pink pills. Delacroix was not allowed to have the whole bag at once, naturally—it was a five-pounder, and he would have gobbled them until he had to go to the infirmary with stomach-gripes. Like almost every murderer we ever had on the Mile, he had absolutely no understanding of moderation. We'd give them out to him half a dozen at a time, and only then if he remembered to ask.

Mr. Jingles was sitting beside Delacroix on the bunk when we got down there, holding one of those pink candies in his paws and munching contentedly away at it. Delacroix was simply overcome with delight—he was like a classical pianist watching his five-year-old son play his first halting exercises. But don't get me wrong; it *was* funny, a

THE GREEN MILE

real hoot. The candy was half the size of Mr. Jingles, and his white-furred belly was already distended from it.

"Take it away from him, Eddie," Brutal said, half-laughing and half-horrified. "Christ almighty Jesus, he'll eat till he busts. I can smell that peppermint from here. How many have you let him have?"

"This his second," Delacroix said, looking a little nervously at Mr. Jingles's belly. "You really think he . . . you know . . . bus' his guts?"

"Might," Brutal said.

That was enough authority for Delacroix. He reached for the half-eaten pink mint. I expected the mouse to nip him, but Mr. Jingles gave over that mint—what remained of it, anyway—as meek as could be. I looked at Brutal, and Brutal gave his head a little shake as if to say no, he didn't understand it, either. Then Mr. Jingles plopped down into his box and lay there on his side in an exhausted way that made all three of us laugh. After that, we got used to seeing the mouse sitting beside Delacroix, holding a mint and munching away on it just as neatly as an old lady at an afternoon tea-party, both of them surrounded by what I later smelled in that hole in the beam—the half-bitter, half-sweet smell of peppermint candy.

There's one more thing to tell you about Mr. Jingles before moving on to the arrival of William Wharton, which was when the cyclone really touched down on E Block. A week or so after the incident of the peppermint candies—around the time when we'd pretty much decided Delacroix wasn't going to feed his pet to death, in other words—the Frenchman called me down to his cell. I was on my own for the time being, Brutal over at the commissary for something, and according to the regs, I was not supposed to approach a prisoner in such circumstances. But since I probably could have shot-putted Delacroix twenty yards one-handed on a good day, I decided to break the rule and see what he wanted.

"Watch this, Boss Edgecombe," he said. "You gonna see what Mr. Jingles can do!" He reached behind the cigar box and brought up a small wooden spool.

"Where'd you get that?" I asked him, although I supposed I knew. There was really only one person he *could* have gotten it from.

"Old Toot-Toot," he said. "Watch this."

I was already watching, and could see Mr. Jingles in his box, standing up with his small front paws propped on the edge, his black eyes fixed on the spool Delacroix was holding between the thumb and first finger of his right hand. I felt a funny little chill go up my back. I had never seen a mere mouse attend to something with such sharpness—with such *intelligence*. I don't really believe that Mr. Jingles was a supernatural visitation, and if I have given you that idea, I'm sorry, but I have never doubted that he was a genius of his kind.

Delacroix bent over and rolled the threadless spool across the floor of his cell. It went easily, like a pair of wheels connected by an axle. The mouse was out of his box in a flash and across the floor after it, like a dog chasing after a stick. I exclaimed with surprise, and Delacroix grinned.

The spool hit the wall and rebounded. Mr. Jingles went around it and pushed it back to the bunk, switching from one end of the spool to the other whenever it looked like it was going to veer off-course. He pushed the spool until it hit Delacroix's foot. Then he looked up at him for a moment, as if to make sure Delacroix had no more immediate tasks for him (a few arithmetic problems to solve, perhaps, or some Latin to parse). Apparently satisfied on this score, Mr. Jingles went back to the cigar box and settled down in it again.

"You taught him that," I said.

"Yessir, Boss Edgecombe," Delacroix said, his smile only slightly dissembling. "He fetch it every time. Smart as hell, ain't he?"

"And the spool?" I asked. "How did you know to fetch that for *him*, Eddie?"

"He whisper in my ear that he want it," Delacroix said serenely. "Same as he whisper his name."

Delacroix showed all the other guys his mouse's trick . . . all except Percy. To Delacroix, it didn't matter that Percy had suggested the cigar box and procured the cotton with which to line it. Delacroix was like some dogs: kick them once and they never trust you again, no matter how nice you are to them.

I can hear Delacroix now, yelling, *Hey, you guys! Come and see what Mr.*

Jingles can do! And them going down in a bluesuit cluster—Brutal, Harry, Dean, even Bill Dodge. All of them had been properly amazed, too, the same as I had been.

Three or four days after Mr. Jingles started doing the trick with the spool, Harry Terwilliger rummaged through the arts and crafts stuff we kept in the restraint room, found the Crayolas, and brought them to Delacroix with a smile that was almost embarrassed. "I thought you might like to make that spool different colors," he said. "Then your little pal'd be like a circus mouse, or something."

"A circus mouse!" Delacroix said, looking completely, rapturously happy. I suppose he *was* completely happy, maybe for the first time in his whole miserable life. "That just what he is, too! A circus mouse! When I get outta here, he gonna make me rich, like inna circus! You see if he don't."

Percy Wetmore would no doubt have pointed out to Delacroix that when he left Cold Mountain, he'd be riding in an ambulance that didn't need to run its light or siren, but Harry knew better. He just told Delacroix to make the spool as colorful as he could as quick as he could, because he'd have to take the crayons back after dinner.

Del made it colorful, all right. When he was done, one end of the spool was yellow, the other end was green, and the drum in the middle was firehouse red. We got used to hearing Delacroix trumpet, *"Maintenant, m'sieurs et mesdames! Le cirque présentement le mous' amusant et amazeant!"* That wasn't exactly it, but it gives you an idea of that stewpot French of his. Then he'd make this sound way down in his throat—I think it was supposed to represent a drumroll—and fling the spool. Mr. Jingles would be after it in a flash, either nosing it back or rolling it with his paws. That second way really was something you would have paid to see in a circus, I think. Delacroix and his mouse and his mouse's brightly colored spool were our chief amusements at the time that John Coffey came into our care and custody, and that was the way things remained for awhile. Then my urinary infection, which had lain still for awhile, came back, and William Wharton arrived, and all hell broke loose.

10

THE DATES have mostly slipped out of my head. I suppose I could have my granddaughter, Danielle, look some of them out of the old newspaper files, but what would be the point? The most important of them, like the day we came down to Delacroix's cell and found the mouse sitting on his shoulder, or the day William Wharton came on the block and almost killed Dean Stanton, would not be in the papers, anyway. Maybe it's better to go on just as I have been; in the end, I guess the dates don't matter much, if you can remember the things you saw and keep them in the right order.

I know that things got squeezed together a little. When Delacroix's DOE papers finally came to me from Curtis Anderson's office, I was amazed to see that our Cajun pal's date with Old Sparky had been advanced from when we had expected, a thing that was almost unheard of, even in those days when you didn't have to move half of heaven and all the earth to execute a man. It was a matter of two days, I think, from the twenty-seventh of October to the twenty-fifth. Don't hold me to it exactly, but I know that's close; I remember thinking that Toot was going to get his Corona box back even sooner than he had expected.

Wharton, meanwhile, got to us later than expected. For one thing, his trial ran longer than Anderson's usually reliable sources had thought it would (when it came to Wild Billy, *nothing* was reliable, we would soon discover, including our time-tested and supposedly foolproof methods of prisoner control). Then, after he had been found guilty—that much, at least, went according to the script—he was taken to Indianola

General Hospital for tests. He had had a number of supposed seizures during the trial, twice serious enough to send him crashing to the floor, where he lay shaking and flopping and drumming his feet on the boards. Wharton's court-appointed lawyer claimed he suffered from "epilepsy spells" and had committed his crimes while of unsound mind; the prosecution claimed the fits were the sham acting of a coward desperate to save his own life. After observing the so-called "epilepsy spells" at first hand, the jury decided the fits were an act. The judge concurred but ordered a series of pre-sentencing tests after the verdict came down. God knows why; perhaps he was only curious.

It's a blue-eyed wonder that Wharton didn't escape from the hospital (and the irony that Warden Moores's wife, Melinda, was in the same hospital at the same time did not escape any of us), but he didn't. They had him surrounded by guards, I suppose, and perhaps he still had hopes of being declared incompetent by reason of epilepsy, if there is such a thing.

He wasn't. The doctors found nothing wrong with his brain—physiologically, at least—and Billy "the Kid" Wharton was at last bound for Cold Mountain. That might have been around the sixteenth or the eighteenth; it's my recollection that Wharton arrived about two weeks after John Coffey and a week or ten days before Delacroix walked the Green Mile.

The day our new psychopath joined us was an eventful one for me. I woke up at four that morning with my groin throbbing and my penis feeling hot and clogged and swollen. Even before I swung my feet out of bed, I knew that my urinary infection wasn't getting better, as I had hoped. It had been a brief turn for the better, that was all, and it was over.

I went out to the privy to do my business—this was at least three years before we put in our first water-closet—and had gotten no further than the woodpile at the corner of the house when I realized I couldn't hold it any longer. I lowered my pajama pants just as the urine started to flow, and that flow was accompanied by the most excruciating pain of my entire life. I passed a gallstone in 1956, and I know people say that is the worst, but that gallstone was like a touch of acid indigestion compared to this outrage.

My knees came unhinged and I fell heavily onto them, tearing out the seat of my pajama pants when I spread my legs to keep from losing my balance and going face-first into a puddle of my own piss. I still might have gone over if I hadn't grabbed one of the woodpile logs with my left hand. All that, though, could have been going on in Australia, or even on another planet. All I was concerned with was the pain that had set me on fire; my lower belly was burning, and my penis—an organ which had gone mostly forgotten by me except when providing me the most intense physical pleasure a man can experience—now felt as if it were melting; I expected to look down and see blood gushing from its tip, but it appeared to be a perfectly ordinary stream of urine.

I hung onto the woodpile with one hand and put the other across my mouth, concentrating on keeping my mouth shut. I did not want to frighten my wife awake with a scream. It seemed that I went on pissing forever, but at last the stream dried up. By then the pain had sunk deep into my stomach and my testicles, biting like rusty teeth. For a long while—it might have been as long as a minute—I was physically incapable of getting up. At last the pain began to abate, and I struggled to my feet. I looked at my urine, already soaking into the ground, and wondered if any sane God could make a world where such a little bit of dampness could come at the cost of such horrendous pain.

I would call in sick, I thought, and go see Dr. Sadler after all. I didn't want the stink and the queasiness of Dr. Sadler's sulfa tablets, but anything would be better than kneeling beside the woodpile, trying not to scream while my prick was reporting that it had apparently been doused with coal-oil and set afire.

Then, as I was swallowing aspirin in our kitchen and listening to Jan snore lightly in the other room, I remembered that today was the day William Wharton was scheduled on the block, and that Brutal wouldn't be there—the roster had him over on the other side of the prison, helping to move the rest of the library and some leftover infirmary equipment to the new building. One thing I didn't feel right about in spite of my pain was leaving Wharton to Dean and Harry. They were good men, but Curtis Anderson's report had suggested that

William Wharton was exceptionally bad news. <u>This man just doesn't care,</u> he had written, underlining for emphasis.

By then the pain had abated some, and I could think. The best idea, it seemed to me, was to leave for the prison early. I could get there at six, which was the time Warden Moores usually came in. He could get Brutus Howell reassigned to E Block long enough for Wharton's reception, and I'd make my long-overdue trip to the doctor. Cold Mountain was actually on my way.

Twice on the twenty-mile ride to the penitentiary, that sudden need to urinate overcame me. Both times I was able to pull over and take care of the problem without embarrassing myself (for one thing, traffic on country roads at such an hour was all but nonexistent). Neither of these two voidings was as painful as the one that had taken me off my feet on the way to the privy, but both times I had to clutch the passenger-side doorhandle of my little Ford coupe to hold myself up, and I could feel sweat running down my hot face. I was sick, all right, good and sick.

I made it, though, drove in through the south gate, parked in my usual place, and went right up to see the warden. It was going on six o'clock by then. Miss Hannah's office was empty—she wouldn't be in until the relatively civilized hour of seven—but the light was on in Moores's office; I could see it through the pebbled glass. I gave a perfunctory knock and opened the door. Moores looked up, startled to see anyone at that unusual hour, and I would have given a great deal not to have been the one to see him in that condition, with his face naked and unguarded. His white hair, usually so neatly combed, was sticking up in tufts and tangles; his hands were in it, yanking and pulling, when I walked in. His eyes were raw, the skin beneath them puffy and swollen. His palsy was the worst I had ever seen it; he looked like a man who had just come inside after a long walk on a terribly cold night.

"Hal, I'm sorry, I'll come back—" I began.

"No," he said. "Please, Paul. Come in. Shut the door and come in. I need someone now, if I ever needed anyone in my whole life. Shut the door and come in."

I did as he asked, forgetting my own pain for the first time since I'd awakened that morning.

"It's a brain tumor," Moores said. "They got X-ray pictures of it. They seemed real pleased with their pictures, actually. One of them said they may be the best ones anyone's ever gotten, at least so far; said they're going to publish them in some biggety medical journal up in New England. It's the size of a lemon, they said, and way down deep inside, where they can't operate. They say she'll be dead by Christmas. I haven't told her. I can't think how. I can't think how for the life of me."

Then he began to cry, big, gasping sobs that filled me with both pity and a kind of terror—when a man who keeps himself as tightly guarded as Hal Moores finally does lose control, it's frightening to watch. I stood there for a moment, then went to him and put my arm around his shoulders. He groped out for me with both of his own arms, like a drowning man, and began to sob against my stomach, all restraint washed away. Later, after he got himself under control, he apologized. He did it without quite meeting my eyes, as a man does when he feels he has embarrassed himself dreadfully, maybe so deeply that he can never quite live it down. A man can end up hating the fellow who has seen him in such a state. I thought Warden Moores was better than that, but it never crossed my mind to do the business I had originally come for, and when I left Moores's office, I walked over to E Block instead of back to my car. The aspirin was working by then, and the pain in my midsection was down to a low throb. I would get through the day somehow, I reckoned, get Wharton settled in, check back with Hal Moores that afternoon, and get my sick-leave for tomorrow. The worst was pretty much over, I thought, with no slightest idea that the worst of that day's mischief hadn't even begun.

11

"WE THOUGHT he was still doped from the tests," Dean said late that afternoon. His voice was low, rasping, almost a bark, and there were blackish-purple bruises rising on his neck. I could see it was hurting him to talk and thought of telling him to let it go, but sometimes it hurts more to be quiet. I judged that this was one of those times, and kept my own mouth shut. "We all thought he was doped, didn't we?"

Harry Terwilliger nodded. Even Percy, sitting off by himself in his own sullen little party of one, nodded.

Brutal glanced at me, and for a moment I met his eyes. We were thinking pretty much that same thing, that this was the way it happened. You were cruising along, everything going according to Hoyle, you made one mistake, and bang, the sky fell down on you. They had thought he was doped, it was a reasonable assumption to make, but no one had *asked* if he was doped. I thought I saw something else in Brutal's eyes, as well: Harry and Dean would learn from their mistake. Especially Dean, who could easily have gone home to his family dead. Percy wouldn't. Percy maybe couldn't. All Percy could do was sit in the corner and sulk because he was in the shit again.

There were seven of them that went up to Indianola to take charge of Wild Bill Wharton: Harry, Dean, Percy, two other guards in the back (I have forgotten their names, although I'm sure I knew them once), plus two up front. They took what we used to call the stagecoach—a Ford panel-truck which had been steel-reinforced and equipped with supposedly bulletproof glass. It looked like a cross between a milk-wagon and an armored car.

Harry Terwilliger was technically in charge of the expedition. He handed his paperwork over to the county sheriff (not Homer Cribus but some other elected yokel like him, I imagine), who in turn handed over Mr. William Wharton, hellraiser *extraordinaire*, as Delacroix might have put it. A Cold Mountain prison uniform had been sent ahead, but the sheriff and his men hadn't bothered to put Wharton in it; they left that to our boys. Wharton was dressed in a cotton hospital johnny and cheap felt slippers when they first met him on the second floor of the General Hospital, a scrawny man with a narrow, pimply face and a lot of long, tangly blond hair. His ass, also narrow and also covered with pimples, stuck out the back of the johnny. That was the part of him Harry and the others saw first, because Wharton was standing at the window and looking out at the parking lot when they came in. He didn't turn but just stood there, holding the curtains back with one hand, silent as a doll, while Harry bitched at the county sheriff about being too lazy to get Wharton into his prison blues and the county sheriff lectured—as every county official I've ever met seems bound to do—about what was his job and what was not.

When Harry got tired of that part (I doubt it took him long), he told Wharton to turn around. Wharton did. He looked, Dean told us in his raspy bark of a half-choked voice, like any one of a thousand back-country stampeders who had wound their way through Cold Mountain during our years there. Boil that look down and what you got was a dullard with a mean streak. Sometimes you also discovered a yellow streak in them, once their backs were to the wall, but more often there was nothing there but fight and mean and then more fight and more mean. There are people who see nobility in folks like Billy Wharton, but I am not one of them. A rat will fight, too, if it is cornered. This man's face seemed to have no more personality than his acne-studded backside, Dean told us. His jaw was slack, his eyes distant, his shoulders slumped, his hands dangling. He looked shot up with morphine, all right, every bit as coo-coo as any dopefiend any of them had ever seen.

At this, Percy gave another of his sullen nods.

"Put this on," Harry said, indicating the uniform on the foot of the bed—it had been taken out of the brown paper it was wrapped in, but otherwise not touched—it was still folded just as it had been in the prison laundry, with a pair of white cotton boxer shorts poking out of one shirtsleeve and a pair of white socks poking out of the other.

Wharton seemed willing enough to comply, but wasn't able to get very far without help. He managed the boxers, but when it came to the pants, he kept trying to put both legs into the same hole. Finally Dean helped him, getting his feet to go where they belonged and then yanking the trousers up, doing the fly, and snapping the waistband. Wharton only stood there, not even trying to help once he saw that Dean was doing it for him. He stared vacantly across the room, hands lax, and it didn't occur to any of them that he was shamming. Not in hopes of escape (at least I don't believe that was it) but only in hopes of making the maximum amount of trouble when the right time came.

The papers were signed. William Wharton, who had become county property when he was arrested, now became the state's property. He was taken down the back stairs and through the kitchen, surrounded by bluesuits. He walked with his head down and his long-fingered hands dangling. The first time his cap fell off, Dean put it back on him. The second time, he just tucked it into his own back pocket.

He had another chance to make trouble in the back of the stagecoach, when they were shackling him, and didn't. If he thought (even now I'm not sure if he did, or if he did, how much), he must have thought that the space was too small and the numbers too great to cause a satisfactory hooraw. So on went the chains, one set running between his ankles and another set—too long, it turned out—between his wrists.

The drive to Cold Mountain took an hour. During that whole time, Wharton sat on the lefthand bench up by the cab, head lowered, cuffed hands dangling between his knees. Every now and then he hummed a little, Harry said, and Percy roused himself enough from his funk to say that the lugoon dripped spittle from his lax lower lip, a drop at a time, until it had made a puddle between his feet. Like a dog dripping off the end of its tongue on a hot summer day.

They drove in through the south gate when they got to the pen, right past my car, I guess. The guard on the south pass ran back the big door between the lot and the exercise yard, and the stagecoach drove through. It was a slack time in the yard, not many men out and most of them hoeing in the garden. Pumpkin time, it would have been. They drove straight across to E Block and stopped. The driver opened the door and told them he was going to take the stagecoach over to the motor-pool to have the oil changed, it had been good working with them. The extra guards went with the vehicle, two of them sitting in the back eating apples, the doors now swinging open.

That left Dean, Harry, and Percy with one shackled prisoner. It should have been enough, *would* have been enough, if they hadn't been lulled by the stick-thin country boy standing head-down there in the dirt with chains on his wrists and ankles. They marched him the twelve or so paces to the door that opened into E Block, falling into the same formation we used when escorting prisoners down the Green Mile. Harry was on his left, Dean was on his right, and Percy was behind, with his baton in his hand. No one told me that, but I know damned well he had it out; Percy loved that hickory stick. As for me, I was sitting in what would be Wharton's home until it came time for him to check into the hot place—first cell on the right as you headed down the corridor toward the restraint room. I had my clipboard in my hands and was thinking of nothing but making my little set speech and getting the hell out. The pain in my groin was building up again, and all I wanted was to go into my office and wait for it to pass.

Dean stepped forward to unlock the door. He selected the right key from the bunch on his belt and slid it into the lock. Wharton came alive just as Dean turned the key and pulled the handle. He voiced a screaming, gibbering cry—a kind of Rebel yell—that froze Harry to temporary immobility and pretty much finished Percy Wetmore for the entire encounter. I heard that scream through the partly opened door and didn't associate it with anything human at first; I thought a dog had gotten into the yard somehow and had been hurt; that perhaps some mean-tempered con had hit it with a hoe.

Wharton lifted his arms, dropped the chain which hung between his wrists over Dean's head, and commenced to choke him with it. Dean gave a strangled cry and lurched forward, into the cool electric light of our little world. Wharton was happy to go with him, even gave him a shove, all the time yelling and gibbering, even laughing. He had his arms cocked at the elbows with his fists up by Dean's ears, yanking the chain as tight as he could, whipsawing it back and forth.

Harry landed on Wharton's back, wrapping one hand in our new boy's greasy blond hair and slamming his other fist into the side of Wharton's face as hard as he could. He had both a baton of his own and a sidearm pistol, but in his excitement drew neither. We'd had trouble with prisoners before, you bet, but never one who'd taken any of us by surprise the way that Wharton did. The man's slyness was beyond our experience. I had never seen its like before, and have never seen it again.

And he was strong. All that slack looseness was gone. Harry said later that it was like jumping onto a coiled nest of steel springs that had somehow come to life. Wharton, now inside and near the duty desk, whirled to his left and flung Harry off. Harry hit the desk and went sprawling.

"Whoooee, boys!" Wharton laughed. *"Ain't this a party, now? Is it, or what?"*

Still screaming and laughing, Wharton went back to choking Dean with his chain. Why not? Wharton knew what we all knew: they could only fry him once.

"Hit him, Percy, hit him!" Harry screamed, struggling to his feet. But Percy only stood there, hickory baton in hand, eyes as wide as soup-plates. Here was the chance he'd been looking for, you would have said, his golden opportunity to put that tallywhacker of his to good use, and he was too scared and confused to do it. This wasn't some terrified little Frenchman or a black giant who hardly seemed to be in his own body; this was a whirling devil.

I came out of Wharton's cell, dropping my clipboard and pulling my .38. I had forgotten the infection that was heating up my middle for the second time that day. I didn't doubt the story the others told of Wharton's blank face and dull eyes when they told it, but that wasn't the Wharton I saw. What I saw was the face of an animal—not an intelligent animal, but one filled with cunning . . . and meanness . . . and joy. Yes. He was doing what he had been made to do. The place and the circumstances didn't matter. The other thing I saw was Dean Stanton's red, swelling face. He was dying in front of my eyes. Wharton saw the gun and turned Dean toward it, so that I'd almost certainly have to hit one to hit the other. From over Dean's shoulder, one blazing blue eye dared me to shoot.

PART THREE

COFFEY'S HANDS

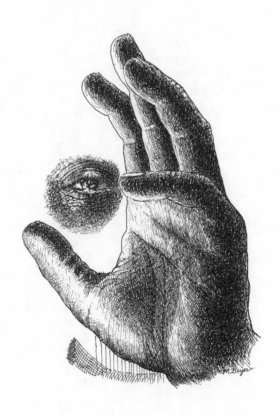

1

LOOKING BACK through what I've written, I see that I called Georgia Pines, where I now live, a nursing home. The folks who run the place wouldn't be very happy with that! According to the brochures they keep in the lobby and send out to prospective clients, it's a "state-of-the-art retirement complex for the elderly." It even has a Resource Center—the brochure says so. The folks who have to live here (the brochure doesn't call us "inmates," but sometimes I do) just call it the TV room.

Folks think I'm stand-offy because I don't go down to the TV room much in the day, but it's the programs I can't stand, not the folks. Oprah, Ricki Lake, Carnie Wilson, Rolanda—the world is falling down around our ears, and all these people care for is talking about fucking to women in short skirts and men with their shirts hanging open. Well, hell—judge not, lest ye be judged, the Bible says, so I'll get down off my soapbox. It's just that if I wanted to spend time with trailer trash, I'd move two miles down to the Happy Wheels Motor Court, where the police cars always seem to be headed on Friday and Saturday nights with their sirens screaming and their blue lights flashing. My special friend, Elaine Connelly, feels the same way. Elaine is eighty, tall and slim, still erect and clear-eyed, very intelligent and refined. She walks very slowly because there's something wrong with her hips, and I know that the arthritis in her hands gives her terrible misery, but she has a beautiful long neck—a swan neck, almost—and long, pretty hair that falls to her shoulders when she lets it down.

Best of all, she doesn't think I'm peculiar, or stand-offy. We spend a

137

lot of time together, Elaine and I. If I hadn't reached such a grotesque age, I suppose I might speak of her as my ladyfriend. Still, having a special friend—just that—is not so bad, and in some ways, it's even better. A lot of the problems and heartaches that go with being boyfriend and girlfriend have simply burned out of us. And although I know that no one under the age of, say, fifty would believe this, sometimes the embers are better than the campfire. It's strange, but it's true.

So I don't watch TV during the day. Sometimes I walk; sometimes I read; mostly what I've been doing for the last month or so is writing this memoir among the plants in the solarium. I think there's more oxygen in that room, and it helps the old memory. It beats the hell out of Geraldo Rivera, I can tell you that.

But when I can't sleep, I sometimes creep downstairs and put on the television. There's no Home Box Office or anything at Georgia Pines— I guess that's a resource just a wee bit too expensive for our Resource Center—but we have the basic cable services, and that means we have the American Movie Channel. That's the one (just in case you don't have the basic cable services yourself) where most of the films are in black and white and none of the women take their clothes off. For an old fart like me, that's sort of soothing. There have been a good many nights when I've slipped right off to sleep on the ugly green sofa in front of the TV while Francis the Talking Mule once more pulls Donald O'Connor's skillet out of the fire, or John Wayne cleans up Dodge, or Jimmy Cagney calls someone a dirty rat and then pulls a gun. Some of them are movies I saw with my wife, Janice (not just my ladyfriend but my *best* friend), and they calm me. The clothes they wear, the way they walk and talk, even the music on the soundtrack—all those things calm me. They remind me, I suppose, of when I was a man still walking on the skin of the world, instead of a moth-eaten relic mouldering away in an old folks' home where many of the residents wear diapers and rubber pants.

There was nothing soothing about what I saw this morning, though. Nothing at all.

Elaine sometimes joins me for AMC's so-called Early Bird Matinee, which starts at 4:00 a.m.—she doesn't say much about it, but I know her arthritis hurts her something terrible, and that the drugs they give her don't help much anymore.

When she came in this morning, gliding like a ghost in her white terrycloth robe, she found me sitting on the lumpy sofa, bent over the scrawny sticks that used to be legs, and clutching my knees to try and still the shakes that were running through me like a high wind. I felt cold all over, except for my groin, which seemed to burn with the ghost of the urinary infection which had so troubled my life in the fall of 1932—the fall of John Coffey, Percy Wetmore, and Mr. Jingles, the trained mouse.

The fall of William Wharton, it had been, too.

"Paul!" Elaine cried, and hurried over to me—hurried as fast as the rusty nails and ground glass in her hips would allow, anyway. "Paul, what's wrong?"

"I'll be all right," I said, but the words didn't sound very convincing—they came out all uneven, through teeth that wanted to chatter. "Just give me a minute or two, I'll be right as rain."

She sat next to me and put her arm around my shoulders. "I'm sure," she said. "But what happened? For heaven's sake, Paul, you look like you saw a ghost."

I did, I thought, and didn't realize until her eyes widened that I'd said it out loud.

"Not really," I said, and patted her hand (gently—so gently!). "But for a minute, Elaine—God!"

"Was it from the time when you were a guard at the prison?" she asked. "The time that you've been writing about in the solarium?"

I nodded. "I worked on our version of Death Row—"

"I know—"

"Only we called it the Green Mile. Because of the linoleum on the floor. In the fall of '32, we got this fellow—we got this *wildman*—named William Wharton. Liked to think of himself as Billy the Kid, even had it tattooed on his arm. Just a kid, but dangerous. I can still remember what Curtis Anderson—he was the assistant warden back in those days—wrote about him. 'Crazy-wild and proud of it. Wharton is nineteen years old, and *he just doesn't care.*' He'd underlined that part."

The hand which had gone around my shoulders was now rubbing

my back. I was beginning to calm. In that moment I loved Elaine Connelly, and could have kissed her all over her face as I told her so. Maybe I should have. It's terrible to be alone and frightened at any age, but I think it's worse when you're old. But I had this other thing on my mind, this load of old and still unfinished business.

"Anyway," I said, "you're right—I've been scribbling about how Wharton came on the block and almost killed Dean Stanton—one of the guys I worked with back then—when he did."

"How could he do that?" Elaine asked.

"Meanness and carelessness," I said grimly. "Wharton supplied the meanness, and the guards who brought him in supplied the carelessness. The real mistake was Wharton's wrist-chain—it was a little too long. When Dean unlocked the door to E Block, Wharton was behind him. There were guards on either side of him, but Anderson was right—Wild Billy just didn't care about such things. He dropped that wrist-chain down over Dean's head and started choking him with it."

Elaine shuddered.

"Anyway, I got thinking about all that and couldn't sleep, so I came down here. I turned on AMC, thinking you might come down and we'd have us a little date—"

She laughed and kissed my forehead just above the eyebrow. It used to make me prickle all over when Janice did that, and it still made me prickle all over when Elaine did it early this morning. I guess some things don't ever change.

"—and what came on was this old black-and-white gangster movie from the forties. *Kiss of Death,* it's called."

I could feel myself wanting to start shaking again and tried to suppress it.

"Richard Widmark's in it," I said. "It was his first big part, I think. I never went to see it with Jan—we gave the cops and robbers a miss, usually—but I remember reading somewhere that Widmark gave one hell of a performance as the punk. He sure did. He's pale . . . doesn't seem to walk so much as go *gliding* around . . . he's always calling people 'squirt' . . . talking about squealers . . . how much he hates the squealers . . ."

I was starting to shiver again in spite of my best efforts. I just couldn't help it.

"Blond hair," I whispered. "Lank blond hair. I watched until the part where he pushed this old woman in a wheelchair down a flight of stairs, then I turned it off."

"He reminded you of Wharton?"

"He *was* Wharton," I said. "To the life."

"Paul—" she began, and stopped. She looked at the blank screen of the TV (the cable box on top of it was still on, the red numerals still showing 10, the number of the AMC channel), then back at me.

"What?" I asked. "What, Elaine?" Thinking, *She's going to tell me I ought to quit writing about it. That I ought to tear up the pages I've written so far and just quit on it.*

What she said was "Don't let this stop you."

I gawped at her.

"Close your mouth, Paul—you'll catch a fly."

"Sorry. It's just that . . . well . . ."

"You thought I was going to tell you just the opposite, didn't you?"

"Yes."

She took my hands in hers (gently, so gently—her long and beautiful fingers, her bunched and ugly knuckles) and leaned forward, fixing my blue eyes with her hazel ones, the left slightly dimmed by the mist of a coalescing cataract. "I may be too old and brittle to live," she said, "but I'm not too old to think. What's a few sleepless nights at our age? What's seeing a ghost on the TV, for that matter? Are you going to tell me it's the only one you've ever seen?"

I thought about Warden Moores, and Harry Terwilliger, and Brutus Howell; I thought about my mother, and about Jan, my wife, who died in Alabama. I knew about ghosts, all right.

"No," I said. "It wasn't the first ghost I've ever seen. But Elaine—it *was* a shock. Because it was *him.*"

She kissed me again, then stood up, wincing as she did so and pressing the heels of her hands to the tops of her hips, as if she were afraid they might actually explode out through her skin if she wasn't very careful.

"I think I've changed my mind about the television," she said. "I've got an extra pill that I've been keeping for a rainy day . . . or night. I think I'll take it and go back to bed. Maybe you should do the same."

"Yes," I said. "I suppose I should." For one wild moment I thought of suggesting that we go back to bed together, and then I saw the dull pain in her eyes and thought better of it. Because she might have said yes, and she would only have said that for me. Not so good.

We left the TV room (I won't dignify it with that other name, not even to be ironic) side by side, me matching my steps to hers, which were slow and painfully careful. The building was quiet except for someone moaning in the grip of a bad dream behind some closed door.

"Will you be able to sleep, do you think?" she asked.

"Yes, I think so," I said, but of course I wasn't able to; I lay in my bed until sunup, thinking about *Kiss of Death*. I'd see Richard Widmark, giggling madly, tying the old lady into her wheelchair and then pushing her down the stairs—"This is what we do to squealers," he told her—and then his face would merge into the face of William Wharton as he'd looked on the day when he came to E Block and the Green Mile—Wharton giggling like Widmark, Wharton screaming, *Ain't this a party, now? Is it, or what?* I didn't bother with breakfast, not after that; I just came down here to the solarium and began to write.

Ghosts? Sure.

I know all about ghosts.

2

"Whoooee, boys!" Wharton laughed. *"Ain't this a party, now? Is it, or what?"*

Still screaming and laughing, Wharton went back to choking Dean with his chain. Why not? Wharton knew what Dean and Harry and my friend Brutus Howell knew—they could only fry a man once.

"Hit him!" Harry Terwilliger screamed. He had grappled with Wharton, tried to stop things before they got fairly started, but Wharton had thrown him off and now Harry was trying to find his feet. "Percy, hit him!"

But Percy only stood there, hickory baton in hand, eyes as wide as soup-plates. He loved that damned baton of his, and you would have said this was the chance to use it he'd been pining for ever since he came to Cold Mountain Penitentiary . . . but now that it had come, he was too scared to use the opportunity. This wasn't some terrified little Frenchman like Delacroix or a black giant who hardly seemed to know he was in his own body, like John Coffey; this was a whirling devil.

I came out of Wharton's cell, dropping my clipboard and pulling my .38. For the second time that day I had forgotten the infection that was heating up my middle. I didn't doubt the story the others told of Wharton's blank face and dull eyes when they recounted it later, but that wasn't the Wharton I saw. What I saw was the face of an animal—not an intelligent animal, but one filled with cunning . . . and meanness . . . and joy. Yes. He was doing what he had been made to do. The place and the circumstances didn't matter. The other thing I saw was Dean

Stanton's red, swelling face. He was dying in front of my eyes. Wharton saw the gun in my hand and turned Dean toward it, so that I'd almost certainly have to hit one to hit the other. From over Dean's shoulder, one blazing blue eye dared me to shoot. Wharton's other eye was hidden by Dean's hair. Behind them I saw Percy standing irresolute, with his baton half-raised. And then, filling the open doorway to the prison yard, a miracle in the flesh: Brutus Howell. They had finished moving the last of the infirmary equipment, and he had come over to see who wanted coffee.

He acted without a moment's hesitation—shoved Percy aside and into the wall with tooth-rattling force, pulled his own baton out of its loop, and brought it crashing down on the back of Wharton's head with all the force in his massive right arm. There was a dull *whock!* sound—an almost hollow sound, as if there were no brain at all under Wharton's skull—and the chain finally loosened around Dean's neck. Wharton went down like a sack of meal and Dean crawled away, hacking harshly and holding one hand to his throat, his eyes bulging.

I knelt by him and he shook his head violently. "Okay," he rasped. "Take care . . . him!" He motioned at Wharton. "Lock! Cell!"

I didn't think he'd need a cell, as hard as Brutal had hit him; I thought he'd need a coffin. No such luck, though. Wharton was conked out, but a long way from dead. He lay sprawled on his side, one arm thrown out so that the tips of his fingers touched the linoleum of the Green Mile, his eyes shut, his breathing slow but regular. There was even a peaceful little smile on his face, as if he'd gone to sleep listening to his favorite lullaby. A tiny red rill of blood was seeping out of his hair and staining the collar of his new prison shirt. That was all.

"Percy," I said. "Help me!"

Percy didn't move, only stood against the wall, staring with wide, stunned eyes. I don't think he knew exactly where he was.

"Percy, goddammit, grab hold of him!"

He got moving, then, and Harry helped him. Together the three of us hauled the unconscious Mr. Wharton into his cell while Brutal helped Dean to his feet and held him as gently as any mother while Dean bent over and hacked air back into his lungs.

Our new problem child didn't wake up for almost three hours, but when he did, he showed absolutely no ill effects from Brutal's savage hit. He came to the way he moved—fast. At one moment he was lying on his bunk, dead to the world. At the next he was standing at the bars—he was silent as a cat—and staring out at me as I sat at the duty desk, writing a report on the incident. When I finally sensed someone looking at me and glanced up, there he was, his grin displaying a set of blackening, dying teeth with several gaps among them already. It gave me a jump to see him there like that. I tried not to show it, but I think he knew. "Hey, flunky," he said. "Next time it'll be you. And I won't miss."

"Hello, Wharton," I said, as evenly as I could. "Under the circumstances, I guess I can skip the speech and the Welcome Wagon, don't you think?"

His grin faltered just a little. It wasn't the sort of response he had expected, and probably wasn't the one I would have given under other circumstances. But something had happened while Wharton was unconscious. It is, I suppose, one of the major things I have trudged through all these pages to tell you about. Now let's just see if you believe it.

3

EXCEPT FOR SHOUTING once at Delacroix, Percy kept his mouth shut once the excitement was over. This was probably the result of shock rather than any effort at tact—Percy Wetmore knew as much about tact as I do about the native tribes of darkest Africa, in my opinion—but it was a damned good thing, just the same. If he'd started in whining about how Brutal had pushed him into the wall or wondering why no one had told him that nasty men like Wild Billy Wharton sometimes turned up on E Block, I think we would have killed him. Then we could have toured the Green Mile in a whole new way. That's sort of a funny idea, when you consider it. I missed my chance to make like James Cagney in *White Heat*.

Anyway, when we were sure that Dean was going to keep breathing and that he wasn't going to pass out on the spot, Harry and Brutal escorted him over to the infirmary. Delacroix, who had been absolutely silent during the scuffle (he had been in prison lots of times, that one, and knew when it was prudent to keep his yap shut and when it was relatively safe to open it again), began bawling loudly down the corridor as Harry and Brutal helped Dean out. Delacroix wanted to know what had happened. You would have thought his constitutional rights had been violated.

"Shut up, you little queer!" Percy yelled back, so furious that the veins stood out on the sides of his neck. I put a hand on his arm and felt it quivering beneath his shirt. Some of this was residual fright, of course (every now and then I had to remind myself that part of Percy's problem was that he was only twenty-one, not much older than Wharton), but I think most of it was rage. He hated Delacroix. I don't know just why, but he did.

"Go see if Warden Moores is still here," I told Percy. "If he is, give him a complete verbal report on what happened. Tell him he'll have my written report on his desk tomorrow, if I can manage it."

Percy swelled visibly at this responsibility; for a horrible moment or two, I actually thought he might salute. "Yes, sir. I will."

"Begin by telling him that the situation in E Block is normal. It's not a story, and the warden won't appreciate you dragging it out to heighten the suspense."

"I won't."

"Okay. Off you go."

He started for the door, then turned back. The one thing you could count on with him was contrariness. I desperately wanted him gone, my groin was on fire, and now he didn't seem to want to go.

"Are you all right, Paul?" he asked. "Running a fever, maybe? Got a touch of the grippe? Cause there's sweat all over your face."

"I might have a touch of something, but mostly I'm fine," I said. "Go on, Percy, tell the warden."

He nodded and left—thank Christ for small favors. As soon as the door was closed, I lunged into my office. Leaving the duty desk unmanned was against regulations, but I was beyond caring about that. It was bad—like it had been that morning.

I managed to get into the little toilet cubicle behind the desk and to get my business out of my pants before the urine started to gush, but it was a near thing. I had to put a hand over my mouth to stifle a scream as I began to flow, and grabbed blindly for the lip of the washstand with the other. It wasn't like my house, where I could fall to my knees and piss a puddle beside the woodpile; if I went to my knees here, the urine would go all over the floor.

I managed to keep my feet and not to scream, but it was a close thing on both counts. It felt like my urine had been filled with tiny slivers of broken glass. The smell coming up from the toilet bowl was swampy and unpleasant, and I could see white stuff—pus, I guess—floating on the surface of the water.

I took the towel off the rack and wiped my face with it. I was sweating, all right; it was pouring off me. I looked into the metal mirror and saw the flushed face of a man running a high fever looking back at me. Hundred and three? Hundred and four? Better not to know, maybe. I put the towel back on its bar, flushed the toilet, and walked slowly back across my office to the cellblock door. I was afraid Bill Dodge or someone else might have come in and seen three prisoners with no attendants, but the place was empty. Wharton still lay unconscious on his bunk, Delacroix had fallen silent, and John Coffey had never made a single noise at all, I suddenly realized. Not a peep. Which was worrisome.

I went down the Mile and glanced into Coffey's cell, half-expecting to discover he'd committed suicide in one of the two common Death Row ways—either hanging himself with his pants, or gnawing into his wrists. No such thing, it turned out. Coffey merely sat on the end of his bunk with his hands in his lap, the largest man I'd ever seen in my life, looking at me with his strange, wet eyes.

"Cap'n?" he said.

"What's up, big boy?"

"I need to see you."

"Ain't you looking right at me, John Coffey?"

He said nothing to this, only went on studying me with his strange, leaky gaze. I sighed.

"In a second, big boy."

I looked over at Delacroix, who was standing at the bars of his cell. Mr. Jingles, his pet mouse (Delacroix would tell you he'd trained Mr. Jingles to do tricks, but us folks who worked on the Green Mile were pretty much unanimous in the opinion that Mr. Jingles had trained himself), was jumping restlessly back and forth from one of Del's outstretched hands to the other, like an acrobat doing leaps from platforms high above the center ring. His eyes were huge, his ears laid back against his sleek brown skull. I hadn't any doubt that the mouse was reacting to Delacroix's nerves. As I watched, he ran down Delacroix's pantsleg and across the cell to where the brightly colored spool lay against one wall. He pushed the spool back to Delacroix's foot and then looked up at him

eagerly, but the little Cajun took no notice of his friend, at least for the
time being.

"What happen, boss?" Delacroix asked. "Who been hurt?"

"Everything's jake," I said. "Our new boy came in like a lion, but
now he's passed out like a lamb. All's well that ends well."

"It ain't over yet," Delacroix said, looking up the Mile toward the
cell where Wharton was jugged. *"L'homme mauvais, c'est vrai!"*

"Well," I said, "don't let it get you down, Del. Nobody's going to
make you play skiprope with him out in the yard."

There was a creaking sound from behind me as Coffey got off his
bunk. "Boss Edgecombe!" he said again. This time he sounded urgent.
"I need to talk to you!"

I turned to him, thinking, all right, no problem, talking was my
business. All the time trying not to shiver, because the fever had turned
cold, as they sometimes will. Except for my groin, which still felt as if it
had been slit open, filled with hot coals, and then sewed back up again.

"So talk, John Coffey," I said, trying to keep my voice light and calm.
For the first time since he'd come onto E Block, Coffey looked as
though he was really here, really among us. The almost ceaseless trickle
of tears from the corners of his eyes *had* ceased, at least for the time being,
and I knew he was seeing what he was looking at—Mr. Paul Edgecombe,
E Block's bull-goose screw, and not some place he wished he could return
to, and take back the terrible thing he'd done.

"No," he said. "You got to come in here."

"Now, you know I can't do that," I said, still trying for the light
tone, "at least not right this minute. I'm on my own here for the time
being, and you outweigh me by just about a ton and a half. We've had
us one hooraw this afternoon, and that's enough. So we'll just have us a
chat through the bars, if it's all the same to you, and—"

"Please!" He was holding the bars so tightly that his knuckles were
pale and his fingernails were white. His face was long with distress,
those strange eyes sharp with some need I could not understand. I
remember thinking that maybe I *could've* understood it if I hadn't been
so sick, and knowing that would have given me a way of helping him
through the rest of it. When you know what a man needs, you know

the man, more often than not. "Please, Boss Edgecombe! *You have to come in!*"

That's the nuttiest thing I ever heard, I thought, and then realized something even nuttier: I was going to do it. I had my keys off my belt and I was hunting through them for the ones that opened John Coffey's cell. He could have picked me up and broken me over his knee like kindling on a day when I was well and feeling fine, and this wasn't that day. All the same, I was going to do it. On my own, and less than half an hour after a graphic demonstration of where stupidity and laxness could get you when you were dealing with condemned murderers, I was going to open this black giant's cell, go in, and sit with him. If I was discovered, I might well lose my job even if he didn't do anything crazy, but I was going to do it, just the same.

Stop, I said to myself, you just stop now, Paul. But I didn't. I used one key on the top lock, another on the bottom lock, and then I slid the door back on its track.

"You know, boss, that maybe not such a good idear," Delacroix said in a voice so nervous and prissy it would probably have made me laugh under other circumstances.

"You mind your business and I'll mind mine," I said without looking around. My eyes were fixed on John Coffey's, and fixed so hard they might have been nailed there. It was like being hypnotized. My voice sounded to my own ears like something which had come echoing down a long valley. Hell, maybe I *was* hypnotized. "You just lie down and take you a rest."

"Christ, this place is crazy," Delacroix said in a trembling voice. "Mr. Jingles, I just about wish they'd fry me and be done widdit!"

I went into Coffey's cell. He stepped away as I stepped forward. When he was backed up against his bunk—it hit him in the calves, that's how tall he was—he sat down on it. He patted the mattress beside him, his eyes never once leaving mine. I sat down there next to him, and he put his arm around my shoulders, as if we were at the movies and I was his girl.

"What do you want, John Coffey?" I asked, still looking into his eyes—those sad, serene eyes.

"Just to help," he said. He sighed like a man will when he's faced with a job he doesn't much want to do, and then he put his hand down in my crotch, on that shelf of bone a foot or so below the navel.

"Hey!" I cried. "Get your goddam hand—"

A jolt slammed through me then, a big painless whack of something. It made me jerk on the cot and bow my back, made me think of Old Toot shouting that he was frying, he was frying, he was a done tom turkey. There was no heat, no feeling of electricity, but for a moment the color seemed to jump out of everything, as if the world had been somehow squeezed and made to sweat. I could see every pore on John Coffey's face, I could see every bloodshot snap in his haunted eyes, I could see a tiny healing scrape on his chin. I was aware that my fingers were hooked down into claws on thin air, and that my feet were drumming on the floor of Coffey's cell.

Then it was over. So was my urinary infection. Both the heat and the miserable throbbing pain were gone from my crotch, and the fever was likewise gone from my head. I could still feel the sweat it had drawn out of my skin, and I could smell it, but it was gone, all right.

"What's going on?" Delacroix called shrilly. His voice still came from far away, but when John Coffey bent forward, breaking eye-contact with me, the little Cajun's voice suddenly came clear. It was as if someone had pulled wads of cotton or a pair of shooters' plugs out of my ears. "What's he doing to you?"

I didn't answer. Coffey was bent forward over his own lap with his face working and his throat bulging. His eyes were bulging, too. He looked like a man with a chicken bone caught in his throat.

"John!" I said. I clapped him on the back; it was all I could think of to do. "John, what's wrong?"

He hitched under my hand, then made an unpleasant gagging, retching sound. His mouth opened the way horses sometimes open their mouths to allow the bit—reluctantly, with the lips peeling back from the teeth in a kind of desperate sneer. Then his teeth parted, too, and he exhaled a cloud of tiny black insects that looked like gnats or noseeums. They swirled furiously between his knees, turned white, and disappeared.

Suddenly all the strength went out of my midsection. It was as if the muscles there had turned to water. I slumped back against the stone side of Coffey's cell. I remember thinking the name of the Savior—Christ, Christ, Christ, over and over, like that—and I remember thinking that the fever had driven me delirious. That was all.

Then I became aware that Delacroix was bawling for help; he was telling the world that John Coffey was killing me, and telling it at the top of his lungs. Coffey was bending over me, all right, but only to make sure I was okay.

"Shut up, Del," I said, and got on my feet. I waited for the pain to rip into my guts, but it didn't happen. I was better. Really. There was a moment of dizziness, but that passed even before I was able to reach out and grab the bars of Coffey's cell door for balance. "I'm totally okey-doke."

"You get on outta dere," Delacroix said, sounding like a nervy old woman telling a kid to climb down out of that-ere apple tree. "You ain't suppose to be in there wit no one else on the block."

I looked at John Coffey, who sat on the bunk with his huge hands on the tree stumps of his knees. John Coffey looked back at me. He had to tilt his head up a little, but not much.

"What did you do, big boy?" I asked in a low voice. "What did you do to me?"

"Helped," he said. "I helped it, didn't I?"

"Yeah, I guess, but *how? How* did you help it?"

He shook his head—right, left, back to dead center. He didn't know how he'd helped it (how he'd *cured* it) and his placid face suggested that he didn't give a rat's ass—any more than I'd give a rat's ass about the mechanics of running when I was leading in the last fifty yards of a Fourth of July Two-Miler. I thought about asking him how he'd known I was sick in the first place, except that would undoubtedly have gotten the same headshake. There's a phrase I read somewhere and never forgot, something about "an enigma wrapped in a mystery." That's what John Coffey was, and I suppose the only reason he could sleep at night was because he didn't care. Percy called him the ijit, which was cruel but not too far off the mark. Our big boy knew his name, and knew it wasn't spelled like the drink, and that was just about all he cared to know.

As if to emphasize this for me, he shook his head in that deliberate way one more time, then lay down on his bunk with his hands clasped under his left cheek like a pillow and his face to the wall. His legs dangled off the end of the bunk from the shins on down, but that never seemed to bother him. The back of his shirt had pulled up, and I could see the scars that crisscrossed his skin.

I left the cell, turned the locks, then faced Delacroix, who was standing across the way with his hands wrapped around the bars of his cell, looking at me anxiously. Perhaps even fearfully. Mr. Jingles perched on his shoulder with his fine whiskers quivering like filaments. "What dat darkie-man do to you?" Delacroix asked. "Waddit gris-gris? He th'ow some gris-gris on you?" Spoken in that Cajun accent of his, *gris-gris* rhymed with *pee-pee.*

"I don't know what you're talking about, Del."

"Devil you don't! Lookit you! All change! Even walk different, boss!"

I probably *was* walking different, at that. There was a beautiful feeling of calm in my groin, a sense of peace so remarkable it was almost ecstasy—anyone who's suffered bad pain and then recovered will know what I'm talking about.

"Everything's all right, Del," I insisted. "John Coffey had a nightmare, that's all."

"He a gris-gris man!" Delacroix said vehemently. There was a nestle of sweat-beads on his upper lip. He hadn't seen much, just enough to scare him half to death. "He a hoodoo man!"

"What makes you say that?"

Delacroix reached up and took the mouse in one hand. He cupped it in his palm and lifted it to his face. From his pocket, Delacroix took out a pink fragment—one of those peppermint candies. He held it out, but at first the mouse ignored it, stretching out its neck toward the man instead, sniffing at his breath the way a person might sniff at a bouquet of flowers. Its little oildrop eyes slitted most of the way closed in an expression that looked like ecstasy. Delacroix kissed its nose, and the mouse allowed its nose to be kissed. Then it took the offered piece of candy and began to munch it. Delacroix looked at it a moment longer, then looked at me. All at once I got it.

"The mouse told you," I said. "Am I right?"

"*Oui.*"

"Like he whispered his name to you."

"*Oui,* in my ear he whisper it."

"Lie down, Del," I said. "Have you a little rest. All that whispering back and forth must wear you out."

He said something else—accused me of not believing him, I suppose. His voice seemed to be coming from a long way off again. And when I went back up to the duty desk, I hardly seemed to be walking at all—it was more like I was floating, or maybe not even moving, the cells just rolling past me on either side, movie props on hidden wheels.

I started to sit like normal, but halfway into it my knees unlocked and I dropped onto the blue cushion Harry had brought from home the year before and plopped onto the seat of the chair. If the chair hadn't been there, I reckon I would have plopped straight to the floor without passing Go or collecting two hundred dollars.

I sat there, feeling the nothing in my groin where a forest fire had been blazing not ten minutes before. *I helped it, didn't I?* John Coffey had said, and that was true, as far as my body went. My peace of mind was a different story, though. *That* he hadn't helped at all.

My eyes fell on the stack of forms under the tin ashtray we kept on the corner of the desk. BLOCK REPORT was printed at the top, and about halfway down was a blank space headed *Report All Unusual Occurrences.* I would use that space in tonight's report, telling the story of William Wharton's colorful and action-packed arrival. But suppose I also told what had happened to me in John Coffey's cell? I saw myself picking up the pencil—the one whose tip Brutal was always licking—and writing a single word in big capital letters: MIRACLE.

That should have been funny, but instead of smiling, all at once I felt sure that I was going to cry. I put my hands to my face, palms against my mouth to stifle the sobs—I didn't want to scare Del again just when he was starting to get settled down—but no sobs came. No tears, either. After a few moments I lowered my hands back to the desk and folded them. I didn't know what I was feeling, and the only clear thought in my head was a wish that no one should come back onto the block until I was a little more in control of myself. I was afraid of what they might see in my face.

I drew a Block Report form toward me. I would wait until I had settled down a bit more to write about how my latest problem child had almost strangled Dean Stanton, but I could fill out the rest of the boilerplate foolishness in the meantime. I thought my handwriting might look funny—trembly—but it came out about the same as always.

About five minutes after I started, I put the pencil down and went into the W.C. adjacent to my office to take a leak. I didn't need to go very bad, but I could manage enough to test what had happened to me, I thought. As I stood there, waiting for my water to flow, I became sure that it would hurt just the way it had that morning, as if I were passing tiny shards of broken glass; what he'd done to me would turn out to be only hypnosis, after all, and that might be a relief in spite of the pain.

Except there was no pain, and what went into the bowl was clear, with no sign of pus. I buttoned my fly, pulled the chain that flushed the commode, went back to the duty desk, and sat down again.

I knew what had happened; I suppose I knew even when I was trying to tell myself I'd been hypnotized. I'd experienced a healing, an authentic Praise Jesus, The Lord Is Mighty. As a boy who'd grown up going to whatever Baptist or Pentecostal church my mother and her sisters happened to be in favor of during any given month, I had heard plenty of Praise Jesus, The Lord Is Mighty miracle stories. I didn't believe all of them, but there were plenty of people I did believe. One of these was a man named Roy Delfines, who lived with his family about two miles down the road from us when I was six or so. Delfines had chopped his son's little finger off with a hatchet, an accident which had occurred when the boy unexpectedly moved his hand on a log he'd been holding on the backyard chopping block for his dad. Roy Delfines said he had practically worn out the carpet with his knees that fall and winter, and in the spring the boy's finger had grown back. Even the nail had grown back. I believed Roy Delfines when he testified at Thursday-night rejoicing. There was a naked, uncomplicated honesty in what he said as he stood there talking with his hands jammed deep into the pockets of his biballs that was impossible *not* to believe. "It itch him some when thet finger started coming, kep him awake nights," Roy Delfines said, "but he knowed it was the Lord's itch and let it be." Praise Jesus, The Lord Is Mighty.

Roy Delfines's story was only one of many; I grew up in a tradition of miracles and healings. I grew up believing in gris-gris, as well (only, up in the hills we said it to rhyme with *kiss-kiss*): stump-water for warts, moss under your pillow to ease the heartache of lost love, and, of course, what we used to call *haints*—but I did not believe John Coffey was a gris-gris man. I had looked into his eyes. More important, I had felt his touch. Being touched by him was like being touched by some strange and wonderful doctor.

I helped it, didn't I?

That kept chiming in my head, like a snatch of song you can't get rid of, or words you'd speak to set a spell.

I helped it, didn't I?

Except *he* hadn't. *God* had. John Coffey's use of "I" could be chalked up to ignorance rather than pride, but I knew—believed, at least—what I had learned about healing in those churches of Praise Jesus, The Lord Is Mighty, piney-woods amen corners much beloved by my twenty-two-year-old mother and my aunts: that healing is never about the healed or the healer, but about God's will. For one to rejoice at the sick made well is normal, quite the expected thing, but the person healed has an obligation to then ask why—to meditate on God's will, and the extraordinary lengths to which God has gone to realize His will.

What did God want of me, in this case? What did He want badly enough to put healing power in the hands of a child-murderer? To be on the block, instead of at home, sick as a dog, shivering in bed with the stink of sulfa running out of my pores? Perhaps; I was maybe supposed to be here instead of home in case Wild Bill Wharton decided to kick up more dickens, or to make sure Percy Wetmore didn't get up to some foolish and potentially destructive piece of fuckery. All right, then. So be it. I would keep my eyes open . . . and my mouth shut, especially about miracle cures.

No one was apt to question my looking and sounding better; I'd been telling the world I was getting better, and until that very day I'd honestly believed it. I had even told Warden Moores that I was on the mend. Delacroix had seen something, but I thought he would keep his mouth shut, too (probably afraid John Coffey would throw a spell on him if he didn't). As for Coffey himself, he'd probably already forgotten it. He was nothing but a conduit, after all, and there isn't a culvert in the world that remembers the water that flowed through it once the rain has stopped. So I resolved to keep my mouth completely shut on the subject, with never an idea of how soon I'd be telling the story, or who I'd be telling it to.

But I was curious about my big boy, and there's no sense not admitting it. After what had happened to me there in his cell, I was more curious than ever.

4

BEFORE LEAVING that night, I arranged with Brutal to cover for me the next day, should I come in a little late, and when I got up the following morning, I set out for Tefton, down in Trapingus County.

"I'm not sure I like you worrying so much about this fellow Coffey," my wife said, handing me the lunch she'd put up for me—Janice never believed in roadside hamburger stands; she used to say there was a bellyache waiting in every one. "It's not like you, Paul."

"I'm not worried about him," I said. "I'm curious, that's all."

"In my experience, one leads to the other," Janice said tartly, then gave me a good, hearty kiss on the mouth. "You look better, at least, I'll say that. For awhile there, you had me nervous. Waterworks all cured up?"

"All cured up," I said, and off I went, singing songs like "Come, Josephine, in My Flying Machine" and "We're in the Money" to keep myself company.

I went to the offices of the Tefton *Intelligencer* first, and they told me that Burt Hammersmith, the fellow I was looking for, was most likely over at the county courthouse. At the courthouse they told me that Hammersmith had been there but had left when a burst waterpipe had closed down the main proceedings, which happened to be a rape trial (in the pages of the *Intelligencer* the crime would be referred to as "assault on a woman," which was how such things were done in the days before Ricki Lake and Carnie Wilson came on the scene). They guessed he'd probably gone on home. I got some directions out a dirt road so rutted and narrow I just about didn't dare take my Ford up it, and there I found my man. Hammersmith had written most of the stories on the Coffey trial, and it was from him I found out most of the details about the brief manhunt that had netted Coffey in the first place. The details the *Intelligencer* considered too gruesome to print is what I mean, of course.

Mrs. Hammersmith was a young woman with a tired, pretty face and hands red from lye soap. She didn't ask my business, just led me through a small house fragrant with the smell of baking and onto the back porch, where her husband sat with a bottle of pop in his hand and an unopened copy of *Liberty* magazine on his lap. There was a small, sloping backyard; at the foot of it, two little ones were squabbling and laughing over a swing. From the porch, it was impossible to tell their sexes, but I thought they were boy and girl. Maybe even twins, which cast an interesting sort of light on their father's part, peripheral as it had been, in the Coffey trial. Nearer at hand, set like an island in the middle of a turd-studded patch of bare, beatup-looking ground, was a doghouse. No sign of Fido; it was another unseasonably hot day, and I guessed he was probably inside, snoozing.

"Burt, yew-all got you a cump'ny," Mrs. Hammersmith said.

"All right," he said. He glanced at me, glanced at his wife, then looked back at his kids, which was where his heart obviously lay. He was a thin man—almost painfully thin, as if he had just begun to recover from a serious illness—and his hair had started to recede. His wife touched his shoulder tentatively with one of her red, wash-swollen hands. He didn't look at it or reach up to touch it, and after a moment she took it back. It occurred to me, fleetingly, that they looked more like brother and sister than husband and wife—he'd gotten the brains, she'd gotten the looks, but neither of them had escaped some underlying resemblance, a heredity that could never be escaped. Later, going home, I realized they didn't look alike at all; what made them seem to was the aftermath of stress and the lingering of sorrow. It's strange how pain marks our faces, and makes us look like family.

She said, "Yew-all want a cold drink, Mr.—?"

"It's Edgecombe," I said. "Paul Edgecombe. And thank you. A cold drink would be wonderful, ma'am."

She went back inside. I held out my hand to Hammersmith, who gave it a brief shake. His grip was limp and cold. He never took his eyes off the kids down at the bottom of the yard.

"Mr. Hammersmith, I'm E Block superintendent at Cold Mountain State Penitentiary. That's—"

"I know what it is," he said, looking at me with a little more interest. "So—the bull-goose screw of the Green Mile is standing on my back porch, just as big as life. What brings you fifty miles to talk to the local rag's only full-time reporter?"

"John Coffey," I said.

I think I expected some sort of strong reaction (the kids who could have been twins working at the back of my mind . . . and perhaps the doghouse, too; the Dettericks had had a dog), but Hammersmith only raised his eyebrows and sipped at his drink. "Coffey's *your* problem now, isn't he?" Hammersmith asked.

"He's not much of a problem," I said. "He doesn't like the dark, and he cries a lot of the time, but neither thing makes much of a problem in our line of work. We see worse."

"Cries a lot, does he?" Hammersmith asked. "Well, he's got a lot to cry about, I'd say. Considering what he did. What do you want to know?"

"Anything you can tell me. I've read your newspaper stories, so I guess what I want is anything that wasn't in them."

He gave me a sharp, dry look. "Like how the little girls looked? Like exactly what he did to them? That the kind of stuff you're interested in, Mr. Edgecombe?"

"No," I said, keeping my voice mild. "It's not the Detterick girls I'm interested in, sir. Poor little mites are dead. But Coffey's not—not yet—and I'm curious about him."

"All right," he said. "Pull up a chair and sit, Mr. Edgecombe. You'll forgive me if I sounded a little sharp just now, but I get to see plenty of vultures in my line of work. Hell, I've been accused of being one of em often enough, myself. I just wanted to make sure of you."

"And are you?"

"Sure enough, I guess," he said, sounding almost indifferent. The story he told me is pretty much the one I set down earlier in this account—how Mrs. Detterick found the porch empty, with the screen door pulled off its upper hinge, the blankets cast into one corner, and blood on the steps; how her son and husband had taken after the girls' abductor; how the posse had caught up to them first and to John Coffey not much later. How Coffey had been sitting on the riverbank and wailing, with the bodies curled in his massive arms like big dolls. The reporter, rack-thin in his open-collared white shirt and gray town pants, spoke in a low, unemotional voice . . . but his eyes never left his own two children as they squabbled and laughed and took turns with the swing down there in the shade at the foot of the slope. Sometime in the middle of the story, Mrs. Hammersmith came back with a bottle of homemade root beer, cold and strong and delicious. She stood listening for awhile, then interrupted long enough to call down to the kids and tell them to come up directly, she had cookies due out of the oven. "We will, Mamma!" called a little girl's voice, and the woman went back inside again.

When Hammersmith had finished, he said: "So why do you want to know? I never had me a visit from a Big House screw before, it's a first."

"I told you—"

"Curiosity, yep. Folks get curious, I know it, I even thank God for it, I'd be out of a job and might actually have to go to work for a living without it. But fifty miles is a long way to come to satisfy simple curiosity, especially when the last twenty is over bad roads. So why don't you tell me the truth, Edgecombe? I satisfied yours, so now you satisfy mine."

Well, I could say, *I had this urinary infection, and John Coffey put his hands on me and healed it. The man who raped and murdered those two little girls did that. So I wondered about him, of course—anyone would. I even wondered if maybe Homer Cribus and Deputy Rob McGee didn't maybe collar the wrong man. In spite of all the evidence against him I wonder that. Because a man who has a power like that in his hands, you don't usually think of him as the kind of man who rapes and murders children.*

No, maybe that wouldn't do.

"There are two things I've wondered about," I said. "The first is if he ever did anything like that before."

Hammersmith turned to me, his eyes suddenly sharp and bright with interest, and I saw he *was* a smart fellow. Maybe even a brilliant fellow, in a quiet way. "Why?" he asked. "What do you know, Edgecombe? What has he said?"

"Nothing. But a man who does this sort of thing once has usually done it before. They get a taste for it."

"Yes," he said. "They do. They certainly do."

"And it occurred to me that it would be easy enough to follow his backtrail and find out. A man his size, and a Negro to boot, can't be that hard to trace."

"You'd think so, but you'd be wrong," he said. "In Coffey's case, anyhow. I know."

"You tried?"

"I did, and came up all but empty. There were a couple of railroad fellows who thought they saw him in the Knoxville yards two days before the Detterick girls were killed. No surprise there; he was just across the river from the Great Southern tracks when they collared him, and that's probably how he came down here from Tennessee. I got a letter from a man who said he'd hired a big bald black man to shift crates for him in the early spring of this year—this was in Kentucky. I sent him a picture of Coffey and he said that was the man. But other than that—" Hammersmith shrugged and shook his head.

"Doesn't that strike you as a little odd?"

"Strikes me as a *lot* odd, Mr. Edgecombe. It's like he dropped out of the sky. And he's no help; he can't remember last week once this week comes."

"No, he can't," I said. "How do you explain it?"

"We're in a Depression," he said, "*that's* how I explain it. People all over the roads. The Okies want to pick peaches in California, the poor whites from up in the brakes want to build cars in Detroit, the black folks from Mississippi want to go up to New England and work in the shoe factories or the textile mills. Everyone—black as well as white—thinks it's going to be better over the next jump of land. It's the American damn way. Even a giant like Coffey doesn't get noticed everywhere he goes . . . until, that is, he decides to kill a couple of little girls. Little *white* girls."

"Do you believe that?" I asked.

He gave me a bland look from his too-thin face. "Sometimes I do," he said.

His wife leaned out of the kitchen window like an engineer from the cab of a locomotive and called, *"Kids! Cookies are ready!"* She turned to me. "Would you like an oatmeal-raisin cookie, Mr. Edgecombe?"

"I'm sure they're delicious, ma'am, but I'll take a pass this time."

"All right," she said, and drew her head back inside.

"Have you seen the scars on him?" Hammersmith asked abruptly. He was still watching his kids, who couldn't quite bring themselves to abandon the pleasures of the swing—not even for oatmeal-raisin cookies.

"Yes." But I was surprised he had.

He saw my reaction and laughed. "The defense attorney's one big victory was getting Coffey to take off his shirt and show those scars to the jury. The prosecutor, George Peterson, objected like hell, but the judge allowed it. Old George could have saved his breath—juries around these parts don't buy all that psychology crap about how people who've been mistreated just can't help themselves. They believe people *can* help themselves. It's a point of view I have a lot of sympathy for . . . but those scars were pretty ghastly, just the same. Notice anything about them, Edgecombe?"

I had seen the man naked in the shower, and I'd noticed, all right; I knew just what he was talking about. "They're all broken up. Latticed, almost."

"You know what that means?"

"Somebody whopped the living hell out of him when he was a kid," I said. "Before he grew."

"But they didn't manage to whop the devil out of him, did they, Edgecombe? Should have spared the rod and just drowned him in the river like a stray kitten, don't you think?"

I suppose it would have been politic to simply agree and get out of there, but I couldn't. I'd seen him. And I'd *felt* him, as well. Felt the touch of his hands.

"He's . . . strange," I said. "But there doesn't seem to be any real violence in him. I know how he was found, and it's hard to jibe that with what I see, day in and day out, on the block. I know violent men, Mr. Hammersmith." It was Wharton I was thinking about, of course, Wharton strangling Dean Stanton with his wrist-chain and bellowing *Whoooee, boys! Ain't this a party, now?*

He was looking at me closely now, and smiling a little, incredulous smile that I didn't care for very much. "You didn't come up here to get an idea about whether or not he might have killed some other little girls somewhere else," he said. "You came up here to see if I think he did it at all. That's it, isn't it? 'Fess up, Edgecombe."

I swallowed the last of my cold drink, put the bottle down on the little table, and said: "Well? Do you?"

"Kids!" he called down the hill, leaning forward a little in his chair to do it. *"Y'all come on up here now n get your cookies!"* Then he leaned back in his chair again and looked at me. That little smile—the one I didn't much care for—had reappeared.

"Tell you something," he said. "You want to listen close, too, because this might just be something you need to know."

"I'm listening."

"We had us a dog named Sir Galahad," he said, and cocked a thumb at the doghouse. "A good dog. No particular breed, but gentle. Calm. Ready to lick your hand or fetch a stick. There are plenty of mongrel dogs like him, wouldn't you say?"

I shrugged, nodded.

"In many ways, a good mongrel dog is like your negro," he said. "You get to know it, and often you grow to love it. It is of no particular use, but you keep it around because you *think* it loves *you*. If you're lucky, Mr. Edgecombe, you never have to find out any different. Cynthia and I, we were not lucky." He sighed—a long and somehow skeletal sound, like the wind rummaging through fallen leaves. He pointed toward the doghouse again, and I wondered how I had missed its general air of abandonment earlier, or the fact that many of the turds had grown whitish and powdery at their tops.

"I used to clean up after him," Hammersmith said, "and keep the roof of his house repaired against the rain. In that way also Sir Galahad was like your Southern negro, who will not do those things for himself. Now

164

I don't touch it, I haven't been near it since the accident . . . if you can call it an accident. I went over there with my rifle and shot him, but I haven't been over there since. I can't bring myself to. I suppose I will, in time. I'll clean up his messes and tear down his house."

Here came the kids, and all at once I didn't want them to come; all at once that was the last thing on earth I wanted. The little girl was all right, but the boy—

They pounded up the steps, looked at me, giggled, then went on toward the kitchen door.

"Caleb," Hammersmith said. "Come here. Just for a second."

The little girl—surely his twin, they had to be of an age—went on into the kitchen. The little boy came to his father, looking down at his feet. He knew he was ugly. He was only four, I guess, but four is old enough to know that you're ugly. His father put two fingers under the boy's chin and tried to raise his face. At first the boy resisted, but when his father said "Please, son," in tones of sweetness and calmness and love, he did as he was asked.

A huge, circular scar ran out of his hair, down his forehead, through one dead and indifferently cocked eye, and to the corner of his mouth, which had been disfigured into the knowing leer of a gambler or perhaps a whoremaster. One cheek was smooth and pretty; the other was bunched up like the stump of a tree. I guessed there had been a hole in it, but that, at least, had healed.

"He has the one eye," Hammersmith said, caressing the boy's bunched cheek with a lover's kind fingers. "I suppose he's lucky not to be blind. We get down on our knees and thank God for that much, at least. Eh, Caleb?"

"Yes, sir," the boy said shyly—the boy who would be beaten mercilessly on the play-yard by laughing, jeering bullies for all his miserable years of education, the boy who would never be asked to play Spin the Bottle or Post Office and would probably never sleep with a woman not bought and paid for once he was grown to manhood's times and needs, the boy who would always stand outside the warm and lighted circle of his peers, the boy who would look at himself in his mirror for the next fifty or sixty or seventy years of his life and think *ugly, ugly, ugly.*

"Go on in and get your cookies," his father said, and kissed his son's sneering mouth.

"Yes, sir," Caleb said, and dashed inside.

Hammersmith took a handkerchief from his back pocket and wiped at his eyes with it—they were dry, but I suppose he'd gotten used to them being wet.

"The dog was here when they were born," he said. "I brought him in the house to smell them when Cynthia brought them home from the hospital, and Sir Galahad licked their hands. Their little hands." He nodded, as if confirming this to himself. "He played with them; used to lick Arden's face until she giggled. Caleb used to pull his ears, and when he was first learning to walk, he'd sometimes go around the yard, holding to Galahad's tail. The dog never so much as *growled* at him. Either of them."

Now the tears were coming; he wiped at them automatically, as a man does when he's had lots of practice.

"There was no reason," he said. "Caleb didn't hurt him, yell at him, anything. I know. I was there. If I hadn't have been, the boy would almost certainly have been killed. What happened, Mr. Edgecombe, was *nothing*. The boy just got his face set the right way in front of the dog's face, and it came into Sir Galahad's mind—whatever serves a dog for a mind—to lunge and bite. To kill, if he could. The boy was there in front of him and the dog bit. And that's what happened with Coffey. He was there, he saw them on the porch, he took them, he raped them, he killed them. You say there should be some hint that he did something like it before, and I know what you mean, but maybe he *didn't* do it before. My dog never bit before; just that once. Maybe, if Coffey was let go, he'd never do it again. Maybe my dog never would have bit again. But I didn't concern myself with that, you know. I went out with my rifle and grabbed his collar and blew his head off."

He was breathing hard.

"I'm as enlightened as the next man, Mr. Edgecombe, went to college in Bowling Green, took history as well as journalism, some philosophy, too. I like to think of myself as enlightened. I don't suppose folks up North would, but I like to think of myself as enlightened. I'd not bring slavery back for all the tea in China. I think we have to be humane and generous in our efforts to solve the race problem. But we have to remember that your negro will bite if he gets the chance, just like a mongrel dog will bite if he gets the chance and it crosses his mind to do so. You want to know if he did it, your weepy Mr. Coffey with the scars all over him?"

I nodded.

"Oh, yes," Hammersmith said. "He did it. Don't you doubt it, and don't you turn your back on him. You might get away with it once or a hundred times . . . even a thousand . . . but in the end—" He raised a hand before my eyes and snapped the fingers together rapidly against the thumb, turning the hand into a biting mouth. "You understand?"

I nodded again.

"He raped them, he killed them, and afterward he was sorry . . . but those little girls stayed raped, those little girls stayed dead. But you'll fix him, won't you, Edgecombe? In a few weeks you'll fix him so he never does anything like that again." He got up, went to the porch rail, and looked vaguely at the doghouse, standing at the center of its beaten patch, in the middle of those aging turds. "Perhaps you'll excuse me," he said. "Since I don't have to spend the afternoon in court, I thought I might visit with my family for a little bit. A man's children are only young once."

"You go ahead," I said. My lips felt numb and distant. "And thank you for your time."

"Don't mention it," he said.

I drove directly from Hammersmith's house to the prison. It was a long drive, and this time I wasn't able to shorten it by singing songs. It felt like all the songs had gone out of me, at least for awhile. I kept seeing that poor little boy's disfigured face. And Hammersmith's hand, the fingers going up and down against the thumb in a biting motion.

5

WILD BILL WHARTON took his first trip down to the restraint room the very next day. He spent the morning and afternoon being as quiet and good as Mary's little lamb, a state we soon discovered was not natural to him, and meant trouble. Then, around seven-thirty that evening, Harry felt something warm splash on the cuffs of uniform pants he had put on clean just that day. It was piss. William Wharton was standing at his cell, showing his darkening teeth in a wide grin, and pissing all over Harry Terwilliger's pants and shoes.

"The dirty sonofabitch must have been saving it up all day," Harry said later, still disgusted and outraged.

Well, that was it. It was time to show William Wharton who ran the show on E Block. Harry got Brutal and me, and I alerted Dean and Percy, who were also on. We had three prisoners by then, remember, and were into what we called full coverage, with my group on from seven in the evening to three in the morning—when trouble was most apt to break out—and two other crews covering the rest of the day. Those other crews consisted mostly of floaters, with Bill Dodge usually in charge. It wasn't a bad way to run things, all and all, and I felt that, once I could shift Percy over to days, life would be even better. I never got around to that, however. I sometimes wonder if it would have changed things, if I had.

Anyway, there was a big watermain in the storage room, on the side away from Old Sparky, and Dean and Percy hooked up a length of canvas firehose to it. Then they stood by the valve that would open it, if needed.

Brutal and I hurried down to Wharton's cell, where Wharton still stood, still grinning and still with his tool hanging out of his pants. I had liberated the straitjacket from the restraint room and tossed it on a shelf in my office last thing before going home the night before, thinking we might be needing it for our new problem child. Now I had it in one hand, my index finger hooked under one of the canvas straps. Harry came behind us, hauling the nozzle of the firehose, which ran back through my office, down the storage-room steps, and to the drum where Dean and Percy were paying it out as fast as they could.

"Hey, d'jall like that?" Wild Bill asked. He was laughing like a kid at a carnival, laughing so hard he could barely talk; big tears went rolling down his cheeks. "You come on s'fast I guess you must've. I'm currently cookin some turds to go with it. Nice soft ones. I'll have them out to y'all tomorrow—"

He saw that I was unlocking his cell door and his eyes narrowed. He saw that Brutal was holding his revolver in one hand and his nightstick in the other, and they narrowed even more.

"You can come in here on your legs, but you'll go out on your backs, Billy the Kid is goan guarantee you that," he told us. His eyes shifted back to me. "And if you think you're gonna put that nut-coat on me, you got another think coming, old hoss."

"You're not the one who says go or jump back around here," I told him. "You should know that, but I guess you're too dumb to pick it up without a little teaching."

I finished unlocking the door and ran it back on its track. Wharton retreated to the bunk, his cock still hanging out of his pants, put his hands out to me, palms up, then beckoned with his fingers. "Come on, you ugly motherfucker," he said. "They be schoolin, all right, but this old boy's well set up to be the teacher." He shifted his gaze and his dark-toothed grin to Brutal. "Come on, big fella, you first. This time you cain't sneak up behind me. Put down that gun—you ain't gonna shoot it any-way, not you—and we'll go man-to-man. See who's the better fel—"

Brutal stepped into the cell, but not toward Wharton. He moved to the left once he was through the door, and Wharton's narrow eyes widened as he saw the firehose pointed at him.

"No, you don't," he said. "Oh no, you d—"

"Dean!" I yelled. *"Turn it on! All the way!"*

Wharton jumped forward, and Brutal hit him a good smart lick—the kind of lick I'm sure Percy dreamed of—across his forehead, laying his baton right over Wharton's eyebrows. Wharton, who seemed to think we'd never seen trouble until we'd seen him, went to his knees, his eyes open but blind. Then the water came, Harry staggering back a step under its power and then holding steady, the nozzle firm in his hands, pointed like a gun. The stream caught Wild Bill Wharton square in the middle of his chest, spun him halfway around, and drove him back under his bunk. Down the hall, Delacroix was jumping from foot to foot, cackling shrilly, and cursing at John Coffey, demanding that Coffey tell him what was going on, who was winning, and how dat *gran' fou* new boy like dat Chinee water treatment. John said nothing, just stood there quietly in his too-short pants and his prison slippers. I only had one quick glance at him, but that was enough to observe his same old expression, both sad and serene. It was as if he'd seen the whole thing before, not just once or twice but a thousand times.

"Kill the water!" Brutal shouted back over his shoulder, then raced forward into the cell. He sank his hands into the semi-conscious Wharton's armpits and dragged him out from under his bunk. Wharton was coughing and making a glub-glub sound. Blood was dribbling into his dazed eyes from above his brows, where Brutal's stick had popped the skin open in a line.

We had the straitjacket business down to a science, did Brutus Howell and me; we'd practiced it like a couple of vaudeville hoofers working up a new dance routine. Every now and then, that practice paid off. Now, for instance. Brutal sat Wharton up and held out his arms toward me the way a kid might hold out the arms of a Raggedy Andy doll. Awareness was just starting to seep back into Wharton's eyes, the knowledge that if he didn't start fighting right away, it was going to be too late, but the lines were still down between his brain and his muscles, and before he could repair them, I had rammed the sleeves of the coat up his arms and Brutal was doing the buckles up the back. While he took care of that, I grabbed the cuff-straps, pulled Wharton's arms around his sides, and linked his wrists together with another canvas strap. He ended up looking like he was hugging himself.

"Goddam you, big dummy, how dey doin widdim?" Delacroix screamed. I heard Mr. Jingles squeaking, as if he wanted to know, too.

Percy arrived, his shirt wet and sticking to him from his struggles with the watermain, his face glowing with excitement. Dean came along behind him, wearing a bracelet of purplish bruises around his throat and looking a lot less thrilled.

"Come on, now, Wild Bill," I said, and yanked Wharton to his feet. "Little walky-walky."

"Don't you call me that!" Wharton screamed shrilly, and I think that for the first time we were seeing real feelings, and not just a clever animal's camouflage spots. "Wild Bill Hickok wasn't no range-rider! He never fought him no bear with a Bowie knife, either! He was just another bushwhackin John Law! Dumb sonofabitch sat with his back to the door and got kilt by a drunk!"

"Oh my suds and body, a *history lesson*!" Brutal exclaimed, and shoved Wharton out of his cell. "A feller just never knows what he's going to get when he clocks in here, only that it's apt to be nice. But with so many nice people like you around, I guess that kind of stands to reason, don't it? And you know what? Pretty soon you'll be history yourself, Wild Bill. Meantime, you get on down the hall. We got a room for you. Kind of a cooling-off room."

Wharton gave a furious, inarticulate scream and threw himself at Brutal, even though he was snugly buckled into the coat now, and his arms were wrapped around behind him. Percy made to draw his baton—the Wetmore Solution for all of life's problems—and Dean put a hand on his wrist. Percy gave him a puzzled, half-indignant look, as if to say that after what Wharton had done to Dean, Dean should be the last person in the world to want to hold him back.

Brutal pushed Wharton backward. I caught him and pushed him to Harry. And Harry propelled him on down the Green Mile, past the gleeful Delacroix and the impassive Coffey. Wharton ran to keep from falling on his face, spitting curses the whole way. Spitting them the way a welder's torch spits sparks. We banged him into the last cell on the right while Dean, Harry, and Percy (who for once wasn't complaining about being unfairly overworked) yanked all of the crap out of the restraint room. While they did that, I had a brief conversation with Wharton.

"You think you're tough," I said, "and maybe you are, sonny, but in here tough don't matter. Your stampeding days are over. If you take it easy on us, we'll take it easy on you. If you make it hard, you'll die in the end just the same, only we'll sharpen you like a pencil before you go."

"You're gonna be so happy to see the end of me," Wharton said in a hoarse voice. He was struggling against the straitjacket even though he must have known it would do no good, and his face was as red as a tomato. "And until I'm gone, I'll make your lives miserable." He bared his teeth at me like an angry baboon.

"If that's all you want, to make our lives miserable, you can quit now, because you've already succeeded," Brutal said. "But as far as your time on the Mile goes, Wharton, we don't care if you spend all of it in the room with the soft walls. And you can wear that damned nut-coat until your arms gangrene from lack of circulation and fall right off." He paused. "No one much comes down here, you know. And if you think anyone gives much of a shit what happens to you, one way or another, you best reconsider. To the world in general, you're already one dead outlaw."

Wharton was studying Brutal carefully, and the choler was fading out of his face. "Lemme out of it," he said in a placatory voice—a voice too sane and too reasonable to trust. "I'll be good. Honest Injun."

Harry appeared in the cell doorway. The end of the corridor looked like a rummage sale, but we'd set things to rights with good speed once we got started. We had before; we knew the drill. "All ready," Harry said.

Brutal grabbed the bulge in the canvas where Wharton's right elbow was and yanked him to his feet. "Come on, Wild Billy. And look on the good side. You're gonna have at least twenty-four hours to remind yourself never to sit with your back to the door, and to never hold onto no aces and eights."

"Lemme out of it," Wharton said. He looked from Brutal to Harry to me, the red creeping back into his face. "I'll be good—I tell you I've learned my lesson. I . . . I . . . *ummmmmmahhhhhh*—"

He suddenly collapsed, half of him in the cell, half of him on the played-out lino of the Green Mile, kicking his feet and bucking his body.

"Holy Christ, he's pitchin a fit," Percy whispered.

"Sure, and my sister's the Whore of Babylon," Brutal said. "She dances the hootchie-kootchie for Moses on Saturday nights in a long white veil." He bent down and hooked a hand into one of Wharton's armpits. I got the other one. Wharton threshed between us like a hooked fish. Carrying his jerking body, listening to him grunt from one end and fart from the other was one of my life's less pleasant experiences.

I looked up and met John Coffey's eyes for a second. They were bloodshot, and his dark cheeks were wet. He had been crying again. I thought of Hammersmith making that biting gesture with his hand and shivered a little. Then I turned my attention back to Wharton.

We threw him into the restraint room like he was cargo, and watched him lie on the floor, bucking hard in the straitjacket next to the drain we had once checked for the mouse which had started its E Block life as Steamboat Willy.

"I don't much care if he swallows his tongue or something and dies," Dean said in his hoarse and raspy voice, "but think of the paperwork, boys! It'd never end."

"Never mind the paperwork, think of the hearing," Harry said gloomily. "We'd lose our damned jobs. End up picking peas down Mississippi. You know what Mississippi is, don't you? It's the Indian word for asshole."

"He ain't gonna die, and he ain't gonna swallow his tongue, either," Brutal said. "When we open this door tomorrow, he's gonna be just fine. Take my word for it."

That's the way it was, too. The man we took back to his cell the next night at nine was quiet, pallid, and seemingly chastened. He walked with his head down, made no effort to attack anyone when the straitjacket came off, and only stared listlessly at me when I told him it would go just the same the next time, and he just had to ask himself how much time he wanted to spend pissing in his pants and eating baby-food a spoonful at a time.

"I'll be good, boss, I learnt my lesson," he whispered in a humble little voice as we put him back in his cell. Brutal looked at me and winked.

Late the next day, William Wharton, who was Billy the Kid to himself and never that bushwhacking John Law Wild Bill Hickok, bought a Moon Pie from Old Toot-Toot. Wharton had been expressly forbidden any such commerce, but the afternoon crew was composed of floaters, as I think I have said, and the deal went down. Toot himself undoubtedly knew better, but to him the snack-wagon was always a case of a nickel is a nickel, a dime is a dime, I'd sing another chorus but I don't have the time.

That night, when Brutal ran his check-round, Wharton was standing at the door of his cell. He waited until Brutal looked up at him, then slammed the heels of his hands into his bulging cheeks and shot a thick and amazingly long stream of chocolate sludge into Brutal's face. He had crammed the entire Moon Pie into his trap, held it there until it liquefied, and then used it like chewing tobacco.

Wharton fell back on his bunk wearing a chocolate goatee, kicking his legs and screaming with laughter and pointing to Brutal, who was wearing a lot more than a goatee. "Li'l Black Sambo, yassuh, boss, yassuh, how*doo* you do?" Wharton held his belly and howled. "Gosh, if it had only been ka-ka! I wish it had been! If I'd had me some of that—"

"You *are* ka-ka," Brutal growled, "and I hope you got your bags packed, because you're going back down to your favorite toilet."

Once again Wharton was bundled into the straitjacket, and once again we stowed him in the room with the soft walls. Two days, this time. Sometimes we could hear him raving in there, sometimes we could hear him promising that he'd be good, that he'd come to his senses and be good, and sometimes we could hear him screaming that he needed a doctor, that he was dying. Mostly, though, he was silent. And he was silent when we took him out again, too, walking back to his cell with his head down and his eyes dull, not responding when Harry said, "Remember, it's up to you." He would be all right for a while, and then he'd try something else. There was nothing he did that hadn't been tried before (well, except for the thing with the Moon Pie, maybe; even Brutal admitted that was pretty original), but his sheer persistence was scary. I was afraid that sooner or later someone's attention might lapse and there would be hell to pay. And the situation might continue for quite awhile, because somewhere he had a lawyer who was beating the bushes, telling folks how wrong it would be to kill this fellow upon whose brow the dew of youth had not yet dried . . . and who was, incidentally, as white as old Jeff Davis. There was no sense complaining about it, because keeping Wharton out of the chair was his lawyer's job. Keeping him safely jugged was ours. And in the end, Old Sparky would almost certainly have him, lawyer or no lawyer.

6

THAT WAS THE WEEK Melinda Moores, the warden's wife, came home from Indianola. The doctors were done with her; they had their interesting, newfangled X-ray photographs of the tumor in her head; they had documented the weakness in her hand and the paralyzing pains that racked her almost constantly by then, and were done with her. They gave her husband a bunch of pills with morphine in them and sent Melinda home to die. Hal Moores had some sick-leave piled up— not a lot, they didn't give you a lot in those days, but he took what he had so he could help her do what she had to do.

My wife and I went to see her three days or so after she came home. I called ahead and Hal said yes, that would be fine, Melinda was having a pretty good day and would enjoy seeing us.

"I hate calls like this," I said to Janice as we drove to the little house where the Mooreses had spent most of their marriage.

"So does everyone, honey," she said, and patted my hand. "We'll bear up under it, and so will she."

"I hope so."

We found Melinda in the sitting room, planted in a bright slant of unseasonably warm October sun, and my first shocked thought was that she had lost ninety pounds. She hadn't, of course—if she'd lost that much weight, she hardly would have been there at all—but that was my brain's initial reaction to what my eyes were reporting. Her face had fallen away to show the shape of the underlying skull, and her skin was as white as parchment. There were dark circles under her eyes.

And it was the first time I ever saw her in her rocker when she didn't have a lapful of sewing or afghan squares or rags for braiding into a rug. She was just sitting there. Like a person in a train-station.

"Melinda," my wife said warmly. I think she was as shocked as I was—more, perhaps—but she hid it splendidly, as some women seem able to do. She went to Melinda, dropped on one knee beside the rocking chair in which the warden's wife sat, and took one of her hands. As she did, my eye happened on the blue hearthrug by the fireplace. It occurred to me that it should have been the shade of tired old limes, because now this room was just another version of the Green Mile.

"I brought you some tea," Jan said, "the kind I put up myself. It's a nice sleepy tea. I've left it in the kitchen."

"Thank you so much, darlin," Melinda said. Her voice sounded old and rusty.

"How you feeling, dear?" my wife asked.

"Better," Melinda said in her rusty, grating voice. "Not so's I want to go out to a barn dance, but at least there's no pain today. They give me some pills for the headaches. Sometimes they even work."

"That's good, isn't it?"

"But I can't grip so well. Something's happened . . . to my hand." She raised it, looked at it as if she had never seen it before, then lowered it back into her lap. "Something's happened . . . all over me." She began to cry in a soundless way that made me think of John Coffey. It started to chime in my head again, that thing he'd said: *I helped it, didn't I? I helped it, didn't I?* Like a rhyme you can't get rid of.

Hal came in then. He collared me, and you can believe me when I say I was glad to be collared. We went into the kitchen, and he poured me half a shot of white whiskey, hot stuff fresh out of some countryman's still. We clinked our glasses together and drank. The shine went down like coal-oil, but the bloom in the belly was heaven. Still, when Moores tipped the mason jar at me, wordlessly asking if I wanted the other half, I shook my head and waved it off. Wild Bill Wharton was out of restraints—for the time being, anyway—and it wouldn't be safe to go near where he was with a booze-clouded head. Not even with bars between us.

"I don't know how long I can take this, Paul," he said in a low voice. "There's a girl who comes in mornings to help me with her, but the doctors say she may lose control of her bowels, and . . . and . . ." He stopped, his throat working, trying hard not to cry in front of me again.

"Go with it as best you can," I said. I reached out across the table and briefly squeezed his palsied, liverspotted hand. "Do that day by day and give the rest over to God. There's nothing else you can do, is there?"

"I guess not. But it's hard, Paul. I pray you never have to find out how hard."

He made an effort to collect himself.

"Now tell me the news. How are you doing with William Wharton? And how are you making out with Percy Wetmore?"

We talked shop for a while, and got through the visit. After, all the way home, with my wife sitting silent, for the most part—wet-eyed and thoughtful—in the passenger seat beside me, Coffey's words ran around in my head like Mr. Jingles running around in Delacroix's cell: *I helped it, didn't I?*

"It's terrible," my wife said dully at one point. "And there's nothing anyone can do to help her."

I nodded agreement and thought, *I helped it, didn't I?* But that was crazy, and I tried as best I could to put it out of my mind.

As we turned into our dooryard, she finally spoke a second time— not about her old friend Melinda, but about my urinary infection. She wanted to know if it was really gone. Really gone, I told her.

"That's fine, then," she said, and kissed me over the eyebrow, in that shivery place of mine. "Maybe we ought to, you know, get up to a little something. If you have the time and the inclination, that is."

Having plenty of the latter and just enough of the former, I took her by the hand and led her into the back bedroom and took her clothes off as she stroked the part of me that swelled and throbbed but didn't hurt anymore. And as I moved in her sweetness, slipping through it in that slow way she liked—that we both liked—I thought of John Coffey, saying he'd helped it, he'd helped it, hadn't he? Like a snatch of song that won't leave your mind until it's damned good and ready.

Later, as I drove to the prison, I got to thinking that very soon we would have to start rehearsing for Delacroix's execution. That thought led to how Percy was going to be out front this time, and I felt a shiver of dread. I told myself to just go with it, one execution and we'd very likely be shut of Percy Wetmore for good . . . but still I felt that shiver, as if the infection I'd been suffering with wasn't gone at all, but had only switched locations, from boiling my groin to freezing my backbone.

7

"COME ON," Brutal told Delacroix the following evening. "We're going for a little walk. You and me and Mr. Jingles."

Delacroix looked at him distrustfully, then reached down into the cigar box for the mouse. He cupped it in the palm of one hand and looked at Brutal with narrowed eyes.

"Whatchoo talking about?" he asked.

"It's a big night for you and Mr. Jingles," Dean said, as he and Harry joined Brutal. The chain of bruises around Dean's neck had gone an unpleasant yellow color, but at least he could talk again without sounding like a dog barking at a cat. He looked at Brutal. "Think we ought to put the shackles on him, Brute?"

Brutal appeared to consider. "Naw," he said at last. "He's gonna be good, ain't you, Del? You and the mouse, both. After all, you're gonna be showin off for some high muck-a-mucks tonight."

Percy and I were standing up by the duty desk, watching this, Percy with his arms folded and a small, contemptuous smile on his lips. After a bit, he took out his horn comb and went to work on his hair with it. John Coffey was watching, too, standing silently at the bars of his cell. Wharton was lying on his bunk, staring up at the ceiling and ignoring the whole show. He was still "being good," although what he called *good* was what the docs at Briar Ridge called *catatonic*. And there was one other person there, as well. He was tucked out of sight in my office, but his skinny shadow fell out the door and onto the Green Mile.

"What dis about, you *gran' fou?*" Del asked querulously, drawing his feet up on the bunk as Brutal undid the double locks on his cell door and ran it open. His eyes flicked back and forth among the three of them.

"Well, I tell you," Brutal said. "Mr. Moores is gone for awhile—his wife is under the weather, as you may have heard. So Mr. Anderson is in charge, Mr. Curtis Anderson."

"Yeah? What that got to do with me?"

"Well," Harry said, "Boss Anderson's heard about your mouse, Del, and wants to see him perform. He and about six other fellows are over in Admin, just waiting for you to show up. Not just plain old bluesuit guards, either. These are pretty big bugs, just like Brute said. One of them, I believe, is a politician all the way from the state capital."

Delacroix swelled visibly at this, and I saw not so much as a single shred of doubt on his face. Of *course* they wanted to see Mr. Jingles; who would not?

He scrummed around, first under his bunk and then under his pillow. He eventually found one of those big pink peppermints and the wildly colored spool. He looked at Brutal questioningly, and Brutal nodded.

"Yep. It's the spool trick they're really wild to see, I guess, but the way he eats those mints is pretty damned cute, too. And don't forget the cigar box. You'll want it to carry him in, right?"

Delacroix got the box and put Mr. Jingles's props in it, but the mouse he settled on the shoulder of his shirt. Then he stepped out of his cell, his puffed-out chest leading the way, and regarded Dean and Harry. "You boys coming?"

"Naw," Dean said. "Got other fish to fry. But you knock em for a loop, Del—show em what happens when a Louisiana boy puts the hammer down and really goes to work."

"You bet." A smile shone out of his face, so sudden and so simple in its happiness that I felt my heart break for him a little, in spite of the terrible thing he had done. What a world we live in—what a world!

Delacroix turned to John Coffey, with whom he had struck up a diffident friendship not much different from a hundred other deathhouse acquaintances I'd seen.

"You knock em for a loop, Del," Coffey said in a serious voice. "You show em all his tricks."

Delacroix nodded and held his hand up by his shoulder. Mr. Jingles stepped onto it like it was a platform, and Delacroix held the hand out toward Coffey's cell. John Coffey stuck out a huge finger, and I'll be damned if that mouse didn't stretch out his neck and lick the end of it, just like a dog.

"Come on, Del, quit lingerin," Brutal said. "These folks're settin back a hot dinner at home to watch your mouse cut his capers." Not true, of course—Anderson would have been there until eight o'clock on any night, and the guards he'd dragged in to watch Delacroix's "show" would be there until eleven or twelve, depending on when their shifts were scheduled to end. The politician from the state capital would most likely turn out to be an office janitor in a borrowed tie. But Delacroix had no way of knowing any of that.

"I'm ready," Delacroix said, speaking with the simplicity of a great star who has somehow managed to retain the common touch. "Let's go." And as Brutal led him up the Green Mile with Mr. Jingles perched there on the little man's shoulder, Delacroix once more began to bugle, "*Messieurs et mesdames! Bienvenue au cirque de mousie!*" Yet, even lost as deeply in his own fantasy world as he was, he gave Percy a wide berth and a mistrustful glance.

Harry and Dean stopped in front of the empty cell across from Wharton's (that worthy had still not so much as stirred). They watched as Brutal unlocked the door to the exercise yard, where another two guards were waiting to join him, and led Delacroix out, bound for his command performance before the grand high poohbahs of Cold Mountain Penitentiary. We waited until the door was locked again, and then I looked toward my office. That shadow was still lying on the floor, thin as famine, and I was glad Delacroix had been too excited to see it.

"Come on out," I said. "And let's move along brisk, folks. I want to get two run-throughs in, and we don't have much time."

Old Toot-Toot, looking as bright-eyed and bushy-tailed as ever, came out, walked to Delacroix's cell, and strolled in through the open door. "Sittin down," he said. "I'm sittin down, I'm sittin down, I'm sittin down."

This is the real circus, I thought, closing my eyes for a second. This is the real circus right here, and we're all just a bunch of trained mice. Then I put the thought out of my mind, and we started to rehearse.

8

THE FIRST REHEARSAL went well, and so did the second. Percy performed better than I could have hoped for in my wildest dreams. That didn't mean things would go right when the time really came for the Cajun to walk the Mile, but it was a big step in the right direction. It occurred to me that it had gone well because Percy was at long last doing something he cared about. I felt a surge of contempt at that, and pushed it away. What did it matter? He would cap Delacroix and roll him, and then both of them would be gone. If that wasn't a happy ending, what was? And, as Moores had pointed out, Delacroix's nuts were going to fry no matter who was out front.

Still, Percy had shown to good advantage in his new role and he knew it. We all did. As for me, I was too relieved to dislike him much, at least for the time being. It looked as if things were going to go all right. I was further relieved to find that Percy actually listened when we suggested some things he could do that might improve his performance even more, or at least cut down the possibility of something going wrong. If you want to know the truth, we got pretty enthusiastic about it—even Dean, who ordinarily stood well back from Percy . . . physically as well as mentally, if he could. None of it that surprising, either, I suppose— for most men, nothing is more flattering than having a young person actually pay attention to his advice, and we were no different in that regard. As a result, not a one of us noticed that Wild Bill Wharton was no longer looking up at the ceiling. That includes me, but I know he wasn't. He was looking at us as we stood there by the duty desk, gassing and giving Percy advice. Giving him advice! And him pretending to listen! Quite a laugh, considering how things turned out!

The sound of a key rattling into the lock of the door to the exercise yard put an end to our little post-rehearsal critique. Dean gave Percy a warning glance. "Not a word or a wrong look," he said. "We don't want him to know what we've been doing. It's not good for them. Upsets them."

Percy nodded and ran a finger across his lips in a mum's-the-word gesture that was supposed to be funny and wasn't. The exercise-yard door opened and Delacroix came in, escorted by Brutal, who was carrying the cigar box with the colored spool in it, the way the magician's assistant in a vaudeville show might carry the boss's props offstage at the end of the act. Mr. Jingles was perched on Delacroix's shoulder. And Delacroix himself? I tell you what—Lillie Langtry couldn't have looked any glowier after performing at the White House. "They love Mr. Jingles!" Delacroix proclaimed. "They laugh and cheer and clap they hands!"

"Well, that's aces," Percy said. He spoke in an indulgent, proprietary way that didn't sound like the old Percy at all. "Pop on back in your cell, old-timer."

Delacroix gave him a comical look of distrust, and the old Percy came busting out. He bared his teeth in a mock snarl and made as if to grab Delacroix. It was a joke, of course, Percy was happy, not in a serious grabbing mood at all, but Delacroix didn't know that. He jerked away with an expression of fear and dismay, and tripped over one of Brutal's big feet. He went down hard, hitting the linoleum with the back of his head. Mr. Jingles leaped away in time to avoid being crushed, and went squeaking off down the Green Mile to Delacroix's cell.

Delacroix got to his feet, gave the chuckling Percy a single hate-filled glance, then scurried off after his pet, calling for him and rubbing the back of his head. Brutal (who didn't know that Percy had shown exciting signs of competency for a change) gave Percy a wordless look of contempt and went after Del, shaking his keys out.

I think what happened next happened because Percy was actually moved to apologize—I know it's hard to believe, but he was in an extraordinary humor that day. If true, it only proves a cynical old adage I heard once, something about how no good deed goes unpunished. Remember me telling you about how, after he'd chased the mouse down to the restraint room on one of those two occasions before Delacroix joined us, Percy got a little too close to The Pres's cell? Doing that was dangerous, which was why the Green Mile was so wide—when you walked straight down the middle of it, you couldn't be reached from the cells. The Pres hadn't done anything to Percy, but I remember thinking that Arlen Bitterbuck might have, had it been him Percy had gotten too close to. Just to teach him a lesson.

Well, The Pres and The Chief had both moved on, but Wild Bill Wharton had taken their place. He was worse-mannered than The Pres or The Chief had ever dreamed of being, and he'd been watching the whole little play, hoping for a chance to get on stage himself. That chance now fell into his lap, courtesy of Percy Wetmore.

"Hey, Del!" Percy called, half-laughing, starting after Brutal and Delacroix and drifting much too close to Wharton's side of the Green Mile without realizing it. "Hey, you numb shit, I didn't mean nothin by it! Are you all ri—"

Wharton was up off his bunk and over to the bars of his cell in a flash—never in my time as a guard did I see anyone move so fast, and that includes some of the athletic young men Brutal and I worked with later at Boys' Correctional. He shot his arms out through the bars and grabbed Percy, first by the shoulders of his uniform blouse and then by the throat. Wharton dragged him back against his cell door. Percy squealed like a pig in a slaughter-chute, and I saw from his eyes that he thought he was going to die.

"Ain't you sweet," Wharton whispered. One hand left Percy's throat and ruffled through his hair. "Soft!" he said, half-laughing. "Like a girl's. I druther fuck your asshole than your sister's pussy, I think." And he actually kissed Percy's ear.

I think Percy—who had beat Delacroix onto the block for accidentally brushing his crotch, remember—knew exactly what was happening. I doubt that he wanted to, but I think he did. All the color had drained from his face, and the blemishes on his cheeks stood out like

186

birthmarks. His eyes were huge and wet. A line of spittle leaked from one corner of his twitching mouth. All this happened quick—it was begun and done in less than ten seconds, I'd say.

Harry and I stepped forward, our billies raised. Dean drew his gun. But before things could go so much as an inch further, Wharton let go of Percy and stepped back, raising his hands to his shoulders and grinning his dank grin. "I let im go, I 'us just playin and I let im go," he said. "Never hurt airy single hair on that boy's purty head, so don't you go stickin me down in that goddam soft room again."

Percy Wetmore darted across the Green Mile and cringed against the barred door of the empty cell on the other side, breathing so fast and so loud that it sounded almost like sobbing. He had finally gotten his lesson in keeping to the center of the Green Mile and away from the frumious bandersnatch, the jaws that bite and the claws that catch. I had an idea it was a lesson that would stick with him longer than all the advice we'd given him after our rehearsals. There was an expression of utter terror on his face, and his precious hair was seriously mussed up for the first time since I'd met him, all in spikes and tangles. He looked like someone who has just escaped being raped.

There was a moment of utter stop then, a quiet so thick that the only sound was the sobbing whistle of Percy's breathing. What broke it was cackling laughter, so sudden and so completely its own mad thing that it was shocking. *Wharton* was my first thought, but it wasn't him. It was Delacroix, standing in the open door of his cell and pointing at Percy. The mouse was back on his shoulder, and Delacroix looked like a small but malevolent male witch, complete with imp.

"Lookit him, he done piss his pants!" Delacroix howled. "Lookit what the big man done! Bus' other people wid 'is stick, *mais oui* some *mauvais homme,* but when someone touch him, he make water in 'is pants jus' like a baby!"

He laughed and pointed, all his fear and hatred of Percy coming out in that derisive laughter. Percy stared at him, seemingly incapable of moving or speaking. Wharton stepped back to the bars of his cell, looked down at the dark splotch on the front of Percy's trousers—it was small but it was there, and no question about what it was—and grinned. "Somebody ought to buy the tough boy a didy," he said, and went back to his bunk, chuffing laughter.

Brutal went down to Delacroix's cell, but the Cajun had ducked inside and thrown himself on his bunk before Brutal could get there.

I reached out and grasped Percy's shoulder. "Percy—" I began, but that was as far as I got. He came to life, shaking my hand off. He looked down at the front of his pants, saw the spot spreading there, and blushed a dark, fiery red. He looked up at me again, then at Harry and Dean. I remember being glad that Old Toot-Toot was gone. If he'd been around, the story would have been all over the prison in a single day. And, given Percy's last name—an unfortunate one, in this con-text—it was a story that would have been told with the relish of high glee for years to come.

"You talk about this to anyone, and you'll all be on the breadlines in a week," he whispered fiercely. It was the sort of crack that would have made me want to swat him under other circumstances, but under these, I only pitied him. I think he saw that pity, and it made it worse with him—like having an open wound scoured with nettles.

"What goes on here stays here," Dean said quietly. "You don't have to worry about that."

Percy looked back over his shoulder, toward Delacroix's cell. Brutal was just locking the door, and from inside, deadly clear, we could still hear Delacroix giggling. Percy's look was as black as thunder. I thought of telling him that you reaped what you sowed in this life, and then decided this might not be the right time for a scripture lesson.

"As for him—" he began, but never finished. He left, instead, head down, to go into the storage room and look for a dry pair of pants.

"He's so *purty,*" Wharton said in a dreamy voice. Harry told him to shut the fuck up before he went down to the restraint room just on general damned principles. Wharton folded his arms on his chest, closed his eyes, and appeared to go to sleep.

9

THE NIGHT BEFORE Delacroix's execution came down hotter and muggier than ever—eighty-one degrees by the thermometer outside the Admin ready-room window when I clocked in at six. Eighty-one degrees at the end of October, think of that, and thunder rumbling in the west like it does in July. I'd met a member of my congregation in town that afternoon, and he had asked me, with apparent seriousness, if I thought such unseasonable weather could be a sign of the Last Times. I said that I was sure not, but it crossed my mind that it was Last Times for Eduard Delacroix, all right. Yes indeed it was.

Bill Dodge was standing in the door to the exercise yard, drinking coffee and smoking him a little smoke. He looked around at me and said, "Well, lookit here. Paul Edgecombe, big as life and twice as ugly."

"How'd the day go, Billy?"

"All right."

"Delacroix?"

"Fine. He seems to understand it's tomorrow, and yet it's like he *don't* understand. You know how most of em are when the end finally comes for them."

I nodded. "Wharton?"

Bill laughed. "What a comedian. Makes Jack Benny sound like a Quaker. He told Rolfe Wettermark that he ate strawberry jam out of his wife's pussy."

"What did Rolfe say?"

"That he wasn't married. Said it must have been his mother Wharton was thinking of."

I laughed, and hard. That really was funny, in a low sort of way. And it was good just to be able to laugh without feeling like someone was lighting matches way down low in my gut. Bill laughed with me, then turned the rest of his coffee out in the yard, which was empty except for a few shuffling trusties, most of whom had been there for a thousand years or so.

Thunder rumbled somewhere far off, and unfocused heat lightning flashed in the darkening sky overhead. Bill looked up uneasily, his laughter dying.

"I tell you what, though," he said, "I don't like this weather much. Feels like something's gonna happen. Something bad."

About that he was right. The bad thing happened right around quarter of ten that night. That was when Percy killed Mr. Jingles.

10

AT FIRST it seemed like it was going to be a pretty good night in spite of the heat—John Coffey was being his usual quiet self, Wild Bill was making out to be Mild Bill, and Delacroix was in good spirits for a man who had a date with Old Sparky in a little more than twenty-four hours.

He *did* understand what was going to happen to him, at least on the most basic level; he had ordered chili for his last meal and gave me special instructions for the kitchen. "Tell em to lay on dat hot-sauce," he said. "Tell em the kind dat really jump up your t'roat an' say howdy— the green stuff, none of dat mild. Dat stuff gripe me like a motherfucker, I can't get off the toilet the nex' day, but I don't think I gonna have a problem this time, *n'est-ce pas?*"

Most of them worry about their immortal souls with a kind of moronic ferocity, but Delacroix pretty much dismissed my questions about what he wanted for spiritual comfort in his last hours. If "dat fella" Schuster had been good enough for Big Chief Bitterbuck, Del reckoned, Schuster would be good enough for him. No, what he cared about— you've guessed already, I'm sure—was what was going to happen to Mr. Jingles after he, Delacroix, passed on. I was used to spending long hours with the condemned on the night before their last march, but this was the first time I'd spent those long hours pondering the fate of a mouse.

Del considered scenario after scenario, patiently working the possibilities through his dim mind. And while he thought aloud, wanting to provide for his pet mouse's future as if it were a child that had to be put

191

through college, he threw that colored spool against the wall. Each time he did it, Mr. Jingles would spring after it, track it down, and then roll it back to Del's foot. It started to get on my nerves after awhile—first the clack of the spool against the stone wall, then the minute clitter of Mr. Jingles's paws. Although it was a cute trick, it palled after ninety minutes or so. And Mr. Jingles never seemed to get tired. He paused every now and then to refresh himself with a drink of water out of a coffee saucer Delacroix kept for just that purpose, or to munch a pink crumb of peppermint candy, and then back to it he went. Several times it was on the tip of my tongue to tell Delacroix to give it a rest, and each time I reminded myself that he had this night and tomorrow to play the spool-game with Mr. Jingles, and that was all. Near the end, though, it began to be really difficult to hold onto that thought—you know how it is, with a noise that's repeated over and over. After a while it shoots your nerve. I started to speak after all, then something made me look over my shoulder and out the cell door. John Coffey was standing at *his* cell door across the way, and he shook his head at me: right, left, back to center. As if he had read my mind and was telling me to think again.

I would see that Mr. Jingles got to Delacroix's maiden aunt, I said, the one who had sent him the big bag of candy. His colored spool could go as well, even his "house"—we'd take up a collection and see that Toot gave up his claim on the Corona box. No, said Delacroix after some consideration (he had time to throw the spool against the wall at least five times, with Mr. Jingles either nosing it back or pushing it with his paws), that wouldn't do. Aunt Hermione was too old, she wouldn't understand Mr. Jingles's frisky ways, and suppose Mr. Jingles outlived her? What would happen to him then? No, no, Aunt Hermione just wouldn't do.

Well, then, I asked, suppose one of us took it? One of us guards? We could keep him right here on E Block. No, Delacroix said, he thanked me kindly for the thought, *certainement,* but Mr. Jingles was a mouse that yearned to be free. He, Eduard Delacroix, knew this, because Mr. Jingles had—you guessed it—whispered the information in his ear.

"All right," I said, "one of us will take him home, Del. Dean, maybe. He's got a little boy that would just love a pet mouse, I bet."

Delacroix actually turned pale with horror at the thought. A little kid in charge of a rodent genius like Mr. Jingles? How in the name of *le bon Dieu* could a little kid be expected to keep up with his training, let alone teach him new tricks? And suppose the kid lost interest and forgot to feed him for two or three days at a stretch? Delacroix, who had roasted six human beings alive in an effort to cover up his original crime, shuddered with the delicate revulsion of an ardent anti-vivisectionist.

All right, I said, I'd take him myself (promise them anything, remember; in their last forty-eight hours, promise them anything). How would that be?

"No, sir, Boss Edgecombe," Del said apologetically. He threw the spool again. It hit the wall, bounced, spun; then Mr. Jingles was on it like white on rice and nosing it back to Delacroix. "Thank you kindly— *merci beaucoup*—but you live out in the woods, and Mr. Jingles, he be scared to live out *dans la forêt*. I know, because—"

"I think I can guess how you know, Del," I said.

Delacroix nodded, smiling. "But we gonna figure this out. You bet!" He threw the spool. Mr. Jingles clittered after it. I tried not to wince.

In the end it was Brutal who saved the day. He had been up by the duty desk, watching Dean and Harry play cribbage. Percy was there, too, and Brutal finally tired of trying to start a conversation with him and getting nothing but sullen grunts in response. He strolled down to where I sat on a stool outside of Delacroix's cell and stood there listening to us with his arms folded.

"How about Mouseville?" Brutal asked into the considering silence which followed Del's rejection of my spooky old house out in the woods. He threw the comment out in a casual just-an-idea tone of voice.

"Mouseville?" Delacroix asked, giving Brutal a look both startled and interested. "What Mouseville?"

"It's this tourist attraction down in Florida," he said. "Tallahassee, I think. Is that right, Paul? Tallahassee?"

"Yep," I said, speaking without a moment's hesitation, thinking God bless Brutus Howell. "Tallahassee. Right down the road apiece from the dog university." Brutal's mouth twitched at that, and I thought he was going to queer the pitch by laughing, but he got it under control and nodded. I'd hear about the dog university later, though, I imagined.

This time Del didn't throw the spool, although Mr. Jingles stood on Del's slipper with his front paws raised, clearly lusting for another chance to chase. The Cajun looked from Brutal to me and back to Brutal again. "What dey do in Mouseville?" he asked.

"You think they'd take Mr. Jingles?" Brutal asked me, simultaneously ignoring Del and drawing him on. "Think he's got the stuff, Paul?"

I tried to appear considering. "You know," I said, "the more I think of it, the more it seems like a brilliant idea." From the corner of my eye I saw Percy come partway down the Green Mile (giving Wharton's cell a very wide berth). He stood with one shoulder leaning against an empty cell, listening with a small, contemptuous smile on his lips.

"What dis Mouseville?" Del asked, now frantic to know.

"A tourist attraction, like I told you," Brutal said. "There's, oh I dunno, a hundred or so mice there. Wouldn't you say, Paul?"

"More like a hundred and fifty these days," I said. "It's a big success. I understand they're thinking of opening one out in California and calling it Mouseville West, that's how much business is booming. Trained mice are the coming thing with the smart set, I guess—I don't understand it, myself."

Del sat with the colored spool in his hand, looking at us, his own situation forgotten for the time being.

"They only take the smartest mice," Brutal cautioned, "the ones that can do tricks. And they can't be white mice, because those are pet-shop mice."

"Pet-shop mice, yeah, you bet!" Delacroix said fiercely. "I hate dem pet-shop mice!"

"And what they got," Brutal said, his eyes distant now as he imagined it, "is this tent you go into—"

"Yeah, yeah, like inna *cirque*! Do you gotta pay to get in?"

"You shittin me? *Course* you gotta pay to get in. A dime apiece, two cents for the kiddies. And there's, like, this whole city made out of Bakelite boxes and toilet-paper rolls, with windows made out of isinglass so you can see what they're up to in there—"

"Yeah! Yeah!" Delacroix was in ecstasy now. Then he turned to me. "What ivy-glass?"

"Like on the front of a stove, where you can see in," I said.

"Oh sure! Dat shit!" He cranked his hand at Brutal, wanting him to go on, and Mr. Jingles's little oildrop eyes practically spun in their sockets, trying to keep that spool in view. It was pretty funny. Percy came a little closer, as if wanting to get a better look, and I saw John Coffey frowning at him, but I was too wrapped up in Brutal's fantasy to pay much attention. This took telling the condemned man what he wanted to hear to new heights, and I was all admiration, believe me.

"Well," Brutal said, "there's the mouse city, but what the kids really like is the Mouseville All-Star Circus, where there's mice that swing on trapezes, and mice that roll these little barrels, and mice that stack coins—"

"Yeah, dat's it! Dat's the place for Mr. Jingles!" Delacroix said. His eyes sparkled and his cheeks were high with color. It occurred to me that Brutus Howell was a kind of saint. "You gonna be a circus mouse after all, Mr. Jingles! Gonna live in a mouse city down Florida! All ivy-glass windows! Hurrah!"

He threw the spool extra-hard. It hit low on the wall, took a crazy bounce, and squirted out between the bars of his cell door and onto the Mile. Mr. Jingles raced out after it, and Percy saw his chance.

"No, you fool!" Brutal yelled, but Percy paid no attention. Just as Mr. Jingles reached the spool—too intent on it to realize his old enemy was at hand—Percy brought the sole of one hard black workshoe down on it. There was an audible snap as Mr. Jingles's back broke, and blood gushed from his mouth. His tiny dark eyes bulged in their sockets, and in them I read an expression of surprised agony that was all too human.

Delacroix screamed with horror and grief. He threw himself at the door of his cell and thrust his arms out between the bars, reaching as far as he could, crying the mouse's name over and over.

Percy turned toward him, smiling. Toward the three of us. "There," he said. "I knew I'd get him, sooner or later. Just a matter of time, really." He turned and walked back up the Green Mile, not hurrying, leaving Mr. Jingles lying on the linoleum in a spreading pool of his own blood.

PART FOUR

THE BAD DEATH
OF EDUARD DELACROIX

1

ALL THIS OTHER WRITING ASIDE, I've kept a little diary since I took up residence at Georgia Pines—no big deal, just a couple of paragraphs a day, mostly about the weather—and I looked back through it last evening. I wanted to see just how long it has been since my grandchildren Christopher and Danielle more or less forced me into Georgia Pines. "For your own good, Gramps," they said. Of course they did. Isn't that what people mostly say when they have finally figured out how to get rid of a problem that walks and talks?

It's been a little over two years. The eerie thing is that I don't know if it *feels* like two years, or longer than that, or shorter. My sense of time seems to be *melting,* like a kid's snowman in a January thaw. It's as if time as it always was—Eastern Standard Time, Daylight Saving Time, Working-Man Time—doesn't exist anymore. Here there is only Georgia Pines Time, which is Old Man Time, Old Lady Time, and Piss the Bed Time. The rest . . . all gone.

This is a dangerous damned place. You don't realize it at first, at first you think it's only a boring place, about as dangerous as a nursery school at nap-time, but it's dangerous, all right. I've seen a lot of people slide into senility since I came here, and sometimes they do more than slide—sometimes they go down with the speed of a crash-diving submarine. They come here mostly all right—dim-eyed and welded to the cane, maybe a little loose in the bladder, but otherwise okay—and then something happens to them. A month later they're just sitting in the TV room, staring up at Oprah Winfrey on the TV with dull eyes, a slack jaw, and a forgotten glass of orange juice tilted and dribbling in one hand. A month after that, you have to tell them their kids' names when the kids come to visit. And a month after that, it's their own damned names you have to refresh them on. Something happens to them, all right: Georgia Pines Time happens to them. Time here is like a weak acid that erases first memory and then the desire to go on living.

You have to fight it. That's what I tell Elaine Connelly, my special friend. It's gotten better for me since I started writing about what happened to me in 1932, the year John Coffey came on the Green Mile. Some of the memories are awful, but I can feel them sharpening my mind and my awareness the way a knife sharpens a pencil, and that makes the pain worthwhile. Writing and memory alone aren't enough, though. I also have a body, wasted and grotesque, though it may now be, and I exercise it as much as I can. It was hard at first—old fogies like me aren't much shakes when it comes to exercise just for the sake of exercise—but it's easier now that there's a purpose to my walks.

I go out before breakfast—as soon as it's light, most days—for my first stroll. It was raining this morning, and the damp makes my joints ache, but I hooked a poncho from the rack by the kitchen door and went out, anyway. When a man has a chore, he has to do it, and if it hurts, too bad. Besides, there are compensations. The chief one is keeping that sense of Real Time, as opposed to Georgia Pines Time. And I like the rain, aches or no aches. Especially in the early morning, when the day is young and seems full of possibilities, even to a washed-up old boy like me.

I went through the kitchen, stopping to beg two slices of toast from one of the sleepy-eyed cooks, and then went out. I crossed the croquet course, then the weedy little putting green. Beyond that is a small stand of woods, with a narrow path winding through it and a couple of sheds, no longer used and mouldering away quietly, along the way. I walked down this path slowly, listening to the sleek and secret patter of the rain in the pines, chewing away at a piece of toast with my few remaining teeth. My legs ached, but it was a low ache, manageable. Mostly I felt pretty well. I drew the moist gray air as deep as I could, taking it in like food.

And when I got to the second of those old sheds, I went in for awhile, and I took care of my business there.

When I walked back up the path twenty minutes later, I could feel a worm of hunger stirring in my belly, and thought I could eat something a little more substantial than toast. A dish of oatmeal, perhaps even a scrambled egg with a sausage on the side. I love sausage, always have, but if I eat more than one these days, I'm apt to get the squitters. One would be safe enough, though. Then, with my belly full and with the damp air still perking up my brain (or so I hoped), I would go up to the solarium and write about the execution of Eduard Delacroix. I would do it as fast as I could, so as not to lose my courage.

It was Mr. Jingles I was thinking about as I crossed the croquet course to the kitchen door—how Percy Wetmore had stamped on him and broken his back, and how Delacroix had screamed when he realized what his enemy had done—and I didn't see Brad Dolan standing there, half-hidden by the Dumpster, until he reached out and grabbed my wrist.

"Out for a little stroll, Paulie?" he asked.

I jerked back from him, yanking my wrist out of his hand. Some of it was just being startled—anyone will jerk when they're startled—but that wasn't all of it. I'd been thinking about Percy Wetmore, remember, and it's Percy that Brad always reminds me of. Some of it's how Brad always goes around with a paperback stuffed into his pocket (with Percy it was always a men's adventure magazine; with Brad it's books of jokes that are only funny if you're stupid and mean-hearted), some of it's how he acts like he's King Shit of Turd Mountain, but mostly it's that he's sneaky, and he likes to hurt.

He'd just gotten to work, I saw, hadn't even changed into his orderly's whites yet. He was wearing jeans and a cheesy-looking Western-style shirt. In one hand was the remains of a Danish he'd hooked out of the kitchen. He'd been standing under the eave, eating it where he wouldn't get wet. And where he could watch for me, I'm pretty sure of that now. I'm pretty sure of something else, as well: I'll have to watch out for Mr. Brad Dolan. He doesn't like me much. I don't know why, but I never knew why Percy Wetmore didn't like Delacroix, either. And *dislike* is

STEPHEN KING

really too weak a word. Percy hated Del's guts from the very first moment the little Frenchman came onto the Green Mile.

"What's with this poncho you got on, Paulie?" he asked, flicking the collar. "This isn't yours."

"I got it in the hall outside the kitchen," I said. I hate it when he calls me Paulie, and I think he knows it, but I was damned if I'd give him the satisfaction of seeing it. "There's a whole row of them. I'm not hurting it any, would you say? Rain's what it's made for, after all."

"But it wasn't made for *you*, Paulie," he said, giving it another little flick. "That's the thing. Those slickers're for the employees, not the residents."

"I still don't see what harm it does."

He gave me a thin little smile. "It's not about *harm*, it's about the *rules*. What would life be without rules? Paulie, Paulie, Paulie." He shook his head, as if just looking at me made him feel sorry to be alive. "You probably think an old fart like you doesn't have to mind about the rules anymore, but that's just not true. *Paulie*."

Smiling at me. Disliking me. Maybe even hating me. And why? I don't know. Sometimes there *is* no why. That's the scary part.

"Well, I'm sorry if I broke the rules," I said. It came out sounding whiney, a little shrill, and I hated myself for sounding that way, but I'm old, and old people whine easily. Old people *scare* easily.

Brad nodded. "Apology accepted. Now go hang that back up. You got no business out walking in the rain, anyway. Specially not in those woods. What if you were to slip and fall and break your damned hip? Huh? Who do you think'd have to hoss your elderly freight back up the hill?"

"I don't know," I said. I just wanted to get away from him. The more I listened to him, the more he sounded like Percy. William Wharton, the crazyman who came to the Green Mile in the fall of '32, once grabbed Percy and scared him so bad that Percy squirted in his pants. *You talk about this to anyone*, Percy told the rest of us afterward, *and you'll all be on the breadlines in a week.* Now, these many years later, I could almost hear Brad Dolan saying those same words, in that same tone of voice. It's as if, by writing about those old times, I have unlocked some unspeakable

202

door that connects the past to the present—Percy Wetmore to Brad Dolan, Janice Edgecombe to Elaine Connelly, Cold Mountain Penitentiary to the Georgia Pines old folks' home. And if that thought doesn't keep me awake tonight, I guess nothing will.

I made as if to go in through the kitchen door and Brad grabbed me by the wrist again. I don't know about the first one, but this time he was doing it on purpose, squeezing to hurt. His eyes shifting back and forth, making sure no one was around in the early-morning wet, no one to see he was abusing one of the old folks he was supposed to be taking care of.

"What do you do down that path?" he asked. "I know you don't go down there and jerk off, those days are long behind you, so what do you do?"

"Nothing," I said, telling myself to be calm, not to show him how bad he was hurting me and to be calm, to remember he'd only mentioned the path, he didn't know about the shed. "I just walk. To clear my mind."

"Too late for that, Paulie, your mind's never gonna be clear again." He squeezed my thin old man's wrist again, grinding the brittle bones, eyes continually shifting from side to side, wanting to make sure he was safe. Brad wasn't afraid of breaking the rules; he was only afraid of being *caught* breaking them. And in that, too, he was like Percy Wetmore, who would never let you forget he was the governor's nephew. "Old as you are, it's a miracle you can remember *who* you are. You're *too* goddam old. Even for a museum like this. You give me the fucking creeps, Paulie."

"Let go of me," I said, trying to keep the whine out of my voice. It wasn't just pride, either. I thought if he heard it, it might inflame him, the way the smell of sweat can sometimes inflame a bad-tempered dog—one which would otherwise only growl—to bite. That made me think of a reporter who'd covered John Coffey's trial. The reporter was a terrible man named Hammersmith, and the most terrible thing about him was that he hadn't known he was terrible.

Instead of letting go, Dolan squeezed my wrist again. I groaned. I didn't want to, but I couldn't help it. It hurt all the way down to my ankles.

"What do you do down there, Paulie? Tell me."

"Nothing!" I said. I wasn't crying, not yet, but I was afraid I'd start soon if he kept bearing down like that. "Nothing, I just walk, I like to walk, let go of me!"

He did, but only long enough so he could grab my other hand. That one was rolled closed. "Open up," he said. "Let Poppa see."

I did, and he grunted with disgust. It was nothing but the remains of my second piece of toast. I'd clenched it in my right hand when he started squeezing my left wrist, and there was butter—well, oleo, they don't have real butter here, of course—on my fingers.

"Go on inside and wash your damned hands," he said, stepping back and taking another bite of his Danish. "Jesus Christ."

I went up the steps. My legs were shaking, my heart pounding like an engine with leaky valves and shaky old pistons. As I grasped the knob that would let me into the kitchen—and safety—Dolan said: "If you tell anyone I squeezed your po' old wrist, Paulie, I'll tell them you're having delusions. Onset of senile dementia, likely. And you know they'll believe me. If there are bruises, they'll think you made them yourself."

Yes. Those things were true. And once again, it could have been Percy Wetmore saying them, a Percy that had somehow stayed young and mean while I'd grown old and brittle.

"I'm not going to say anything to anyone," I muttered. "Got nothing to say."

"That's right, you old sweetie." His voice light and mocking, the voice of a lugoon (to use Percy's word) who thought he was going to be young forever. "And I'm going to find out what you're up to. I'm going to make it my business. You hear?"

I heard, all right, but wouldn't give him the satisfaction of saying so. I went in, passed through the kitchen (I could now smell eggs and sausage cooking, but no longer wanted any), and hung the poncho back up on its hook. Then I went upstairs to my room—resting at every step, giving my heart time to slow—and gathered my writing materials together.

I went down to the solarium and was just sitting at the little table by the windows when my friend Elaine poked her head in. She looked tired, and, I thought, unwell. She'd combed her hair out but was still in her robe. We old sweeties don't stand much on ceremony; for the most part, we can't afford to.

"I won't disturb you," she said, "I see you're getting set to write—"

"Don't be silly," I said. "I've got more time than Carter's got liver pills. Come on in."

She did, but stood by the door. "It's just that I couldn't sleep— again—and happened to be looking out my window a little earlier . . . and . . ."

"And you saw Mr. Dolan and me having our pleasant little chat," I said. I hoped seeing was all she'd done; that her window had been closed and she hadn't heard me whining to be let go.

"It didn't look pleasant and it didn't look friendly," she said. "Paul, that Mr. Dolan's been asking around about you. He asked *me* about you—last week, this was. I didn't think much about it then, just that he's got himself a nasty long nose for other people's business, but now I wonder."

"Asking about me?" I hoped I didn't sound as uneasy as I felt. "Asking what?"

"Where you go walking, for one thing. And *why* you go walking."

I tried to laugh. "There's a man who doesn't believe in exercise, that much is clear."

"He thinks you've got a secret." She paused. "So do I."

I opened my mouth—to say what, I don't know—but Elaine raised one of her gnarled but oddly beautiful hands before I could get a single word out. "If you do, I don't want to know what it is, Paul. Your business is your business. I was raised to think that way, but not everyone was. Be careful. That's all I want to tell you. And now I'll let you alone to do your work."

She turned to go, but before she could get out the door, I called her name. She turned back, eyes questioning.

"When I finish what I'm writing—" I began, then shook my head a little. That was wrong. "*If* I finish what I'm writing, would you read it?"

She seemed to consider, then gave me the sort of smile a man could easily fall in love with, even a man as old as me. "That would be my honor."

"You'd better wait until you read it before you talk about honor," I said, and it was Delacroix's death I was thinking of.

"I'll read it, though," she said. "Every word. I promise. But you have to finish writing it, first."

She left me to it, but it was a long time before I wrote anything. I sat staring out the windows for almost an hour, tapping my pen against the side of the table, watching the gray day brighten a little at a time, thinking about Brad Dolan, who calls me Paulie and never tires of jokes about chinks and slopes and spicks and micks, thinking about what Elaine Connelly had said. *He thinks you've got a secret. So do I.*

And maybe I do. Yes, maybe I do. And of course Brad Dolan wants it. Not because he thinks it's important (and it's not, I guess, except to me), but because he doesn't think very old men like myself should have secrets. No taking the ponchos off the hook outside the kitchen; no secrets, either. No getting the idea that the likes of us are still human. And why shouldn't we be allowed such an idea? He doesn't know. And in that, too, he is like Percy.

So my thoughts, like a river that takes an oxbow turn, finally led back to where they had been when Brad Dolan reached out from beneath the kitchen eave and grabbed my wrist: to Percy, mean-spirited Percy Wetmore, and how he had taken his revenge on the man who had laughed at him. Delacroix had been throwing the colored spool he had—the one Mr. Jingles would fetch—and it bounced out of the cell and into the corridor. That was all it took; Percy saw his chance.

2

"*No, you fool!*" Brutal yelled, but Percy paid no attention. Just as Mr. Jingles reached the spool—too intent on it to realize his old enemy was at hand—Percy brought the sole of one hard black workshoe down on him. There was an audible snap as Mr. Jingles's back broke, and blood gushed from his mouth. His tiny black eyes bulged in their sockets, and in them I read an expression of surprised agony that was all too human.

Delacroix screamed with horror and grief. He threw himself at the door of his cell and thrust his arms out through the bars, reaching as far as he could, crying the mouse's name over and over.

Percy turned toward him, smiling. Toward me and Brutal, as well. "There," he said. "I knew I'd get him, sooner or later. Just a matter of time, really." He turned and walked back up the Green Mile, leaving Mr. Jingles lying on the linoleum, his spreading blood red over green.

Dean got up from the duty desk, hitting the side of it with his knee and knocking the cribbage board to the floor. The pegs spilled out of their holes and rolled in all directions. Neither Dean nor Harry, who had been just about to go out, paid the slightest attention to the over-turn of the game. "What'd you do this time?" Dean shouted at Percy. "What the hell'd you do this time, you stoopnagel?"

Percy didn't answer. He strode past the desk without saying a word, patting his hair with his fingers. He went through my office and into the storage shed. William Wharton answered for him. "Boss Dean? I think what he did was teach a certain french-fry it ain't smart to laugh at him," he said, and then began to laugh himself. It was a good laugh, a *country* laugh, cheery and deep. There were people I met during that period of my life (very scary people, for the most part) who only sounded normal when they laughed. Wild Bill Wharton was one of those.

I looked down at the mouse again, stunned. It was still breathing, but there were little minute beads of blood caught in the filaments of its whiskers, and a dull glaze was creeping over its previously brilliant oil-drop eyes. Brutal picked up the colored spool, looked at it, then looked at me. He looked as dumbfounded as I felt. Behind us, Delacroix went on screaming out his grief and horror. It wasn't just the mouse, of course; Percy had smashed a hole in Delacroix's defenses and all his terror was pouring out. But Mr. Jingles was the focusing point for those pent-up feelings, and it was terrible to listen to him.

"Oh no," he cried over and over again, amid the screams and the garbled pleas and prayers in Cajun French. "Oh no, oh no, poor Mr. Jingles, poor old Mr. Jingles, oh no."

"Give im to me."

I looked up, puzzled by that deep voice, at first not sure who it belonged to. I saw John Coffey. Like Delacroix, he had put his arms through the bars of his cell door, but unlike Del, he wasn't waving them around. He simply held them out as far as he could, the hands at the ends of them open. It was a purposeful pose, an almost urgent pose. And his voice had the same quality, which was why, I suppose, I didn't recognize it as belonging to Coffey at first. He seemed a different man from the lost, weepy soul that had occupied this cell for the last few weeks.

"Give im to me, Mr. Edgecombe! While there's still time!"

Then I remembered what he'd done for me, and understood. I supposed it couldn't hurt, but I didn't think it would do much good, either. When I picked the mouse up, I winced at the feel—there were so many splintered bones poking at various spots on Mr. Jingles's hide that it was like picking up a fur-covered pincushion. This was no urinary infection. Still—

"What are you doing?" Brutal asked as I put Mr. Jingles in Coffey's huge right hand. "What the hell?"

Coffey pulled the mouse back through the bars. He lay limp on Coffey's palm, tail hanging over the arc between Coffey's thumb and first finger, the tip twitching weakly in midair. Then Coffey covered his right hand with his left, creating a kind of cup in which the mouse lay. We could no longer see Mr. Jingles himself, only the tail, hanging down and twitching at the tip like a dying pendulum. Coffey lifted his hands toward his face, spreading the fingers of the right as he did so, creating spaces like those between prison bars. The tail of the mouse now hung from the side of his hands that was facing us.

Brutal stepped next to me, still holding the colored spool between his fingers. "What's he think he's doing?"

"Shh," I said.

Delacroix had stopped screaming. "Please, John," he whispered. "Oh Johnny, help him, please help him, oh *s'il vous plaît*."

Dean and Harry joined us, Harry with our old deck of Airplane cards still in one hand. "What's going on?" Dean asked, but I only shook my head. I was feeling hypnotized again, damned if I wasn't.

Coffey put his mouth between two of his fingers and inhaled sharply. For a moment everything hung suspended. Then he raised his head away from his hands and I saw the face of a man who looked desperately sick, or in terrible pain. His eyes were sharp and blazing; his upper teeth bit at his full lower lip; his dark face had faded to an unpleasant color that looked like ash stirred into mud. He made a choked sound way back in his throat.

"Dear Jesus Lord and Savior," Brutal whispered. His eyes appeared to be in danger of dropping right out of his face.

"What?" Harry almost barked. *"What?"*

"The tail! Don't you see it? The *tail!*"

Mr. Jingles's tail was no longer a dying pendulum; it was snapping briskly from side to side, like the tail of a cat in a bird-catching mood. And then, from inside Coffey's cupped hands, came a perfectly familiar squeak.

Coffey made that choking, gagging sound again, then turned his head to one side like a man that has coughed up a wad of phlegm and means to spit it out. Instead, he exhaled a cloud of black insects—I *think* they were insects, and the others said the same, but to this day I am not sure—from his mouth and nose. They boiled around him in a dark cloud that temporarily obscured his features.

"Christ, what're those?" Dean asked in a shrill, scared voice.

"It's all right," I heard myself say. "Don't panic, it's all right, in a few seconds they'll be gone."

As when Coffey had cured my urinary infection for me, the "bugs" turned white and then disappeared.

"Holy shit," Harry whispered.

"Paul?" Brutal asked in an unsteady voice. "Paul?"

Coffey looked okay again—like a fellow who has successfully coughed up a wad of meat that has been choking him. He bent down, put his cupped hands on the floor, peeked through his fingers, then opened them. Mr. Jingles, absolutely all right—not a single twist to his backbone, not a single lump poking at his hide—ran out. He paused for a moment at the door of Coffey's cell, then ran across the Green Mile to Delacroix's cell. As he went, I noticed there were still beads of blood in his whiskers.

Delacroix gathered him up, laughing and crying at the same time, covering the mouse with shameless, smacking kisses. Dean and Harry and Brutal watched with silent wonder. Then Brutal stepped forward and handed the colored spool through the bars. Delacroix didn't see it at first; he was too taken up with Mr. Jingles. He was like a father whose son has been saved from drowning. Brutal tapped him on the shoulder with the spool. Delacroix looked, saw it, took it, and went back to Mr. Jingles again, stroking his fur and devouring him with his eyes, needing to constantly refresh his perception that yes, the mouse was all right, the mouse was whole and fine and all right.

"Toss it," Brutal said. "I want to see how he runs."

"He all right, Boss Howell, he all right, praise God—"

"Toss it," Brutal repeated. "Mind me, Del."

Delacroix bent, clearly reluctant, clearly not wanting to let Mr. Jingles out of his hands again, at least not yet. Then, very gently, he tossed the spool. It rolled across the cell, past the Corona cigar box, and to the wall. Mr. Jingles was after it, but not quite with the speed he had shown previously. He appeared to be limping just a bit on his left rear leg, and that was what struck me the hardest—it was, I suppose, what made it real. That little limp.

He got to the spool, though, got to it just fine and nosed it back to Delacroix with all his old enthusiasm. I turned to John Coffey, who was standing at his cell door and smiling. It was a tired smile, and not what I'd call really happy, but the sharp urgency I'd seen in his face as he begged for the mouse to be given to him was gone, and so was the look of pain and fear, as if he were choking. It was our John Coffey again, with his not-quite-there face and strange, far-looking eyes.

"You helped it," I said. "Didn't you, big boy?"

"That's right," Coffey said. The smile widened a little, and for a moment or two it *was* happy. "I helped it. I helped Del's mouse. I helped . . ." He trailed off, unable to remember the name.

"Mr. Jingles," Dean said. He was looking at John with careful, wondering eyes, as if he expected Coffey to burst into flames or maybe begin to float in his cell.

"That's right," Coffey said. "Mr. Jingles. He's a circus mouse. Goan live in ivy-glass."

"You bet your bobcat," Harry said, joining us in looking at John Coffey. Behind us, Delacroix lay down on his bunk with Mr. Jingles on his chest. Del was crooning to him, singing him some French song that sounded like a lullaby.

Coffey looked up the Green Mile toward the duty desk and the door which led into my office and the storage room beyond. "Boss Percy's bad," he said. "Boss Percy's mean. He stepped on Del's mouse. He stepped on Mr. Jingles."

And then, before we could say anything else to him—if we could have thought of anything to say—John Coffey went back to his bunk, lay down, and rolled on his side to face the wall.

3

PERCY WAS STANDING with his back to us when Brutal and I came into the storage room about twenty minutes later. He had found a can of paste furniture polish on a shelf above the hamper where we put our dirty uniforms (and, sometimes, our civilian clothes; the prison laundry didn't care what it washed), and was polishing the oak arms and legs of the electric chair. This probably sounds bizarre to you, perhaps even macabre, but to Brutal and me, it seemed the most normal thing Percy had done all night. Old Sparky would be meeting his public tomorrow, and Percy would at least appear to be in charge.

"Percy," I said quietly.

He turned, the little tune he'd been humming dying in his throat, and looked at us. I didn't see the fear I'd expected, at least not at first. I realized that Percy looked older, somehow. And, I thought, John Coffey was right. He looked mean. Meanness is like an addicting drug— no one on earth is more qualified to say that than me—and I thought that, after a certain amount of experimentation, Percy had gotten hooked on it. He liked what he had done to Delacroix's mouse. What he liked even more was Delacroix's dismayed screams.

"Don't start in on me," he said in a tone of voice that was almost pleasant. "I mean, hey, it was just a mouse. It never belonged here in the first place, as you boys well know."

"The mouse is fine," I said. My heart was thumping hard in my chest but I made my voice come out mild, almost disinterested. "Just fine.

Running and squeaking and chasing its spool again. You're no better at mouse-killing than you are at most of the other things you do around here."

He was looking at me, amazed and disbelieving. "You expect me to believe that? The goddam thing *crunched*! I heard it! So you can just—"

"Shut up."

He stared at me, his eyes wide. "*What?* What did you say to me?"

I took a step closer to him. I could feel a vein throbbing in the middle of my forehead. I couldn't remember the last time I'd felt so angry. "Aren't you glad Mr. Jingles is okay? After all the talks we've had about how our job is to keep the prisoners calm, especially when it gets near the end for them, I thought you'd be glad. Relieved. With Del having to take the walk tomorrow, and all."

Percy looked from me to Brutal, his studied calmness dissolving into uncertainty. "What the hell game do you boys think you're playing?" he asked.

"None of this is a game, my friend," Brutal said. "You thinking it is . . . well, that's just one of the reasons you can't be trusted. You want to know the absolute truth? I think you're a pretty sad case."

"You want to watch it," Percy said. Now there was a rawness in his voice. Fear creeping back in, after all—fear of what we might want with him, fear of what we might be up to. I was glad to hear it. It would make him easier to deal with. "I know people. Important people."

"So you say, but you're *such* a dreamer," Brutal said. He sounded as if he was on the verge of laughter.

Percy dropped the polishing rag onto the seat of the chair with the clamps attached to the arms and legs. "I killed that mouse," he said in a voice that was not quite steady.

"Go on and check for yourself," I said. "It's a free country."

"I will," he said. "I will."

He stalked past us, mouth set, small hands (Wharton was right, they *were* pretty) fiddling with his comb. He went up the steps and ducked through into my office. Brutal and I stood by Old Sparky, waiting for him to come back and not talking. I don't know about Brutal, but I couldn't think of a thing to say. I didn't even know how to think about what we had just seen.

Three minutes passed. Brutal picked up Percy's rag and began to polish the thick back-slats of the electric chair. He had time to finish one and start another before Percy came back. He stumbled and almost fell coming down the steps from the office to the storage-room floor, and when he crossed to us he came at an uneven strut. His face was shocked and unbelieving.

"You switched them," he said in a shrill, accusatory voice. "You switched mice somehow, you bastards. You're playing with me, and you're going to be goddam sorry if you don't stop! I'll see you on the goddam breadlines if you don't stop! Who do you think you are?"

He quit, panting for breath, his hands clenched.

"I'll tell you who we are," I said. "We're the people you work with, Percy . . . but not for very much longer." I reached out and clamped my hands on his shoulders. Not real hard; but it was a clamp, all right. Yes it was.

Percy reached up to break it. "Take your—"

Brutal grabbed his right hand—the whole thing, small and soft and white, disappeared into Brutal's tanned fist. "Shut up your cakehole, sonny. If you know what's good for you, you'll take this one last opportunity to dig the wax out of your ears."

I turned him around, lifted him onto the platform, then backed him up until the backs of his knees struck the seat of the electric chair and he had to sit down. His calm was gone; the meanness and the arrogance, too. Those things were real enough, but you have to remember that Percy was very young. At his age they were still only a thin veneer, like an ugly shade of enamel paint. You could still chip through. And I judged that Percy was now ready to listen.

"I want your word," I said.

"My word about what?" His mouth was still trying to sneer, but his eyes were terrified. The power in the switch room was locked off, but Old Sparky's wooden seat had its own power, and right then I judged that Percy was feeling it.

"Your word that if we put you out front for it tomorrow night, you'll really go on to Briar Ridge and leave us alone," Brutal said, speaking with a vehemence I had never heard from him before. "That you'll put in for a transfer the very next day."

"And if I won't? If I should just call up certain people and tell them you're harassing me and threatening me? *Bullying* me?"

"We might get the bum's rush if your connections are as good as you seem to think they are," I said, "but we'd make sure you left your fair share of blood on the floor, too, Percy."

"About that mouse? Huh! You think anyone is going to care that I stepped on a condemned murderer's pet mouse? Outside of this looney-bin, that is?"

"No. But three men saw you just standing there with your thumb up your ass while Wild Bill Wharton was trying to strangle Dean Stanton with his wrist-chains. About that people *will* care, Percy, I promise you. About that even your offsides uncle the governor is going to care."

Percy's cheeks and brow flushed a patchy red. "You think they'd believe you?" he asked, but his voice had lost a lot of its angry force. Clearly *he* thought someone might believe us. And Percy didn't like being in trouble. Breaking the rules was okay. Getting caught breaking them was not.

"Well, I've got some photos of Dean's neck before the bruising went down," Brutal said—I had no idea if this was true or not, but it certainly sounded good. "You know what those pix say? That Wharton got a pretty good shot at it before anyone pulled him off, although you were right there, and on Wharton's blind side. You'd have some hard questions to answer, wouldn't you? And a thing like that could follow a man for quite a spell. Chances are it'd still be there long after his relatives were out of the state capital and back home drinking mint juleps on the front porch. A man's work-record can be a mighty interesting thing, and a lot of people get a chance to look at it over the course of a lifetime."

Percy's eyes flicked back and forth mistrustfully between us. His left hand went to his hair and smoothed it. He said nothing, but I thought we almost had him.

"Come on, let's quit this," I said. "You don't want to be here any more than we want you here, isn't that so?"

"I hate it here!" he burst out. "I hate the way you treat me, the way you never gave me a chance!"

That last was far from true, but I judged this wasn't the time to argue the matter.

"But I don't like to be pushed around, either. My Daddy taught me that once you start down that road you most likely end up letting people push you around your whole life." His eyes, not as pretty as his hands but almost, flashed. "I especially don't like being pushed around by big apes like this guy." He glanced at my old friend and grunted. "Brutal—you got the right nickname, at least."

"You have to understand something, Percy," I said. "The way we look at it, you've been pushing *us* around. We keep telling you the way we do things around here and you keep doing things your own way, then hiding behind your political connections when things turn out wrong. Stepping on Delacroix's mouse—" Brutal caught my eye and I backtracked in a hurry. "*Trying* to step on Delacroix's mouse is just a case in point. You push and push and push; we're finally pushing back, that's all. But listen, if you do right, you'll come out of this looking good—like a young man on his way up—and smelling like a rose. Nobody'll ever know about this little talk we're having. So what do you say? Act like a grownup. Promise you'll leave after Del."

He thought it over. And after a moment or two, a look came into his eyes, the sort of look a fellow gets when he's just had a good idea. I didn't like it much, because any idea which seemed good to Percy wouldn't seem good to us.

"If nothing else," Brutal said, "just think how nice it'd be to get away from that sack of pus Wharton."

Percy nodded, and I let him get out of the chair. He straightened his uniform shirt, tucked it in at the back, gave his hair a pass-through with his comb. Then he looked at us. "Okay, I agree. I'm out front for Del tomorrow night; I'll put in for Briar Ridge the very next day. We call it quits right there. Good enough?"

"Good enough," I said. That look was still in his eyes, but right then I was too relieved to care.

He stuck out his hand. "Shake on it?"

I did. So did Brutal.

More fools us.

4

THE NEXT DAY was the thickest yet, and the last of our strange October heat. Thunder was rumbling in the west when I came to work, and the dark clouds were beginning to stack up there. They moved closer as the night came down, and we could see blue-white forks of lightning jabbing out of them. There was a tornado in Trapingus County around ten that night—it killed four people and tore the roof off the livery stable in Tefton—and vicious thunderstorms and gale-force winds at Cold Mountain. Later it seemed to me as if the very heavens had protested the bad death of Eduard Delacroix.

Everything went just fine to begin with. Del had spent a quiet day in his cell, sometimes playing with Mr. Jingles but mostly just lying on his bunk and petting him. Wharton tried to get trouble started a couple of times—once he hollered down to Del about the mouseburgers they were going to have after old Lucky Pierre was dancing the two-step in hell—but the little Cajun didn't respond and Wharton, apparently deciding that was his best shot, gave it up.

At quarter past ten, Brother Schuster showed up and delighted us all by saying he would recite the Lord's Prayer with Del in Cajun French. It seemed like a good omen. In that we were wrong, of course.

The witnesses began to arrive around eleven, most talking in low tones about the impending weather, and speculating about the possibility of a power outage postponing the electrocution. None of them seemed to know that Old Sparky ran off a generator, and unless that took a direct lightning-hit, the show would go on. Harry was in the switch room that night, so he and Bill Dodge and Percy Wetmore acted as ushers, seeing folks into their seats and asking each one if he'd like a cold drink of water. There were two women present: the sister of the girl Del had raped and murdered, and the mother of one of the fire victims. The latter lady was large and pale and determined. She told Harry Terwilliger that she hoped the man she'd come to see was good and scared, that he knew the fires in the furnace were stoked for him, and that Satan's imps were waiting for him. Then she burst into tears and buried her face in a lace hanky that was almost the size of a pillowslip.

Thunder, hardly muffled at all by the tin roof, banged harsh and loud. People glanced up uneasily. Men who looked uncomfortable wearing ties this late at night wiped at their florid cheeks. It was hotter than blue blazes in the storage shed. And, of course, they kept turning their eyes to Old Sparky. They might have made jokes about this chore earlier in the week, but the jokes were gone by eleven-thirty or so that night. I started all this by telling you that the humor went out of the situation in a hurry for the people who had to sit down in that oak chair, but the condemned prisoners weren't the only ones who lost the smiles off their faces when the time actually came. It just seemed so *bald,* somehow, squatting up there on its platform, with the clamps on the legs sticking off to either side, looking like the things a person with polio would have to wear. There wasn't much talk, and when the thunder boomed again, as sharp and personal as a splintering tree, the sister of Delacroix's victim gave a little scream. The last person to take his seat in the witnesses' section was Curtis Anderson, Warden Moores's stand-in.

At eleven-thirty, I approached Delacroix's cell with Brutal and Dean walking slightly behind me. Del was sitting on his bunk, with Mr. Jingles in his lap. The mouse's head was stretched forward toward the condemned man, his little oilspot eyes rapt on Del's face. Del was stroking the top of Mr. Jingles's head between his ears. Large silent tears were rolling down Del's face, and it was these the mouse seemed to be peering at. Del looked up at the sound of our footsteps. He was very pale. From behind me, I sensed rather than saw John Coffey standing at his cell door, watching.

Del winced at the sound of my keys clashing against metal, but held steady, continuing to stroke Mr. Jingles's head, as I turned the locks and ran the door open.

"Hi dere, Boss Edgecombe," he said. "Hi dere, boys. Say hi, Mr. Jingles." But Mr. Jingles only continued to look raptly up at the balding little man's face, as if wondering at the source of his tears. The colored spool had been neatly laid aside in the Corona box—laid aside for the last time, I thought, and felt a pang.

"Eduard Delacroix, as an officer of the court . . ."

"Boss Edgecombe?"

I thought about just running on with the set speech, then thought again. "What is it, Del?"

He held the mouse out to me. "Here. Don't let nothing happen to Mr. Jingles."

"Del, I don't think he'll come to me. He's not—"

"*Mais oui,* he say he will. He say he know all about you, Boss Edgecombe, and you gonna take him down to dat place in Florida where the mousies do their tricks. He say he trust you." He held his hand out farther, and I'll be damned if the mouse didn't step off his palm and onto my shoulder. It was so light I couldn't even feel it through my uniform coat, but I sensed it, like a small heat. "And boss? Don't let that bad 'un near him again. Don't let that bad 'un hurt my mouse."

"No, Del. I won't." The question was, what was I supposed to do with him right then? I couldn't very well march Delacroix past the witnesses with a mouse perched on my shoulder.

"I'll take him, boss," a voice rumbled from behind me. It was John Coffey's voice, and it was eerie the way it came right then, as though he had read my mind. "Just for now. If Del don't mind."

Del nodded, relieved. "Yeah, you take im, John, 'til dis foolishment done—*bien*! And den after . . ." His gaze shifted back to Brutal and me. "You gonna take him down to Florida. To dat Mouseville Place."

"Yeah, most likely Paul and I will do it together," Brutal said, watching with a troubled and unquiet eye as Mr. Jingles stepped off my shoulder and into Coffey's huge outstretched palm. Mr. Jingles did this with no protest or attempt to run; indeed, he scampered as readily up

John Coffey's arm as he had stepped onto my shoulder. "We'll take some of our vacation time. Won't we, Paul?"

I nodded. Del nodded, too, eyes bright, just a trace of a smile on his lips. "People pay a dime apiece to see him. Two cents for the kiddies. Ain't dat right, Boss Howell?"

"That's right, Del."

"You a good man, Boss Howell," Del said. "You, too, Boss Edgecombe. You yell at me sometimes, *oui,* but not 'less you have to. You all good men except for dat Percy. I wish I coulda met you someplace else. *Mauvais temps, mauvaise chance.*"

"I got something to say to you, Del," I told him. "They're just the words I have to say to everyone before we walk. No big deal, but it's part of my job. Okay?"

"Oui, monsieur," he said, and looked at Mr. Jingles, perched on John Coffey's broad shoulder, for the last time. *"Au revoir, mon ami,"* he said, beginning to cry harder. *"Je t'aime, mon petit."* He blew the mouse a kiss. It should have been funny, that blown kiss, or maybe just grotesque, but it wasn't. I met Dean's eye for a moment, then had to look away. Dean stared down the corridor toward the restraint room and smiled strangely. I believe he was on the verge of tears. As for me, I said what I had to say, beginning with the part about how I was an officer of the court, and when I was done, Delacroix stepped out of his cell for the last time.

"Hold on a second longer, hoss," Brutal said, and checked the crown of Del's head, where the cap would go. He nodded at me, then clapped Del on the shoulder. "Right with Eversharp. We're on our way."

So Eduard Delacroix took his last walk on the Green Mile with little streams of mingled sweat and tears running down his cheeks and big thunder rolling in the sky overhead. Brutal walked on the condemned man's left, I was on his right, Dean was to the rear.

Schuster was in my office, with guards Ringgold and Battle standing in the corners and keeping watch. Schuster looked up at Del, smiled, and then addressed him in French. It sounded stilted to me, but it worked wonders. Del smiled back, then went to Schuster, put his arms around him, hugged him. Ringgold and Battle tensed, but I raised my hands to them and shook my head.

Schuster listened to Del's flood of tear-choked French, nodded as if he understood perfectly, and patted him on the back. He looked at me over the little man's shoulder and said, "I hardly understand a quarter of what he's saying."

"Don't think it matters," Brutal rumbled.

"Neither do I, son," Schuster said with a grin. He was the best of them, and now I realize I have no idea what became of him. I hope he kept his faith, whatever else befell.

He urged Delacroix onto his knees, then folded his hands. Delacroix did the same.

"Not' Père, qui êtes aux cieux," Schuster began, and Delacroix joined him. They spoke the Lord's Prayer together in that liquid-sounding Cajun French, all the way to *"mais déliverez-nous du mal, ainsi soit-il."* By then, Del's tears had mostly stopped and he looked calm. Some Bible verses (in English) followed, not neglecting the old standby about the still waters. When that was done, Schuster started to get up, but Del held onto the sleeve of his shirt and said something in French. Schuster listened carefully, frowning. He responded. Del said something else, then just looked at him hopefully.

Schuster turned to me and said: "He's got something else, Mr. Edgecombe. A prayer I can't help him with, because of my faith. Is it all right?"

I looked at the clock on the wall and saw it was seventeen minutes to midnight. "Yes," I said, "but it'll have to be quick. We've got a schedule to keep here, you know."

"Yes. I do." He turned to Delacroix and gave him a nod.

Del closed his eyes as if to pray, but for a moment said nothing. A frown creased his forehead and I had a sense of him reaching far back in his mind, as a man may search a small attic room for an object which hasn't been used (or needed) for a long, long time. I glanced at the clock again and almost said something—would have, if Brutal hadn't twitched my sleeve and shaken his head.

Then Del began, speaking softly but quickly in that Cajun which was as round and soft and sensual as a young woman's breast: *"Marie! Je vous salue, Marie, oui, pleine de grâce; le Seigneur est avec vous; vous êtes*

bénie entre toutes les femmes, et mon cher Jésus, le fruit de vos entrailles, est béni."
He was crying again, but I don't think he knew it. *"Sainte Marie, Ô ma*
mère, Mère de Dieu, priez pour moi, priez pour nous, pauv' pécheurs, maint'ant
et à l'heure . . . l'heure de nôtre mort. L'heure de mon mort." He took a deep,
shuddering breath. *"Ainsi soit-il."*

Lightning spilled through the room's one window in a brief blue-white
glare as Delacroix got to his feet. Everyone jumped and cringed except
for Del himself; he still seemed lost in the old prayer. He reached out
with one hand, not looking to see where it went. Brutal took it and
squeezed it briefly. Delacroix looked at him and smiled a little. *"Nous*
voyons—" he began, then stopped. With a conscious effort, he switched
back to English. "We can go now, Boss Howell, Boss Edgecombe. I'm
right wit God."

"That's good," I said, wondering how right with God Del was going
to feel twenty minutes from now, when he stood on the other side of
the electricity. I hoped his last prayer had been heard, and that Mother
Mary was praying for him with all her heart and soul, because Eduard
Delacroix, rapist and murderer, right then needed all the praying he
could get his hands on. Outside, thunder bashed across the sky again.
"Come on, Del. Not far now."

"Fine, boss, dat fine. Because I ain't ascairt no more." So he said, but
I saw in his eyes that—Our Father or no Our Father, Hail Mary or no
Hail Mary—he lied. By the time they cross the rest of the green carpet
and duck through the little door, almost all of them are scared.

"Stop at the bottom, Del," I told him in a low voice as he went
through, but it was advice I needn't have given him. He stopped at the
foot of the stairs, all right, stopped cold, and what did it was the sight
of Percy Wetmore standing there on the platform, with the sponge-
bucket by one foot and the phone that went to the governor just visible
beyond his right hip.

"Non," Del said in a low, horrified voice. *"Non, non,* not him!"

"Walk on," Brutal said. "You just keep your eyes on me and Paul.
Forget he's there at all."

"But—"

People had turned to look at us, but by moving my body a bit, I could still grip Delacroix's left elbow without being seen. "Steady," I said in a voice only Del—and perhaps Brutal—could hear. "The only thing most of these people will remember about you is how you go out, so give them something good."

The loudest crack of thunder yet broke overhead at that moment, loud enough to make the storage room's tin roof vibrate. Percy jumped as if someone had goosed him, and Del gave a small, contemptuous snort of laughter. "It get much louder dan dat, he gonna piddle in his pants again," he said, and then squared his shoulders—not that he had much to square. "Come on. Let's get it over."

We walked to the platform. Delacroix ran a nervous eye over the witnesses—about twenty-five of them this time—as we went, but Brutal, Dean, and I kept our own eyes trained on the chair. All looked in order to me. I raised one thumb and a questioning eyebrow to Percy, who gave a little one-sided grimace, as if to say *What do you mean, is everything all right? Of course it is.*

I hoped he was right.

Brutal and I reached automatically for Delacroix's elbows as he stepped up onto the platform. It's only eight or so inches up from the floor, but you'd be surprised how many of them, even the toughest of tough babies, need help to make that last step up of their lives.

Del did okay, though. He stood in front of the chair for a moment (resolutely not looking at Percy), then actually spoke to it, as if introducing himself: *"C'est moi,"* he said. Percy reached for him, but Delacroix turned around on his own and sat down. I knelt on what was now his left side, and Brutal knelt on his right. I guarded my crotch and my throat in the manner I have already described, then swung the clamp in so that its open jaws encircled the skinny white flesh just above the Cajun's ankle. Thunder bellowed and I jumped. Sweat ran in my eye, stinging. Mouseville, I kept thinking for some reason. Mouseville, and how it cost a dime to get in. Two cents for the kiddies, who would look at Mr. Jingles through his ivy-glass windows.

The clamp was balky, wouldn't shut. I could hear Del breathing in great dry pulls of air, lungs that would be charred bags less than four minutes from now laboring to keep up with his fear-driven heart. The fact that he had killed half a dozen people seemed at that moment the least important thing about him. I'm not trying to say anything about right and wrong here, but only to tell how it was.

Dean knelt next to me and whispered, "What's wrong, Paul?"

"I can't—" I began, and then the clamp closed with an audible snapping sound. It must have also pinched a fold of Delacroix's skin in its jaws, because he flinched and made a little hissing noise. "Sorry," I said.

"It okay, boss," Del said. "It only gonna hurt for a minute."

Brutal's side had the clamp with the electrode in it, which always took a little longer, and so we stood up, all three of us, at almost exactly the same time. Dean reached for the wrist-clamp on Del's left, and Percy went to the one on his right. I was ready to move forward if Percy should need help, but he did better with his wrist-clamp than I'd done with my ankle-clamp. I could see Del trembling all over now, as if a low current were already passing through him. I could smell his sweat, too. It was sour and strong and reminded me of weak pickle juice.

Dean nodded to Percy. Percy turned back over his shoulder—I could see a place just under the angle of his jaw where he'd cut himself shaving that day—and said in a low, firm voice: "Roll on one!"

There was a hum, sort of like the sound an old refrigerator makes when it kicks on, and the hanging lights in the storage room brightened. There were a few low gasps and murmurs from the audience. Del jerked in the chair, his hands gripping the ends of the oak arms hard enough to turn the knuckles white. His eyes rolled rapidly from side to side in their sockets, and his dry breathing quickened even more. He was almost panting now.

"Steady," Brutal murmured. "Steady, Del, you're doing just fine. Hang on, you're doing just fine."

Hey you guys! I thought. *Come and see what Mr. Jingles can do!* And overhead, the thunder banged again.

Percy stepped grandly around to the front of the electric chair. This was his big moment, he was at center stage, all eyes were on him. All, that was, but for one set. Delacroix saw who it was and looked down at his lap instead. I would have bet you a dollar to a doughnut that Percy would flub his lines when he actually had to say them for an audience, but he reeled them off without a hitch, in an eerily calm voice.

"Eduard Delacroix, you have been condemned to die in the electric chair, sentence passed by a jury of your peers and imposed by a judge of good standing in this state, God save the people of this state. Do you have anything to say before sentence is carried out?"

Del tried to speak and at first nothing came out but a terrified whisper full of air and vowel-sounds. The shadow of a contemptuous smile touched the corners of Percy's lips, and I could have cheerfully shot him right there. Then Del licked his lips and tried again.

"I sorry for what I do," he said. "I give anything to turn back the clock, but no one can. So now—" Thunder exploded like an airburst mortar shell above us. Del jumped as much as the clamps would allow, eyes starting wildly out of his wet face. "So now I pay the price. God forgive me." He licked his lips again, and looked at Brutal. "Don't forget your promise about Mr. Jingles," he said in a lower voice that was meant just for us.

"We won't, don't worry," I said, and patted Delacroix's clay-cold hand. "He's going to Mouseville—"

"The hell he is," Percy said, speaking from the corner of his mouth like a yardwise con as he hooked the restraining belt across Delacroix's chest. "There's no such place. It's a fairy-tale these guys made up to keep you quiet. Just thought you should know, faggot."

A stricken light in Del's eyes told me that part of him *had* known . . . but would have kept the knowledge from the rest of him, if allowed. I looked at Percy, dumbfounded and furious, and he looked back at me levelly, as if to ask what I meant to do about it. And he had me, of course. There was nothing I *could* do about it, not in front of the witnesses, not with Delacroix now sitting on the furthest edge of life. There was nothing to do now but go on with it, finish it.

Percy took the mask from its hook and rolled it down over Del's face, snugging it tight under the little man's undershot chin so as to stretch the hole in the top. Taking the sponge from the bucket and putting it in the cap was the next, and it was here that Percy diverged from the routine for the first time: instead of just bending over and fishing the sponge out, he took the steel cap from the back of the chair, and bent over with it in his hands. Instead of bringing the sponge to the cap, in other words—which would have been the natural way to do it—he brought the cap to the sponge. I should have realized something was wrong, but I was too upset. It was the only execution I ever took part in where I felt totally out of control. As for Brutal, he never looked at Percy at all, not as Percy bent over the bucket (moving so as to partially block what he was doing from our view), not as he straightened up and turned to Del with the cap in his hands and the brown circle of sponge already inside it. Brutal was looking at the cloth which had replaced Del's face, watching the way the black silk mask drew in, outlining the circle of Del's open mouth, and then puffed out again with his breath. There were big beads of perspiration on Brutal's forehead, and at his temples, just below the hairline. I had never seen him sweat at an execution before. Behind him, Dean looked distracted and ill, as if he was fighting not to lose his supper. We all understood that something was wrong, I know that now. We just couldn't tell what it was. No one knew—not then— about the questions Percy had been asking Jack Van Hay. There were a lot of them, but I suspect most were just camouflage. What Percy wanted to know about—the *only* thing Percy wanted to know about, I believe—was the sponge. The purpose of the sponge. Why it was soaked in brine . . . and what would happen if it was not soaked in brine.

What would happen if the sponge was dry.

Percy jammed the cap down on Del's head. The little man jumped and moaned again, this time louder. Some of the witnesses stirred uneasily on their folding chairs. Dean took a half-step forward, meaning to help with the chin-strap, and Percy motioned him curtly to step back. Dean did, hunching a little and wincing as another blast of thunder shook the storage shed. This time it was followed by the first spatters of rain across the roof. They sounded hard, like someone flinging handfuls of goobers onto a washboard.

You've heard people say "My blood ran cold" about things, haven't you? Sure. All of us have, but the only time in all my years that I actually felt it happen to me was on that new and thunderstruck morning in October of 1932, at about ten seconds past midnight. It wasn't the look of poison triumph on Percy Wetmore's face as he stepped away from the capped, clamped, and hooded figure sitting there in Old Sparky; it was what I should have seen and didn't. There was no water running down Del's cheeks from out of the cap. That was when I finally got it.

"Edward Delacroix," Percy was saying, "electricity shall now be passed through your body until you are dead, according to state law."

I looked over at Brutal in an agony that made my urinary infection seem like a bumped finger. *The sponge is dry!* I mouthed at him, but he only shook his head, not understanding, and looked back at the mask over the Frenchman's face, where the man's last few breaths were pulling the black silk in and then blousing it out again.

I reached for Percy's elbow and he stepped away from me, giving me a flat look as he did so. It was only a momentary glance, but it told me everything. Later he would tell his lies and his half-truths, and most would be believed by the people who mattered, but I knew a different story. Percy was a good student when he was doing something he cared about, we'd found that out at the rehearsals, and he had listened carefully when Jack Van Hay explained how the brine-soaked sponge conducted the juice, channelling it, turning the charge into a kind of electric bullet to the brain. Oh yes, Percy knew exactly what he was doing. I think I believed him later when he said he didn't know how far it would go, but that doesn't even count in the good-intentions column, does it? I don't think so. Yet, short of screaming in front of the assistant warden and all the witnesses for Jack Van Hay not to pull the switch, there was nothing I could do. Given another five seconds, I think I might have screamed just that, but Percy didn't give me another five seconds.

"May God have mercy on your soul," he told the panting, terrified figure in the electric chair, then looked past him at the mesh-covered rectangle where Harry and Jack were standing, Jack with his hand on the switch marked MABEL'S HAIR DRIER. The doctor was standing to the right of that window, eyes fixed on the black bag between his feet, as silent and self-effacing as ever. "Roll on two!"

At first it was the same as always—the humming that was a little louder than the original cycle-up, but not much, and the mindless forward surge of Del's body as his muscles spasmed.

Then things started going wrong.

The humming lost its steadiness and began to waver. It was joined by a crackling sound, like cellophane being crinkled. I could smell something horrible that I didn't identify as a mixture of burning hair and organic sponge until I saw blue tendrils of smoke curling out from beneath the edges of the cap. More smoke was streaming out of the hole in the top of the cap that the wire came in through; it looked like smoke coming out of the hole in an Indian's teepee.

Delacroix began to jitter and twist in the chair, his mask-covered face snapping from side to side as if in some vehement refusal. His legs began to piston up and down in short strokes that were hampered by the clamps on his ankles. Thunder banged overhead, and now the rain began to pour down harder.

I looked at Dean Stanton; he stared wildly back. There was a muffled pop from under the cap, like a pine knot exploding in a hot fire, and now I could see smoke coming through the mask, as well, seeping out in little curls.

I lunged toward the mesh between us and the switch room, but before I could open my mouth, Brutus Howell seized my elbow. His grip was hard enough to make the nerves in there tingle. He was as white as tallow but not in a panic—not even close to being in a panic. "Don't you tell Jack to stop," he said in a low voice. "Whatever you do, don't tell him that. It's too late to stop."

At first, when Del began to scream, the witnesses didn't hear him. The rain on the tin roof had swelled to a roar, and the thunder was damned near continuous. But those of us on the platform heard him, all right—choked howls of pain from beneath the smoking mask, sounds an animal caught and mangled in a hay-baler might make.

The hum from the cap was ragged and wild now, broken by bursts of what sounded like radio static. Delacroix began to slam back and forth in the chair like a kid doing a tantrum. The platform shook, and he hit the leather restraining belt almost hard enough to pop it. The current was also twisting him from side to side, and I heard the crunching snap as his right shoulder either broke or dislocated. It went with a sound like someone hitting a wooden crate with a sledgehammer. The crotch of his pants, no more than a blur because of the short pistoning strokes of his legs, darkened. Then he began to squeal, horrible sounds, high-pitched and ratlike, that were audible even over the rushing downpour.

"What the hell's happening to him?" someone cried.

"Are those clamps going to hold?"

"Christ, the *smell*! Phew!"

Then, one of the two women: "Is this normal?"

Delacroix snapped forward, dropped back, snapped forward, fell back. Percy was staring at him with slack-jawed horror. He had expected *something,* sure, but not this.

The mask burst into flame on Delacroix's face. The smell of cooking hair and sponge was now joined by the smell of cooking flesh. Brutal grabbed the bucket the sponge had been in—it was empty now, of course—and charged for the extra-deep janitor's sink in the corner.

"Shouldn't I kill the juice, Paul?" Van Hay called through the mesh. He sounded completely rattled. "Shouldn't I—"

"No!" I shouted back. Brutal had understood it first, but I hadn't been far behind: we had to finish it. Whatever else we might do in all the rest of our lives was secondary to that one thing: we had to finish with Delacroix. "Roll, for Christ's sake! Roll, roll, roll!"

I turned to Brutal, hardly aware of the people talking behind us now, some on their feet, a couple screaming. *"Quit that!"* I yelled at Brutal. *"No water! No water! Are you nuts?"*

Brutal turned toward me, a kind of dazed understanding on his face. Throw water on a man who was getting the juice. Oh yes. That would be very smart. He looked around, saw the chemical fire extinguisher hanging on the wall, and got that instead. Good boy.

The mask had peeled away from Delacroix's face enough to reveal features that had gone blacker than John Coffey's. His eyes, now nothing but misshapen globs of white, filmy jelly, had been blown out of their sockets and lay on his cheeks. His eyelashes were gone, and as I looked, the lids themselves caught fire and began to burn. Smoke puffed from the open V of his shirt. And still the humming of the electricity went on and on, filling my head, vibrating in there. I think it's the sound mad people must hear, that or something like it.

Dean started forward, thinking in some dazed way that he could beat the fire out of Del's shirt with his hands, and I yanked him away almost hard enough to pull him off his feet. Touching Delacroix at that point would have been like Brer Rabbit punching into the Tar-Baby. An electrified Tar-Baby, in this case.

I still didn't turn around to see what was going on behind us, but it sounded like pandemonium, chairs falling over, people bellowing, a woman crying *"Stop it, stop it, oh can't you see he's had enough?"* at the top of her lungs. Curtis Anderson grabbed my shoulder and asked what was happening, for Christ's sake, what was happening, and why didn't I order Jack to shut down?

"Because I can't," I said. "We've gone too far to turn back, can't you see that? It'll be over in a few more seconds, anyway."

But it was at least two minutes before it was over, the longest two minutes of my whole life, and through most of it I think Delacroix was conscious. He screamed and jittered and rocked from side to side. Smoke poured from his nostrils and from a mouth that had gone the purple-black of ripe plums. Smoke drifted up from his tongue the way smoke rises from a hot griddle. All the buttons on his shirt either burst or melted. His undershirt did not quite catch fire, but it charred and smoke poured through it and we could smell his chest-hair roasting. Behind us, people were heading for the door like cattle in a stampede. They couldn't get out through it, of course—we were in a damn prison, after all—so they simply clustered around it while Delacroix fried (*Now I'm fryin,* Old Toot had said when we were rehearsing for Arlen Bitterbuck, *I'm a done tom turkey*) and the thunder rolled and the rain ran down out of the sky in a perfect fury.

At some point I thought of the doc and looked around for him. He was still there, but crumpled on the floor beside his black bag. He'd fainted.

Brutal came up and stood beside me, holding the fire extinguisher.

"Not yet," I said.

"I know."

We looked around for Percy and saw him standing almost behind Sparky now, frozen, eyes huge, one knuckle crammed into his mouth.

Then, at last, Delacroix slumped back in the chair, his bulging, misshapen face lying over on one shoulder. He was still jittering, but we'd seen this before; it was the current running through him. The cap had come askew on his head, but when we took it off a little later, most of his scalp and his remaining fringe of hair came with it, bonded to the metal as if by some powerful adhesive.

"Kill it!" I called to Jack when thirty seconds had gone by with nothing but electric jitters coming from the smoking, man-shaped lump of charcoal lolling in the electric chair. The hum died immediately, and I nodded to Brutal.

He turned and slammed the fire extinguisher into Percy's arms so hard that Percy staggered backward and almost fell off the platform. "You do it," Brutal said. "You're running the show, after all, ain't you?"

Percy gave him a look that was both sick and murderous, then armed the extinguisher, pumped it, cocked it, and shot a huge cloud of white foam over the man in the chair. I saw Del's foot twitch once as the spray hit his face and thought *Oh no, we might have to go again,* but there was only that single twitch.

Anderson had turned around and was bawling at the panicky witnesses, telling them everything was all right, everything was under control, just a power-surge from the electrical storm, nothing to worry about. Next thing, he'd be telling them that what they smelled—a devil's mixture of burned hair, fried meat, and fresh-baked shit—was Chanel No. 5.

"Get doc's stethoscope," I told Dean as the extinguisher ran dry. Delacroix was coated with white now, and the worst of the stench was being overlaid by a thin and bitter chemical smell.

"Doc . . . should I . . ."

"Never mind doc, just get his stethoscope," I said. "Let's get this over . . . get him out of here."

Dean nodded. *Over* and *out of here* were two concepts that appealed to him just then. They appealed to both of us. He went over to doc's bag and began rummaging in it. Doc was beginning to move again, so at least he hadn't had a stroke or a heart-storm. That was good. But the way Brutal was looking at Percy wasn't.

"Get down in the tunnel and wait by the gurney," I said.

Percy swallowed. "Paul, listen. I didn't know—"

"Shut up. Get down in the tunnel and wait by the gurney. Now."

He swallowed, grimaced as if it hurt, and then walked toward the door which led to the stairs and the tunnel. He carried the empty fire extinguisher in his arms, as if it were a baby. Dean passed him, coming back to me with the stethoscope. I snatched it and set the earpieces. I'd done this before, in the army, and it's sort of like riding a bike—you don't forget.

I wiped at the foam on Delacroix's chest, then had to gag back vomit as a large, hot section of his skin simply slid away from the flesh beneath, the way the skin will slide off a . . . well, you know. A done tom turkey.

"Oh my God!" a voice I didn't recognize almost sobbed behind me. "Is it always this way? Why didn't somebody tell me? I never would have come!"

Too late now, friend, I thought. "Get that man out of here," I said to Dean or Brutal or whoever might be listening—I said it when I was sure I could speak without puking into Delacroix's smoking lap. "Get them all back by the door."

I steeled myself as best I could, then put the disc of the stethoscope on the red-black patch of raw flesh I'd made on Del's chest. I listened, praying I would hear nothing, and that's just what I did hear.

"He's dead," I told Brutal.

"Thank Christ."

"Yes. Thank Christ. You and Dean get the stretcher. Let's unbuckle him and get him out of here, fast."

5

WE GOT HIS BODY down the twelve stairs and onto the gurney all right. My nightmare was that his cooked flesh might slough right off his bones as we lugged him—it was Old Toot's done tom turkey that had gotten into my head—but of course that didn't happen.

Curtis Anderson was upstairs soothing the spectators—trying to, anyway—and that was good for Brutal, because Anderson wasn't there to see when Brutal took a step toward the head of the gurney and pulled his arm back to slug Percy, who was standing there looking stunned. I caught his arm, and that was good for both of them. It was good for Percy because Brutal meant to deliver a blow of near-decapitory force, and good for Brutal because he would have lost his job if the blow had connected, and maybe ended up in prison himself.

"No," I said.

"What do you mean, no?" he asked me furiously. "How can you say no? You saw what he did! What are you telling me? That you're still going to let his *connections* protect him? After what he *did*?"

"Yes."

Brutal stared at me, mouth agape, eyes so angry they were watering.

"Listen to me, Brutus—you take a poke at him, and most likely we all go. You, me, Dean, Harry, maybe even Jack Van Hay. Everyone else moves a rung or two up the ladder, starting with Bill Dodge, and the Prison Commission hires three or four Breadline Barneys to fill the spots at the bottom. Maybe you can live with that, but—" I cocked my thumb at Dean, who was staring down the dripping, brick-lined tunnel. He was holding his specs in one hand, and looked almost as dazed as Percy. "But what about Dean? He's got two kids, one in high school and one just about to go."

"So what's it come down to?" Brutal asked. "We let him get away with it?"

"I didn't know the sponge was supposed to be wet," Percy said in a faint, mechanical voice. This was the story he had rehearsed beforehand, of course, when he was expecting a painful prank instead of the cataclysm we had just witnessed. "It was never wet when we rehearsed."

"Aw, you sucker—" Brutal began, and started for Percy. I grabbed him again and yanked him back. Footsteps clacked on the steps. I looked up, desperately afraid of seeing Curtis Anderson, but it was Harry Terwilliger. His cheeks were paper-white and his lips were purplish, as if he'd been eating blackberry cobbler.

I switched my attention back to Brutal. "For God's sake, Brutal, Delacroix's *dead,* nothing can change that, and Percy's not worth it." Was the plan, or the beginnings of it, in my head even then? I've wondered about that since, let me tell you. I've wondered over the course of a lot of years, and have never been able to come up with a satisfactory answer. I suppose it doesn't matter much. A lot of things don't matter, but it doesn't keep a man from wondering about them, I've noticed.

"You guys talk about me like I was a chump," Percy said. He still sounded dazed and winded—as if someone had punched him deep in the gut—but he was coming back a little.

"You *are* a chump, Percy," I said.

"Hey, you can't—"

I controlled my own urge to hit him only with the greatest effort. Water dripped hollowly from the bricks down in the tunnel; our shadows danced huge and misshapen on the walls, like shadows in that Poe story about the big ape in the Rue Morgue. Thunder bashed, but down here it was muffled.

"I only want to hear one thing from you, Percy, and that's you repeating your promise to put in for Briar Ridge tomorrow."

"Don't worry about that," he said sullenly. He looked at the sheeted figure on the gurney, looked away, flicked his eyes up toward my face for a moment, then looked away again.

"That *would* be for the best," Harry said. "Otherwise, you might get to know Wild Bill Wharton a whole lot better than you want to." A slight pause. "We could see to it."

Percy was afraid of us, and he was probably afraid of what we might do if he was still around when we found out he'd been talking to Jack Van Hay about what the sponge was for and why we always soaked it in brine, but Harry's mention of Wharton woke real terror in his eyes. I could see him remembering how Wharton had held him, ruffling his hair and crooning to him.

"You wouldn't dare," Percy whispered.

"Yes I would," Harry replied calmly. "And do you know what? I'd get away with it. Because you've already shown yourself to be careless as hell around the prisoners. Incompetent, too."

Percy's fists bunched and his cheeks colored in a thin pink. "I am not—"

"Sure you are," Dean said, joining us. We formed a rough semicircle around Percy at the foot of the stairs, and even a retreat up the tunnel was blocked; the gurney was behind him, with its load of smoking flesh hidden under an old sheet. "You just burned Delacroix alive. If that ain't incompetent, what is?"

Percy's eyes flickered. He had been planning to cover himself by pleading ignorance, and now he saw he was hoist by his own petard. I don't know what he might have said next, because Curtis Anderson came lunging down the stairs just then. We heard him and drew back from Percy a little, so as not to look quite so threatening.

"What in the blue fuck was *that* all about?" Anderson roared. "Jesus Christ, there's puke all over the floor up there! And the smell! I got Magnusson and Old Toot-Toot to open both doors, but that smell won't come out for five damn years, that's what I'm betting. And that asshole Wharton is *singing* about it! I can hear him!"

"Can he carry a tune, Curt?" Brutal asked. You know how you can burn off illuminating gas with a single spark and not be hurt if you do it before the concentration gets too heavy? This was like that. We took an instant to gape at Brutus, and then we were all howling. Our high, hysterical laughter flapped up and down the gloomy tunnel like bats. Our shadows bobbed and flickered on the walls. Near the end, even Percy joined in. At last it died, and in its aftermath we all felt a little better. Felt *sane* again.

"Okay, boys," Anderson said, mopping at his teary eyes with his handkerchief and still snorting out an occasional hiccup of laughter, "what the hell happened?"

"An execution," Brutal said. I think his even tone surprised Anderson, but it didn't surprise me, at least not much; Brutal had always been good at turning down his dials in a hurry. "A successful one."

"How in the name of Christ can you call a direct-current abortion like that a success? We've got witnesses that won't sleep for a month! Hell, that fat old broad probably won't sleep for a year!"

Brutal pointed at the gurney, and the shape under the sheet. "He's dead, ain't he? As for your witnesses, most of them will be telling their friends tomorrow night that it was poetic justice—Del there burned a bunch of people alive, so we turned around and burned *him* alive. Except they won't say it was us. They'll say it was the will of God, working *through* us. Maybe there's even some truth to that. And you want to know the best part? The absolute cat's pajamas? Most of their friends will wish they'd been here to see it." He gave Percy a look both distasteful and sardonic as he said this last.

"And if their feathers are a little ruffled, so what?" Harry asked. "They volunteered for the damn job, nobody drafted them."

"I didn't know the sponge was supposed to be wet," Percy said in his robot's voice. "It's never wet in rehearsal."

Dean looked at him with utter disgust. "How many years did you spend pissing on the toilet seat before someone told you to put it up before you start?" he snarled.

Percy opened his mouth to reply, but I told him to shut up. For a wonder, he did. I turned to Anderson.

"Percy fucked up, Curtis—that's what happened, pure and simple."

I turned toward Percy, daring him to contradict me. He didn't, maybe because he read my eyes: better that Anderson hear *stupid mistake* than *on purpose*. And besides, whatever was said down here in the tunnel didn't matter. What mattered, what always matters to the Percy Wetmores of the world, is what gets written down or overheard by the big bugs—the people who matter. What matters to the Percys of the world is how it plays in the newspapers.

Anderson looked at the five of us uncertainly. He even looked at Del, but Del wasn't talking. "I guess it could be worse," Anderson said.

"That's right," I agreed. "He could still be alive."

Curtis blinked—that possibility seemed not to have crossed his mind. "I want a complete report about this on my desk tomorrow," he said. "And none of you are going to talk to Warden Moores about it until I've had my chance. Are you?"

We shook our heads vehemently. If Curtis Anderson wanted to tell the warden, why, that was fine by us.

"If none of those asshole scribblers put it in their papers—"

"They won't," I said. "If they tried, their editors'd kill it. Too gruesome for a family audience. But they won't even try—they were all vets tonight. Sometimes things go wrong, that's all. They know it as well as we do."

Anderson considered a moment longer, then nodded. He turned his attention to Percy, an expression of disgust on his usually pleasant face. "You're a little asshole," he said, "and I don't like you a bit." He nodded at Percy's look of flabbergasted surprise. "If you tell any of your candy-ass friends I said that, I'll deny it until Aunt Rhody's old gray goose comes back to life, and these men will back me up. You've got a problem, son."

He turned and started up the stairs. I let him get four steps and then said: "Curtis?"

He turned back, eyebrows raised, saying nothing.

"You don't want to worry too much about Percy," I said. "He's moving on to Briar Ridge soon. Bigger and better things. Isn't that right, Percy?"

"As soon as his transfer comes through," Brutal added.

"And until it comes, he's going to call in sick every night," Dean put in.

That roused Percy, who hadn't been working at the prison long enough to have accumulated any paid sick-time. He looked at Dean with bright distaste. "Don't you *wish*," he said.

6

WE WERE BACK on the block by one-fifteen or so (except for Percy, who had been ordered to clean up the storage room and was sulking his way through the job), me with a report to write. I decided to do it at the duty desk; if I sat in my more comfortable office chair, I'd likely doze off. That probably sounds peculiar to you, given what had happened only an hour before, but I felt as if I'd lived three lifetimes since eleven o'clock the previous night, all of them without sleep.

John Coffey was standing at his cell door, tears streaming from his strange, distant eyes—it was like watching blood run out of some unhealable but strangely painless wound. Closer to the desk, Wharton was sitting on his bunk, rocking from side to side, and singing a song apparently of his own invention, and not quite nonsense. As well as I can remember, it went something like this:

> "Bar-be-cue! Me and you!
> Stinky, pinky, phew-phew-phew!
> It wasn't Billy or Philadelphia Philly,
> it wasn't Jackie or Roy!
> It was a warm little number, a hot cucumber,
> by the name of Delacroix!"

"Shut up, you jerk," I said.

Wharton grinned, showing his mouthful of dingy teeth. *He* wasn't dying, at least not yet; he was up, happy, practically tap-dancing.

"Come on in here and make me, why don't you?" he said happily, and then began another verse of "The Barbecue Song," making up words not quite at random. There was something going on in there, all right. A kind of green and stinking intelligence that was, in its own way, almost brilliant.

I went down to John Coffey. He wiped away his tears with the heels of his hands. His eyes were red and sore-looking, and it came to me that he was exhausted, too. Why he should have been, a man who trudged around the exercise yard maybe two hours a day and either sat or lay down in his cell the rest of the time, I didn't know, but I didn't doubt what I was seeing. It was too clear.

"Poor Del," he said in a low, hoarse voice. "Poor old Del."

"Yes," I said. "Poor old Del. John, are *you* okay?"

"He's out of it," Coffey said. "Del's out of it. Isn't he, boss?"

"Yes. Answer my question, John. Are you okay?"

"Del's out of it, he's the lucky one. No matter how it happened, he's the lucky one."

I thought Delacroix might have given him an argument on that, but didn't say so. I glanced around Coffey's cell, instead. "Where's Mr. Jingles?"

"Ran down there." He pointed through the bars, down the hall to the restraint-room door.

I nodded. "Well, he'll be back."

But he wasn't; Mr. Jingles's days on the Green Mile were over. The only trace of him we ever happened on was what Brutal found that winter: a few brightly colored splinters of wood, and a smell of peppermint candy wafting out of a hole in a beam.

I meant to walk away then, but I didn't. I looked at John Coffey, and he back at me as if he knew everything I was thinking. I told myself to get moving, to just call it a night and get moving, back to the duty desk and my report. Instead I said his name: "John Coffey."

"Yes, boss," he said at once.

Sometimes a man is cursed with needing to know a thing, and that was how it was with me right then. I dropped down on one knee and began taking off one of my shoes.

7

THE RAIN HAD QUIT by the time I got home, and a late grin of moon had appeared over the ridges to the north. My sleepiness seemed to have gone with the clouds. I was wide awake, and I could smell Delacroix on me. I thought I might smell him on my skin—barbecue, me and you, stinky, pinky, phew-phew-phew—for a long time to come.

Janice was waiting up, as she always did on execution nights. I meant not to tell her the story, saw no sense in harrowing her with it, but she got a clear look at my face as I came in the kitchen door and would have it all. So I sat down, took her warm hands in my cold ones (the heater in my old Ford barely worked, and the weather had turned a hundred and eighty degrees since the storm), and told her what she thought she wanted to hear. About halfway through I broke down crying, which I hadn't expected. I was a little ashamed, but only a little; it was her, you see, and she never taxed me with the times that I slipped from the way I thought a man should be . . . the way I thought *I* should be, at any rate. A man with a good wife is the luckiest of God's creatures, and one without must be among the most miserable, I think, the only true blessing of their lives that they don't know how poorly off they are. I cried, and she held my head against her breast, and when my own storm passed, I felt better . . . a little, anyway. And I believe that was when I had the first conscious sight of my idea. Not the shoe; I don't mean that. The shoe was related, but different. All my *real* idea was right then, however, was an odd realization: that John Coffey and Melinda Moores, different as they might have been in size and sex and skin color, had exactly the same eyes: woeful, sad, and distant. Dying eyes.

"Come to bed," my wife said at last. "Come to bed with me, Paul."

So I did, and we made love, and when it was over she went to sleep. As I lay there watching the moon grin and listening to the walls tick— they were at last pulling in, exchanging summer for fall—I thought about John Coffey saying he had helped it. *I helped Del's mouse. I helped Mr. Jingles. He's a circus mouse.* Sure. And maybe, I thought, we were all circus mice, running around with only the dimmest awareness that God and all His heavenly host were watching us in our Bakelite houses through our ivy-glass windows.

I slept a little as the day began to lighten—two hours, I guess, maybe three; and I slept the way I always sleep these days here in Georgia Pines and hardly ever did then, in thin little licks. What I went to sleep thinking about was the churches of my youth. The names changed, depending on the whims of my mother and her sisters, but they were all really the same, all The First Backwoods Church of Praise Jesus, The Lord Is Mighty. In the shadow of those blunt, square steeples, the concept of atonement came up as regularly as the toll of the bell which called the faithful to worship. Only God could forgive sins, could and did, washing them away in the agonal blood of His crucified Son, but that did not change the responsibility of His children to atone for those sins (and even their simple errors of judgement) whenever possible. Atonement was powerful; it was the lock on the door you closed against the past.

I fell asleep thinking of piney-woods atonement, and Eduard Delacroix on fire as he rode the lightning, and Melinda Moores, and my big boy with the endlessly weeping eyes. These thoughts twisted their way into a dream. In it, John Coffey was sitting on a riverbank and bawling his inarticulate mooncalf's grief up at the early-summer sky while on the other bank a freight-train stormed endlessly toward a rusty trestle spanning the Trapingus. In the crook of each arm the black man held the body of a naked, blonde-haired girlchild. His fists, huge brown rocks at the ends of those arms, were closed. All around him crickets chirred and noseeums flocked; the day hummed with heat. In my dream I went to him, knelt before him, and took his hands. His fists relaxed and gave up their secrets. In one was a spool colored green and red and yellow. In the other was a prison guard's shoe.

"I couldn't help it," John Coffey said. "I tried to take it back, but it was too late."

And this time, in my dream, I understood him.

8

At nine o'clock the next morning, while I was having a third cup of coffee in the kitchen (my wife said nothing, but I could see disapproval writ large on her face when she brought it to me), the telephone rang. I went into the parlor to take it, and Central told someone that their party was holding the line. She then told me to have a birdlarky day and rang off . . . presumably. With Central, you could never quite tell for sure.

Hal Moores's voice shocked me. Wavery and hoarse, it sounded like the voice of an octogenarian. It occurred to me that it was good that things had gone all right with Curtis Anderson in the tunnel last night, good that he felt about the same as we did about Percy, because this man I was talking to would very likely never work another day at Cold Mountain.

"Paul, I understand there was trouble last night. I also understand that our friend Mr. Wetmore was involved."

"A spot of trouble," I admitted, holding the receiver tight to my ear and leaning in toward the horn, "but the job got done. That's the important thing."

"Yes. Of course."

"Can I ask who told you?" So I can tie a can to his tail? I didn't add.

"You can ask, but since it's really none of your beeswax, I think I'll keep my mouth shut on that score. But when I called my office to see if there were any messages or urgent business, I was told an interesting thing."

"Oh?"

"Yes. Seems a transferral application landed in my basket. Percy Wetmore wants to go to Briar Ridge as soon as possible. Must have filled out the application even before last night's shift was over, wouldn't you think?"

"It sounds that way," I agreed.

"Ordinarily I'd let Curtis handle it, but considering the . . . atmosphere on E Block just lately, I asked Hannah to run it over to me personally on her lunch hour. She has graciously agreed to do so. I'll approve it and see it's forwarded on to the state capital this afternoon. I expect you'll get a look at Percy's backside going out the door in no more than a month. Maybe less."

He expected me to be pleased with this news, and had a right to expect it. He had taken time out from tending his wife to expedite a matter that might otherwise have taken upwards of half a year, even with Percy's vaunted connections. Nevertheless, my heart sank. A month! But maybe it didn't matter much, one way or the other. It removed a perfectly natural desire to wait and put off a risky endeavor, and what I was now thinking about would be very risky indeed. Sometimes, when that's the case, it's better to jump before you can lose your nerve. If we were going to have to deal with Percy in any case (always assuming I could get the others to go along with my insanity—always assuming there was a we, in other words), it might as well be tonight.

"Paul? Are you there?" His voice lowered a little, as if he thought he was now talking to himself. "Damn, I think I lost the connection."

"No, I'm here, Hal. That's great news."

"Yes," he agreed, and I was again struck by how old he sounded. How *papery*, somehow. "Oh, I know what you're thinking."

No, you don't, Warden, I thought. Never in a million years could you know what I'm thinking.

"You're thinking that our young friend will still be around for the Coffey execution. That's probably true—Coffey will go well before Thanksgiving, I imagine—but you can put him back in the switch room. No one will object. Including him, I should think."

"I'll do that," I said. "Hal, how's Melinda?"

246

There was a long pause—so long I might have thought *I'd* lost *him,* except for the sound of his breathing. When he spoke this time, it was in a much lower tone of voice. "She's sinking," he said.

Sinking. That chilly word the old-timers used not to describe a person who was dying, exactly, but one who had begun to uncouple from living.

"The headaches seem a little better . . . for now, anyway . . . but she can't walk without help, she can't pick things up, she loses control of her water while she sleeps . . ." There was another pause, and then, in an even lower voice, Hal said something that sounded like "She wears."

"Wears what, Hal?" I asked, frowning. My wife had come into the parlor doorway. She stood there wiping her hands on a dishtowel and looking at me.

"No," he said in a voice that seemed to waver between anger and tears. "She *swears.*"

"Oh." I still didn't know what he meant, but had no intention of pursuing it. I didn't have to; he did it for me.

"She'll be all right, perfectly normal, talking about her flower-garden or a dress she saw in the catalogue, or maybe about how she heard Roosevelt on the radio and how wonderful he sounds, and then, all at once, she'll start to say the most awful things, the most awful . . . words. She doesn't raise her voice. It would almost be better if she did, I think, because then . . . you see, *then* . . ."

"She wouldn't sound so much like herself."

"That's it," he said gratefully. "But to hear her saying those awful gutter-language things in her sweet voice . . . pardon me, Paul." His voice trailed away and I heard him noisily clearing his throat. Then he came back, sounding a little stronger but just as distressed. "She wants to have Pastor Donaldson over, and I know he's a comfort to her, but how can I ask him? Suppose that he's sitting there, reading Scripture with her, and she calls him a foul name? She could; she called me one last night. She said, 'Hand me that *Liberty* magazine, you cocksucker, would you?' Paul, where could she have ever heard such language? How could she know those words?"

"I don't know. Hal, are you going to be home this evening?"

When he was well and in charge of himself, not distracted by worry or grief, Hal Moores had a cutting and sarcastic facet to his personality; his subordinates feared that side of him even more than his anger or his contempt, I think. His sarcasm, usually impatient and often harsh, could sting like acid. A little of that now splashed on me. It was unexpected, but on the whole I was glad to hear it. All the fight hadn't gone out of him after all, it seemed.

"No," he said, "I'm taking Melinda out square-dancing. We're going to do-si-do, allemand left, and then tell the fiddler he's a rooster-dick motherfucker."

I clapped my hand over my mouth to keep from laughing. Mercifully, it was an urge that passed in a hurry.

"I'm sorry," he said. "I haven't been getting much sleep lately. It's made me grouchy. Of course we're going to be home. Why do you ask?"

"It doesn't matter, I guess," I said.

"You weren't thinking of coming by, were you? Because if you were on last night, you'll be on tonight. Unless you've switched with somebody?"

"No, I haven't switched," I said. "I'm on tonight."

"It wouldn't be a good idea, anyway. Not the way she is right now."

"Maybe not. Thanks for your news."

"You're welcome. Pray for my Melinda, Paul."

I said I would, thinking that I might do quite a bit more than pray. God helps those who help themselves, as they say in The Church of Praise Jesus, The Lord Is Mighty. I hung up and looked at Janice.

"How's Melly?" she asked.

"Not good." I told her what Hal had told me, including the part about the swearing, although I left out cock-sucker and rooster-dick motherfucker. I finished with Hal's word, *sinking,* and Jan nodded sadly. Then she took a closer look at me.

"What are you thinking about? You're thinking about *something,* probably no good. It's in your face."

Lying was out of the question; it wasn't the way we were with each other. I just told her it was best she not know, at least for the time being.

"Is it . . . could it get you in trouble?" She didn't sound particularly alarmed at the idea—more interested than anything—which is one of the things I have always loved about her.

"Maybe," I said.

"Is it a good thing?"

"Maybe," I repeated. I was standing there, still turning the phone's crank idly with one finger, while I held down the connecting points with a finger of my other hand.

"Would you like me to leave you alone while you use the telephone?" she asked. "Be a good little woman and butt out? Do some dishes? Knit some booties?"

I nodded. "That's not the way I'd put it, but—"

"Are we having extras for lunch, Paul?"

"I hope so," I said.

9

I GOT BRUTAL AND DEAN right away, because both of them were on the exchange. Harry wasn't, not then, at least, but I had the number of his closest neighbor who was. Harry called me back about twenty minutes later, highly embarrassed at having to reverse the charges and sputtering promises to "pay his share" when our next bill came. I told him we'd count those chickens when they hatched; in the meantime, could he come over to my place for lunch? Brutal and Dean would be here, and Janice had promised to put out some of her famous slaw . . . not to mention her even more famous apple pie.

"Lunch just for the hell of it?" Harry sounded skeptical.

I admitted I had something I wanted to talk to them about, but it was best not gone into, even lightly, over the phone. Harry agreed to come. I dropped the receiver onto the prongs, went to the window, and looked out thoughtfully. Although we'd had the late shift, I hadn't wakened either Brutal or Dean, and Harry hadn't sounded like a fellow freshly turned out of dreamland, either. It seemed that I wasn't the only one having problems with what had happened last night, and considering the craziness I had in mind, that was probably good.

Brutal, who lived closest to me, arrived at quarter past eleven. Dean showed up fifteen minutes later, and Harry—already dressed for work—about fifteen minutes after Dean. Janice served us cold beef sandwiches, slaw, and iced tea in the kitchen. Only a day before, we would have had it out on the side porch and been glad of a breeze, but the temperature had dropped a good fifteen degrees since the thunderstorm, and a keen-edged wind was snuffling down from the ridges.

"You're welcome to sit down with us," I told my wife.

She shook her head. "I don't think I want to know what you're up to—I'll worry less if I'm in the dark. I'll have a bite in the parlor. I'm visiting with Miss Jane Austen this week, and she's very good company."

"Who's Jane Austen?" Harry asked when she had left. "Your side or Janice's, Paul? A cousin? Is she pretty?"

"She's a writer, you nit," Brutal told him. "Been dead practically since Betsy Ross basted the stars on the first flag."

"Oh." Harry looked embarrassed. "I'm not much of a reader. Radio manuals, mostly."

"What's on your mind, Paul?" Dean asked.

"John Coffey and Mr. Jingles, to start with." They looked surprised, which I had expected—they'd been thinking I wanted to discuss either Delacroix or Percy. Maybe both. I looked at Dean and Harry. "The thing with Mr. Jingles—what Coffey did—happened pretty fast. I don't know if you got there in time to see how broken up the mouse was or not."

Dean shook his head. "I saw the blood on the floor, though."

I turned to Brutal.

"That son of a bitch Percy crushed it," he said simply. "It should have died, but it didn't. Coffey did something to it. Healed it somehow. I know how that sounds, but I saw it with my own eyes."

I said: "He healed me, as well, and I didn't just see it, I *felt* it." I told them about my urinary infection—how it had come back, how bad it had been (I pointed through the window at the woodpile I'd had to hold onto the morning the pain drove me to my knees), and how it had gone away completely after Coffey touched me. And stayed away.

It didn't take long to tell. When I was done, they sat and thought about it awhile, chewing on their sandwiches as they did. Then Dean said, "Black things came out of his mouth. Like bugs."

"That's right," Harry agreed. "They were black to start with, anyway. Then they turned white and disappeared." He looked around, considering. "It's like I damned near forgot the whole thing until you brought it up, Paul. Ain't that funny?"

"Nothing funny or strange about it," Brutal said. "I think that's what people most always do with the stuff they can't make out—just forget it. Doesn't do a person much good to remember stuff that doesn't make any sense. What about it, Paul? Were there bugs when he fixed you?"

"Yes. I think they're the sickness . . . the pain . . . the hurt. He takes it in, then lets it out into the open air again."

"Where it dies," Harry said.

I shrugged. I didn't know if it died or not, wasn't sure it even mattered.

"Did he suck it out of you?" Brutal asked. "He looked like he was sucking it right out of the mouse. The hurt. The . . . you know. The death."

"No," I said. "He just touched me. And I felt it. A kind of jolt, like electricity only not painful. But I wasn't dying, only hurting."

Brutal nodded. "The touch and the breath. Just like you hear those backwoods gospel-shouters going on about."

"Praise Jesus, the Lord is mighty," I said.

"I dunno if Jesus comes into it," Brutal said, "but it seems to me like John Coffey is one mighty man."

"All right," Dean said. "If you say all this happened, I guess I believe it. God works in mysterious ways His wonders to perform. But what's it got to do with us?"

Well, that was the big question, wasn't it? I took in a deep breath and told them what I wanted to do. They listened, dumbfounded. Even Brutal, who liked to read those magazines with the stories about little green men from space, looked dumbfounded. There was a longer silence when I finished this time, and no one chewing any sandwiches.

At last, in a gentle and reasonable voice, Brutus Howell said: "We'd lose our jobs if we were caught, Paul, and we'd be very goddam lucky if that was all that happened. We'd probably end up over in A Block as guests of the state, making wallets and showering in pairs."

"Yes," I said. "That could happen."

"I can understand how you feel, a little," he went on. "You know Moores better than us—he's your friend as well as the big boss—and I know you think a lot of his wife . . ."

"She's the sweetest woman you could ever hope to meet," I said, "and she means the world to him."

"But we don't know her the way you and Janice do," Brutal said. "Do we, Paul?"

"You'd like her if you did," I said. "At least, you'd like her if you'd met her before this thing got its claws into her. She does a lot of community things, she's a good friend, and she's religious. More than that, she's funny. Used to be, anyway. She could tell you things that'd make you laugh until the tears rolled down your cheeks. But none of those things are the reason I want to help save her, if she can be saved. What's happening to her is an *offense,* goddammit, an *offense.* To the eyes and the ears and the heart."

"Very noble, but I doubt like hell if that's what put this bee in your bonnet," Brutal said. "I think it's what happened to Del. You want to balance it off somehow."

And he was right. Of course he was. I knew Melinda Moores better than the others did, but maybe not, in the end, well enough to ask them to risk their jobs for her . . . and possibly their freedom, as well. Or my own job and freedom, for that matter. I had two children, and the last thing on God's earth that I wanted my wife to have to do was to write them the news that their father was going on trial for . . . well, what would it be? I didn't know for sure. Aiding and abetting an escape attempt seemed the most likely.

But the death of Eduard Delacroix had been the ugliest, foulest thing I had ever seen in my life—not just my working life but my whole, entire life—and I had been a party to it. We had *all* been a party to it, because we had allowed Percy Wetmore to stay even after we knew he was horribly unfit to work in a place like E Block. We had played the game. Even Warden Moores had been a party to it. "His nuts are going to cook whether Wetmore's on the team or not," he had said, and maybe that was well enough, considering what the little Frenchman had done, but in the end Percy had done a lot more than cook Del's nuts; he had blown the little man's eyeballs right out of their sockets and set his damned face on fire. And why? Because Del was a murderer half a dozen times over? No. Because Percy had wet his pants and the little Cajun had had the temerity to laugh at him. We'd been part of a monstrous act, and Percy was going to get away with it. Off to Briar Ridge he would go, happy as a clam at high tide, and there he would have a whole asylum filled with lunatics to practice his cruelties upon. There was nothing we could do about that, but perhaps it was not too late to wash some of the muck off our own hands.

"In my church they call it atonement instead of balancing," I said, "but I guess it comes to the same thing."

"Do you really think Coffey *could* save her?" Dean asked in a soft, awed voice. "Just . . . what? . . . suck that brain tumor out of her head? Like it was a . . . a peach-pit?"

"I think he could. It's not for sure, of course, but after what he did to me . . . and to Mr. Jingles . . ."

"That mouse was seriously busted up, all right," Brutal said.

"But *would* he do it?" Harry mused. "*Would* he?"

"If he can, he will," I said.

"Why? Coffey doesn't even know her!"

"Because it's what he does. It's what God made him for."

Brutal made a show of looking around, reminding us all that someone was missing. "What about Percy? You think he's just gonna let this go down?" he asked, and so I told them what I had in mind for Percy. By the time I finished, Harry and Dean were looking at me in amazement, and a reluctant grin of admiration had dawned on Brutal's face.

"Pretty audacious, Brother Paul!" he said. "Fair takes my breath away!"

"But wouldn't it be the bee's knees!" Dean almost whispered, then laughed aloud and clapped his hands like a child. "I mean, voh-doh-dee-oh-doh and twenty-three-skidoo!" You want to remember that Dean had a special interest in the part of my plan that involved Percy—Percy could have gotten Dean killed, after all, freezing up the way he had.

"Yeah, but what about after?" Harry said. He sounded gloomy, but his eyes gave him away; they were sparkling, the eyes of a man who wants to be convinced. "What then?"

"They say dead men tell no tales," Brutal rumbled, and I took a quick look at him to make sure he was joking.

"I think he'll keep his mouth shut," I said.

"Really?" Dean looked skeptical. He took off his glasses and began to polish them. "Convince me."

"First, he won't know what really happened—he's going to judge us by himself and think it was just a prank. Second—and more important—*he'll be afraid to say anything*. That's what I'm really counting on. We tell him that if he starts writing letters and making phone calls, *we* start writing letters and making phone calls."

"About the execution," Harry said.

"And about the way he froze when Wharton attacked Dean," Brutal said. "I think people finding out about that is what Percy Wetmore's really afraid of." He nodded slowly and thoughtfully. "It could work. But Paul . . . wouldn't it make more sense to bring Mrs. Moores to Coffey than Coffey to Mrs. Moores? We could take care of Percy pretty much the way you laid it out, then bring her in through the tunnel instead of taking Coffey out that way."

I shook my head. "Never happen. Not in a million years."

"Because of Warden Moores?"

"That's right. He's so hardheaded he makes old Doubting Thomas look like Joan of Arc. If we bring Coffey to his house, I think we can surprise him into at least letting Coffey make the try. Otherwise . . ."

"What were you thinking about using for a vehicle?" Brutal asked.

"My first thought was the stagecoach," I said, "but we'd never get it out of the yard without being noticed, and everyone within a twenty-mile radius knows what it looks like, anyway. I guess maybe we can use my Ford."

"Guess again," Dean said, popping his specs back onto his nose. "You couldn't get John Coffey into your car if you stripped him naked, covered him with lard, and used a shoehorn. You're so used to looking at him that you've forgotten how big he is."

I had no reply to that. Most of my attention that morning had been focused on the problem of Percy—and the lesser but not inconsiderable problem of Wild Bill Wharton. Now I realized that transportation wasn't going to be as simple as I had hoped.

Harry Terwilliger picked up the remains of his second sandwich, looked at it for a second, then put it down again. "If we was to actually do this crazy thing," he said, "I guess we could use my pickup truck. Sit him in the back of that. Wouldn't be nobody much on the roads at that hour. We're talking about well after midnight, ain't we?"

"Yes," I said.

"You guys're forgetting one thing," Dean said. "I know Coffey's been pretty quiet ever since he came on the block, doesn't do much but lay there on his bunk and leak from the eyes, but he's a *murderer*. Also, he's *huge*. If he decided he wanted to escape out of the back of Harry's truck, the only way we could stop him would be to shoot him dead. And a guy like that would take a lot of killing, even with a .45. Suppose we weren't able to put him down? And suppose he killed someone else? I'd hate losing my job, and I'd hate going to jail—I got a wife and kids depending on me to put bread in their mouths—but I don't think I'd hate either of those things near as much as having another dead little girl on my conscience."

"That won't happen," I said.

"How in God's name can you be so sure of that?"

I didn't answer. I didn't know just how to begin. I had known this would come up, of course I did, but I still didn't know how to start telling them what I knew. Brutal helped me.

"You don't think he did it, do you, Paul?" He looked incredulous. "You think that big lug is innocent."

"I'm positive he's innocent," I said.

"How in the name of Jesus *can* you be?"

"There are two things," I said. "One of them is my shoe." I leaned forward over the table and began talking.

PART FIVE

NIGHT
JOURNEY

1

MR. H. G. WELLS once wrote a story about a man who invented a time machine, and I have discovered that, in the writing of these memoirs, I have created my own time machine. Unlike Wells's, it can only travel into the past—back to 1932, as a matter of fact, when I was the bull-goose screw in E Block of Cold Mountain State Penitentiary—but it's eerily efficient, for all that. Still, this time machine reminds me of the old Ford I had in those days: you could be sure that it would start eventually, but you never knew if a turn of the key would be enough to fire the motor, or if you were going to have to get out and crank until your arm practically fell off.

I've had a lot of easy starts since I started telling the story of John Coffey, but yesterday I had to crank. I think it was because I'd gotten to Delacroix's execution, and part of my mind didn't want to have to relive that. It was a bad death, a *terrible* death, and it happened the way it did because of Percy Wetmore, a young man who loved to comb his hair but couldn't stand to be laughed at—not even by a half-bald little Frenchman who was never going to see another Christmas.

As with most dirty jobs, however, the hardest part is just getting started. It doesn't matter to an engine whether you use the key or have to crank; once you get it going, it'll usually run just as sweet either way. That's how it worked for me yesterday. At first the words came in little bursts of phrasing, then in whole sentences, then in a torrent. Writing is a special and rather terrifying form of remembrance, I've discovered—there is a totality to it that seems almost like rape. Perhaps I only feel that way because I've become a very old man (a thing that happened behind my own back, I sometimes feel), but I don't think so. I believe that the combination of pencil and memory creates a kind of practical magic, and magic is dangerous. As a man who knew John Coffey and saw what he could do—to mice and to men—I feel very qualified to say that.

Magic is dangerous.

In any case, I wrote all day yesterday, the words simply flooding out of me, the sunroom of this glorified old folks' home gone, replaced by the storage room at the end of the Green Mile where so many of my problem children took their last sit-me-downs, and the bottom of the stairs which led to the tunnel under the road. That was where Dean and Harry and Brutal and I confronted Percy Wetmore over Eduard Delacroix's smoking body and made Percy renew his promise to put in for transfer to the Briar Ridge state mental facility.

There are always fresh flowers in the sunroom, but by noon yesterday all I could smell was the noxious aroma of the dead man's cooked flesh. The sound of the power mower on the lawn down below had been replaced by the hollow plink of dripping water as it seeped slowly through the tunnel's curved roof. The trip was on. I had travelled back to 1932, in soul and mind, if not body.

I skipped lunch, wrote until four o'clock or so, and when I finally put my pencil down, my hand was aching. I walked slowly down to the end of the second-floor corridor. There's a window there that looks out on the employee parking lot. Brad Dolan, the orderly who reminds me of Percy—and the one who is altogether too curious about where I go and what I do on my walks—drives an old Chevrolet with a bumper sticker that says I HAVE SEEN GOD AND HIS NAME IS NEWT. It was gone; Brad's shift was over and he'd taken himself off to whatever garden spot he calls home. I envision an Airstream trailer with *Hustler* gatefolds Scotch-taped to the walls and Dixie Beer cans in the corners.

I went out through the kitchen, where dinner preparations were getting started. "What you got in that bag, Mr. Edgecombe?" Norton asked me.

"It's an empty bottle," I said. "I've discovered the Fountain of Youth down there in the woods. I pop down every afternoon about this time and draw a little. I drink it at bedtime. Good stuff, I can tell you."

"May be keepin you young," said George, the other cook, "but it ain't doin *shit* for your looks."

We all had a laugh at that, and I went out. I found myself looking around for Dolan even though his car was gone, called myself a chump for letting him get so far under my skin, and crossed the croquet course. Beyond it is a scraggy little putting green that looks ever so much nicer in the Georgia Pines brochures, and beyond that is a path that winds into the little copse of woods east of the nursing home. There are a couple of old sheds along this path, neither of them used for anything these days. At the second, which stands close to the high stone wall between the Georgia Pines grounds and Georgia Highway 47, I went in and stayed for a little while.

I ate a good dinner that night, watched a little TV, and went to bed early. On many nights I'll wake up and creep back down to the TV room, where I watch old movies on the American Movie Channel. Not last night, though; last night I slept like a stone, and with none of the dreams that have so haunted me since I started my adventures in literature. All that writing must have worn me out; I'm not as young as I used to be, you know.

When I woke and saw that the patch of sun which usually lies on the floor at six in the morning had made it all the way up to the foot of my bed, I hit the deck in a hurry, so alarmed I hardly noticed the arthritic flare of pain in my hips and knees and ankles. I dressed as fast as I could, then hurried down the hall to the window that overlooks the employees' parking lot, hoping the slot where Dolan parks his old Chevrolet would still be empty. Sometimes he's as much as half an hour late—

No such luck. The car was there, gleaming rustily in the morning sun. Because Mr. Brad Dolan has something to arrive on time for these days, doesn't he? Yes. Old Paulie Edgecombe goes somewhere in the early mornings, old Paulie Edgecombe is up to something, and Mr. Brad Dolan intends to find out what it is. *What do you do down there, Paulie? Tell me.* He would likely be watching for me already. It would be smart to stay right where I was . . . except I couldn't.

"Paul?"

I turned around so fast I almost fell down. It was my friend Elaine Connelly. Her eyes widened and she put out her hands, as if to catch me. Lucky for her I caught my balance; Elaine's arthritis is terrible, and I probably would have broken her in two like a dry stick if I'd fallen into her arms. Romance doesn't die when you pass into the strange country that lies beyond eighty, but you can forget the *Gone with the Wind* crap.

"I'm sorry," she said. "I didn't mean to startle you."

"That's all right," I said, and gave her a feeble smile. "It's a better wake-up than a faceful of cold water. I should hire you to do it every morning."

"You were looking for his car, weren't you? Dolan's car."

There was no sense kidding her about it, so I nodded. "I wish I could be sure he's over in the west wing. I'd like to slip out for a little while, but I don't want him to see me."

She smiled—a ghost of the teasing imp's smile she must have had as a girl. "Nosy bastard, isn't he?"

"Yes."

"He's not in the west wing, either. I've already been down to breakfast, sleepyhead, and I can tell you where he is, because I peeked. He's in the kitchen."

I looked at her, dismayed. I had known Dolan was curious, but not how curious.

"Can you put your morning walk off?" Elaine asked.

I thought about it. "*I could*, I suppose, but . . ."

"You shouldn't."

"No. I shouldn't."

Now, I thought, *she'll ask me where I go, what I have to do down in those woods that's so damned important.*

But she didn't. Instead she gave me that imp's smile again. It looked strange and absolutely wonderful on her too-gaunt, pain-haunted face. "Do you know Mr. Howland?" she asked.

"Sure," I said, although I didn't see him much; he was in the west wing, which at Georgia Pines was almost like a neighboring country. "Why?"

"Do you know what's special about him?"

I shook my head.

"Mr. Howland," Elaine said, smiling more widely than ever, "is one of only five residents left at Georgia Pines who have permission to smoke. That's because he was a resident before the rules changed."

A grandfather clause, I thought. And what place was more fitted for one than an old-age home?

She reached into the pocket of her blue-and-white-striped dress and pulled two items partway out: a cigarette and a book of matches. "Thief of green, thief of red," she sang in a lilting, funny voice. "Little Ellie's going to wet the bed."

"Elaine, what—"

"Walk an old girl downstairs," she said, putting the cigarette and matches back into her pocket and taking my arm in one of her gnarled hands. We began to walk back down the hall. As we did, I decided to give up and put myself in her hands. She was old and brittle, but not stupid.

As we went down, walking with the glassy care of the relics we have now become, Elaine said: "Wait at the foot. I'm going over to the west wing, to the hall toilet there. You know the one I mean, don't you?"

"Yes," I said. "The one just outside the spa. But why?"

"I haven't had a cigarette in over fifteen years," she said, "but I feel like one this morning. I don't know how many puffs it'll take to set off the smoke detector in there, but I intend to find out."

I looked at her with dawning admiration, thinking how much she reminded me of my wife—Jan might have done exactly the same thing. Elaine looked back at me, smiling her saucy imp's smile. I cupped my hand around the back of her lovely long neck, drew her face to mine, and kissed her mouth lightly. "I love you, Ellie," I said.

"Oooh, such big talk," she said, but I could tell she was pleased.

"What about Chuck Howland?" I asked. "Is he going to get in trouble?"

"No, because he's in the TV room, watching *Good Morning America* with about two dozen other folks. And I'm going to make myself scarce as soon as the smoke detector turns on the west-wing fire alarm."

"Don't you fall down and hurt yourself, woman. I'd never forgive myself if—"

"Oh, stop your fussing," she said, and this time *she* kissed *me*. Love among the ruins. It probably sounds funny to some of you and grotesque to the rest of you, but I'll tell you something, my friend: weird love's better than no love at all.

I watched her walk away, moving slowly and stiffly (but she will only use a cane on wet days, and only then if the pain is terrible; it's one of her vanities), and waited. Five minutes went by, then ten, and just as I was deciding she had either lost her courage or discovered that the battery of the smoke detector in the toilet was dead, the fire alarm went off in the west wing with a loud, buzzing burr.

I started toward the kitchen at once, but slowly—there was no reason to hurry until I was sure Dolan was out of my way. A gaggle of old folks, most still in their robes, came out of the TV room (here it's called the Resource Center; now *that's* grotesque) to see what was going on. Chuck Howland was among them, I was happy to see.

"Edgecombe!" Kent Avery rasped, hanging onto his walker with one hand and yanking obsessively at the crotch of his pajama pants with the other. "Real alarm or just another falsie? What do you think?"

"No way of knowing, I guess," I said.

Just about then three orderlies went trotting past, all headed for the west wing, yelling at the folks clustered around the TV-room door to go outside and wait for the all-clear. The third in line was Brad Dolan. He didn't even look at me as he went past, a fact that pleased me to no end. As I went on down toward the kitchen, it occurred to me that the team of Elaine Connelly and Paul Edgecombe would probably be a match for a dozen Brad Dolans, with half a dozen Percy Wetmores thrown in for good measure.

The cooks in the kitchen were continuing to clear up breakfast, paying no attention to the howling fire alarm at all.

"Say, Mr. Edgecombe," George said. "I believe Brad Dolan been lookin for you. In fact, you just missed him."

Lucky me, I thought. What I said out loud was that I'd probably see

Mr. Dolan later. Then I asked if there was any leftover toast lying around from breakfast.

"Sure," Norton said, "but it's stone-cold dead in the market. You runnin late this morning?"

"I am," I agreed, "but I'm hungry."

"Only take a minute to make some fresh and hot," George said, reaching for the bread.

"Nope, cold will be fine," I said, and when he handed me a couple of slices (looking mystified—actually both of them looked mystified), I hurried out the door, feeling like the boy I once was, skipping school to go fishing with a jelly fold-over wrapped in waxed paper slipped into the front of my shirt.

Outside the kitchen door I took a quick, reflexive look around for Dolan, saw nothing to alarm me, and hurried across the croquet course and putting green, gnawing on one of my pieces of toast as I went. I slowed a little as I entered the shelter of the woods, and as I walked down the path, I found my mind turning to the day after Eduard Delacroix's terrible execution.

I had spoken to Hal Moores that morning, and he had told me that Melinda's brain tumor had caused her to lapse into bouts of cursing and foul language ... what my wife had later labelled (rather tentatively; she wasn't sure it was really the same thing) as Tourette's Syndrome. The quavering in his voice, coupled with the memory of how John Coffey had healed both my urinary infection and the broken back of Delacroix's pet mouse, had finally pushed me over the line that runs between just thinking about a thing and actually *doing* a thing.

And there was something else. Something that had to do with John Coffey's hands, and my shoe.

So I had called the men I worked with, the men I had trusted my life to over the years—Dean Stanton, Harry Terwilliger, Brutus Howell. They came to lunch at my house on the day after Delacroix's execution, and they at least listened to me when I outlined my plan. Of course, they all knew that Coffey had healed the mouse; Brutal had actually seen it. So when I suggested that another miracle might result if we took John

Coffey to Melinda Moores, they didn't outright laugh. It was Dean Stanton who raised the most troubling question: What if John Coffey escaped while we had him out on his field-trip?

"Suppose he killed someone else?" Dean asked. "I'd hate losing my job, and I'd hate going to jail—I got a wife and kids depending on me to put bread in their mouths—but I don't think I'd hate either of those things near as much as having another little dead girl on my conscience."

There was silence, then, all of them looking at me, waiting to see how I'd respond. I knew everything would change if I said what was on the tip of my tongue; we had reached a point beyond which retreat would likely become impossible.

Except retreat, for me, at least, was already impossible. I opened my mouth and said

2

"That won't happen."

"How in God's name can you be so sure?" Dean asked.

I didn't answer. I didn't know just how to begin. I had known this would come up, of course I had, but I still didn't know how to start telling them what was in my head and heart. Brutal helped.

"You don't think he did it, do you, Paul?" He looked incredulous. "You think that big lug is innocent."

"I'm positive he's innocent," I said.

"How *can* you be?"

"There are two things," I said. "One of them is my shoe."

"Your *shoe*?" Brutal exclaimed. "What has your *shoe* got to do with whether or not John Coffey killed those two little girls?"

"I took off one of my shoes and gave it to him last night," I said. "After the execution, this was, when things had settled back down a little. I pushed it through the bars, and he picked it up in those big hands of his. I told him to tie it. I had to make sure, you see, because all our problem children normally wear is slippers—a man who really wants to commit suicide can do it with shoelaces, if he's dedicated. That's something all of us know."

They were nodding.

"He put it on his lap and got the ends of the laces crossed over all right, but then he was stuck. He said he was pretty sure someone had showed him how to do it when he was a lad—maybe his father or maybe one of the boyfriends his mother had after the father was gone—but he'd forgot the knack."

267

"I'm with Brutal—I still don't see what your shoe has to do with whether or not Coffey killed the Detterick twins," Dean said.

So I went over the story of the abduction and murder again—what I'd read that hot day in the prison library with my groin sizzling and Gibbons snoring in the corner, and all that the reporter, Hammersmith, told me later.

"The Dettericks' dog wasn't much of a biter, but it was a world-class barker," I said. "The man who took the girls kept it quiet by feeding it sausages. He crept a little closer every time he gave it one, I imagine, and while the mutt was eating the last one, he reached out, grabbed it by the head, and twisted. Broke its neck.

"Later, when they caught up with Coffey, the deputy in charge of the posse—Rob McGee, his name was—spotted a bulge in the chest pocket of the biballs Coffey was wearing. McGee thought at first it might be a gun. Coffey said it was a lunch, and that's what it turned out to be—a couple of sandwiches and a pickle, wrapped up in newspaper and tied with butcher's string. Coffey couldn't remember who gave it to him, only that it was a woman wearing an apron."

"Sandwiches and a pickle but no sausages," Brutal said.

"No sausages," I agreed.

"Course not," Dean said. "He fed those to the dog."

"Well, that's what the prosecutor said at the trial," I agreed, "but if Coffey opened his lunch and fed the sausages to the dog, how'd he tie the newspaper back up again with that butcher's twine? I don't know when he even would have had the chance, but leave that out of it, for the time being. This man can't even tie a simple granny knot."

There was a long moment of thunderstruck silence, broken at last by Brutus. "Holy shit," he said in a low voice. "How come no one brought that up at the trial?"

"Nobody thought of it," I said, and found myself again thinking of Hammersmith, the reporter—Hammersmith who had been to college in Bowling Green, Hammersmith who liked to think of himself as enlightened, Hammersmith who had told me that mongrel dogs and Negroes were about the same, that either might take a chomp out of you suddenly, and for no reason. Except he kept calling them *your*

Negroes, as if they were still property . . . but not *his* property. No, not his. Never his. And at that time, the South was full of Hammersmiths. "Nobody was really *equipped* to think of it, Coffey's own attorney included."

"But *you* did," Harry said. "Goddam, boys, we're sittin here with Mr. Sherlock Holmes." He sounded simultaneously joshing and awed.

"Oh, put a cork in it," I said. "I wouldn't have thought of it either, if I hadn't put together what he told Deputy McGee that day with what he said after he cured my infection, and what he said after he healed the mouse."

"What?" Dean asked.

"When I went into his cell, it was like I was hypnotized. I didn't feel like I could have stopped doing what he wanted, even if I'd tried."

"I don't like the sound of that," Harry said, and shifted uneasily in his seat.

"I asked him what he wanted, and he said 'Just to help.' I remember that very clearly. And when it was over and I was better, he knew. 'I helped it,' he said. 'I helped it, didn't I?' "

Brutal was nodding. "Just like with the mouse. You said 'You helped it,' and Coffey said it back to you like he was a parrot. 'I helped Del's mouse.' Is that when you knew? It was, wasn't it?"

"Yeah, I guess so. I remembered what he said to McGee when McGee asked him what had happened. It was in every story about the murders, just about. 'I couldn't help it. I tried to take it back, but it was too late.' A man saying a thing like that with two little dead girls in his arms, them white and blonde, him as big as a house, no wonder they got it wrong. They heard what he was saying in a way that would agree with what they were seeing, and what they were seeing was black. They thought he was confessing, that he was saying he'd had a compulsion to take those girls, rape them, and kill them. That he'd come to his senses and tried to stop—"

"But by then it was too late," Brutal murmured.

"Yes. Except what he was *really* trying to tell them was that he'd found them, tried to heal them—to bring them back—and had no success. They were too far gone in death."

"Paul, do you believe that?" Dean asked. "Do you really, honest-to-God believe that?"

I examined my heart as well as I could one final time, then nodded my head. Not only did I know it now, there was an intuitive part of me that had known something wasn't right with John Coffey's situation from the very beginning, when Percy had come onto the block hauling on Coffey's arm and blaring "Dead man walking!" at the top of his lungs. I had shaken hands with him, hadn't I? I had never shaken the hand of a man coming on the Green Mile before, but I had shaken Coffey's.

"Jesus," Dean said. "Good Jesus Christ."

"Your shoe's one thing," Harry said. "What's the other?"

"Not long before the posse found Coffey and the girls, the men came out of the woods near the south bank of the Trapingus River. They found a patch of flattened-down grass there, a lot of blood, and the rest of Cora Detterick's nightie. The dogs got confused for a bit. Most wanted to go southeast, downstream along the bank. But two of them—the coon-dogs—wanted to go *upstream*. Bobo Marchant was running the dogs, and when he gave the coonies a sniff of the night-gown, they turned with the others."

"The coonies got mixed up, didn't they?" Brutal asked. A strange, sickened little smile was playing around the corners of his mouth. "They ain't built to be trackers, strictly speaking, and they got mixed up on what their job was."

"Yes."

"I don't get it," Dean said.

"The coonies forgot whatever it was Bobo ran under their noses to get them started," Brutal said. "By the time they came out on the riverbank, the coonies were tracking the *killer*, not the girls. That wasn't a problem as long as the killer and the girls were together, but . . ."

The light was dawning in Dean's eyes. Harry had already gotten it.

"When you think about it," I said, "you wonder how anybody, even a jury wanting to pin the crime on a wandering black fellow, could have believed John Coffey was their man for even a minute. Just the idea of keeping the dog quiet with food until he could snap its neck would have been beyond Coffey.

"He was never any closer to the Detterick farm than the south bank of the Trapingus, that's what I think. Six or more miles away. He was just mooning along, maybe meaning to go down to the railroad tracks and catch a freight to somewhere else—when they come off the trestle, they're going slow enough to hop—when he heard a commotion to the north."

"The killer?" Brutal asked.

"The killer. He might have raped them already, or maybe the rape was what Coffey heard. In any case, that bloody patch in the grass was where the killer finished the business; dashed their heads together, dropped them, and then hightailed it."

"Hightailed it northwest," Brutal said. "The direction the coon-dogs wanted to go."

"Right. John Coffey comes through a stand of alders that grows a little way southeast of the spot where the girls were left, probably curious about all the noise, and he finds their bodies. One of them might still have been alive; I suppose it's possible both of them were, although not for much longer. John Coffey wouldn't have known if they were dead, that's for sure. All he knows is that he's got a healing power in his hands, and he tried to use it on Cora and Kathe Detterick. When it didn't work, he broke down, crying and hysterical. Which is how they found him."

"Why didn't he stay there, where he found them?" Brutal asked. "Why take them south along the riverbank? Any idea?"

"I bet he did stay put, at first," I said. "At the trial, they kept talking about a *big* trampled area, all the grass squashed flat. And John Coffey's a big man."

"John Coffey's a fucking giant," Harry said, pitching his voice very low so my wife wouldn't hear him cuss if she happened to be listening.

"Maybe he panicked when he saw that what he was doing wasn't working. Or maybe he got the idea that the killer was still there, in the woods upstream, watching him. Coffey's big, you know, but not real brave. Harry, remember him asking if we left a light on in the block after bedtime?"

"Yeah. I remember thinking how funny that was, what with the size of him." Harry looked shaken and thoughtful.

"Well, if he didn't kill the little girls, who did?" Dean asked.

I shook my head. "Someone else. Someone *white* would be my best guess. The prosecutor made a big deal about how it would have taken a strong man to kill a dog as big as the one the Dettericks kept, but—"

"That's crap," Brutus rumbled. "A strong twelve-year-old girl could break a big dog's neck, if she took the dog by surprise and knew where to grab. If Coffey didn't do it, it could have been damned near anyone . . . any man, that is. We'll probably never know."

I said, "Unless he does it again."

"We wouldn't know even then, if he did it down Texas or over in California," Harry said.

Brutal leaned back, screwed his fists into his eyes like a tired child, then dropped them into his lap again. "This is a nightmare," he said. "We've got a man who may be innocent—who probably *is* innocent—and he's going to walk the Green Mile just as sure as God made tall trees and little fishes. What are we supposed to do about it? If we start in with that healing-fingers shit, everyone is going to laugh their asses off, and he'll end up in the Fry-O-Lator just the same."

"Let's worry about that later," I said, because I didn't have the slightest idea how to answer him. "The question right now is what we do—or don't do—about Melly. I'd say step back and take a few days to think it over, but I believe every day we wait raises the chances that he won't be able to help her."

"Remember him holding his hands out for the mouse?" Brutal asked. " 'Give im to me while there's still time,' he said. *While there's still time.*"

"I remember."

Brutal considered, then nodded. "I'm in. I feel bad about Del, too, but mostly I think I just want to see what happens when he touches her. Probably nothing will, but maybe . . ."

"I doubt like hell we even get the big dummy off the block," Harry said, then sighed and nodded. "But who gives a shit? Count me in."

"Me, too," Dean said. "Who stays on the block, Paul? Do we draw straws for it?"

"No, sir," I said. "No straws. You stay."

"Just like that? The hell you say!" Dean replied, hurt and angry. He whipped off his spectacles and began to polish them furiously on his shirt. "What kind of a bum deal is that?"

"The kind you get if you're young enough to have kids still in school," Brutal said. "Harry and me's bachelors. Paul's married, but his kids are grown and off on their own, at least. This is a *mucho* crazy stunt we're planning here; I think we're almost sure to get caught." He gazed at me soberly. "One thing you didn't mention, Paul, is that if we do manage to get him out of the slam and then Coffey's healing fingers don't work, Hal Moores is apt to turn us in himself." He gave me a chance to reply to this, maybe to rebut it, but I couldn't and so I kept my mouth shut. Brutal turned back to Dean and went on. "Don't get me wrong, you're apt to lose your job, too, but at least you'd have a chance to get clear of prison if the heat really came down. Percy's going to think it was a prank; if you're on the duty desk, you can say you thought the same thing and we never told you any different."

"I still don't like it," Dean said, but it was clear he'd go along with it, like it or not. The thought of his kiddies had convinced him. "And it's to be tonight? You're sure?"

"If we're going to do it, it had *better* be tonight," Harry said. "If I get a chance to think about it, I'll most likely lose my nerve."

"Let me be the one to go by the infirmary," Dean said. "I can do that much at least, can't I?"

"As long as you can do what needs doing without getting caught," Brutal said.

Dean looked offended, and I clapped him on the shoulder. "As soon after you clock in as you can . . . all right?"

"You bet."

My wife popped her head through the door as if I'd given her a cue to do so. "Who's for more iced tea?" she asked brightly. "What about you, Brutus?"

"No, thanks," he said. "What I'd like is a good hard knock of whiskey, but under the circumstances, that might not be a good idea."

Janice looked at me; smiling mouth, worried eyes. "What are you getting these boys into, Paul?" But before I could even think of framing a reply, she raised her hand and said, "Never mind, I don't want to know."

3

LATER, LONG AFTER the others were gone and while I was dressing for work, she took me by the arm, swung me around, and looked into my eyes with fierce intensity.

"Melinda?" she asked.

I nodded.

"Can you do something for her, Paul? Really do something for her, or is it all wishful dreaming brought on by what you saw last night?"

I thought of Coffey's eyes, of Coffey's hands, and of the hypnotized way I'd gone to him when he'd wanted me. I thought of him holding out his hands for Mr. Jingles's broken, dying body. *While there's still time,* he had said. And the black swirling things that turned white and disappeared.

"I think we might be the only chance she has left," I said at last.

"Then take it," she said, buttoning the front of my new fall coat. It had been in the closet since my birthday at the beginning of September, but this was only the third or fourth time I'd actually worn it. "Take it."

And she practically pushed me out the door.

4

I CLOCKED IN that night—in many ways the strangest night of my entire life—at twenty past six. I thought I could still smell the faint, lingering odor of burned flesh on the air. It had to be an illusion—the doors to the outside, both on the block and in the storage room, had been open most of the day, and the previous two shifts had spent hours scrubbing in there—but that didn't change what my nose was telling me, and I didn't think I could have eaten any dinner even if I hadn't been scared almost to death about the evening which lay ahead.

Brutal came on the block at quarter to seven, Dean at ten 'til. I asked Dean if he would go over to the infirmary and see if they had a heating pad for my back, which I seemed to have strained that early morning, helping to carry Delacroix's body down into the tunnel. Dean said he'd be happy to. I believe he wanted to tip me a wink, but restrained himself.

Harry clocked on at three minutes to seven.

"The truck?" I asked.

"Where we talked about."

So far, so good. There followed a little passage of time when we stood by the duty desk, drinking coffee and studiously not mentioning what we were all thinking and hoping: that Percy was late, that maybe Percy wasn't going to show up at all. Considering the hostile reviews he'd gotten on the way he'd handled the electrocution, that seemed at least possible.

But Percy apparently subscribed to that old axiom about how you should get right back on the horse that had thrown you, because here he came through the door at six minutes past seven, resplendent in his blue uniform, with his sidearm on one hip and his hickory stick in its ridiculous custom-made holster on the other. He punched his time-card, then looked around at us warily (except for Dean, who hadn't come back from the infirmary yet). "My starter busted," he said. "I had to crank."

"Aw," Harry said, "po' baby."

"Should have stayed home and got the cussed thing fixed," Brutal said blandly. "We wouldn't want you straining your arm none, would we, boys?"

"Yeah, you'd like that, wouldn't you?" Percy sneered, but I thought he seemed reassured by the relative mildness of Brutal's response. That was good. For the next few hours we'd have to walk a line with him—not too hostile, but not too friendly, either. After last night, he'd find anything even approaching warmth suspect. We weren't going to get him with his guard down, we all knew that, but I thought we could catch him with it a long piece from all the way up if we played things just right. It was important that we move fast, but it was also important—to me, at least—that nobody be hurt. Not even Percy Wetmore.

Dean came back and gave me a little nod.

"Percy," I said, "I want you to go on in the storeroom and mop down the floor. Stairs to the tunnel, too. Then you can write your report on last night."

"*That* should be creative," Brutal remarked, hooking his thumbs into his belt and looking up at the ceiling.

"You guys are funnier'n a fuck in church," Percy said, but beyond that he didn't protest. Didn't even point out the obvious, which was that the floor in there had already been washed at least twice that day. My guess is that he was glad for the chance to be away from us.

I went over the previous shift report, saw nothing that concerned me, and then took a walk down to Wharton's cell. He was sitting there on his bunk with his knees drawn up and his arms clasped around his shins, looking at me with a bright, hostile smile.

"Well, if it ain't the big boss," he said. "Big as life and twice as ugly.

You look happier'n a pig knee-deep in shit, Boss Edgecombe. Wife give your pecker a pull before you left home, did she?"

"How you doing, Kid?" I asked evenly, and at that he brightened for real. He let go of his legs, stood up, and stretched. His smile broadened, and some of the hostility went out of it.

"Well, damn!" he said. "You got my name right for once! What's the matter with you, Boss Edgecombe? You sick or sumpin?"

No, not sick. I'd *been* sick, but John Coffey had taken care of that. His hands no longer knew the trick of tying a shoe, if they ever had, but they knew other tricks. Yes indeed they did.

"My friend," I told him, "if you want to be a Billy the Kid instead of a Wild Bill, it's all the same to me."

He puffed visibly, like one of those loathsome fish that live in South American rivers and can sting you almost to death with the spines along their backs and sides. I dealt with a lot of dangerous men during my time on the Mile, but few if any so repellent as William Wharton, who considered himself a great outlaw, but whose jailhouse behavior rarely rose above pissing or spitting through the bars of his cell. So far we hadn't given him the awed respect he felt was his by right, but on that particular night I wanted him tractable. If that meant lathering on the soft-soap, I would gladly lather it on.

"I got a lot in common with the Kid, and you just better believe it," Wharton said. "I didn't get here for stealing candy out of a dimestore." As proud as a man who's been conscripted into the Heroes' Brigade of the French Foreign Legion instead of one whose ass has been slammed into a cell seventy long steps from the electric chair. "Where's my supper?"

"Come on, Kid, report says you had it at five-fifty. Meatloaf with gravy, mashed, peas. You don't con me that easy."

He laughed expansively and sat down on his bunk again. "Put on the radio, then." He said radio in the way people did back then when they were joking, so it rhymed with the fifties slang word "Daddy-O." It's funny how much a person can remember about times when his nerves were tuned so tight they almost sang.

"Maybe later, big boy," I said. I stepped away from his cell and looked down the corridor. Brutal had strolled down to the far end, where he checked to make sure the restraint-room door was on the single lock instead of the double. I knew it was, because I'd already checked it myself. Later on, we'd want to be able to open that door as quickly as we could. There would be no time spent emptying out the attic-type rick-rack that had accumulated in there over the years; we'd taken it out, sorted it, and stored it in other places not long after Wharton joined our happy band. It had seemed to us the room with the soft walls was apt to get a lot of use, at least until "Billy the Kid" strolled the Mile.

John Coffey, who would usually have been lying down at this time, long, thick legs dangling and face to the wall, was sitting on the end of his bunk with his hands clasped, watching Brutal with an alertness—a *thereness*—that wasn't typical of him. He wasn't leaking around the eyes, either.

Brutal tried the door to the restraint room, then came on back up the Mile. He glanced at Coffey as he passed Coffey's cell, and Coffey said a curious thing: "Sure. I'd *like* a ride." As if responding to something Brutal had said.

Brutal's eyes met mine. *He knows,* I could almost hear him saying. *Somehow he knows.*

I shrugged and spread my hands, as if to say *Of course he knows.*

5

OLD TOOT-TOOT made his last trip of the night down to E Block with his cart at about quarter to nine. We bought enough of his crap to make him smile with avarice.

"Say, you boys seen that mouse?" he asked.

We shook our heads.

"Maybe Pretty Boy has," Toot said, and gestured with his head in the direction of the storage room, where Percy was either washing the floor, writing his report, or picking his ass.

"What do you care? It's none of your affair, either way," Brutal said. "Roll wheels, Toot. You're stinkin the place up."

Toot smiled his peculiarly unpleasant smile, toothless and sunken, and made a business of sniffing the air. "That ain't me you smell," he said. "That be Del, sayin so-long."

Cackling, he rolled his cart out the door and into the exercise yard. And he went on rolling it for another ten years, long after I was gone—hell, long after Cold Mountain was gone—selling Moon Pies and pops to the guards and prisoners who could afford them. Sometimes even now I hear him in my dreams, yelling that he's fryin, he's fryin, he's a done tom turkey.

The time stretched out after Toot was gone, the clock seeming to crawl. We had the radio for an hour and a half, Wharton braying laughter at Fred Allen and *Allen's Alley*, even though I doubt like hell he understood many of the jokes. John Coffey sat on the end of his bunk, hands clasped, eyes rarely leaving whoever was at the duty desk.

I have seen men waiting that way in bus stations for their buses to be called.

Percy came in from the storage room around quarter to eleven and handed me a report which had been laboriously written in pencil. Eraser-crumbs lay over the sheet of paper in gritty smears. He saw me run my thumb over one of these, and said hastily: "That's just a first pass, like. I'm going to copy it over. What do you think?"

What I thought was that it was the most outrageous goddam whitewash I'd read in all my born days. What I told him was that it was fine, and he went away, satisfied.

Dean and Harry played cribbage, talking too loud, squabbling over the count too often, and looking at the crawling hands of the clock every five seconds or so. On at least one of their games that night, they appeared to go around the board three times instead of twice. There was so much tension in the air that I felt I could almost have carved it like clay, and the only people who didn't seem to feel it were Percy and Wild Bill.

When it got to be ten of twelve, I could stand it no longer and gave Dean a little nod. He went into my office with a bottle of R.C. Cola bought off Toot's cart, and came back out a minute or two later. The cola was now in a tin cup, which a prisoner can't break and then slash with.

I took it and glanced around. Harry, Dean, and Brutal were all watching me. So, for that matter, was John Coffey. Not Percy, though. Percy had returned to the storage room, where he probably felt more at ease on this particular night. I gave the tin cup a quick sniff and got no odor except for the R.C., which had an odd but pleasant cinnamon smell back in those days.

I took it down to Wharton's cell. He was lying on his bunk. He wasn't masturbating—yet, anyway—but had raised quite a boner inside his shorts and was giving it a good healthy twang every now and again, like a dopey bass-fiddler hammering an extra-thick E-string.

"Kid," I said.

"Don't bother me," he said.

"Okay," I agreed. "I brought you a pop for behaving like a human being all night—damn near a record for you—but I'll just drink it myself."

I made as if to do just that, raising the tin cup (battered all up and down the sides from many angry bangings on many sets of cell bars) to my lips. Wharton was off the bunk in a flash, which didn't surprise me. It wasn't a high-risk bluff; most deep cons—lifers, rapists, and the men slated for Old Sparky—are pigs for their sweets, and this one was no exception.

"Gimme that, you clunk," Wharton said. He spoke as if he were the foreman and I was just another lowly peon. "Give it to the Kid."

I held it just outside the bars, letting him be the one to reach through. Doing it the other way around is a recipe for disaster, as any long-time prison screw will tell you. That was the kind of stuff we thought of without even knowing we were thinking of it—the way we knew not to let the cons call us by our first names, the way we knew that the sound of rapidly jingling keys meant trouble on the block, because it was the sound of a prison guard running and prison guards *never* run unless there's trouble in the valley. Stuff Percy Wetmore was never going to get wise to.

Tonight, however, Wharton had no interest in grabbing or choking. He snatched the tin cup, downed the pop in three long swallows, then voiced a resounding belch. *"Excellent!"* he said.

I held my hand out. "Cup."

He held it for a moment, teasing with his eyes. "Suppose I keep it?"

I shrugged. "We'll come in and take it back. You'll go down to the little room. And you will have drunk your last R.C. Unless they serve it down in hell, that is."

His smile faded. "I don't like jokes about hell, screwtip." He thrust the cup out through the bars. "Here. Take it."

I took it. From behind me, Percy said: "Why in God's name did you want to give a lugoon like him a soda-pop?"

Because it was loaded with enough infirmary dope to put him on his back for forty-eight hours, and he never tasted a thing, I thought.

"With Paul," Brutal said, "the quality of mercy is not strained; it droppeth like the gentle rain from heaven."

"Huh?" Percy asked, frowning.

"Means he's a soft touch. Always has been, always will be. Want to play a game of Crazy Eights, Percy?"

Percy snorted. "Except for Go Fish and Old Maid, that's the stupidest card-game ever made."

"That's why I thought you might like a few hands," Brutal said, smiling sweetly.

"Everybody's a wisenheimer," Percy said, and sulked off into my office. I didn't care much for the little rat parking his ass behind my desk, but I kept my mouth shut.

The clock crawled. Twelve-twenty; twelve-thirty. At twelve-forty, John Coffey got up off his bunk and stood at his cell door, hands grasping the bars loosely. Brutal and I walked down to Wharton's cell and looked in. He lay there on his bunk, smiling up at the ceiling. His eyes were open, but they looked like big glass balls. One hand lay on his chest; the other dangled limply off the side of his bunk, knuckles brushing the floor.

"Gosh," Brutal said, "from Billy the Kid to Willie the Weeper in less than an hour. I wonder how many of those morphine pills Dean put in that tonic."

"Enough," I said. There was a little tremble in my voice. I didn't know if Brutal heard it, but I sure did. "Come on. We're going to do it."

"You don't want to wait for beautiful there to pass out?"

"He's passed out now, Brute. He's just too buzzed to close his eyes."

"You're the boss." He looked around for Harry, but Harry was already there. Dean was sitting bolt-upright at the duty desk, shuffling the cards so hard and fast it was a wonder they didn't catch fire, throwing a little glance to his left, at my office, with every flutter-shuffle. Keeping an eye out for Percy.

"Is it time?" Harry asked. His long, horsey face was very pale above his blue uniform blouse, but he looked determined.

"Yes," I said. "If we're going through with it, it's time."

Harry crossed himself and kissed his thumb. Then he went down to the restraint room, unlocked it, and came back with the straitjacket. He handed it to Brutal. The three of us walked up the Green Mile. Coffey stood at his cell door, watching us go, and said not a word. When we reached the duty desk, Brutal put the straitjacket behind his back, which was broad enough to conceal it easily.

"Luck," Dean said. He was as pale as Harry, and looked just as determined.

Percy was behind my desk, all right, sitting in my chair and frowning over the book he'd been toting around with him the last few nights—not *Argosy* or *Stag* but *Caring for the Mental Patient in Institutions.* You would have thought, from the guilty, worried glance he threw our way when we walked in, that it had been *The Last Days of Sodom and Gomorrah.*

"What?" he asked, closing the book in a hurry. "What do you want?"

"To talk to you, Percy," I said, "that's all."

But he read a hell of a lot more than a desire to talk on our faces, and was up like a shot, hurrying—not quite running, but almost—toward the open door to the storeroom. He thought we had come to give him a ragging at the very least, and more likely a good roughing up.

Harry cut around behind him and blocked the doorway, arms folded on his chest.

"Saaay!" Percy turned to me, alarmed but trying not to show it. "What *is* this?"

"Don't ask, Percy," I said. I had thought I'd be okay—back to normal, anyway—once we actually got rolling on this crazy business, but it wasn't working out that way. I couldn't believe what I was doing. It was like a bad dream. I kept expecting my wife to shake me awake and tell me I'd been moaning in my sleep. "It'll be easier if you just go along with it."

"What's Howell got behind his back?" Percy asked in a ragged voice, turning to get a better look at Brutal.

"Nothing," Brutal said. "Well . . . *this*, I suppose—"

He whipped the straitjacket out and shook it beside one hip, like a matador shaking his cape to make the bull charge.

Percy's eyes widened, and he lunged. He meant to run, but Harry grabbed his arms and a lunge was all he was able to manage.

"Let go of me!" Percy shouted, trying to jerk out of Harry's grasp. It wasn't going to happen, Harry outweighed him by almost a hundred pounds and had the muscles of a man who spent most of his spare time plowing and chopping, but Percy gave it a good enough effort to drag Harry halfway across the room and to rough up the unpleasant green carpet I kept meaning to replace. For a moment I thought he was even going to get one arm free—panic can be one hell of a motivator.

"Settle down, Percy," I said. "It'll go easier if—"

"Don't you tell me to settle down, you ignoramus!" Percy yelled, jerking his shoulders and trying to free his arms. "Just get away from me! All of you! I know people! *Big* people! If you don't quit this, you'll have to go all the way to South Carolina just to get a meal in a soup kitchen!"

He gave another forward lunge and ran his upper thighs into my desk. The book he'd been reading, *Caring for the Mental Patient in Institutions*, gave a jump, and the smaller, pamphlet-sized book which had been hidden inside it popped out. No wonder Percy had looked guilty when we came in. It wasn't *The Last Days of Sodom and Gomorrah*, but it was the one we sometimes gave to inmates who were feeling especially horny and who had been well-behaved enough to deserve a treat. I've mentioned it, I think—the little cartoon book where Olive Oyl does everybody except Sweet Pea, the kid.

I found it sad that Percy had been in my office and pursuing such pallid porn, and Harry—what I could see of him from over Percy's straining shoulder—looked mildly disgusted, but Brutal hooted with laughter, and that took the fight out of Percy, at least for the time being.

"Oh Poicy," he said. "What would your mother say? For that matter, what would the governor say?"

Percy was blushing a dark red. "Just shut up. And leave my mother out of it."

Brutal tossed me the straitjacket and pushed his face up into Percy's. "Sure thing. Just stick out your arms like a good boy."

Percy's lips were trembling, and his eyes were too bright. He was, I realized, on the verge of tears. "I won't," he said in a childish, trembling voice, "and you can't make me." Then he raised his voice and began to scream for help. Harry winced and so did I. If we ever came close to just dropping the whole thing, it was then. We might have, except for

Brutal. He never hesitated. He stepped behind Percy so he was shoulder to shoulder with Harry, who still had Percy's hands pinned behind him. Brutal reached up and took Percy's ears in his hands.

"Stop that yelling," Brutal said. "Unless you want to have a pair of the world's most unique teabag caddies."

Percy quit yelling for help and just stood there, trembling and looking down at the cover of the crude cartoon book, which showed Popeye and Olive doing it in a creative way I had heard of but never tried. "Oooh, Popeye!" read the balloon over Olive's head. "Uck-uck-uck-uck!" read the one over Popeye's. He was still smoking his pipe.

"Hold out your arms," Brutal said, "and let's have no more foolishness about it. Do it now."

"I won't," Percy said. "I won't, and you can't make me."

"You're dead wrong about that, you know," Brutal said, then clamped down on Percy's ears and twisted them the way you might twist the dials on an oven. An oven that wasn't cooking the way you wanted. Percy let out a miserable shriek of pain and surprise that I would have given a great deal not to have heard. It wasn't *just* pain and surprise, you see; it was understanding. For the first time in his life, Percy was realizing that awful things didn't just happen to other people, those not fortunate enough to be related to the governor. I wanted to tell Brutal to stop, but of course I couldn't. Things had gone much too far for that. All I could do was to remind myself that Percy had put Delacroix through God knew what agonies simply because Delacroix had laughed at him. The reminder didn't go very far toward soothing the way I felt. Perhaps it might have, if I'd been built more along the lines of Percy.

"Stick those arms out there, honey," Brutal said, "or you get another."

Harry had already let go of young Mr. Wetmore. Sobbing like a little kid, the tears which had been standing in his eyes now spilling down his cheeks, Percy shot his hands out straight in front of him, like a sleepwalker in a movie comedy. I had the sleeves of the straitjacket up his arms in a trice. I hardly had it over his shoulders before Brutal had let go of Percy's ears and grabbed the straps hanging down from the jacket's cuffs. He yanked Percy's hands around to his sides, so that his arms were crossed tightly on his chest. Harry, meanwhile, did up the back and snapped the cross-straps. Once Percy gave in and stuck out his arms, the whole thing took less than ten seconds.

"Okay, hon," Brutal said. "Forward harch."

But he wouldn't. He looked at Brutal, then turned his terrified, streaming eyes on me. Nothing about his connections now, or how we'd have to go all the way to South Carolina just to get a free meal; he was far past that.

"Please," he whispered in a hoarse, wet voice. "Don't put me in with him, Paul."

Then I understood why he had panicked, why he'd fought us so hard. He thought we were going to put him in with Wild Bill Wharton; that his punishment for the dry sponge was to be a dry cornholing from the resident psychopath. Instead of feeling sympathy for Percy at this realization, I felt disgusted and a hardening of my resolve. He was, after all, judging us by the way he would have behaved, had our positions been reversed.

"Not Wharton," I said. "The restraint room, Percy. You're going to spend three or four hours in there, all by yourself in the dark, thinking about what you did to Del. It's probably too late for you to learn any new lessons about how people are supposed to behave—Brute thinks so, anyway—but I'm an optimist. Now move."

He did, muttering under his breath that we'd be sorry for this, plenty sorry, just wait and see, but on the whole he seemed relieved and reassured.

When we herded him out into the hall, Dean gave us a look of such wide-eyed surprise and dewy innocence that I could have laughed, if the business hadn't been so serious. I've seen better acting in backwoods Grange revues.

"Say, don't you think the joke's gone far enough?" Dean asked.

"You just shut up, if you know what's good for you," Brutal growled. These were lines we'd scripted at lunch, and that was just what they sounded like to me, scripted lines, but if Percy was scared enough and confused enough, they still might save Dean Stanton's job in a pinch. I myself didn't think so, but anything was possible. Any time I've doubted that, then or since, I just think about John Coffey, and Delacroix's mouse.

We ran Percy down the Green Mile, him stumbling and gasping for us to slow down, he was going to go flat on his face if we didn't slow down. Wharton was on his bunk, but we went by too fast for me to see if he was awake or asleep. John Coffey was standing at his cell door and watching. "You're a bad man and you deserve to go in that dark place," he said, but I don't think Percy heard him.

Into the restraint room we went, Percy's cheeks red and wet with tears, his eyes rolling into their sockets, his pampered locks all flopping down on his forehead. Harry pulled Percy's gun with one hand and his treasured hickory head-knocker with the other. "You'll get em back, don't worry," Harry said. He sounded a trifle embarrassed.

"I wish I could say the same about your job," Percy replied. "*All* your jobs. You can't do this to me! You *can't*!"

He was obviously prepared to go on in that vein for quite awhile, but we didn't have time to listen to his sermon. In my pocket was a roll of friction-tape, the thirties ancestor of the strapping-tape folks use today. Percy saw it and started to back away. Brutal grabbed him from behind and hugged him until I had slapped the tape over his mouth, winding the roll around to the back of his head, just to be sure. He was going to have a few less swatches of hair when the tape came off, and a pair of *seriously* chapped lips into the bargain, but I no longer much cared. I'd had a gutful of Percy Wetmore.

We backed away from him. He stood in the middle of the room, under the caged light, wearing the straitjacket, breathing through flared nostrils, and making muffled *mmmph! mmmph!* sounds from behind the tape. All in all, he looked as crazy as any other prisoner we'd ever jugged in that room.

"The quieter you are, the sooner you get out," I said. "Try to remember that, Percy."

"And if you get lonely, think about Olive Oyl," Harry advised. "Uck-uck-uck-uck."

Then we went out. I closed the door and Brutal locked it. Dean was standing a little way up the Mile, just outside of Coffey's cell. He had already put the master key in the top lock. The four of us looked at each other, no one saying anything. There was no need to. We had started the machinery; all we could do now was hope that it ran the course we had laid out instead of jumping the tracks somewhere along the line.

"You still want to go for that ride, John?" Brutal asked.

"Yes, sir," Coffey said. "I reckon."

"Good," Dean said. He turned the first lock, removed the key, and seated it in the second.

"Do we need to chain you up, John?" I asked.

Coffey appeared to think about this. "Can if you want to," he said at last. "Don't *need* to."

I nodded at Brutal, who opened the cell door, then turned to Harry, who was more or less pointing Percy's .45 at Coffey as Coffey emerged from his cell.

"Give those to Dean," I said.

Harry blinked like someone awakening from a momentary doze, saw Percy's gun and stick still in his hands, and passed them over to Dean. Coffey, meanwhile, hulked in the corridor with his bald skull almost brushing one of the caged overhead lights. Standing there with his hands in front of him and his shoulders sloped forward to either side of his barrel chest, he made me think again, as I had the first time I saw him, of a huge captured bear.

"Lock Percy's toys in the duty desk until we get back," I said.

"*If* we get back," Harry added.

"I will," Dean said to me, taking no notice of Harry.

"And if someone shows up—probably no one will, but if someone does—what do you say?"

"That Coffey got upset around midnight," Dean said. He looked as studious as a college student taking a big exam. "We had to give him the jacket and put him in the restraint room. If there's noise, whoever hears it'll just think it's him." He raised his chin at John Coffey.

"And what about us?" Brutal asked.

"Paul's over in Admin, pulling Del's file and going over the witnesses," Dean said. "It's especially important this time, because the execution was such a balls-up. He said he'd probably be there the rest of the shift. You and Harry and Percy are over in the laundry, washing your clothes."

Well, that was what folks said, anyway. There was a crap-game in the laundry supply room some nights; on others it was blackjack or poker or acey-deucey. Whatever it was, the guards who participated were said to be washing their clothes. There was usually moonshine at these get-togethers, and on occasion a joystick would go around the circle. It's been the same in prisons since prisons were invented, I suppose. When you spend your life taking care of mud-men, you can't help getting a little dirty yourself. In any case, we weren't likely to be checked up on. "Clothes washing" was treated with great discretion at Cold Mountain.

"Right with Eversharp," I said, turning Coffey around and putting him in motion. "And if it all falls down, Dean, you don't know nothing about nothing."

"That's easy to say, but—"

At that moment, a skinny arm shot out from between the bars of Wharton's cell and grabbed Coffey's slab of a bicep. We all gasped. Wharton should have been dead to the world, all but comatose, yet here he stood, swaying back and forth on his feet like a hard-tagged fighter, grinning blearily.

Coffey's reaction was remarkable. He didn't pull away, but he also gasped, pulling air in over his teeth like someone who has touched something cold and unpleasant. His eyes widened, and for a moment he looked as if he and dumb had never even met, let alone got up together every morning and lain down together every night. He had looked alive—*there*—when he had wanted me to come into his cell so he could touch me. Help me, in Coffeyspeak. He had looked that way again when he'd been holding his hands out for the mouse. Now, for the third time, his face had lit up, as if a spotlight had suddenly been turned on inside his brain. Except it was different this time. It was *colder* this time, and for the first time I wondered what might happen if John Coffey were suddenly to run amok. We had our guns, we could shoot him, but actually taking him down might not be easy to do.

I saw similar thoughts on Brutal's face, but Wharton just went on grinning his stoned, loose-lipped grin. "Where do you think you're going?" he asked. It came out something like *Wherra fink yerr gone?*

Coffey stood still, looking first at Wharton, then at Wharton's hand, then back into Wharton's face. I could not read that expression. I mean I could see the intelligence in it, but I couldn't *read* it. As for Wharton, I wasn't worried about him at all. He wouldn't remember any of this later; he was like a drunk walking in a blackout.

"You're a bad man," Coffey whispered, and I couldn't tell what I heard in his voice—pain or anger or fear. Maybe all three. Coffey looked down at the hand on his arm again, the way you might look at a bug which could give you a really nasty bite, had it a mind.

"That's right, nigger," Wharton said with a bleary, cocky smile. "Bad as you'd want."

I was suddenly positive that something awful was going to happen, something that would change the planned course of this early morning as completely as a cataclysmic earthquake can change the course of a river. It was going to happen, and nothing I or any of us did would stop it.

Then Brutal reached down, plucked Wharton's hand off John Coffey's arm, and that feeling stopped. It was as if some potentially dangerous circuit had been broken. I told you that in my time in E Block, the governor's line never rang. That was true, but I imagine that if it ever had, I would have felt the same relief that washed over me when Brutal removed Wharton's hand from the big man towering beside me. Coffey's eyes dulled over at once; it was as if the searchlight inside his head had been turned off.

"Lie down, Billy," Brutal said. "Take you some rest." That was my usual line of patter, but under the circumstances, I didn't mind Brutal using it.

"Maybe I will," Wharton agreed. He stepped back, swayed, almost went over, and caught his balance at the last second. "Whoo, daddy. Whole room's spinnin around. Like bein drunk."

He backed toward his bunk, keeping his bleary regard on Coffey as he went. "Niggers ought to have they own 'lectric chair," he opined. Then the backs of his knees struck his bunk and he swooped down onto it. He was snoring before his head touched his thin prison pillow, deep blue shadows brushed under the hollows of his eyes and the tip of his tongue lolling out.

"Christ, how'd he get up with so much dope in him?" Dean whispered.

"It doesn't matter, he's out now," I said. "If he starts to come around, give him another pill dissolved in a glass of water. No more than one, though. We don't want to kill him."

"Speak for yourself," Brutal rumbled, and gave Wharton a contemptuous look. "You can't kill a monkey like him with dope, anyway. They thrive on it."

"He's a bad man," Coffey said, but in a lower voice this time, as if he was not quite sure of what he was saying, or what it meant.

"That's right," Brutal said. "Most wicked. But that's not a problem now, because we ain't going to tango with him anymore." We started walking again, the four of us surrounding Coffey like worshippers circling an idol that's come to some stumbling kind of half life. "Tell me something, John—do you know where we're taking you?"

"To help," he said. "I think . . . to help . . . a lady?" He looked at Brutal with hopeful anxiety.

Brutal nodded. "That's right. But how do you know that? How do you *know*?"

John Coffey considered the question carefully, then shook his head. "I don't know," he told Brutal. "To tell you the truth, boss, I don't know much of anything. Never have."

And with that we had to be content.

6

I HAD KNOWN the little door between the office and the steps down to the storage room hadn't been built with the likes of Coffey in mind, but I hadn't realized how great the disparity was until he stood before it, looking at it thoughtfully.

Harry laughed, but John himself seemed to see no humor in the big man standing in front of the little door. He wouldn't have, of course; even if he'd been quite a few degrees brighter than he was, he wouldn't have. He'd been that big man for most of his life, and this door was just a scrap littler than most.

He sat down, scooted through it that way, stood up again, and went down the stairs to where Brutal was waiting for him. There he stopped, looking across the empty room at the platform where Old Sparky waited, as silent—and as eerie—as the throne in the castle of a dead king. The cap hung with hollow jauntiness from one of the back-posts, looking less like a king's crown than a jester's cap, however, something a fool would wear, or shake to make his high-born audience laugh harder at his jokes. The chair's shadow, elongated and spidery, climbed one wall like a threat. And yes, I thought I could still smell burned flesh in the air. It was faint, but I thought it was more than just my imagination.

Harry ducked through the door, then me. I didn't like the frozen, wide-eyed way John was looking at Old Sparky. Even less did I like what I saw on his arms when I got close to him: goosebumps.

"Come on, big boy," I said. I took his wrist and attempted to pull him in the direction of the door leading down to the tunnel. At first he wouldn't go, and I might as well have been trying to pull a boulder out of the ground with my bare hands.

"Come on, John, we gotta go, 'less you want the coach-and-four to turn back into a pumpkin," Harry said, giving his nervous laugh again. He took John's other arm and tugged, but John still wouldn't come. And then he said something in a low and dreaming voice. It wasn't me he was speaking to, it wasn't any of us, but I have still never forgotten it.

"They're still in there. Pieces of them, still in there. I hear them screaming."

Harry's nervous chuckles ceased, leaving him with a smile that hung on his mouth like a crooked shutter hangs on an empty house. Brutal gave me a look that was almost terrified, and stepped away from John Coffey. For the second time in less than five minutes, I sensed the whole enterprise on the verge of collapse. This time I was the one who stepped in; when disaster threatened a third time, a little later on, it would be Harry. We all got our chance that night, believe me.

I slid in between John and his view of the chair, standing on my tip-toes to make sure I was completely blocking his sight-line. Then I snapped my fingers in front of his eyes, twice, sharply.

"Come on!" I said. "Walk! You said you didn't need to be chained, now prove it! Walk, big boy! Walk, John Coffey! Over there! That door!"

His eyes cleared. "Yes, boss." And praise God, he began to walk.

"Look at the door, John Coffey, just at the door and nowhere else."

"Yes, boss." John fixed his eyes obediently on the door.

"Brutal," I said, and pointed.

He hurried in advance, shaking out his keyring, finding the right one. John kept his gaze fixed on the door to the tunnel and I kept my gaze fixed on John, but from the corner of one eye I could see Harry throwing nervous glances at the chair, as if he had never seen it before in his life.

There are pieces of them still in there . . . I hear them screaming.

If that was true, then Eduard Delacroix had to be screaming longest and loudest of all, and I was glad I couldn't hear what John Coffey did.

Brutal opened the door. We went down the stairs with Coffey in the lead. At the bottom, he looked glumly down the tunnel, with its low brick ceiling. He was going to have a crick in his back by the time we got to the other end, unless—

I pulled the gurney over. The sheet upon which we'd laid Del had been stripped (and probably incinerated), so the gurney's black leather pads were visible. "Get on," I told John. He looked at me doubtfully, and I nodded encouragement. "It'll be easier for you and no harder for us."

"Okay, Boss Edgecombe." He sat down, then lay back, looking up at us with worried brown eyes. His feet, clad in cheap prison slippers, dangled almost all the way to the floor. Brutal got in between them and pushed John Coffey along the dank corridor as he had pushed so many others. The only difference was that the current rider was still breathing. About halfway along—under the highway, we would have been, and able to hear the muffled drone of passing cars, had there been any at that hour—John began to smile. "Say," he said, "this is fun." He wouldn't think so the next time he rode the gurney; that was the thought which crossed my mind. In fact, the next time he rode the gurney, he wouldn't think or feel anything. Or would he? There are pieces of them still in there, he had said; he could hear them screaming.

Walking behind the others and unseen by them, I shivered.

"I hope you remembered Aladdin, Boss Edgecombe," Brutal said as we reached the far end of the tunnel.

"Don't worry," I said. Aladdin looked no different from the other keys I carried in those days—and I had a bunch that must have weighed four pounds—but it was the master key of master keys, the one that opened everything. There was one Aladdin key for each of the five cellblocks in those days, each the property of the block super. Other guards could borrow it, but only the bull-goose screw didn't have to sign it out.

There was a steel-barred gate at the far end of the tunnel. It always reminded me of pictures I'd seen of old castles; you know, in days of old when knights were bold and chivalry was in flower. Only Cold Mountain was a long way from Camelot. Beyond the gate, a flight of stairs led up to an unobtrusive bulkhead-style door with signs reading NO TRESPASSING and STATE PROPERTY and ELECTRIFIED WIRE on the outside.

I opened the gate and Harry swung it back. We went up, John Coffey once more in the lead, shoulders slumped and head bent. At the top, Harry got around him (not without some difficulty, either, although he was the smallest of the three of us) and unlocked the bulkhead. It was heavy. He could move it, but wasn't able to flip it up.

"Here, boss," John said. He pushed to the front again—bumping Harry into the wall with one hip as he did so—and raised the bulkhead with one hand. You would have thought it was painted cardboard instead of sheet steel.

Cold night air, moving with the ridge-running wind we would now get most of the time until March or April, blew down into our faces. A swirl of dead leaves came with it, and John Coffey caught one of them with his free hand. I will never forget the way he looked at it, or how he crumpled it beneath his broad, handsome nose so it would release its smell.

"Come on," Brutal said. "Let's go, forward harch."

We climbed out. John lowered the bulkhead and Brutal locked it— no need for the Aladdin key on this door, but it was needed to unlock the gate in the pole-and-wire cage which surrounded the bulkhead.

"Hands to your sides while you go through, big fella," Harry murmured. "Don't touch the wire, if you don't want a nasty burn."

Then we were clear, standing on the shoulder of the road in a little cluster (three foothills around a mountain is what I imagine we looked like), staring across at the walls and lights and guard-towers of Cold Mountain Penitentiary. I could actually see the vague shape of a guard inside one of those towers, blowing on his hands, but only for a moment; the road-facing windows in the towers were small and unimportant. Still, we would have to be very, very quiet. And if a car *did* come along now, we could be in deep trouble.

"Come on," I whispered. "Lead the way, Harry."

We slunk north along the highway in a little conga-line, Harry first, then John Coffey, then Brutal, then me. We breasted the first rise and walked down the other side, where all we could see of the prison was the bright glow of the lights in the tops of the trees. And still Harry led us onward.

"Where'd you park it?" Brutal stage-whispered, vapor puffing from his mouth in a white cloud. "Baltimore?"

"It's right up ahead," Harry replied, sounding nervous and irritable. "Hold your damn water, Brutus."

But Coffey, from what I'd seen of him, would have been happy to walk until the sun came up, maybe until it went down again. He looked everywhere, starting—not in fear but in delight, I am quite sure—when an owl hoo'd. It came to me that, while he might be afraid of the dark inside, he wasn't afraid of it out here, not at all. He was caressing the night, rubbing his senses across it the way a man might rub his face across the swells and concavities of a woman's breasts.

"We turn here," Harry muttered.

A little finger of road—narrow, unpaved, weeds running up the center crown—angled off to the right. We turned up this and walked another quarter of a mile. Brutal was beginning to grumble again when Harry stopped, went to the left side of the track, and began to remove sprays of broken-off pine boughs. John and Brutal pitched in, and before I could join them, they had uncovered the dented snout of an old Farmall truck, its wired-on headlights staring at us like buggy eyes.

"I wanted to be as careful as I could, you know," Harry said to Brutal in a thin, scolding voice. "This may be a big joke to you, Brutus Howell, but I come from a very religious family, I got cousins back in the hollers so damn holy they make the Christians look like lions, and if I get caught playing at something like this—!"

"It's okay," Brutal said. "I'm just jumpy, that's all."

"Me too," Harry said stiffly. "Now if this cussed old thing will just start—"

He walked around the hood of the truck, still muttering, and Brutal tipped me a wink. As far as Coffey was concerned, we had ceased to exist. His head was tilted back and he was drinking in the sight of the stars sprawling across the sky.

"I'll ride in back with him, if you want," Brutal offered. Behind us, the Farmall's starter whined briefly, sounding like an old dog trying to find its feet on a cold winter morning; then the engine exploded into life. Harry raced it once and let it settle into a ragged idle. "No need for both of us to do it."

"Get up front," I said. "You can ride with him on the return trip. If we don't end up making that one locked into the back of our own stagecoach, that is."

"Don't talk that way," he said, looking genuinely upset. It was as if he had realized for the first time how serious this would be for us if we were caught. "Christ, Paul!"

"Go on," I said. "In the cab."

He did as he was told. I yanked on John Coffey's arm until I could get his attention back to the earth for a bit, then led him around to the rear of the truck, which was stake-sided. Harry had draped canvas over the posts, and that would be of some help if we passed cars or trucks going the other way. He hadn't been able to do anything about the open back, though.

"Upsy-daisy, big boy," I said.

"Goin for the ride now?"

"That's right."

"Good." He smiled. It was sweet and lovely, that smile, perhaps the more so because it wasn't complicated by much in the way of thought. He got up in back. I followed him, went to the front of the truckbed, and banged on top of the cab. Harry ground the transmission into first and the truck pulled out of the little bower he had hidden it in, shaking and juddering.

John Coffey stood spread-legged in the middle of the truckbed, head cocked up at the stars again, smiling broadly, unmindful of the boughs that whipped at him as Harry turned his truck toward the highway. "Look, boss!" he cried in a low, rapturous voice, pointing up into the black night. "It's Cassie, the lady in the rockin chair!"

He was right; I could see her in the lane of stars between the dark bulk of the passing trees. But it wasn't Cassiopeia I thought of when he spoke of the lady in the rocking chair; it was Melinda Moores.

"I see her, John," I said, and tugged on his arm. "But you have to sit down now, all right?"

He sat with his back against the cab, never taking his eyes off the night sky. On his face was a look of sublime unthinking happiness. The Green Mile fell farther behind us with each revolution of the Farmall's bald tires, and for the time being, at least, the seemingly endless flow of John Coffey's tears had stopped.

7

IT WAS TWENTY-FIVE MILES to Hal Moores's house on Chimney Ridge, and in Harry Terwilliger's slow and rattly farm truck, the trip took over an hour. It was an eerie ride, and although it seems to me now that every moment of it is still etched in my memory—every turn, every bump, every dip, the scary times (two of them) when trucks passed us going the other way—I don't think I could come even close to describing how I felt, sitting back there with John Coffey, both of us bundled up like Indians in the old blankets Harry had been thoughtful enough to bring along.

It was, most of all, a sense of *lostness*—the deep and terrible ache a child feels when he realizes he has gone wrong somewhere, all the landmarks are strange, and he no longer knows how to find his way home. I was out in the night with a prisoner—not just *any* prisoner, but one who had been tried and convicted for the murder of two little girls, and sentenced to die for the crime. My belief that he was innocent wouldn't matter if we were caught; we would go to jail ourselves, and probably Dean Stanton would, too. I had thrown over a life of work and belief because of one bad execution and because I believed the overgrown lummox sitting beside me *might* be able to cure a woman's inoperable brain tumor. Yet watching John watch the stars, I realized with dismay that I no longer *did* believe that, if I ever really had; my urinary infection seemed faraway and unimportant now, as such harsh and painful things always do once they are past (if a woman could really remember how bad it hurt to have her first baby, my mother once said, she'd never have a second). As for Mr. Jingles, wasn't it possible, even likely, that we had been wrong about how badly Percy had hurt him? Or that John—who really did have some kind of hypnotic power, there was no doubt of that much, at least—had somehow fooled us into thinking we'd seen something we hadn't seen at all? Then there was the matter of Hal Moores. On the day I'd surprised him in his office, I'd encountered a palsied, weepy old man. But I didn't think that was the truest side of the warden. I thought the real Warden Moores was the man who'd once broken the wrist of a skatehound who tried to stab him; the man who had pointed out to me with cynical accuracy that Delacroix's nuts were going to cook no matter who was out front on the execution team. Did I think that Hal Moores would stand meekly aside and let us bring a convicted child-murderer into his house to lay hands on his wife?

My doubt grew like a sickness as we rode along. I simply did not understand why I had done the things I had, or why I'd persuaded the others to go along with me on this crazy night journey, and I did not believe we had a chance of getting away with it—not a hound's chance of heaven, as the oldtimers used to say. Yet I made no effort to cry it off, either, which I might have been able to do; things wouldn't pass irrevocably out of our hands until we showed up at Moores's house. Something—I think it might have been no more than the waves of exhilaration coming off the giant sitting next to me—kept me from hammering on top of the cab and yelling at Harry to turn around and go back to the prison while there was still time.

Such was my frame of mind as we passed off the highway and onto County 5, and from County 5 onto Chimney Ridge Road. Some fifteen minutes after that, I saw the shape of a roof blotting out the stars and knew we had arrived.

Harry shifted down from second to low (I think he only made it all the way into top gear once during the whole trip). The engine lugged, sending a shudder through the whole truck, as if it, too, dreaded what now lay directly ahead of us.

Harry swung into Moores's gravelled driveway and parked the grumbling truck behind the warden's sensible black Buick. Ahead and slightly to our right was a neat-as-a-pin house in the style which I believe is called Cape Cod. That sort of house should have looked out of place in our ridge country, perhaps, but it didn't. The moon had come up, its grin a little fatter this morning, and by its light I could see that the yard, always so beautifully kept, now looked uncared for. It was just leaves, mostly, that hadn't been raked away. Under normal circumstances that would have been Melly's job, but Melly hadn't been up to any leaf-raking this fall, and she would never see the leaves fall again. That was the truth of the matter, and I had been mad to think this vacant-eyed idiot could change it.

Maybe it still wasn't too late to save ourselves, though. I made as if to get up, the blanket I'd been wearing slipping off my shoulders. I would lean over, tap on the driver's-side window, tell Harry to get the hell out before—

John Coffey grabbed my forearm in one of his hamhock fists, pulling me back down as effortlessly as I might have done to a toddler. "Look, boss," he said, pointing. "Someone's up."

I followed the direction of his finger and felt a sinking—not just of the belly, but of the heart. There was a spark of light in one of the back windows. The room where Melinda now spent her days and nights, most likely; she would be no more capable of using the stairs than she would of going out to rake the leaves which had fallen during the recent storm.

They'd heard the truck, of course—Harry Terwilliger's goddam Farmall, its engine bellowing and farting down the length of an exhaust pipe unencumbered by anything so frivolous as a muffler. Hell, the Mooreses probably weren't sleeping that well these nights, anyway.

A light closer to the front of the house went on (the kitchen), then the living-room overhead, then the one in the front hall, then the one over the stoop. I watched these forward-marching lights the way a man standing against a cement wall and smoking his last cigarette might watch the lockstep approach of the firing squad. Yet I did not entirely acknowledge to myself even then that it was too late until the uneven chop of the Farmall's engine faded into silence, and the doors creaked, and the gravel crunched as Harry and Brutal got out.

John was up, pulling me with him. In the dim light, his face looked lively and eager. Why not? I remember thinking. Why shouldn't he look eager? He's a fool.

Brutal and Harry were standing shoulder to shoulder at the foot of the truck, like kids in a thunderstorm, and I saw that both of them looked as scared, confused, and uneasy as I felt. That made me feel even worse.

John got down. For him it was more of a step than a jump. I followed, stiff-legged and miserable. I would have sprawled on the cold gravel if he hadn't caught me by the arm.

"This is a mistake," Brutal said in a hissy little voice. His eyes were very wide and very frightened. "Christ Almighty, Paul, what were we thinking?"

"Too late now," I said. I pushed one of Coffey's hips, and he went obediently enough to stand beside Harry. Then I grabbed Brutal's elbow like this was a date we were on and got the two of us walking toward the stoop where that light was now burning. "Let me do the talking. Understand?"

"Yeah," Brutal said. "Right now that's just about the only thing I *do* understand."

I looked back over my shoulder. "Harry, stay by the truck with him until I call for you. I don't want Moores to see him until I'm ready." Except I was never going to be ready. I knew that now.

Brutal and I had just reached the foot of the steps when the front door was hauled open hard enough to flap the brass knocker against its plate. There stood Hal Moores in blue pajama pants and a strap-style tee-shirt, his iron-gray hair standing up in tufts and twists. He was a man who had made a thousand enemies over the course of his career, and he knew it. Clasped in his right hand, the abnormally long barrel not quite pointing at the floor, was the pistol which had always been mounted over the mantel. It was the sort of gun known as a Ned Buntline Special, it had been his grandfather's, and right then (I saw this with a further sinking in my gut) it was fully cocked.

"Who the hell goes there at two-thirty in the goddam morning?" he asked. I heard no fear at all in his voice. And—for the time being, at least—his shakes had stopped. The hand holding the gun was as steady as a stone. "Answer me, or—" The barrel of the gun began to rise.

"Stop it, Warden!" Brutal raised his hands, palms out, toward the man with the gun. I have never heard his voice sound the way it did then; it was as if the shakes turned out of Moores's hands had somehow found their way into Brutus Howell's throat. "It's us! It's Paul and me and . . . it's us!"

He took the first step up, so that the light over the stoop could fall fully on his face. I joined him. Hal Moores looked back and forth between us, his angry determination giving way to bewilderment. "What are you doing here?" he asked. "Not only is it the shank of the morning, you boys have the duty. I know you do, I've got the roster pinned up in my workshop. So what in the name of . . . oh, Jesus. It's not a lockdown, is it? Or a riot?" He looked between us, and his gaze sharpened. "Who else is down by that truck?"

Let me do the talking. So I had instructed Brutal, but now the time to talk was here and I couldn't even open my mouth. On my way into work that afternoon I had carefully planned out what I was going to say when we got here, and had thought that it didn't sound too crazy. Not normal—nothing about it was normal—but maybe *close enough* to normal to get us through the door and give us a chance. Give *John* a chance. But now all my carefully rehearsed words were lost in a roaring confusion. Thoughts and images—Del burning, the mouse dying, Toot jerking in Old Sparky's lap and screaming that he was a done tom turkey—whirled inside my head like sand caught in a dust-devil. I believe there is good in the world, all of it flowing in one way or another from a loving God. But I believe there's another force as well, one every bit as real as the God I have prayed to my whole life, and that it works consciously to bring all our decent impulses to ruin. Not Satan, I don't mean Satan (although I believe he is real, too), but a kind of demon of discord, a prankish and stupid thing that laughs with glee when an old man sets himself on fire trying to light his pipe or when a much-loved baby puts its first Christmas toy in its mouth and chokes to death on it. I've had a lot of years to think on this, all the way from Cold Mountain to Georgia Pines, and I believe that force was actively at work among us on that morning, swirling everywhere like a fog, trying to keep John Coffey away from Melinda Moores.

"Warden . . . Hal . . . I . . ." Nothing I tried made any sense.

He raised the pistol again, pointing it between Brutal and me, not listening. His bloodshot eyes had gotten very wide. And here came Harry Terwilliger, being more or less pulled along by our big boy, who was wearing his wide and daffily charming smile.

"Coffey," Moores breathed. "John Coffey." He pulled in breath and yelled in a voice that was reedy but strong: "Halt! Halt right there, or I shoot!"

From somewhere behind him, a weak and wavery female voice called: "Hal? What are you doing out there? Who are you talking to, you fucking cocksucker?"

He turned in that direction for just a moment, his face confused and despairing. Just a moment, as I say, but it should have been long enough for me to snatch the long-barrelled gun out of his hand. Except I couldn't lift my own hands. They might have had weights tied to them. My head seemed full of static, like a radio trying to broadcast during an electrical storm. The only emotions I remember feeling were fright and a kind of dull embarrassment for Hal.

Harry and John Coffey reached the foot of the steps. Moores turned away from the sound of his wife's voice and raised the gun again. He said later that yes, he fully intended to shoot Coffey; he suspected we were all prisoners, and that the brains behind whatever was happening were back by the truck, lurking in the shadows. He didn't understand why we should have been brought to his house, but revenge seemed the most likely possibility.

Before he could shoot, Harry Terwilliger stepped up ahead of Coffey and then moved in front of him, shielding most of his body. Coffey didn't make him do it; Harry did it on his own.

"No, Warden Moores!" he said. "It's all right! No one's armed, no one's going to get hurt, we're here to help!"

"Help?" Moores's tangled, tufted eyebrows drew together. His eyes blazed. I couldn't take my eyes off the cocked hammer of the Buntline. "Help *what*? Help *who*?"

As if in answer, the old woman's voice rose again, querulous and certain and utterly lost: "Come in here and poke my mudhole, you son of a bitch! Bring your asshole friends, too! Let them all have a turn!"

I looked at Brutal, shaken to my soul. I'd understood that she swore—that the tumor was somehow *making* her swear—but this was more than swearing. A lot more.

"What are you doing here?" Moores asked us again. A lot of the determination had gone out of his voice—his wife's wavering cries had done that. "I don't understand. Is it a prison break, or . . ."

John set Harry aside—just picked him up and moved him over—and then climbed to the stoop. He stood between Brutal and me, so big he almost pushed us off either side and into Melly's holly bushes. Moores's eyes turned up to follow him, the way a person's eyes do when he's trying to see the top of a tall tree. And suddenly the world fell back into place for me. That spirit of discord, which had jumbled my thoughts like powerful fingers sifting through sand or grains of rice, was gone. I thought I also understood why Harry had been able to act when Brutal and I could only stand, hopeless and indecisive, in front of our boss. Harry had been with John . . . and whatever spirit it is that opposes that other, demonic one, it was in John Coffey that night. And, when John stepped forward to face Warden Moores, it was that other spirit—something white, that's how I think of it, as something white—which took control of the situation. The other thing didn't leave, but I could see it drawing back like a shadow in a sudden strong light.

"I want to help," John Coffey said. Moores looked up at him, eyes fascinated, mouth hanging open. When Coffey plucked the Buntline Special from his hand and passed it to me, I don't think Hal even knew it was gone. I carefully lowered the hammer. Later, when I checked the cylinder, I would find it had been empty all along. Sometimes I wonder if Hal knew that. Meanwhile, John was still murmuring. "I came to help her. Just to help. That's all I want."

"Hal!" she cried from the back bedroom. Her voice sounded a little stronger now, but it also sounded afraid, as if the thing which had so confused and unmanned us had now retreated to her. "Make them go away, whoever they are! We don't need no salesmen in the middle of the night! No Electrolux! No Hoover! No French knickers with come in the crotch! Get them out! Tell them to take a flying fuck at a rolling d . . . d . . ." Something broke—it could have been a waterglass—and then she began to sob.

"Just to help," John Coffey said in a voice so low it was hardly more than a whisper. He ignored the woman's sobbing and profanity equally. "Just to help, boss, that's all."

"You can't," Moores said. "No one can." It was a tone I'd heard before, and after a moment I realized it was how I'd sounded myself when I'd gone into Coffey's cell the night he cured my urinary infection. Hypnotized. *You mind your business and I'll mind mine* was what I'd told Delacroix . . . except it had been *Coffey* who'd been minding my business, just as he was minding Hal Moores's now.

"We think he can," Brutal said. "And we didn't risk our jobs—plus a stretch in the can ourselves, maybe—just to get here and turn around and go back without giving it the old college try."

Only I had been ready to do just that three minutes before. Brutal, too.

John Coffey took the play out of our hands. He pushed into the entry and past Moores, who raised a single strengthless hand to stop him (it trailed across Coffey's hip and fell off; I'm sure the big man never even felt it), and then shuffled down the hall toward the living room, the kitchen beyond it, and the back bedroom beyond that, where that shrill unrecognizable voice raised itself again: "You stay out of here! Whoever you are, just stay out! I'm not dressed, my tits are out and my bitchbox is taking the breeze!"

John paid no attention, just went stolidly along, head bent so he wouldn't smash any of the light fixtures, his round brown skull gleaming, his hands swinging at his sides. After a moment we followed him, me first, Brutal and Hal side by side, and Harry bringing up the rear. I understood one thing perfectly well: it was all out of our hands now, and in John's.

8

THE WOMAN in the back bedroom, propped up against the headboard and staring wall-eyed at the giant who had come into her muddled sight, didn't look at all like the Melly Moores I had known for twenty years; she didn't even look like the Melly Moores Janice and I had visited shortly before Delacroix's execution. The woman propped up in that bed looked like a sick child got up as a Halloween witch. Her livid skin was a hanging dough of wrinkles. It was puckered up around the eye on the right side, as if she were trying to wink. That same side of her mouth turned down; one old yellow eyetooth hung out over her liverish lower lip. Her hair was a wild thin fog around her skull. The room stank of the stuff our bodies dispose of with such decorum when things are running right. The chamberpot by her bed was half full of some vile yellowish goo. We had come too late anyway, I thought, horrified. It had only been a matter of days since she had been recognizable—sick but still herself. Since then, the thing in her head must have moved with horrifying speed to consolidate its position. I didn't think even John Coffey could help her now.

Her expression when Coffey entered was one of fear and horror—as if something inside her had recognized a doctor that might be able to get at it and pry it loose, after all . . . to sprinkle salt on it the way you do on a leech to make it let go its grip. Hear me carefully: I'm not saying that Melly Moores was possessed, and I'm aware that, wrought up as I was, all my perceptions of that night might be suspect. But I have never completely discounted the possibility of demonic possession, either. There was something in her eyes, I tell you, something that looked like fear. On that I think you *can* trust me; it's an emotion I've seen too much of to mistake.

Whatever it was, it was gone in a hurry, replaced by a look of lively, irrational interest. That unspeakable mouth trembled in what might have been a smile.

"Oh, so big!" she cried. She sounded like a little girl just coming down with a bad throat infection. She took her hands—as spongy-white as her face—out from under the counterpane and patted them together. "Pull down your pants! I've heard about nigger-cocks my whole life but never seen one!"

Behind me, Moores made a soft groaning sound, full of despair.

John Coffey paid no attention to any of it. After standing still for a moment, as if to observe her from a little distance, he crossed to the bed, which was illuminated by a single bedside lamp. It threw a bright circle of light on the white counterpane drawn up to the lace at the throat of her nightgown. Beyond the bed, in shadow, I saw the chaise longue which belonged in the parlor. An afghan Melly had knitted with her own hands in happier days lay half on the chaise and half on the floor. It was here Hal had been sleeping—dozing, at least—when we pulled in.

As John approached, her expression underwent a third change. Suddenly I saw Melly, whose kindness had meant so much to me over the years, and even more to Janice when the kids had flown from the nest and she had been left feeling so alone and useless and blue. Melly was still interested, but now her interest seemed sane and aware.

"Who are you?" she asked in a clear, reasonable voice. "And why have you so many scars on your hands and arms? Who hurt you so badly?"

"I don't hardly remember where they all come from, ma'am," John Coffey said in a humble voice, and sat down beside her on her bed.

Melinda smiled as well as she could—the sneering right side of her mouth trembled, but wouldn't quite come up. She touched a white scar, curved like a scimitar, on the back of his left hand. "What a blessing that is! Do you understand why?"

"Reckon if you don't know who hurt you or dog you down, it don't keep you up nights," John Coffey said in his almost-Southern voice.

She laughed at that, the sound as pure as silver in the bad-smelling sickroom. Hal was beside me now, breathing rapidly but not trying to interfere. When Melly laughed, his rapid breathing paused for a moment, indrawn, and one of his big hands gripped my shoulder. He gripped it hard enough to leave a bruise—I saw it the next day—but right then I hardly felt it.

"What's your name?" she asked.

"John Coffey, ma'am."

"Coffey like the drink."

"Yes, ma'am, only spelled different."

She lay back against her pillows, propped up but not quite sitting up, looking at him. He sat beside her, looking back, and the light from the lamp circled them like they were actors on a stage—the hulking black man in the prison overall and the small dying white woman. She stared into John's eyes with shining fascination.

"Ma'am?"

"Yes, John Coffey?" The words barely breathed, barely slipping to us on the bad-smelling air. I felt the muscles bunching on my arms and legs and back. Somewhere, far away, I could feel the warden clutching my arm, and to the side of my vision I could see Harry and Brutal with their arms around each other, like little kids lost in the night. Something was going to happen. Something big. We each felt it in our own way.

John Coffey bent closer to her. The springs of the bed creaked, the bedclothes rustled, and the coldly smiling moon looked in through an upper pane of the bedroom window. Coffey's bloodshot eyes searched her upturned haggard face.

"I see it," he said. Speaking not to her—I don't think so, anyway—but to himself. "I see it, and I can help. Hold still . . . hold right still . . ."

Closer he bent, and closer still. For a moment his huge face stopped less than two inches from hers. He raised one hand off to the side, fingers splayed, as if telling something to wait . . . just wait . . . and then he lowered his face again. His broad, smooth lips pressed against hers and forced them open. For a moment I could see one of her eyes, staring up past Coffey, filling with an expression of what seemed to be surprise. Then his smooth bald head moved, and that was gone, too.

There was a soft whistling sound as he inhaled the air which lay deep within her lungs. That was all for a second or two, and then the floor moved under us and the whole house moved around us. It wasn't my imagination; they all felt it, they all remarked on it later. It was a kind of rippling thump. There was a crash as something very heavy fell over in the parlor—the grandfather clock, it turned out to be. Hal Moores tried to have it repaired, but it never kept time for more than fifteen minutes at a stretch again.

Closer by there was a crack followed by a tinkle as the pane of glass through which the moon had been peeking broke. A picture on the wall—a clipper ship cruising one of the seven seas—fell off its hook and crashed to the floor; the glass over its front shattered.

I smelled something hot and saw smoke rising from the bottom of the white counterpane which covered her. A portion was turning black, down by the jittering lump that was her right foot. Feeling like a man in a dream, I shook free of Moores's hand and stepped to the nighttable. There was a glass of water there, surrounded by three or four bottles of pills which had fallen over during the shake. I picked up the water and dumped it on the place that was smoking. There was a hiss.

John Coffey went on kissing her in that deep and intimate way, inhaling and inhaling, one hand still held out, the other on the bed, propping up his immense weight. The fingers were splayed; the hand looked to me like a brown starfish.

Suddenly, her back arched. One of her own hands flailed out in the air, the fingers clenching and unclenching in a series of spasms. Her feet drummed against the bed. Then something screamed. Again, that's not just me; the other men heard it, as well. To Brutal it sounded like a wolf or coyote with its leg caught in a trap. To me it sounded like an eagle, the way you'd sometimes hear them on still mornings back then, cruising down through the misty cuts with their wings stiffly spread.

Outside, the wind gusted hard enough to give the house a second shake—and that was strange, you know, because until then there had been no wind to speak of at all.

John Coffey pulled away from her, and I saw that her face had smoothed out. The right side of her mouth no longer drooped. Her eyes had regained their normal shape, and she looked ten years younger. He regarded her raptly for a moment or two, and then he began to cough. He turned his head so as not to cough in her face, lost his balance (which wasn't hard; big as he was, he'd been sitting with his butt halfway off the side of the bed to start with), and went down onto the floor. There was enough of him to give the house a third shake. He landed on his knees and hung his head over, coughing like a man in the last stages of TB.

I thought, *Now the bugs. He's going to cough them out, and what a lot there'll be this time.*

But he didn't. He only went on coughing in deep retching barks, hardly finding time between fits to snatch in the next breath of air. His dark, chocolatey skin was graying out. Alarmed, Brutal went to him, dropped to one knee beside him, and put an arm across his broad, spasming back. As if Brutal's moving had broken a spell, Moores went to his wife's bed and sat where Coffey had sat. He hardly seemed to register the coughing, choking giant's presence at all. Although Coffey was kneeling at his very feet, Moores had eyes only for his wife, who was gazing at him with amazement. Looking at her was like looking at a dirty mirror which has been wiped clean.

"John!" Brutal shouted. "Sick it up! Sick it up like you done before!"

John went on barking those choked coughs. His eyes were wet, not with tears but with strain. Spit flew from his mouth in a fine spray, but nothing else came out.

Brutal whammed him on the back a couple of times, then looked around at me. "He's choking! Whatever he sucked out of her, he's choking on it!"

I started forward. Before I got two steps, John knee-walked away from me and into the corner of the room, still coughing harshly and dragging for each breath. He laid his forehead against the wallpaper— wild red roses overspreading a garden wall—and made a gruesome deep hacking sound, as if he were trying to vomit up the lining of his own throat. That'll bring the bugs if anything can, I remember thinking, but there was no sign of them. All the same, his coughing fit seemed to ease a little.

"I'm all right, boss," he said, still leaning with his forehead against the wild roses. His eyes remained closed. I'm not sure how he knew I was there, but he clearly did. "Honest I am. See to the lady."

I looked at him doubtfully, then turned to the bed. Hal was stroking Melly's brow, and I saw an amazing thing above it: some of her hair— not very much, but some—had gone back to black.

"What's happened?" she asked him. As I watched, color began to blush into her cheeks. It was as if she had stolen a couple of roses right out of the wallpaper. "How did I get here? We were going to the hospital up in Indianola, weren't we? A doctor was going to shoot X-rays into my head and take pictures of my brain."

"Shhh," Hal said. "Shhh, dearie, none of that matters now."

"But I don't *understand*!" she nearly wailed. "We stopped at a roadside stand . . . you bought me a dime packet of posies . . . and then . . . I'm here. It's dark! Have you had your supper, Hal? Why am I in the guest room? Did I have the X-ray?" Her eyes moved across Harry almost without seeing him—that was shock, I imagine—and fixed on me. "Paul? Did I have the X-ray?"

"Yes," I said. "It was clear."

"They didn't find a tumor?"

"No," I said. "They say the headaches will likely stop now."

Beside her, Hal burst into tears.

She sat forward and kissed his temple. Then her eyes moved to the corner. "Who is that Negro man? Why is he in the corner?"

I turned and saw John trying to get up on his feet. Brutal helped him and John made it with a final lunge. He stood facing the wall, though, like a child who has been bad. He was still coughing in spasms, but these seemed to be weakening now.

"John," I said. "Turn around, big boy, and see this lady."

He slowly turned. His face was still the color of ashes, and he looked ten years older, like a once powerful man at last losing a long battle with consumption. His eyes were cast down on his prison slippers, and he looked as if he wished for a hat to wring.

"Who are you?" she asked again. "What's your name?"

"John Coffey, ma'am," he said, to which she immediately replied, "But not spelled like the drink."

Hal started beside her. She felt it, and patted his hand reassuringly without taking her eyes from the black man.

"I dreamed of you," she said in a soft, wondering voice. "I dreamed you were wandering in the dark, and so was I. We found each other."

John Coffey said nothing.

"We found each other in the dark," she said. "Stand up, Hal, you're pinning me in here."

He got up and watched with disbelief as she turned back the counterpane. "Melly, you can't—"

"Don't be silly," she said, and swung her legs out. "Of course I can." She smoothed her nightgown, stretched, then got to her feet.

"My God," Hal whispered. "My dear God in heaven, *look* at her."

She went to John Coffey. Brutal stood away from her, an awed expression on his face. She limped with the first step, did no more than favor her right leg a bit with the second, and then even that was gone. I remembered Brutal handing the colored spool to Delacroix and saying, "Toss it—I want to see how he runs." Mr. Jingles had limped then, but on the next night, the night Del walked the Mile, he had been fine.

Melly put her arms around John and hugged him. Coffey stood there for a moment, letting himself be hugged, and then he raised one hand and stroked the top of her head. This he did with infinite gentleness. His face was still gray. I thought he looked dreadfully sick.

She stood away from him, her face turned up to his. "Thank you."

"Right welcome, ma'am."

She turned to Hal and walked back to him. He put his arms around her.

"Paul—" It was Harry. He held his right wrist out to me and tapped the face of his watch. It was pressing on to three o'clock. Light would start showing by four-thirty. If we wanted to get Coffey back to Cold Mountain before that happened, we would have to go soon. And I wanted to get him back. Partly because the longer this went on the worse our chances of getting away with it became, yes, of course. But I also wanted John in a place where I could legitimately call a doctor for him, if the need arose. Looking at him, I thought it might.

The Mooreses were sitting on the edge of the bed, arms around each other. I thought of asking Hal out into the living room for a private word, then realized I could ask until the cows came home and he wouldn't budge from where he was right then. He might be able to take his eyes off her—for a few seconds, at least—by the time the sun came up, but not now.

"Hal," I said. "We have to go now."

He nodded, not looking at me. He was studying the color in his wife's cheeks, the natural unstrained curve of his wife's lips, the new black in his wife's hair.

I tapped him on the shoulder, hard enough to get his attention for a moment, at least.

"Hal, we never came here."

"What—?"

"We never came here," I said. "Later on we'll talk, but for now that's all you need to know. We were never here."

"Yes, all right . . ." He forced himself to focus on me for a moment, with what was clearly an effort. "You got him out. Can you get him back in?"

"I think so. Maybe. But we need to go."

"How did you know he could do this?" Then he shook his head, as if realizing for himself that this wasn't the time. "Paul . . . thank you."

"Don't thank me," I said. "Thank John."

He looked at John Coffey, then put out one hand—just as I had done on the day Harry and Percy escorted John onto the block. "Thank you. Thank you so much."

John looked at the hand. Brutal threw a none-too-subtle elbow into his side. John started, then took the hand and gave it a shake. Up, down, back to center, release. "Welcome," he said in a hoarse voice. It sounded to me like Melly's when she had clapped her hands and told John to pull down his pants. "Welcome," he said to the man who would, in the ordinary course of things, grasp a pen with that hand and then sign John Coffey's execution order with it.

Harry tapped the face of his watch, more urgently this time.

"Brute?" I said. "Ready?"

"Hello, Brutus," Melinda said in a cheerful voice, as if noticing him for the first time. "It's good to see you. Would you gentlemen like tea? Would you, Hal? I could make it." She got up again. "I've been ill, but I feel fine now. Better than I have in years."

"Thank you, Missus Moores, but we have to go," Brutal said. "It's past John's bedtime." He smiled to show it was a joke, but the look he gave John was as anxious as I felt.

"Well . . . if you're sure . . ."

"Yes, ma'am. Come on, John Coffey." He tugged John's arm to get him going, and John went.

"Just a minute!" Melinda shook free of Hal's hand and ran as lightly as a girl to where John stood. She put her arms around him and gave him another hug. Then she reached around to the nape of her neck and pulled a fine-link chain out of her bodice. At the end of it was a silver medallion. She held it out to John, who looked at it uncomprehendingly.

"It's St. Christopher," she said. "I want you to have it, Mr. Coffey, and wear it. He'll keep you safe. Please wear it. For me."

John looked at me, troubled, and I looked at Hal, who first spread his hands and then nodded.

"Take it, John," I said. "It's a present."

John took it, slipped the chain around his bull-neck, and dropped the St. Christopher medallion into the front of his shirt. He had completely stopped coughing now, but I thought he looked grayer and sicker than ever.

"Thank you, ma'am," he said.

"No," she replied. "Thank *you*. Thank *you*, John Coffey."

9

I RODE UP in the cab with Harry going back, and was damned glad to be there. The heater was broken, but we were out of the open air, at least. We had gone about ten miles when Harry spotted a little turnout and veered the truck into it.

"What is it?" I asked. "Is it a bearing?" To my mind, the problem could have been that or anything; every component of the Farmall's engine and transmission sounded on the verge of going cataclysmically wrong or giving up the ghost entirely.

"Nope," Harry said, sounding apologetic. "I got to take a leak, is all. My back teeth are floatin."

It turned out that we all did, except for John. When Brutal asked if he wouldn't like to step down and help us water the bushes, he just shook his head without looking up. He was leaning against the back of the cab and wearing one of the Army blankets over his shoulders like a serape. I couldn't get any kind of read on his complexion, but I could hear his breathing—dry and raspy, like wind blowing through straw. I didn't like it.

I walked into a clump of willows, unbuttoned, and let go. I was still close enough to my urinary infection so that the body's amnesia had not taken full hold, and I could be grateful simply to be able to pee without needing to scream. I stood there, emptying out and looking up at the moon; I was hardly aware of Brutal standing next to me and doing the same thing until he said in a low voice, "He'll never sit in Old Sparky."

I looked around at him, surprised and a little frightened by the low certainty in his tone. "What do you mean?"

"I mean he swallered that stuff instead of spitting out like he done before for a reason. It might take a week—he's awful big and strong—but I bet it's quicker. One of us'll do a check-tour and there he'll be, lying dead as stone on his bunk."

I'd thought I was done peeing, but at that a little shiver twisted up my back and a little more squirted out. As I rebuttoned my fly, I thought that what Brutal was saying made perfect sense. And I hoped, all in all, that he was right. John Coffey didn't deserve to die at all, if I was right in my reasoning about the Detterick girls, but if he *did* die, I didn't want it to be by my hand. I wasn't sure I could lift my hand to do it, if it came to that.

"Come on," Harry murmured out of the dark. "It's gettin late. Let's get this done."

As we walked back to the truck, I realized we had left John entirely alone—stupidity on the Percy Wetmore level. I thought that he would be gone; that he'd spat out the bugs as soon as he saw he was unguarded, and had then just lit out for the territories, like Huck and Jim on the Big Muddy. All we would find was the blanket he had been wearing around his shoulders.

But he was there, still sitting with his back against the cab and his forearms propped on his knees. He looked up at the sound of our approach and tried to give us a smile. It hung there for a moment on his haggard face and then slipped off.

"How you doing, Big John?" Brutal asked, climbing into the back of the truck again and retrieving his own blanket.

"Fine, boss," John said listlessly. "I's fine."

Brutal patted his knee. "We'll be back soon. And when we get squared away, you know what? I'm going to see you get a great big cup of hot coffee. Sugar and cream, too."

You bet, I thought, going around to the passenger side of the cab and climbing in. If we don't get arrested and thrown in jail ourselves first.

But I'd been living with that idea ever since we'd thrown Percy into

317

the restraint room, and it didn't worry me enough to keep me awake. I dozed off and dreamed of Calvary Hill. Thunder in the west and a smell that might have been juniper berries. Brutal and Harry and Dean and I were standing around in robes and tin hats like in a Cecil B. DeMille movie. We were Centurions, I guess. There were three crosses, Percy Wetmore and Eduard Delacroix flanking John Coffey. I looked down at my hand and saw I was holding a bloody hammer.

We got to get him down from there, Paul! Brutal screamed. *We got to get him down!*

Except we couldn't, they'd taken away the stepladder. I started to tell Brutal this, and then an extra-hard jounce of the truck woke me up. We were backing into the place where Harry had hidden the truck earlier on a day that already seemed to stretch back to the beginning of time.

The two of us got out and went around to the back. Brutal hopped down all right, but John Coffey's knees buckled and he almost fell. It took all three of us to catch him, and he was no more than set solid on his feet again before he went off into another of those coughing fits, this one the worst yet. He bent over, the coughing sounds muffled by the heels of his palms, which he held pressed against his mouth.

When his coughing eased, we covered the front of the Farmall with the pine boughs again and walked back the way we had come. The worst part of that whole surreal furlough was—for me, at least—the last two hundred yards, with us scurrying back south along the shoulder of the highway. I could see (or thought I could) the first faint lightening of the sky in the east, and felt sure some early farmer, out to harvest his pumpkins or dig his last few rows of yams, would come along and see us. And even if that didn't happen, we would hear someone (in my imagination it sounded like Curtis Anderson) shout *"Hold it right there!"* as I used the Aladdin key to unlock the enclosure around the bulkhead leading to the tunnel. Then two dozen carbine-toting guards would step out of the woods and our little adventure would be over.

By the time we actually got to the enclosure, my heart was whamming so hard that I could see little white dots exploding in front of my eyes with each pulse it made. My hands felt cold and numb and faraway, and for the longest time I couldn't get the key to go into the lock.

"Oh Christ, headlights!" Harry moaned.

I looked up and saw brightening fans of light on the road. My keyring almost fell out of my hand; I managed to clutch it at the last second.

"Give them to me," Brutal said. "I'll do it."

"No, I've got it," I said. The key at last slipped into its slot and turned. A moment later we were in. We crouched behind the bulkhead and watched as a Sunshine Bread truck went pottering past the prison. Beside me I could hear John Coffey's tortured breathing. He sounded like an engine which has almost run out of oil. He had held the bulk-head door up effortlessly for us on our way out, but we didn't even ask him to help this time; it would have been out of the question. Brutal and I got the door up, and Harry led John down the steps. The big man tottered as he went, but he got down. Brutal and I followed him as fast as we could, then lowered the bulkhead behind us and locked it again.

"Christ, I think we're gonna—" Brutal began, but I cut him off with a sharp elbow to the ribs.

"Don't say it," I said. "Don't even think it, until he's safe back in his cell."

"And there's Percy to think about," Harry said. Our voices had a flat, echoey quality in the brick tunnel. "The evening ain't over as long as we got him to contend with."

As it turned out, our evening was *far* from over.

PART SIX

COFFEY
ON THE MILE

1

I SAT IN THE GEORGIA PINES SUNROOM, my father's fountain pen in my hand, and time was lost to me as I recalled the night Harry and Brutal and I took John Coffey off the Mile and to Melinda Moores, in an effort to save her life. I wrote about the drugging of William Wharton, who fancied himself the second coming of Billy the Kid; I wrote of how we stuck Percy in the straitjacket and jugged him in the restraint room at the end of the Green Mile; I wrote about our strange night journey—both terrifying and exhilarating—and the miracle that befell at the end of it. We saw John Coffey drag a woman back, not just from the edge of her grave, but from what seemed to us to be the very bottom of it.

I wrote and was very faintly aware of the Georgia Pines version of life going on around me. Old folks went down to supper, then trooped off to the Resource Center (yes, you are permitted a chuckle) for their evening dose of network sitcoms. I seem to remember my friend Elaine bringing me a sandwich, and thanking her, and eating it, but I couldn't tell you what time of the evening she brought it, or what was in it. Most of me was back in 1932, when our sandwiches were usually bought off old Toot-Toot's rolling gospel snack-wagon, cold pork a nickel, corned beef a dime.

I remember the place quieting down as the relics who live here made ready for another night of thin and troubled sleep; I heard Mickey—maybe not the best orderly in the place, but certainly the kindest—singing "Red River Valley" in his good tenor as he went around dispensing the evening meds: *"From this valley they say you are going . . . We*

will miss your bright eyes and sweet smile . . ." The song made me think of
Melinda again, and what she had said to John after the miracle had hap-
pened. *I dreamed of you. I dreamed you were wandering in the dark, and so was
I. We found each other.*

Georgia Pines grew quiet, midnight came and passed, and still I
wrote. I got to Harry reminding us that, even though we had gotten
John back to the prison without being discovered, we still had Percy
waiting for us. "The evening ain't over as long as we got him to contend with" is more or less what Harry said.

That's where my long day of driving my father's pen at last caught up
with me. I put it down—just for a few seconds, I thought, so I could flex
some life back into the fingers—and then I put my forehead down on
my arm and closed my eyes to rest them. When I opened them again
and raised my head, morning sun glared in at me through the windows.
I looked at my watch and saw it was past eight. I had slept, head on
arms like an old drunk, for what must have been six hours. I got up,
wincing, trying to stretch some life into my back. I thought about going
down to the kitchen, getting some toast, and going for my morning
walk, then looked down at the sheafs of scribbled pages scattered across
the desk. All at once I decided to put off the walk for awhile. I had a
chore, yes, but it could keep, and I didn't feel like playing hide-and-seek
with Brad Dolan that morning.

Instead of walking, I'd finish my story. Sometimes it's better to push
on through, no matter how much your mind and body may protest.
Sometimes it's the only way to *get* through. And what I remember
most about that morning is how desperately I wanted to get free of
John Coffey's persistent ghost.

"Okay," I said. "One more mile. But first . . ."

I walked down to the toilet at the end of the second-floor hall. As I
stood inside there, urinating, I happened to glance up at the smoke
detector on the ceiling. That made me think of Elaine, and how she had
distracted Dolan so I could go for my walk and do my little chore
the day before. I finished peeing with a grin on my face.

I walked back to the sunroom, feeling better (and a *lot* comfier in my
nether regions). Someone—Elaine, I have no doubt—had set down a

pot of tea beside my pages. I drank greedily, first one cup, then another, before I even sat down. Then I resumed my place, uncapped the fountain pen, and once more began to write.

I was just slipping fully into my story when a shadow fell on me. I looked up and felt a sinking in my stomach. It was Dolan, standing between me and the windows. He was grinning.

"Missed you going on your morning walk, Paulie," he said, "so I thought I'd come and see what you were up to. Make sure you weren't, you know, sick."

"You're all heart and a mile wide," I said. My voice sounded all right—so far, anyway—but my heart was pounding hard. I was afraid of him, and I don't think that realization was entirely new. He reminded me of Percy Wetmore, and I'd never been afraid of *him* . . . but when I knew Percy, I had been young.

Brad's smile widened, but became no less unpleasant.

"Folks tellin me you been in here all night, Paulie, just writing your little report. Now, that's just no good. Old farts like you need their beauty rest."

"Percy—" I began, then saw a frown crease his grin and realized my mistake. I took a deep breath and began again. "Brad, what have you got against me?"

He looked puzzled for a moment, maybe a bit unsettled. Then the grin returned. "Old-timer," he said, "could be I just don't like your face. What you writin, anyway? Last will n testicles?"

He came forward, craning. I slapped my hand over the page I'd been working on. The rest of them I began to rake together with my free hand, crumpling some in my hurry to get them under my arm and under cover.

"Now," he said, as if speaking to a baby, "that ain't going to work, you old sweetheart. If Brad wants to look, Brad is going to look. And you can take that to the everfucking *bank*."

His hand, young and hideously strong, closed over my wrist, and squeezed. Pain sank into my hand like teeth, and I groaned.

"Let go," I managed.

"When you let me see," he replied, and he was no longer smiling. His face was cheerful, though; the kind of good cheer you only see on the faces of folks who enjoy being mean. "Let me see, Paulie. I want to know what you're writing." My hand began to move away from the top page. From our trip with John back through the tunnel under the road. "I want to see if it has anything to do with where you—"

"Let that man alone."

The voice was like a harsh whipcrack on a dry, hot day . . . and the way Brad Dolan jumped, you would have thought his ass had been the target. He let go of my hand, which thumped back down on my paper-work, and we both looked toward the door.

Elaine Connelly was standing there, looking fresh and stronger than she had in days. She wore jeans that showed off her slim hips and long legs; there was a blue ribbon in her hair. She had a tray in her arthritic hands—juice, a scrambled egg, toast, more tea. And her eyes were blazing.

"What do you think you're doing?" Brad asked. "He can't eat up here."

"He can, and he's going to," she said in that same dry tone of command. I had never heard it before, but I welcomed it now. I looked for fear in her eyes and saw not a speck—only rage. "And what you're going to do is get out of here before you go beyond the cockroach level of nuisance to that of slightly larger vermin—*Rattus Americanus*, let us say."

He took a step toward her, looking both unsure of himself and absolutely furious. I thought it a dangerous combination, but Elaine didn't flinch as he approached. "I bet I know who set off that goddam smoke alarm," Dolan said. "Might could have been a certain old bitch with claws for hands. Now get out of here. Me and Paulie haven't finished our little talk, yet."

"His name is *Mr. Edgecombe*," she said, "and if I ever hear you call him Paulie again, I think I can promise you that your days of employment here at Georgia Pines will end, Mr. Dolan."

"Just who do you think you are?" he asked her. He was hulking over her, now, trying to laugh and not quite making it.

"I think," she said calmly, "that I am the grandmother of the man who is currently Speaker of the Georgia House of Representatives. A man who loves his relatives, Mr. Dolan. Especially his *older* relatives."

The effortful smile dropped off his face the way that writing comes off a blackboard swiped with a wet sponge. I saw uncertainty, the possibility that he was being bluffed, the fear that he was not, and a certain dawning logical assumption: it would be easy enough to check, she must know that, ergo she was telling the truth.

Suddenly I began to laugh, and although the sound was rusty, it was right. I was remembering how many times Percy Wetmore had threatened us with his connections, back in the bad old days. Now, for the first time in my long, long life, such a threat was being made again . . . but this time it was being made on my behalf.

Brad Dolan looked at me, glaring, then looked back at her.

"I mean it," Elaine said. "At first I thought I'd just let you be—I'm old, and that seemed easiest. But when my friends are threatened and abused, I *do not* just let be. Now get out of here. And without one more word."

His lips moved like those of a fish—oh, how badly he wanted to say that one more word (perhaps the one that rhymes with *witch*). He didn't, though. He gave me a final look, and then strode past her and out into the hall.

I let out my breath in a long, ragged sigh as Elaine set the tray down in front of me and then set herself down across from me. "Is your grandson really Speaker of the House?" I asked.

"He really is."

"Then what are you doing here?"

"Speaker of the statehouse makes him powerful enough to deal with a roach like Brad Dolan, but it doesn't make him *rich*," she said, laughing. "Besides, I like it here. I like the company."

"I will take that as a compliment," I said, and I did.

"Paul, are you all right? You look so tired." She reached across the table and brushed my hair away from my forehead and eyebrows. Her fingers were twisted, but her touch was cool and wonderful. I closed my eyes for a moment. When I opened them again, I had made a decision.

"I'm all right," I said. "And almost finished. Elaine, would you read something?" I offered her the pages I had clumsily swept together. They were probably no longer in the right order—Dolan really had scared me badly—but they were numbered and she could quickly put them right.

She looked at me consideringly, not taking what I was offering. Yet, anyway. "Are you done?"

"It'll take you until afternoon to read what's there," I said. "If you can make it out at all, that is."

Now she *did* take the pages, and looked down at them. "You write with a very fine hand, even when that hand is obviously tired," she said. "I'll have no trouble with this."

"By the time you finish reading, I will have finished writing," I said. "You can read the rest in a half an hour or so. And then . . . if you're still willing . . . I'd like to show you something."

"Is it to do with where you go most mornings and afternoons?"

I nodded.

She sat thinking about it for what seemed a long time, then nodded herself and got up with the pages in her hand. "I'll go out back," she said. "The sun is very warm this morning."

"And the dragon's been vanquished," I said. "This time by the lady fair."

She smiled, bent, and kissed me over the eyebrow in the sensitive place that always makes me shiver. "We'll hope so," she said, "but in my experience, dragons like Brad Dolan are hard to get rid of." She hesitated. "Good luck, Paul. I hope you can vanquish whatever it is that has been festering in you."

"I hope so, too," I said, and thought of John Coffey. *I couldn't help it,* John had said. *I tried, but it was too late.*

I ate the eggs she'd brought, drank the juice, and pushed the toast aside for later. Then I picked up my pen and began to write again, for what I hoped would be the last time.

One last mile.

A green one.

2

WHEN WE BROUGHT JOHN back to E Block that night, the gurney was a necessity instead of a luxury. I very much doubt if he could have made it the length of the tunnel on his own; it takes more energy to walk at a crouch than it does upright, and it was a damned low ceiling for the likes of John Coffey. I didn't like to think of him collapsing down there. How would we explain that, on top of trying to explain why we had dressed Percy in the madman's dinner-jacket and tossed him in the restraint room?

But we had the gurney—thank God—and John Coffey lay on it like a beached whale as we pushed him back to the storage-room stairs. He got down off it, staggered, then simply stood with his head lowered, breathing harshly. His skin was so gray he looked as if he'd been rolled in flour. I thought he'd be in the infirmary by noon . . . if he wasn't dead by noon, that was.

Brutal gave me a grim, desperate look. I gave it right back. "We can't carry him up, but we can help him," I said. "You under his right arm, me under his left."

"What about me?" Harry asked.

"Walk behind us. If he looks like going over backward, shove him forward again."

"And if that don't work, kinda crouch down where you think he's gonna land and soften the blow," Brutal said.

"Gosh," Harry said thinly, "you oughta go on the Orpheum Circuit, Brute, that's how funny *you* are."

"I got a sense of humor, all right," Brutal admitted.

In the end, we did manage to get John up the stairs. My biggest worry was that he might faint, but he didn't. "Go around me and check to make sure the storage room's empty," I gasped to Harry.

"What should I say if it's not?" Harry asked, squeezing under my arm. " 'Avon calling,' and then pop back in here?"

"Don't be a wisenheimer," Brutal said.

Harry eased the door open a little way and poked his head through. It seemed to me that he stayed that way for a very long time. At last he pulled back, looking almost cheerful. "Coast's clear. And it's *quiet*."

"Let's hope it stays that way," Brutal said. "Come on, John Coffey, almost home."

He was able to cross the storage room under his own power, but we had to help him up the three steps to my office and then almost push him through the little door. When he got to his feet again, he was breathing stertorously, and his eyes had a glassy sheen. Also—I noticed this with real horror—the right side of his mouth had pulled down, making it look like Melinda's had, when we walked into her room and saw her propped up on her pillows.

Dean heard us and came in from the desk at the head of the Green Mile. "Thank God! I thought you were never coming back, I'd half made up my mind you were caught, or the Warden plugged you, or—" He broke off, really seeing John for the first time. "Holy cats, what's wrong with him? He looks like he's dying!"

"He's not dying . . . are you, John?" Brutal said. His eyes flashed Dean a warning.

"Course not, I didn't mean actually *dyin'*"—Dean gave a nervous little laugh—"but, jeepers . . ."

"Never mind," I said. "Help us get him back to his cell."

Once again we were foothills surrounding a mountain, but now it was a mountain that had suffered a few million years' worth of erosion, one that was blunted and sad. John Coffey moved slowly, breathing through his mouth like an old man who smoked too much, but at least he moved.

"What about Percy?" I asked. "Has he been kicking up a ruckus?"

"Some at the start," Dean said. "Trying to yell through the tape you put over his mouth. Cursing, I believe."

"Mercy me," Brutal said. "A good thing our tender ears were elsewhere."

"Since then, just a mulekick at the door every once in awhile, you know." Dean was so relieved to see us that he was babbling. His glasses slipped down to the end of his nose, which was shiny with sweat, and he pushed them back up. We passed Wharton's cell. That worthless young man was flat on his back, snoring like a sousaphone. His eyes were shut this time, all right.

Dean saw me looking and laughed.

"No trouble from that guy! Hasn't moved since he laid back down on his bunk. Dead to the world. As for Percy kicking the door every now and then, I never minded that a bit. Was glad of it, tell you the truth. If he didn't make any noise at all, I'd start wonderin if he hadn't choked to death on that gag you slapped over his cakehole. But that's not the best. You know the best? It's been as quiet as Ash Wednesday morning in New Orleans! Nobody's been down all night!" He said this last in a triumphant, gloating voice. "We got away with it, boys! We did!"

That made him think of why we'd gone through the whole comedy in the first place, and he asked about Melinda.

"She's fine," I said. We had reached John's cell. What Dean had said was just starting to sink in: *We got away with it, boys . . . we did.*

"Was it like . . . you know . . . the mouse?" Dean asked. He glanced briefly at the empty cell where Delacroix had lived with Mr. Jingles, then down at the restraint room, which had been the mouse's seeming point of origin. His voice dropped, the way people's voices do when they enter a big church where even the silence seems to whisper. "Was it a . . ." He gulped. "Shoot, you know what I mean—was it a miracle?"

The three of us looked at each other briefly, confirming what we already knew. "Brought her back from her damn grave is what he did," Harry said. "Yeah, it was a miracle, all right."

Brutal opened the double locks on the cell, and gave John a gentle push inside. "Go on, now, big boy. Rest awhile. You earned it. We'll just settle Percy's hash—"

"He's a bad man," John said in a low, mechanical voice.

"That's right, no doubt, wicked as a warlock," Brutal agreed in his most soothing voice, "but don't you worry a smidge about him, we're not going to let him near you. You just ease down on that bunk of yours and I'll have that cup of coffee to you in no time. Hot and strong. You'll feel like a new man."

John sat heavily on his bunk. I thought he'd fall back on it and roll to the wall as he usually did, but he just sat there for the time being, hands clasped loosely between his knees, head lowered, breathing hard through his mouth. The St. Christopher's medal Melinda had given him had fallen out of the top of his shirt and swung back and forth in the air. He'll keep you safe, that's what she'd told him, but John Coffey didn't look a bit safe. He looked like he had taken Melinda's place on the lip of that grave Harry had spoken of.

But I couldn't think about John Coffey just then.

I turned around to the others. "Dean, get Percy's pistol and hickory stick."

"Okay." He went back up to the desk, unlocked the drawer with the gun and the stick in it, and brought them back.

"Ready?" I asked them. My men—good men, and I was never prouder of them than I was that night—nodded. Harry and Dean both looked nervous; Brutal as stolid as ever. "Okay. I'm going to do the talking. The less the rest of you open your mouths, the better it'll probably be and the quicker it'll probably wrap up . . . for better or worse. Okay?"

They nodded again. I took a deep breath and walked down to the Green Mile restraint room.

Percy looked up, squinting, when the light fell on him. He was sitting on the floor and licking at the tape I had slapped across his mouth. The part I'd wound around to the back of his head had come free (probably the sweat and brilliantine in his hair had loosened it), and he'd gotten a ways toward getting the rest off, as well. Another hour and he would've been bawling for help at the top of his lungs.

He used his feet to shove himself a little way backward when we came in, then stopped, no doubt realizing that there was nowhere to go except for the southeast corner of the room.

I took his gun and stick from Dean and held them out in Percy's direction. "Want these back?" I asked.

He looked at me warily, then nodded his head.

"Brutal," I said. "Harry. Get him on his feet."

They bent, hooked him under the canvas arms of the straitjacket, and up he came. I moved toward him until we were almost nose to nose. I could smell the sour sweat in which he'd been basting. Some of it probably came from his efforts to get free of the quiet-down coat, or to administer the occasional kicks to the door Dean had heard, but I thought most of his sweat had come as a result of plain old fear: fear of what we might do to him when we came back.

I'll be okay, they ain't *killers*, Percy would think . . . and then, maybe, he'd think of Old Sparky and it would cross his mind that yes, in a way we *were* killers. I'd done seventy-seven myself, more than any of the men I'd ever put the chest-strap on, more than Sergeant York himself got credit for in World War I. Killing Percy wouldn't be logical, but we'd already behaved illogically, he would have told himself as he sat there with his arms behind him, working with his tongue to get the tape off his mouth. And besides, logic most likely doesn't have much power over a person's thoughts when that person is sitting on the floor of a room with soft walls, wrapped up as neat and tight as any spider ever wrapped a fly.

Which is to say, if I didn't have him where I wanted now, I never would.

"I'll take the tape off your mouth if you promise not to start yowling," I said. "I want to have a talk with you, not a shouting match. So what do you say? Will you be quiet?"

I saw relief come up in his eyes as he realized that, if I wanted to talk, he really did stand a good chance of getting out of this with a whole skin. He nodded his head.

"If you start noising off, the tape goes back on," I said. "Do you understand that, too?"

Another nod, rather impatient this time.

I reached up, grabbed the end of the runner he'd worked loose, and gave it a hard yank. It made a loud peeling sound. Brutal winced. Percy yipped with pain and his eyes watered.

"Get me out of this nut-coat, you lugoon," he spat.

"In a minute," I said.

"Now! Now! Right n—"

I slapped his face. It was done before I'd even known I was going to do it . . . but of course I'd known it *might* come to that. Even back during the first talk about Percy that I'd had with Warden Moores, the one where Hal advised me to put Percy out for the Delacroix execution, I'd known it *might* come to that. A man's hand is like an animal that's only half-tame; mostly it's good, but sometimes it escapes and bites the first thing it sees.

The sound was a sharp *snap*, like a breaking branch. Dean gasped. Percy stared at me in utter shock, his eyes so wide they looked as if they must fall out of their sockets. His mouth opened and closed, opened and closed, like the mouth of a fish in an aquarium tank.

"Shut up and listen to me," I said. "You deserved to be punished for what you did to Del, and we gave you what you deserved. This was the only way we could do it. We all agreed, except for Dean, and he'll go along with us, because we'll make him sorry if he doesn't. Isn't that so, Dean?"

"Yes," Dean whispered. He was milk-pale. "Guess it is."

"And we'll make *you* sorry you were ever born," I went on. "We'll see that people know about how you sabotaged the Delacroix execution—"

"Sabotaged—!"

"—and how you almost got Dean killed. We'll blab enough to keep you out of almost any job your uncle can get you."

Percy was shaking his head furiously. He didn't believe that, perhaps *couldn't* believe that. My handprint stood out on his pale cheek like a fortune-teller's sign.

"And no matter what, we'd see you beaten within an inch of your life. We wouldn't have to do it ourselves. We know people, too, Percy, are you so foolish you don't realize that? They aren't up in the state capital, but they still know how to legislate certain matters. These are people who have friends in here, people who have brothers in here, people who have fathers in here. They'd be happy to amputate the nose or the penis of a shitheels like you. They'd do it just so someone they care for could get an extra three hours in the exercise yard each week."

Percy had stopped shaking his head. Now he was only staring. Tears stood in his eyes, but didn't fall. I think they were tears of rage and frustration. Or maybe I just hoped they were.

"Okay—now look on the sunny side, Percy. Your lips sting a little from having the tape pulled off them, I imagine, but otherwise there's nothing hurt but your pride . . . and nobody needs to know about that but the people in this room right now. And we'll never tell, will we, boys?"

They shook their heads. "Course not," Brutal said. "Green Mile business stays on the Green Mile. Always has."

"You're going on to Briar Ridge and we're going to leave you alone until you go," I said. "Do you want to leave it at that, Percy, or do you want to play hardball with us?"

There was a long, long silence as he considered—I could almost see the wheels turning in his head as he tried out and rejected possible counters. And at last, I think a more basic truth must have over-whelmed the rest of his calculations: the tape was off his mouth, but he was still wearing the straitjacket and probably he had to piss like a racehorse.

"All right," he said. "We'll consider the matter closed. Now get me out of this coat. It feels like my shoulders are—"

Brutal stepped forward, shouldering me aside, and grabbed Percy's face with one big hand—fingers denting in Percy's right cheek, thumb making a deep dimple in his left.

"In a few seconds," he said. "First, you listen to me. Paul here is the big boss, and so he has to talk elegant sometimes."

I tried to remember anything elegant I might've said to Percy and couldn't come up with much. Still, I thought it might be best to keep my mouth shut; Percy looked suitably terrorized, and I didn't want to spoil the effect.

"People don't always understand that being elegant isn't the same as being soft, and that's where I come in. I don't worry about being ele-gant. I just say things straight out. So here it is, straight out: if you go back on your promise, we'll most likely take an ass-fucking. But then we'll find you—if we have to go all the way to Russia, we'll find you—and *we* will fuck *you*, not just up the ass but in every hole you own. We'll fuck you until you'll wish you were dead, and then we'll rub vinegar in the parts that are bleeding. Do you understand me?"

He nodded. With Brutal's hand digging into the soft sides of his face the way it was, Percy looked eerily like Old Toot-Toot.

Brutal let go of him and stepped back. I nodded to Harry, who went behind Percy and started unsnapping and unbuckling.

"Keep it in mind, Percy," Harry said. "Keep it in mind and let bygones be bygones."

All of it suitably scary, three bogeymen in bluesuits . . . but I felt a kind of knowing despair sweep through me, all the same. He might keep quiet for a day or a week, continuing to calculate the odds on various actions, but in the end two things—his belief in his connections and his inability to walk away from a situation where he saw himself as the loser—would combine. When that happened, he would spill his guts. We had perhaps helped to save Melly Moores's life by taking John to her, and I wouldn't have changed that ("not for all the tea in China," as we used to say back in those days), but in the end we were going to hit the canvas and the ref was going to count us out. Short of murder, there was no way we could make Percy keep his end of the bargain, not once he was away from us and had started to get back what passed for his guts.

I took a little sidelong glance at Brutal and saw he knew this, too. Which didn't surprise me. There were no flies on Mrs. Howell's boy Brutus, never had been. He gave me a tiny shrug, just one shoulder lifting an inch and then dropping, but it was enough. *So what?* that shrug said. *What else is there, Paul? We did what we had to do, and we did it the best we could.*

Yes. Results hadn't been half-bad, either.

Harry undid the last buckle on the straitjacket. Grimacing with disgust and rage, Percy pawed it off and let it drop at his feet. He wouldn't look at any of us, not directly.

"Give me my gun and my baton," he said. I handed them over. He dropped the gun into its holster and shoved the hickory stick into its custom loop.

"Percy, if you think about it—"

"Oh, I intend to," he said, brushing past me. "I intend to think about it very hard. Starting right now. On my way home. One of you boys can clock me out at quitting time." He reached the door of the restraint room and turned to survey us with a look of angry, embarrassed contempt—a deadly combination for the secret we'd had some fool's hope of keeping. "Unless, of course, you want to try explaining why I left early."

He left the room and went striding up the Green Mile, forgetting in his agitation why that green-floored central corridor was so wide. He had made this mistake once before and had gotten away with it. He would not get away with it again.

I followed him out the door, trying to think of a way to soothe him down—I didn't want him leaving E Block the way he was now, sweaty and dishevelled, with the red print of my hand still on his cheek. The other three followed me.

What happened then happened very fast—it was all over in no more than a minute, perhaps even less. Yet I remember all of it to this day—mostly, I think, because I told Janice everything when I got home and that set it in my mind. What happened afterward—the dawn meeting with Curtis Anderson, the inquest, the press-meeting Hal Moores set up for us (he was back by then, of course), and the eventual Board of Enquiry in the state capital—those things have blurred over the years like so much else in my memory. But as to what actually happened next there on the Green Mile, yes, that I remember perfectly well.

Percy was walking up the right side of the Mile with his head lowered, and I'll say this much: no ordinary prisoner could have reached him. John Coffey wasn't an ordinary prisoner, though. John Coffey was a giant, and he had a giant's reach.

I saw his long brown arms shoot out from between the bars and yelled, *"Watch it, Percy, watch it!"* Percy started to turn, his left hand dropping to the butt of his stick. Then he was seized and yanked against the front of John Coffey's cell, the right side of his face smashing into the bars.

He grunted and turned toward Coffey, raising the hickory club. John was certainly vulnerable to it; his own face was pressed so strenuously into the space between two of the center bars that he looked as if he was trying to squeeze his entire head through. It would have been impossible, of course, but that was how it looked. His right hand groped, found the nape of Percy's neck, curled around it, and yanked Percy's head forward. Percy brought the club down between the bars and onto John's temple. Blood flowed, but John paid no attention. His mouth pressed against Percy's mouth. I heard a whispering rush—an exhalatory sound, as of long-held breath. Percy jerked like a fish on a hook, trying to get away, but he never had a chance; John's right hand was pressed to the back of his neck, holding him firm. Their faces seemed to melt together, like the faces of lovers I have seen kissing passionately through bars.

Percy screamed, the sound muffled as it had been through the tape, and made another effort to pull back. For an instant their lips came apart a little, and I saw the black, swirling tide that was flowing out of John Coffey and into Percy Wetmore. What wasn't going into him through his quivering mouth was flowing in by way of his nostrils. Then the hand on the nape of his neck flexed, and Percy was pulled forward onto John's mouth again; was almost impaled on it.

Percy's left hand sprang open. His treasured hickory baton fell to the green linoleum. He never picked it up again.

I tried to lunge forward, I guess I *did* lunge forward, but my movements felt old and creaky to myself. I grabbed for my gun, but the strap was still across the burled-walnut grip, and at first I couldn't get it out of its holster. Beneath me, I seemed to feel the floor shake as it had in the back bedroom of the Warden's neat little Cape Cod. That I'm not sure of, but I know that one of the caged lightbulbs overhead broke. Fragments of glass showered down. Harry yelled in surprise.

At last I managed to thumb loose the safety strap over the butt of my .38, but before I could pull it out of its holster, John had thrust Percy away from him and stepped back into his cell. John was grimacing and rubbing his mouth, as if he had tasted something bad.

"What'd he do?" Brutal shouted. "What'd he do, Paul?"

"Whatever he took out of Melly, Percy's got it now," I said.

Percy was standing against the bars of Delacroix's old cell. His eyes were wide and blank—double zeros. I approached him carefully, expecting him to start coughing and choking the way John had after he'd finished with Melinda, but he didn't. At first he only stood there.

I snapped my fingers in front of his eyes. "Percy! Hey, Percy! Wake up!"

Nothing. Brutal joined me, and reached toward Percy's empty face with both hands.

"That isn't going to work," I said.

Ignoring me, Brutal clapped his hands sharply together twice, right in front of Percy's nose. And it *did* work, or appeared to work. His eyelids fluttered and he stared around—dazed, like someone hit over the head struggling back to consciousness. He looked from Brutal to me. All these years later, I'm pretty sure he didn't see either of us, but I thought he did then; I thought he was coming out of it.

He pushed away from the bars and swayed a little on his feet. Brutal steadied him. "Easy, boy, you all right?" Percy didn't answer, just stepped past Brutal and turned toward the duty desk. He wasn't staggering, exactly, but he was listing to port.

Brutal reached out for him. I pushed his hand away. "Leave him alone." Would I have said the same if I'd known what was going to happen next? I've asked myself that question a thousand times since the fall of 1932. There's never any answer.

Percy made twelve or fourteen paces, then stopped again, head lowered. He was outside of Wild Bill Wharton's cell by then. Wharton was still making those sousaphone noises. He slept through the whole thing. He slept through his own death, now that I think of it, which made him a lot luckier than most of the men who ended up here. Certainly luckier than he deserved.

Before we knew what was happening, Percy drew his gun, stepped to the bars of Wharton's cell, and emptied all six shots into the sleeping man. Just bam-bam-bam, bam-bam-bam, as fast as he could pull the trigger. The sound in that enclosed space was deafening; when I told Janice the story the next morning, I could still hardly hear the sound of my own voice for the ringing in my ears.

We ran at him, all four of us. Dean got there first—I don't know how, as he was behind Brutal and me when Coffey had hold of Percy—but he did. He grabbed Percy's wrist, prepared to wrestle the gun out of Percy's hand, but he didn't have to. Percy just let go, and the gun fell to the floor. His eyes went across us like they were skates and we were ice. There was a low hissing sound and a sharp ammoniac smell as Percy's bladder let go, then a *brrrap* sound and a thicker stink as he filled the other side of his pants, as well. His eyes had settled on a far corner of the corridor. They were eyes that never saw anything in this real world of ours again, so far as I know. Back near the beginning of this I wrote that Percy was at Briar Ridge by the time that Brutal found the colored slivers of Mr. Jingles's spool a couple of months later, and I didn't lie about that. He never got the office with the fan in the corner, though; never got a bunch of lunatic patients to push around, either. But I imagine he at least got his own private room.

He had connections, after all.

Wharton was lying on his side with his back against the wall of his cell. I couldn't see much then but a lot of blood soaking into the sheet and splattered across the cement, but the coroner said Percy had shot like Annie Oakley. Remembering Dean's story of how Percy had thrown his hickory baton at the mouse that time and barely missed, I wasn't too surprised. This time the range had been shorter and the target not moving. One in the groin, one in the gut, one in the chest, three in the head.

Brutal was coughing and waving at the haze of gunsmoke. I was coughing myself, but hadn't noticed it until then.

"End of the line," Brutal said. His voice was calm, but there was no mistaking the glaze of panic in his eyes.

I looked down the hallway and saw John Coffey sitting on the end of his bunk. His hands were clasped between his knees again, but his head was up and he no longer looked a bit sick. He nodded at me slightly, and I surprised myself—as I had on the day I offered him my hand— by returning the nod.

"What are we going to do?" Harry gibbered. "Oh Christ, what are we going to do?"

"Nothing we *can* do," Brutal said in that same calm voice. "We're hung. Aren't we, Paul?"

My mind had begun to move very fast. I looked at Harry and Dean, who were staring at me like scared kids. I looked at Percy, who was standing there with his hands and jaw dangling. Then I looked at my old friend, Brutus Howell.

"We're going to be okay," I said.

Percy at last commenced coughing. He doubled over, hands on his knees, almost retching. His face began to turn red. I opened my mouth, meaning to tell the others to stand back, but I never got a chance. He made a sound that was a cross between a dry-heave and a bullfrog's croak, opened his mouth, and spewed out a cloud of black, swirling stuff. It was so thick that for a moment we couldn't see his head. Harry said "Oh God save us" in a weak and watery voice. Then the stuff turned a white so dazzling it was like January sun on fresh snow. A moment later the cloud was gone. Percy straightened slowly up and resumed his vacant gaze down the length of the Green Mile.

"We didn't see that," Brutal said. "Did we, Paul?"

"No. I didn't and you didn't. Did you see it, Harry?"

"No," Harry said.

"Dean?"

"See what?" Dean took his glasses off and began to polish them. I thought he would drop them out of his trembling hands, but he managed not to.

" 'See what,' that's good. That's just the ticket. Now listen to your scoutmaster, boys, and get it right the first time, because time is short. It's a simple story. Let's not complicate it."

3

I TOLD ALL THIS to Jan at around eleven o'clock that morning—*the next morning*, I almost wrote, but of course it was the same day. The longest one of my whole life, without a doubt. I told it pretty much as I have here, finishing with how William Wharton had ended up lying dead on his bunk, riddled with lead from Percy's sidearm.

No, that's not right. What I *actually* finished with was the stuff that came out of Percy, the bugs or the whatever-it-was. That was a hard thing to tell, even to your wife, but I told it.

As I talked, she brought me black coffee by the half-cup—at first my hands were shaking too badly to pick up a whole one without spilling it. By the time I finished, the shaking had eased some, and I felt that I could even take some food—an egg, maybe, or some soup.

"The thing that saved us was that we didn't really have to lie, any of us."

"Just leave a few things out," she said, and nodded. "Little things, mostly, like how you took a condemned murderer out of prison, and how he cured a dying woman, and how he drove that Percy Wetmore crazy by—what?—spitting a pureed brain tumor down his throat?"

"I don't know, Jan," I said. "I only know that if you keep talking like that, you'll end up either eating that soup yourself, or feeding it to the dog."

"I'm sorry. But I'm right, aren't I?"

"Yeah," I said. "Except we got away with the—" The what? You

342

couldn't call it an escape, and furlough wasn't right, either. "—the field trip. Not even Percy can tell them about that, if he ever comes back."

"If he comes back," she echoed. "How likely is that?"

I shook my head to indicate I had no idea. But I did, actually; I didn't think he *was* going to come back, not in 1932, not in '42 or '52, either. In that I was right. Percy Wetmore stayed at Briar Ridge until it burned flat in 1944. Seventeen inmates were killed in that fire, but Percy wasn't one of them. Still silent and blank in every regard—the word I learned to describe that state is *catatonic*—he was led out by one of the guards long before the fire reached his wing. He went on to another institution—I don't remember the name and guess it doesn't matter, anyway—and died in 1965. So far as I know, the last time he ever spoke was when he told us we could clock him out at quitting time . . . unless we wanted to explain why he had left early.

The irony was that we never had to explain much of anything. Percy had gone crazy and shot William Wharton to death. That was what we told, and so far as it went, every word was true. When Anderson asked Brutal how Percy had seemed before the shooting and Brutal answered with one word—*"Quiet"*—I had a terrible moment when I felt that I might burst out laughing. Because that was true, too, Percy *had* been quiet, for most of his shift he'd had a swatch of friction-tape across his mouth and the best he'd been able to come up with was *mmmph, mmmph, mmmph.*

Curtis kept Percy there until eight o'clock, Percy as silent as a cigar-store Indian but a lot more eerie. By then Hal Moores had arrived, looking grim but competent, ready to climb back into the saddle. Curtis Anderson let him do just that, and with a sigh of relief the rest of us could almost hear. The bewildered, frightened old man was gone; it was the Warden who strode up to Percy, grabbed him by the shoulders with his big hands, and shook him hard.

"Son!" he shouted into Percy's blank face—a face that was already starting to soften like wax, I thought. *"Son!* Do you hear me? Talk to me if you hear me! I want to know what happened!"

Nothing from Percy, of course. Anderson wanted to get the Warden aside, discuss how they were going to handle it—it was a political hot potato if there had ever been one—but Moores put him off, at least for the time being, and drew me down the Mile. John Coffey was lying on his bunk with his face to the wall, legs dangling outrageously, as they always did. He appeared to be sleeping and probably was . . . but he wasn't *always* what he appeared, as we had found out.

"Did what happened at my house have anything to do with what happened here when you got back?" Moores asked in a low voice. "I'll cover you as much as I can, even if it means my job, but I have to know."

I shook my head. When I spoke, I also kept my voice low-pitched. There were now almost a dozen screws milling around at the head of the aisle. Another was photographing Wharton in his cell. Curtis Anderson had turned to watch that, and for the time being, only Brutal was watching us. "No, sir. We got John back into his cell just like you see, then let Percy out of the restraint room, where we'd stashed him for safekeeping. I thought he'd be hot under the collar, but he wasn't. Just asked for his sidearm and baton. He didn't say anything else, just walked off up the corridor. Then, when he got to Wharton's cell, he pulled his gun and started shooting."

"Do you think being in the restraint room . . . did something to his mind?"

"No, sir."

"Did you put him in the straitjacket?"

"No, sir. There was no need."

"He was quiet? Didn't struggle?"

"No struggle."

"Even when he saw you meant to put him in the restraint room, he was quiet and didn't struggle."

"That's right." I felt an urge to embroider on this—to give Percy at least a line or two—and conquered it. Simpler would be better, and I knew it. "There was no fuss. He just went over into one of the far corners and sat down."

"Didn't speak of Wharton then?"

"No, sir."

"Didn't speak of Coffey, either?"

I shook my head.

"Could Percy have been laying for Wharton? Did he have something against the man?"

"That might be," I said, lowering my voice even more. "Percy was careless about where he walked, Hal. One time Wharton reached out, grabbed him up against the bars, and messed him over some." I paused. "Felt him up, you could say."

"No worse than that? Just . . . 'messed him over' . . . and that was all?"

"Yes, but it was pretty bad for Percy, just the same. Wharton said something about how he'd rather screw Percy than Percy's sister."

"Um." Moores kept looking sideways at John Coffey, as if he needed constant reassurance that Coffey was a real person, actually in the world. "It doesn't explain what's happened to him, but it goes a good piece toward explaining why it was Wharton he turned on and not Coffey or one of you men. And speaking of your men, Paul, will they all tell the same story?"

"Yes, sir," I told him. "And they will," I said to Jan, starting in on the soup she brought to the table. "I'll see to it."

"You *did* lie," she said. "You lied to Hal."

Well, that's a wife for you, isn't it? Always poking around for moth-holes in your best suit, and finding one more often than not.

"I guess, if you want to look at it that way. I didn't tell him anything we both won't be able to live with, though. Hal's in the clear, I think. He wasn't even *there*, after all. He was home tending his wife until Curtis called him."

"Did he say how Melinda was?"

"Not then, there wasn't time, but we spoke again just as Brutal and I were leaving. Melly doesn't remember much, but she's fine. Up and walking. Talking about next year's flower beds."

My wife sat watching me eat for some little time. Then she asked, "Does Hal know it's a miracle, Paul? Does he understand that?"

"Yes. We all do, all of us that were there."

"Part of me wishes I'd been there, too," she said, "but I think most of me is glad I wasn't. If I'd seen the scales fall from Saul's eyes on the road to Damascus, I probably would have died of a heart attack."

"Naw," I said, tilting my bowl to capture the last spoonful, "probably would have cooked him some soup. This is pretty fine, hon."

"Good." But she wasn't really thinking about soup or cooking or Saul's conversion on the Damascus road. She was looking out the window toward the ridges, her chin propped on her hand, her eyes as hazy as those ridges look on summer mornings when it's going to be hot. Summer mornings like the one when the Detterick girls had been found, I thought for no reason. I wondered why they hadn't screamed. Their killer had hurt them; there had been blood on the porch, and on the steps. So why hadn't they screamed?

"You think John Coffey really killed that man Wharton, don't you?" Janice asked, looking back from the window at last. "Not that it was an accident, or anything like that; you think he used Percy Wetmore on Wharton like a gun."

"Yes."

"Why?"

"I don't know."

"Tell me again about what happened when you took Coffey off the Mile, would you? Just that part."

So I did. I told her how the skinny arm shooting out from between the bars and grabbing John's bicep had reminded me of a snake—one of the water moccasins we were all scared of when we were kids swimming in the river—and how Coffey had said Wharton was a bad man. Almost whispering it.

"And Wharton said . . . ?" My wife was looking out the window again, but she was listening, all right.

"Wharton said, 'That's right, nigger, bad as you'd want.' "

"And that's all."

"Yes. I had a feeling that something was going to happen right then, but nothing did. Brutal took Wharton's hand off John and told him to lie down, which Wharton did. He was out on his feet to start with. Said something about how niggers should have their own electric chair, and that was all. We went about our business."

"John Coffey called him a bad man."

"Yep. Said the same thing about Percy once, too. Maybe more than once. I can't remember exactly when, but I know he did."

"But Wharton never did anything to John Coffey personally, did he? Like he did to Percy, I mean."

"No. The way their cells were—Wharton up by the duty desk on one side, John down a ways on the other—they could hardly see each other."

"Tell me again how Coffey looked when Wharton grabbed him."

"Janice, this isn't getting us anywhere."

"Maybe it isn't and maybe it is. Tell me again how he looked."

I sighed. "I guess you'd have to say shocked. He gasped. Like you would if you were sunning at the beach and I snuck up and trickled a little cold water down your back. Or like he'd been slapped."

"Well, sure," she said. "Being grabbed out of nowhere like that startled him, woke him up for a second."

"Yes," I said. And then, "No."

"Well which is it? Yes or no?"

"No. It wasn't being *startled*. It was like when he wanted me to come into his cell so he could cure my infection. Or when he wanted me to hand him the mouse. It was being surprised, but not by being touched . . . not *exactly*, anyway . . . oh, Christ, Jan, I don't know."

"All right, we'll leave it," she said. "I just can't imagine why John did it, that's all. It's not as if he's violent by nature. Which leads to another question, Paul: how can you execute him if you're right about those girls? How can you possibly put him in the electric chair if someone else—"

I jerked in my chair. My elbow struck my bowl and knocked it off onto the floor, where it broke. An idea had come to me. It was more intuition than logic at that point, but it had a certain black elegance.

"Paul?" Janice asked, alarmed. "What's wrong?"

"I don't know," I said. "I don't know anything for sure, but I'm going to find out if I can."

4

THE AFTERMATH of the shooting was a three-ring circus, with the governor in one ring, the prison in another, and poor brain-blasted Percy Wetmore in the third. And the ringmaster? Well, the various gentlemen of the press took turns at that job. They weren't as bad then as they are now—they didn't *allow* themselves to be as bad—but even back then before Geraldo and Mike Wallace and the rest of them, they could gallop along pretty good when they really got the bit in their teeth. That was what happened this time, and while the show lasted, it was a good one.

But even the liveliest circus, the one with the scariest freaks, funniest clowns, and wildest animals, has to leave town eventually. This one left after the Board of Enquiry, which sounds pretty special and fearsome, but actually turned out to be pretty tame and perfunctory. Under other circumstances, the governor undoubtedly would have demanded someone's head on a platter, but not this time. His nephew by marriage—his wife's own blood kin—had gone crackers and killed a man. Had killed a killer—there was that, at least, and thank God for it—but Percy had still shot the man as he lay sleeping in his cell, which was not quite sporting. When you added in the fact that the young man in question remained just as mad as a March hare, you could understand why the governor only wanted it to go away, and as soon as possible.

Our trip to Warden Moores's house in Harry Terwilliger's truck never came out. The fact that Percy had been straitjacketed and locked in the restraint room during the time we were away never came out. The fact that William Wharton had been doped to the gills when Percy

348

shot him never came out, either. Why would it? The authorities had no reason to suspect anything in Wharton's system but half a dozen slugs. The coroner removed those, the mortician put him in a pine box, and that was the end of the man with *Billy the Kid* tattooed on his left forearm. Good riddance to bad rubbish, you might say.

All in all, the uproar lasted about two weeks. During that time I didn't dare fart sideways, let alone take a day off to investigate the idea I'd gotten at my kitchen table on the morning after all the upheavals. I knew for sure that the circus had left town when I got to work on a day just shy of the middle of November—the twelfth, I think, but don't hold me to that. That was the day I found the piece of paper I'd been dreading on the middle of my desk: the DOE on John Coffey. Curtis Anderson had signed it instead of Hal Moores, but of course it was just as legal either way, and of course it had needed to go through Hal in order to get to me. I could imagine Hal sitting at his desk in Administration with that piece of paper in his hand, sitting there and thinking of his wife, who had become something of a nine days' wonder to the doctors at Indianola General Hospital. She'd had her own DOE papers handed to her by those doctors, but John Coffey had torn them up. Now, however, it was Coffey's turn to walk the Green Mile, and who among us could stop it? Who among us *would* stop it?

The date on the death warrant was November 20th. Three days after I got it—the fifteenth, I think—I had Janice call me in sick. A cup of coffee later I was driving north in my badly sprung but otherwise reliable Ford. Janice had kissed me on my way and wished me good luck; I'd thanked her but no longer had any clear idea what good luck would be—finding what I was looking for or not finding it. All I knew for sure is that I didn't feel much like singing as I drove. Not that day.

By three that afternoon I was well up in the ridge country. I got to the Purdom County Courthouse just before it closed, looked at some records, then had a visit from the Sheriff, who had been informed by the county clerk that a stranger was poking in amongst the local skeletons. Sheriff Catlett wanted to know what I thought I was doing. I told him. Catlett thought it over and then told me something interesting. He said he'd deny he'd ever said a word if I spread it around, and it wasn't conclusive anyway, but it was something, all right. It was sure something. I thought about it all the way home, and that night there was a lot of thinking and precious little sleeping on my side of the bed.

The next day I got up while the sun was still just a rumor in the east and drove downstate to Trapingus County. I skirted around Homer Cribus, that great bag of guts and waters, speaking to Deputy Sheriff Rob McGee instead. McGee didn't want to hear what I was telling him. Most vehemently didn't want to hear it. At one point I was pretty sure he was going to punch me in the mouth so he could *stop* hearing it, but in the end he agreed to go out and ask Klaus Detterick a couple of questions. Mostly, I think, so he could be sure I wouldn't. "He's only thirty-nine, but he looks like an old man these days," McGee said, "and he don't need a smartass prison guard who thinks he's a detective to stir him up just when some of the sorrow has started to settle. You stay right here in town. I don't want you within hailing distance of the Detterick farm, but I want to be able to find you when I'm done talking to Klaus. If you start feeling restless, have a piece of pie down there in the diner. It'll weight you down." I ended up having two pieces, and it *was* kind of heavy.

When McGee came into the diner and sat down at the counter next to me, I tried to read his face and failed. "Well?" I asked.

"Come on home with me, we'll talk there," he said. "This place is a mite too public for my taste."

We had our conference on Rob McGee's front porch. Both of us were bundled up and chilly, but Mrs. McGee didn't allow smoking anywhere in her house. She was a woman ahead of her time. McGee talked awhile. He did it like a man who doesn't in the least enjoy what he's hearing out of his own mouth.

"It proves nothing, you know that, don't you?" he asked when he was pretty well done. His tone was belligerent, and he poked his home-rolled cigarette at me in an aggressive way as he spoke, but his face was sick. Not all proof is what you see and hear in a court of law, and we both knew it. I have an idea that was the only time in his life when Deputy McGee wished he was as country-dumb as his boss.

"I know," I said.

"And if you're thinking of getting him a new trial on the basis of this one thing, you better think again, *señor*. John Coffey is a Negro, and in Trapingus County we're awful particular about giving new trials to Negroes."

"I know that, too."

"So what are you going to do?"

I pitched my cigarette over the porch rail and into the street. Then I stood up. It was going to be a long, cold ride back home, and the sooner I got going the sooner the trip would be done. "That I wish I did know, Deputy McGee," I said, "but I don't. The only thing I know tonight for a fact is that second piece of pie was a mistake."

"I'll tell you something, smart guy," he said, still speaking in that tone of hollow belligerence. "I don't think you should have opened Pandora's Box in the first place."

"It wasn't me opened it," I said, and then drove home.

I got there late—after midnight—but my wife was waiting up for me. I'd suspected she would be, but it still did my heart good to see her, and to have her put her arms around my neck and her body nice and firm against mine. "Hello, stranger," she said, and then touched me down below. "Nothing wrong with this fellow now, is there? He's just as healthy as can be."

"Yes, ma'am," I said, and lifted her up in my arms. I took her into the bedroom and we made love as sweet as sugar, and as I came to my climax, that delicious feeling of going out and letting go, I thought of John Coffey's endlessly weeping eyes. And of Melinda Moores saying *I dreamed you were wandering in the dark, and so was I.*

Still lying on top of my wife, with her arms around my neck and our thighs together, I began to weep myself.

"Paul!" she said, shocked and afraid. I don't think she'd seen me in tears more than half a dozen times before in the entire course of our marriage. I have never been, in the ordinary course of things, a crying man. "Paul, what is it?"

"I know everything there is to know," I said through my tears. "I know too goddam much, if you want to know the truth. I'm supposed to electrocute John Coffey in less than a week's time, but it was William Wharton who killed the Detterick girls. It was Wild Bill."

5

THE NEXT DAY, the same bunch of screws who had eaten lunch in my kitchen after the botched Delacroix execution ate lunch there again. This time there was a fifth at our council of war: my wife. It was Jan who convinced me to tell the others; my first impulse had been not to. Wasn't it bad enough, I asked her, that *we* knew?

"You're not thinking clear about it," she'd answered. "Probably because you're still upset. They already know the worst thing, that John's on the spot for a crime he didn't commit. If anything, this makes it a little better."

I wasn't so sure, but I deferred to her judgement. I expected an uproar when I told Brutal, Dean, and Harry what I knew (I couldn't prove it, but I knew, all right), but at first there was only thoughtful silence. Then, taking another of Janice's biscuits and beginning to put an outrageous amount of butter on it, Dean said: "Did John see him, do you think? Did he see Wharton drop the girls, maybe even rape them?"

"I think if he'd seen that, he would have tried to stop it," I said. "As for seeing Wharton, maybe as he ran off, I suppose he might have. If he did, he forgot it later."

"Sure," Dean said. "He's special, but that doesn't make him bright. He only found out it was Wharton when Wharton reached through the bars of his cell and touched him."

Brutal was nodding. "That's why John looked so surprised . . . so shocked. Remember the way his eyes opened?"

I nodded. "He used Percy on Wharton like a gun, that was what Janice said, and it was what I kept thinking about. Why would John Coffey want to kill Wild Bill? *Percy*, maybe—Percy stamped on Delacroix's mouse right in front of him, Percy burned Delacroix alive and John knew it—but Wharton? Wharton messed with most of us in one way or another, but he didn't mess with John at all, so far as I know—hardly passed four dozen words with him the whole time they were on the Mile together, and half of those were that last night. Why would he want to? He was from Purdom County, and as far as white boys from up there are concerned, you don't even see a Negro unless he happens to step into your road. So why did he do it? What could he've seen or felt when Wharton touched him that was so bad that he saved back the poison he took out of Melly's body?"

"And half-killed himself doing it, too," Brutal said.

"More like three-quarters. And the Detterick twins were all I could think of that was bad enough to explain what he did. I told myself the idea was nuts, too much of a coincidence, it just couldn't be. Then I remembered something Curtis Anderson wrote in the first memo I ever got about Wharton—that Wharton was crazy-wild, and that he'd rambled all over the state before the holdup where he killed all those people. *Rambled all over the state.* That stuck with me. Then there was the way he tried to choke Dean when he came in. That got me thinking about—"

"The dog," Dean said. He was rubbing his neck where Wharton had wrapped the chain. I don't think he even knew he was doing it. "How the dog's neck was broken."

"Anyway, I went on up to Purdom County to check Wharton's court records—all we had here were the reports on the murders that got him to the Green Mile. The end of his career, in other words. I wanted the beginning."

"Lot of trouble?" Brutal asked.

"Yeah. Vandalism, petty theft, setting haystack fires, even theft of an explosive—he and a friend swiped a stick of dynamite and set it off down by a creek. He got going early, ten years old, but what I wanted wasn't there. Then the Sheriff turned up to see who I was and what I was doing, and that was actually lucky. I fibbed, told him that a cell-search had turned up a bunch of pictures in Wharton's mattress—little girls with no clothes on. I said I'd wanted to see if Wharton had any kind of history as a pederast, because there were a couple of unsolved cases up in Tennessee that I'd heard about. I was careful never to mention the Detterick twins. I don't think they crossed his mind, either."

"Course not," Harry said. "Why would they have? That case is solved, after all."

"I said I guessed there was no sense chasing the idea, since there was nothing in Wharton's back file. I mean, there was *plenty* in the file, but none of it about that sort of thing. Then the Sheriff—Catlett, his name is—laughed and said not everything a bad apple like Bill Wharton did was in the court files, and what did it matter, anyway? He was dead, wasn't he?

"I said I was doing it just to satisfy my own curiosity, nothing else, and that relaxed him. He took me back to his office, sat me down, gave me a cup of coffee and a sinker, and told me that sixteen months ago, when Wharton was barely eighteen, a man in the western part of the county caught him in the barn with his daughter. It wasn't rape, exactly; the fellow described it to Catlett as 'not much more'n stinkfinger.' Sorry, honey."

"That's all right," Janice said. She looked pale, though.

"How old was the girl?" Brutal asked.

"Nine," I said.

He winced.

"The man might've taken off after Wharton himself, if he'd had him some big old brothers or cousins to give him a help, but he didn't. So he went to Catlett, but made it clear he only wanted Wharton warned. No one wants a nasty thing like that right out in public, if it can be helped. Anyway, Sheriff C. had been dealing with Wharton's antics for quite some time—had him in the reform school up that way for eight months or so when Wharton was fifteen—and he decided enough was enough. He got three deputies, they went out to the Wharton place, set Missus Wharton aside when she started to weep and wail, and then they warned Mr. William 'Billy the Kid' Wharton what happens to big pimple-faced galoots who go up in the hayloft with girls not even old enough to have heard about their monthly courses, let alone started them. 'We warned that little punk good,' Catlett told me. 'Warned him until his head was bleedin, his shoulder was dislocated, and his ass was damn near broke.' "

Brutal was laughing in spite of himself. "That sounds like Purdom County, all right," he said. "Like as not."

"It was three months later, give or take, that Wharton broke out and started the spree that ended with the holdup," I said. "That and the murders that got him to us."

"So he'd had something to do with an underage girl once," Harry said. He took off his glasses, huffed on them, polished them. "*Way* underage. Once isn't exactly a pattern, is it?"

"A man doesn't do a thing like that just once," my wife said, then pressed her lips together so tight they almost weren't there.

Next I told them about my visit to Trapingus County. I'd been a lot more frank with Rob McGee—I'd had no choice, really. To this day I have no idea what sort of story he spun for Mr. Detterick, but the McGee who sat down next to me in the diner seemed to have aged seven years.

In mid-May, about a month before the holdup and the murders which finished Wharton's short career as an outlaw, Klaus Detterick had painted his barn (and, incidentally, Bowser's doghouse next to it). He hadn't wanted his son crawling around up on a high scaffolding, and the boy had been in school, anyway, so he had hired a fellow. A nice enough fellow. Very quiet. Three days' work it had been. No, the fellow hadn't slept at the house, Detterick wasn't foolish enough to believe that nice and quiet always meant safe, especially in those days, when there was so much dust-bowl riffraff on the roads. A man with a family had to be careful. In any case, the man hadn't needed lodging; he told Detterick he had taken a room in town, at Eva Price's. There *was* a lady named Eva Price in Tefton, and she *did* rent rooms, but she hadn't had a boarder that May who fit the description of Detterick's hired man, just the usual fellows in checked suits and derby hats, hauling sample cases—drummers, in other words. McGee had been able to tell me that because he stopped at Mrs. Price's and checked on his way back from the Detterick farm— that's how upset he was.

"Even so," he added, "there's no law against a man sleeping rough in the woods, Mr. Edgecombe. I've done it a time or two myself."

The hired man didn't sleep at the Dettericks' house, but he took dinner with them twice. He would have met Howie. He would have met the girls, Cora and Kathe. He would have listened to their chatter, some of which might have been about how much they looked forward to the coming summer, because if they were good and the weather was good, Mommy sometimes let them sleep out on the porch, where they could pretend they were pioneer wives crossing the Great Plains in Conestoga wagons.

I can see him sitting there at the table, eating roast chicken and Mrs. Detterick's rye bread, listening, keeping his wolf's eyes well veiled, nodding, smiling a little, storing it all up.

"This doesn't sound like the wildman you told me about when he first came on the Mile, Paul," Janice said doubtfully. "Not a bit."

"You didn't see him up at Indianola Hospital, ma'am," Harry said. "Just standin there with his mouth open and his bare butt hangin out the back of his johnny. Lettin us dress him. We thought he was either drugged or foolish. Didn't we, Dean?"

Dean nodded.

"The day after he finished the barn and left, a man wearing a bandanna mask robbed Hampey's Freight Office in Jarvis," I told them. "Got away with seventy dollars. He also took an 1892 silver dollar the freight agent carried as a lucky piece. That silver dollar was on Wharton when he was captured, and Jarvis is only thirty miles from Tefton."

"So this robber . . . this wildman . . . you think he stopped for three days to help Klaus Detterick paint his barn," my wife said. "Ate dinner with them and said please pass the peas just like folks."

"The scariest thing about men like him is how unpredictable they are," Brutal said. "He might've been planning to kill the Dettericks and rifle their house, then changed his mind because a cloud came over the sun at the wrong time, or something like. Maybe he just wanted to cool off a little. But most likely he already had his eye on those two girls and was planning to come back. Do you think, Paul?"

I nodded. Of course I thought it. "And then there's the name he gave Detterick."

"What name?" Jan asked.

"Will Bonney."

"Bonney? I don't—"

"It was Billy the Kid's real name."

"Oh." Then her eyes widened. "Oh! So you *can* get John Coffey off! Thank God! All you have to do is show Mr. Detterick a picture of William Wharton . . . his mug-shot should do . . ."

Brutal and I exchanged an uncomfortable look. Dean was looking a bit hopeful, but Harry was staring down at his hands, as if all at once fabulously interested in his fingernails.

"What's wrong?" Janice asked. "Why are you looking at each other that way? Surely this man McGee will have to—"

"Rob McGee struck me as a good man, and I think he's a hell of a law officer," I said, "but he swings no weight in Trapingus County. The power there is Sheriff Cribus, and the day he reopens the Detterick case on the basis of what I was able to find out would be the day it snows in hell."

"But . . . if Wharton was there . . . if Detterick can identify a picture of him and they *know* he was *there* . . ."

"Him being there in May doesn't mean he came back and killed those girls in June," Brutal said. He spoke in a low, gentle voice, the way you speak when you're telling someone there's been a death in the family. "On one hand you've got this fellow who helped Klaus Detterick paint a barn and then went away. Turns out he was committing crimes all over the place, but there's nothing against him for the three days in May he was around Tefton. On the other hand, you've got this big Negro, this *huge* Negro, that you found on the riverbank, holding two little dead girls, both of them naked, in his arms."

He shook his head.

"Paul's right, Jan. McGee may have his doubts, but McGee doesn't matter. Cribus is the only one who can reopen the case, and Cribus doesn't want to mess with what he thinks of as a happy ending—'it was a nigger,' thinks he, 'and not one of our'n in any case. Beautiful, I'll go up there to Cold Mountain, have me a steak and a draft beer at Ma's, then watch him fry, and there's an end to it.' "

Janice listened to all this with a mounting expression of horror on her face, then turned to me. "But McGee believes it, doesn't he, Paul? I could see it on your face. Deputy McGee knows he arrested the wrong man. Won't he stand up to the Sheriff?"

"All he can do by standing up to him is lose his job," I said. "Yes, I think that in his heart he knows it was Wharton. But what he says to himself is that, if he keeps his mouth shut and plays the game until Cribus either retires or eats himself to death, he gets the job. And things will be different then. That's what he tells himself to get to sleep, I imagine. And he's probably not so much different than Homer about one thing. He'll tell himself, 'After all, it's only a Negro. It's not like they're going to burn a white man for it.' "

"Then you'll have to go to them," Janice said, and my heart turned cold at the decisive, no-doubt-about-it tone of her voice. "Go and tell them what you found out."

"And how should we tell them we found it out, Jan?" Brutal asked her in that same low voice. "Should we tell them about how Wharton grabbed John while we were taking him out of the prison to work a miracle on the Warden's wife?"

"No . . . of course not, but . . ." She saw how thin the ice was in that direction and skated in another one. "Lie, then," she said. She looked defiantly at Brutal, then turned that look on me. It was hot enough to smoke a hole in newspaper, you'd have said.

"Lie," I repeated. "Lie about what?"

"About what got you going, first up to Purdom County and then down to Trapingus. Go down there to that fat old Sheriff Cribus and say that Wharton *told* you he raped and murdered the Detterick girls. That he confessed." She switched her hot gaze to Brutal for a moment. "You can back him up, Brutus. You can say you were there when he confessed, you heard it, too. Why, Percy probably heard it as well, and that was probably what set him off. He shot Wharton because he couldn't stand thinking of what Wharton had done to those children. It snapped his mind. Just . . . What? What *now*, in the name of God?"

It wasn't just me and Brutal; Harry and Dean were looking at her, too, with a kind of horror.

"We never *reported* anything like that, ma'am," Harry said. He spoke as if talking to a child. "The first thing people'd ask is why we didn't. We're supposed to report anything our cell-babies say about prior crimes. Theirs or anyone else's."

"Not that we would've believed him," Brutal put in. "A man like Wild Bill Wharton lies about anything, Jan. Crimes he's committed, bigshots he's known, women he's gone to bed with, touchdowns he scored in high school, even the damn weather."

"But . . . but . . ." Her face was agonized. I went to put my arm around her and she pushed it violently away. *"But he was there! He painted their goddamned barn! HE ATE DINNER WITH THEM!"*

"All the more reason why he might take credit for the crime," Brutal said. "After all, what harm? Why not boast? You can't fry a man twice, after all."

"Let me see if I've got this right. We here at this table know that not only did John Coffey not kill those girls, he was trying to save their lives. Deputy McGee doesn't know all that, of course, but he *does* have a pretty good idea that the man condemned to die for the murders didn't do them. And still . . . *still* . . . you can't get him a new trial. Can't even reopen the case."

"Yessum," Dean said. He was polishing his glasses furiously. "That's about the size of it."

She sat with her head lowered, thinking. Brutal started to say something and I raised a hand, shushing him. I didn't believe Janice could think of a way to get John out of the killing box he was in, but I didn't believe it was impossible, either. She was a fearsomely smart lady, my wife. Fearsomely determined, as well. That's a combination that sometimes turns mountains into valleys.

"All right," she said at last. "Then you've got to get him out on your own."

"Ma'am?" Harry looked flabbergasted. Frightened, too.

"You can do it. You did it once, didn't you? You can do it again. Only this time you won't bring him back."

"Would you want to be the one to explain to my kids why their daddy is in prison, Missus Edgecombe?" Dean asked. "Charged with helping a murderer escape jail?"

"There won't be any of that, Dean; we'll work out a plan. Make it look like a real escape."

"Make sure it's a plan that could be worked out by a fellow who can't even remember how to tie his own shoes, then," Harry said. "They'll have to believe that."

She looked at him uncertainly.

"It wouldn't do any good," Brutal said. "Even if we could think of a way, it wouldn't do any good."

"Why not?" She sounded as if she might be going to cry. "Just why the damn hell not?"

"Because he's a six-foot-eight-inch baldheaded black man with barely enough brains to feed himself," I said. "How long do you think it would be before he was recaptured? Two hours? Six?"

"He got along without attracting much attention before," she said. A tear trickled down her cheek. She slapped it away with the heel of her hand.

That much was true. I had written letters to some friends and relatives of mine farther down south, asking if they'd seen anything in the papers about a man fitting John Coffey's description. Anything at all. Janice had done the same. We had come up with just one possible sighting so far, in the town of Muscle Shoals, Alabama. A twister had struck a church there during choir practice—in 1929, this had been—and a large black man had hauled two fellows out of the rubble. Both had looked dead to onlookers at first, but as it turned out, neither had been even seriously hurt. It was like a miracle, one of the witnesses was quoted as saying. The black man, a drifter who had been hired by the church pastor to do a day's worth of chores, had disappeared in the excitement.

"You're right, he got along," Brutal said. "But you have to remember that he did most of his getting along before he was convicted of raping and murdering two little girls."

She sat without answering. She sat that way for almost a full minute, and then she did something which shocked me as badly as my sudden flow of tears must have shocked her. She reached out and shoved every-thing off the table with one sweep of her arm—plates, glasses, cups, silverware, the bowl of collards, the bowl of squash, the platter with the carved ham on it, the milk, the pitcher of cold tea. All off the table and onto the floor, ker-smash.

"Holy shit!" Dean cried, rocking back from the table so hard he damned near went over on his back.

Janice ignored him. It was Brutal and me she was looking at, mostly me. "Do you mean to kill him, you cowards?" she asked. "Do you mean to kill the man who saved Melinda Moores's life, who tried to save those little girls' lives? Well, at least there will be one less black man in the world, won't there? You can console yourselves with that. *One less nigger.*"

She got up, looked at her chair, and kicked it into the wall. It rebounded and fell into the spilled squash. I took her wrist and she yanked it free.

"Don't touch me," she said. "Next week this time you'll be a mur-derer, no better than that man Wharton, so don't touch me."

She went out onto the back stoop, put her apron up to her face, and began to sob into it. The four of us looked at each other. After a little bit I got on my feet and set about cleaning up the mess. Brutal joined me first, then Harry and Dean. When the place looked more or less ship-shape again, they left. None of us said a word the whole time. There was really nothing left to say.

6

THAT WAS MY NIGHT OFF. I sat in the living room of our little house, smoking cigarettes, listening to the radio, and watching the dark come up out of the ground to swallow the sky. Television is all right, I've nothing against it, but I don't like how it turns you away from the rest of the world and toward nothing but its own glassy self. In that one way, at least, radio was better.

Janice came in, knelt beside the arm of my chair, and took my hand. For a little while neither of us said anything, just stayed that way, listening to *Kay Kyser's Kollege of Musical Knowledge* and watching the stars come out. It was all right with me.

"I'm so sorry I called you a coward," she said. "I feel worse about that than anything I've ever said to you in our whole marriage."

"Even the time when we went camping and you called me Old Stinky Sam?" I asked, and then we laughed and had a kiss or two and it was better again between us. She was so beautiful, my Janice, and I still dream of her. Old and tired of living as I am, I'll dream that she walks into my room in this lonely, forgotten place where the hallways all smell of piss and old boiled cabbage, I dream she's young and beautiful with her blue eyes and her fine high breasts that I couldn't hardly keep my hands off of, and she'll say, *Why, honey, I wasn't in that bus crash. You made a mistake, that's all.* Even now I dream that, and sometimes when I wake up and know it was a dream, I cry. I, who hardly ever cried at all when I was young.

"Does Hal know?" she asked at last.

"That John's innocent? I don't see how he can."

"Can he help? Does he have any influence with Cribus?"

"Not a bit, honey."

She nodded, as if she had expected this. "Then don't tell him. If he can't help, for God's sake don't tell him."

"No."

She looked up at me with steady eyes. "And you won't call in sick that night. None of you will. You can't."

"No, we can't. If we're there, we can at least make it quick for him. We can do that much. It won't be like Delacroix." For a moment, mercifully brief, I saw the black silk mask burning away from Del's face and revealing the cooked blobs of jelly which had been his eyes.

"There's no way out for you, is there?" She took my hand, rubbed it down the soft velvet of her cheek. "Poor Paul. Poor old guy."

I said nothing. Never before or after in my life did I feel so much like running from a thing. Just taking Jan with me, the two of us with a single packed carpetbag between us, running to anywhere.

"My poor old guy," she repeated, and then: "Talk to him."

"Who? John?"

"Yes. Talk to him. Find out what *he* wants."

I thought about it, then nodded. She was right. She usually was.

7

TWO DAYS LATER, on the eighteenth, Bill Dodge, Hank Bitterman, and someone else—I don't remember who, some floater—took John Coffey over to D Block for his shower, and we rehearsed his execution while he was gone. We didn't let Toot-Toot stand in for John; all of us knew, even without talking about it, that it would have been an obscenity.

I did it.

"John Coffey," Brutal said in a not-quite-steady voice as I sat clamped into Old Sparky, "you have been condemned to die in the electric chair, sentence passed by a jury of your peers . . ."

John Coffey's peers? What a joke. So far as I knew, there was no one like him on the planet. Then I thought of what John had said while he stood looking at Sparky from the foot of the stairs leading down from my office: *They're still in there. I hear them screaming.*

"Get me out of it," I said hoarsely. "Undo these clamps and let me up."

They did it, but for a moment I felt frozen there, as if Old Sparky did not want to let me go.

As we walked back to the block, Brutal spoke to me in a low voice, so not even Dean and Harry, who were setting up the last of the chairs behind us, would overhear. "I done a few things in my life that I'm not proud of, but this is the first time I ever felt really actually in danger of hell."

I looked at him to make sure he wasn't joking. I didn't think he was. "What do you mean?"

"I mean we're fixing to kill a gift of God," he said. "One that never did any harm to us, or to anyone else. What am I going to say if I end up standing in front of God the Father Almighty and He asks me to explain why I did it? That it was my job? My *job*?"

8

WHEN JOHN GOT BACK from his shower and the floaters had left, I unlocked his cell, went in, and sat down on the bunk beside him. Brutal was on the desk. He looked up, saw me in there on my own, but said nothing. He just went back to whatever paperwork he was currently mangling, licking away at the tip of his pencil the whole time.

John looked at me with his strange eyes—bloodshot, distant, on the verge of tears . . . and yet calm, too, as if crying was not such a bad way of life, not once you got used to it. He even smiled a little. He smelled of Ivory soap, I remember, as clean and fresh as a baby after his evening bath.

"Hello, boss," he said, and then reached out and took both of my hands in both of his. It was done with a perfect unstudied naturalness.

"Hello, John." There was a little block in my throat, and I tried to swallow it away. "I guess you know that we're coming down to it now. Another couple of days."

He said nothing, only sat there holding my hands in his. I think, looking back on it, that something had already begun to happen to me, but I was too fixed—mentally and emotionally—on doing my duty to notice.

"Is there anything special you'd like that night for dinner, John? We can rustle you up most anything. Even bring you a beer, if you want. Just have to put her in a coffee cup, that's all."

"Never got the taste," he said.

"Something special to eat, then?"

His brow creased below that expanse of clean brown skull. Then the lines smoothed out and he smiled. "Meatloaf'd be good."

"Meatloaf it is. With gravy and mashed." I felt a tingle like you get in your arm when you've slept on it, except this one was all over my body. *In* my body. "What else to go with it?"

"Dunno, boss. Whatever you got, I guess. Okra, maybe, but I's not picky."

"All right," I said, and thought he would also have Mrs. Janice Edgecombe's peach cobbler for dessert. "Now, what about a preacher? Someone you could say a little prayer with, night after next? It comforts a man, I've seen that many times. I could get in touch with Reverend Schuster, he's the man who came when Del—"

"Don't want no preacher," John said. "You been good to me, boss. You can say a prayer, if you want. That'd be all right. I could get kneebound with you a bit, I guess."

"*Me!* John, I couldn't—"

He pressed down on my hands a little, and that feeling got stronger. "You *could*," he said. "Couldn't you, boss?"

"I suppose so," I heard myself say. My voice seemed to have developed an echo. "I suppose I could, if it came to that."

The feeling was strong inside me by then, and it was like before, when he'd cured my waterworks, but it was different, too. And not just because there was nothing wrong with me this time. It was different because *this time he didn't know he was doing it*. Suddenly I was terrified, almost choked with a need to get out of there. Lights were going on inside me where there had never been lights before. Not just in my brain; all over my body.

"You and Mr. Howell and the other bosses been good to me," John Coffey said. "I know you been worryin, but you ought to quit on it now. Because I *want* to go, boss."

I tried to speak and couldn't. He could, though. What he said next was the longest I ever heard him speak.

"I'm rightly tired of the pain I hear and feel, boss. I'm tired of bein on the road, lonely as a robin in the rain. Not never havin no buddy to go on with or tell me where we's comin from or goin to or why. I'm tired of people bein ugly to each other. It feels like pieces of glass in my head. I'm tired of all the times I've wanted to help and couldn't. I'm tired of bein in the dark. Mostly it's the pain. There's too much. If I could end it, I would. But I can't."

Stop it, I tried to say. Stop it, let go of my hands, I'm going to drown if you don't. Drown or explode.

"You won't 'splode," he said, smiling a little at the idea . . . but he let go of my hands.

I leaned forward, gasping. Between my knees I could see every crack in the cement floor, every groove, every flash of mica. I looked up at the wall and saw names that had been written there in 1924, 1926, 1931. Those names had been washed away, the men who had written them had also been washed away, in a manner of speaking, but I guess you can never wash anything completely away, not from this dark glass of a world, and now I saw them again, a tangle of names overlying one another, and looking at them was like listening to the dead speak and sing and cry out for mercy. I felt my eyeballs pulsing in their sockets, heard my own heart, felt the windy whoosh of my blood rushing through all the boulevards of my body like letters being mailed to everywhere.

I heard a train-whistle in the distance—the three-fifty to Priceford, I imagine, but I couldn't be sure, because I'd never heard it before. Not from Cold Mountain, I hadn't, because the closest it came to the state pen was ten miles east. I *couldn't* have heard it from the pen, so you would have said and so, until November of '32, I would have believed, but I heard it that day.

Somewhere a lightbulb shattered, loud as a bomb.

"What did you do to me?" I whispered. "Oh John, what did you do?"

"I'm sorry, boss," he said in his calm way. "I wasn't thinkin. Ain't much, I reckon. You feel like regular soon."

I got up and went to the cell door. It felt like walking in a dream. When I got there, he said: "You wonder why they didn't scream. That's the only thing you still wonder about, ain't it? Why those two little girls didn't scream while they were still there on the porch."

I turned and looked at him. I could see every red snap in his eyes, I could see every pore on his face . . . and I could feel his hurt, the pain that he took in from other people like a sponge takes in water. I could see the darkness he had spoken of, too. It lay in all the spaces of the world as he saw it, and in that moment I felt both pity for him and great relief. Yes, it was a terrible thing we'd be doing, nothing would ever change that . . . and yet we would be doing him a favor.

"I seen it when that bad fella, he done grab me," John said. "That's when I knowed it was him done it. I seen him that day, I was in the trees and I seen him drop them down and run away, but—"

"You forgot," I said.

"That's right, boss. Until he touch me, I forgot."

"Why *didn't* they scream, John? He hurt them enough to make them bleed, their parents were right upstairs, so why didn't they scream?"

John looked at me from his haunted eyes. "He say to the one, 'If you make noise, it's your sister I kill, not you.' He say that same to the other. You see?"

"Yes," I whispered, and I *could* see it. The Detterick porch in the dark. Wharton leaning over them like a ghoul. One of them had maybe started to cry out, so Wharton had hit her and she had bled from the nose. That's where most of it had come from.

"He kill them with they love," John said. "They love for each other. You see how it was?"

I nodded, incapable of speech.

He smiled. The tears were flowing again, but he smiled. "That's how it is every day," he said, "all over the worl'." Then he lay down and turned his face to the wall.

I stepped out into the Mile, locked his cell, and walked up to the duty desk. I still felt like a man in a dream. I realized I could hear Brutal's thoughts—a very faint whisper, how to spell some word, *receive*, I think it was. He was thinking i *before* e, *except after* c, *is that how the dadratted thing goes?* Then he looked up, started to smile, and stopped when he got a good look at me. "Paul?" he asked. "Are you all right?"

"Yes." Then I told him what John had told me—not all of it, and certainly not about what his touch had done to me (I never told anyone that part, not even Janice; Elaine Connelly will be the first to know of it—if, that is, she wants to read these last pages after reading all the rest of them), but I repeated what John had said about wanting to go. That seemed to relieve Brutal—a bit, anyway—but I sensed (heard?) him wondering if I hadn't made it up, just to set his mind at ease. Then I felt him deciding to believe it, simply because it would make things a little easier for him when the time came.

"Paul, is that infection of yours coming back?" he asked. "You look all flushed."

"No, I think I'm okay," I said. I wasn't, but I felt sure by then that John was right and I was going to be. I could feel that tingle starting to subside.

"All the same, it might not hurt you to go on in your office there and lie down a bit."

Lying down was the *last* thing I felt like right then—the idea seemed so ridiculous that I almost laughed. What I felt like doing was maybe building myself a little house, then shingling it, and plowing a garden in back, and planting it. All before suppertime.

That's how it is, I thought. *Every day. All over the world. That darkness. All over the world.*

"I'm going to take a turn over to Admin instead. Got a few things to check over there."

"If you say so."

I went to the door and opened it, then looked back. "You've got it right," I said: "r-e-c-e-i-v-e; *i* before *e*, except after *c*. Most of the time, anyway; I guess there's exceptions to all the rules."

I went out, not needing to look back at him to know he was staring with his mouth open.

I kept moving for the rest of that shift, unable to sit down for more than five minutes at a stretch before jumping up again. I went over to Admin, and then I tromped back and forth across the empty exercise yard until the guards in the towers must have thought I was crazy. But by the time my shift was over, I was starting to calm down again, and that rustle of thoughts in my head—like a stirring of leaves, it was— had pretty much quieted down.

Still, halfway home that morning, it came back strong. The way my urinary infection had. I had to park my Ford by the side of the road, get out, and sprint nearly half a mile, head down, arms pumping, breath tearing in and out of my throat as warm as something that you've carried in your armpit. Then, at last, I began to feel really normal. I trotted halfway back to where the Ford was parked and walked the rest of the way, my breath steaming in the chilly air. When I got home, I told Janice that John Coffey had said he was ready, that he wanted to go. She nodded, looking relieved. Was she really? I couldn't say. Six hours before, even three, I would have known, but by then I didn't. And that was good. John had kept saying that he was tired, and now I could understand why. It would have tired anyone out, what he had. Would have made anyone long for rest and for quiet.

When Janice asked me why I looked so flushed and smelled so sweaty, I told her I had stopped the car on my way home and gone running for awhile, running hard. I told her that much—as I may have said (there's too many pages here now for me to want to look back through and make sure), lying wasn't much a part of our marriage—but I didn't tell her why.

And she didn't ask.

9

THERE WERE NO THUNDERSTORMS on the night it came John Coffey's turn to walk the Green Mile. It was seasonally cold for those parts at that time of year, in the thirties, I'd guess, and a million stars spilled across used-up, picked-out fields where frost glittered on fenceposts and glowed like diamonds on the dry skeletons of July's corn.

Brutus Howell was out front for this one—he would do the capping and tell Van Hay to roll when it was time. Bill Dodge was in with Van Hay. And, at around eleven-twenty on the night of November 20th, Dean and Harry and I went down to our one occupied cell, where John Coffey sat on the end of his bunk with his hands clasped between his knees and a tiny dab of meatloaf gravy on the collar of his blue shirt. He looked out through the bars at us, a lot calmer than we felt, it seemed. My hands were cold and my temples were throbbing. It was one thing to know he was willing—it made it at least possible for us to do our job—but it was another to know we were going to electrocute him for someone else's crime.

I had last seen Hal Moores around seven that evening. He was in his office, buttoning up his overcoat. His face was pale, his hands shaking so badly that he was making quite some production of those buttons. I almost wanted to knock his fingers aside and do the coat up myself, like you would with a little kid. The irony was that Melinda had looked better when Jan and I went to see her the previous weekend than Hal had looked earlier on John Coffey's execution evening.

"I won't be staying for this one," he had said. "Curtis will be there, and I know Coffey will be in good hands with you and Brutus."

"Yes, sir, we'll do our best," I said. "Is there any word on Percy?" Is he coming back around? is what I meant, of course. Is he even now sitting in a room somewhere and telling someone—some doctor, most likely—about how we zipped him into the nut-coat and threw him into the restraint room like any other problem child . . . any other lugoon, in Percy's language? And if he is, are they believing him?

But according to Hal, Percy was just the same. Not talking, and not, so far as anyone could tell, in the world at all. He was still at Indianola— "being evaluated," Hal had said, looking mystified at the phrase—but if there was no improvement, he would be moving along soon.

"How's Coffey holding up?" Hal had asked then. He had finally managed to do up the last button of his coat.

I nodded. "He'll be fine, Warden."

He'd nodded back, then gone to the door, looking old and ill. "How can so much good and so much evil live together in the same man? How could the man who cured my wife be the same man who killed those little girls? Do you understand that?"

I had told him I didn't, the ways of God were mysterious, there was good and evil in all of us, ours not to reason why, hotcha, hotcha, row-dee-dow. Most of what I told him were things I'd learned in the church of Praise Jesus, The Lord Is Mighty, Hal nodding the whole time and looking sort of exalted. He could afford to nod, couldn't he? Yes. And look exalted, too. There was a deep sadness on his face—he was shaken, all right; I never doubted it—but there were no tears this time, because he had a wife to go home to, his companion to go home to, and she was fine. Thanks to John Coffey, she was well and fine and the man who had signed John's death warrant could leave and go to her. He didn't have to watch what came next. He would be able to sleep that night in his wife's warmth while John Coffey lay on a slab in the basement of County Hospital, growing cool as the friendless, speechless hours moved toward dawn. And I hated Hal for those things. Just a little, and I'd get over it, but it was hate, all right. The genuine article.

Now I stepped into the cell, followed by Dean and Harry, both of them pale and downcast. "Are you ready, John?" I asked.

He nodded. "Yes, boss. Guess so."

"All right, then. I got a piece to say before we go out."

"You say what you need to, boss."

"John Coffey, as an officer of the court . . ."

I said it right to the end, and when I'd finished, Harry Terwilliger stepped up beside me and held out his hand. John looked surprised for a moment, then smiled and shook it. Dean, looking paler than ever, offered his next. "You deserve better than this, Johnny," he said hoarsely. "I'm sorry."

"I be all right," John said. "This the hard part; I be all right in a little while." He got up, and the St. Christopher's medal Melly had given him swung free of his shirt.

"John, I ought to have that," I said. "I can put it back on you after the . . . after, if you want, but I should take it for now." It was silver, and if it was lying against his skin when Jack Van Hay switched on the juice, it might fuse itself into his skin. Even if it didn't do that, it was apt to electroplate, leaving a kind of charred photograph of itself on the skin of his chest. I had seen it before. I'd seen most everything during my years on the Mile. More than was good for me. I knew that now.

He slipped the chain over his head and put it in my hand. I put the medallion in my pocket and told him to step on out of the cell. There was no need to check his head and make sure the contact would be firm and the induction good; it was as smooth as the palm of my hand.

"You know, I fell asleep this afternoon and had a dream, boss," he said. "I dreamed about Del's mouse."

"Did you, John?" I flanked him on the left. Harry took the right. Dean fell in behind, and then we were walking the Green Mile. For me, it was the last time I ever walked it with a prisoner.

"Yep," he said. "I dreamed he got down to that place Boss Howell talked about, that Mouseville place. I dreamed there was kids, and how they laughed at his tricks! My!" He laughed himself at the thought of it, then grew serious again. "I dreamed those two little blonde-headed girls were there. They 'us laughin, too. I put my arms around em and there 'us no blood comin out they hair and they 'us fine. We all watch Mr. Jingles roll that spool, and how we did laugh. Fit to bus', we was."

"Is that so?" I was thinking I couldn't go through with it, just could not, there was no way. I was going to cry or scream or maybe my heart would burst with sorrow and that would be an end to it.

We went into my office. John looked around for a moment or two, then dropped to his knees without having to be asked. Behind him, Harry was looking at me with haunted eyes. Dean was as white as paper.

I got down on my knees with John and thought there was a funny turnaround brewing here: after all the prisoners I'd had to help up so they could finish the journey, this time I was the one who was apt to need a hand. That's the way it felt, anyway.

"What should we pray for, boss?" John asked.

"Strength," I said without even thinking. I closed my eyes and said, "Lord God of Hosts, please help us finish what we've started, and please welcome this man, John Coffey—like the drink but not spelled the same—into heaven and give him peace. Please help us to see him off the way he deserves and let nothing go wrong. Amen." I opened my eyes and looked at Dean and Harry. Both of them looked a little better. Probably it was having a few moments to catch their breath. I doubt it was my praying.

I started to get up, and John caught my arm. He gave me a look that was both timid and hopeful. "I 'member a prayer someone taught me when I 'us little," he said. "At least I think I do. Can I say it?"

"You go right on and do her," Dean said. "Lots of time yet, John."

John closed his eyes and frowned with concentration. I expected now-I-lay-me-down-to-sleep, or maybe a garbled version of the Lord's prayer, but I got neither; I had never heard what he came out with before, and have never heard it again, not that either the sentiments or expressions were particularly unusual. Holding his hands up in front of his closed eyes, John Coffey said: "Baby Jesus, meek and mild, pray for me, an orphan child. Be my strength, be my friend, be with me until the end. Amen." He opened his eyes, started to get up, then looked at me closely.

I wiped my arm across my eyes. As I listened to him, I had been thinking about Del; he had wanted to pray one more at the end, too. *Holy Mary, mother of God, pray for us sinners now, and at the hour of our death.* "Sorry, John."

"Don't be," he said. He squeezed my arm and smiled. And then, as I'd thought he might have to do, he helped me to my feet.

10

THERE WEREN'T MANY WITNESSES—maybe fourteen in all, half the number that had been in the storage room for the Delacroix execution. Homer Cribus was there, overflowing his chair as per usual, but I didn't see Deputy McGee. Like Warden Moores, he had apparently decided to give this one a miss.

Sitting in the front row was an elderly couple I didn't recognize at first, even though I had seen their pictures in a good many newspaper articles by that day in the third week of November. Then, as we neared the platform where Old Sparky waited, the woman spat, "Die slow, you son of a bitch!" and I realized they were the Dettericks, Klaus and Marjorie. I hadn't recognized them because you don't often see elderly people who haven't yet climbed out of their thirties.

John hunched his shoulders at the sound of the woman's voice and Sheriff Cribus's grunt of approval. Hank Bitterman, who had the guard-post near the front of the meager group of spectators, never took his eyes off Klaus Detterick. That was per my orders, but Detterick never made a move in John's direction that night. Detterick seemed to be on some other planet.

Brutal, standing beside Old Sparky, gave me a small finger-tilt as we stepped up onto the platform. He holstered his sidearm and took John's wrist, escorting him toward the electric chair as gently as a boy leading his date out onto the floor for their first dance as a couple.

"Everything all right, John?" he asked in a low voice.

"Yes, boss, but . . ." His eyes were moving from side to side in their sockets, and for the first time he looked and sounded scared. "But they's a lot of folks here hate me. A *lot*. I can feel it. Hurts. Bores in like bee-stings an' *hurts*."

"Feel how we feel, then," Brutal said in that same low voice. "*We* don't hate you—can you feel that?"

"Yes, boss." But his voice was trembling worse now, and his eyes had begun to leak their slow tears again.

"*Kill him twice, you boys!*" Marjorie Detterick suddenly screamed. Her ragged, strident voice was like a slap. John cringed against me and moaned. "*You go on and kill that raping baby-killer twice, that'd be just fine!*" Klaus, still looking like a man dreaming awake, pulled her against his shoulder. She began to sob.

I saw with dismay that Harry Terwilliger was crying, too. So far none of the spectators had seen his tears—his back was to them—but he was crying, all right. Still, what could we do? Besides push on with it, I mean?

Brutal and I turned John around. Brutal pressed on one of the big man's shoulders and John sat. He gripped Sparky's wide oak arms, his eyes moving from side to side, his tongue darting out to wet first one corner of his mouth, then the other.

Harry and I dropped to our knees. The day before, we'd had one of the shop-trusties weld temporary flexible extensions to the chair's ankle clamps, because John Coffey's ankles were nigh on the size of an ordinary fellow's calves. Still, I had a nightmarish moment when I thought they were still going to come up small, and we'd have to take him back to his cell while Sam Broderick, who was head of the shop guys in those days, was found and tinkered some more. I gave a final, extra-hard shove with the heels of my hands and the clamp on my side closed. John's leg jerked and he gasped. I had pinched him.

"Sorry, John," I murmured, and glanced at Harry. He had gotten his clamp fixed more easily (either the extension on his side was a little bigger or John's right calf was a little smaller), but he was looking at the result with a doubtful expression. I guessed I could understand why; the modified clamps had a *hungry* look, their jaws seeming to gape like the mouths of alligators.

"It'll be all right," I said, hoping that I sounded convincing . . . and that I was telling the truth. "Wipe your face, Harry."

He swabbed at it with his arm, wiping away tears from his cheeks and beads of sweat from his forehead. We turned. Homer Cribus, who had been talking too loudly to the man sitting next to him (the prosecutor, judging from the string tie and rusty black suit), fell silent. It was almost time.

Brutal had clamped one of John's wrists, Dean the other. Over Dean's shoulder I could see the doctor, unobtrusive as ever, standing against the wall with his black bag between his feet. Nowadays I guess they just about run such affairs, especially the ones with the IV drips, but back then you almost had to yank them forward if you wanted them. Maybe back then they had a clearer idea of what was right for a doctor to be doing, and what was a perversion of the special promise they make, the one where they swear first of all to do no harm.

Dean nodded to Brutal. Brutal turned his head, seemed to glance at the telephone that was never going to ring for the likes of John Coffey, and called "Roll on one!" to Jack Van Hay.

There was that hum, like an old fridge kicking on, and the lights burned a little brighter. Our shadows stood out a little sharper, black shapes that climbed the wall and seemed to hover around the shadow of the chair like vultures. John drew in a sharp breath. His knuckles were white.

"Does it hurt yet?" Mrs. Detterick shrieked brokenly from against her husband's shoulder. *"I hope it does! I hope it hurts like hell!"* Her husband squeezed her. One side of his nose was bleeding, I saw, a narrow trickle of red working its way down into his narrow-gauge mustache. When I opened the paper the following March and saw he'd died of a stroke, I was about the least surprised man on earth.

Brutal stepped into John's field of vision. He touched John's shoulder as he spoke. That was irregular, but of the witnesses, only Curtis Anderson knew it, and he did not seem to remark it. I thought he looked like a man who only wants to be done with his current job. Desperately wants to be done with it. He enlisted in the Army after Pearl Harbor, but never got overseas; he died at Fort Bragg, in a truck accident.

John, meanwhile, relaxed beneath Brutal's fingers. I don't think he understood much, if any, of what Brutal was telling him, but he took comfort from Brutal's hand on his shoulder. Brutal, who died of a heart attack about twenty-five years later (he was eating a fish sandwich and watching TV wrestling when it happened, his sister said), was a good man. My friend. Maybe the best of us. He had no trouble understanding how a man could simultaneously want to go and still be terrified of the trip.

"John Coffey, you have been condemned to die in the electric chair, sentence passed by a jury of your peers and imposed by a judge of good standing in this state. God save the people of this state. Do you have anything to say before sentence is carried out?"

John wet his lips again, then spoke clearly. Six words. "I'm sorry for what I am."

"You ought to be!" the mother of the two dead girls screamed. *"Oh you monster, you ought to be! YOU DAMN WELL OUGHT TO BE!"*

John's eyes turned to me. I saw no resignation in them, no hope of heaven, no dawning peace. How I would love to tell you that I did. How I would love to tell myself that. What I saw was fear, misery, incompletion, and incomprehension. They were the eyes of a trapped and terrified animal. I thought of what he'd said about how Wharton had gotten Cora and Kathe Detterick off the porch without rousing the house: *He kill them with they love. That's how it is every day. All over the worl'.*

Brutal took the new mask from its brass hook on the back of the chair, but as soon as John saw it and understood what it was, his eyes widened in horror. He looked at me, and now I could see huge droplets of sweat standing out on the curve of his naked skull. As big as robin's eggs, they looked.

"Please, boss, don't put that thing over my face," he said in a moaning little whisper. "Please don't put me in the dark, don't make me go into the dark, I's afraid of the dark."

Brutal was looking at me, eyebrows raised, frozen in place, the mask in his hands. His eyes said it was my call, he'd go either way. I thought as fast as I could and as well as I could—hard to do, with my head pounding the way it was. The mask was tradition, not law. It was, in fact, to spare the witnesses. And suddenly I decided that they did not need to be spared, not this once. John, after all, hadn't done a damned thing in his life to warrant dying under a mask. They didn't know that, but we did, and I decided I was going to grant this last request. As for Marjorie Detterick, she'd probably send me a thank-you note.

"All right, John," I murmured.

Brutal put the mask back. From behind us, Homer Cribus called out indignantly in his deep-dish cracker voice: "Say, boy! Put that-air mask on him! Think we want to watch his eyes pop?"

"Be quiet, sir," I said without turning. "This is an execution, and you're not in charge of it."

"Any more than you were in charge of catching him, you tub of guts," Harry whispered. Harry died in 1982, close to the age of eighty. An old man. Not in my league, of course, but few are. It was intestinal cancer of some kind.

Brutal bent over and plucked the disk of sponge out of its bucket. He pressed a finger into it and licked the tip, but he hardly had to; I could see the ugly brown thing dripping. He tucked it into the cap, then put the cap on John's head. For the first time I saw that Brutal was pale, too—pasty white, on the verge of passing out. I thought of him saying that he felt, for the first time in his life, that he was in danger of hell, because we were fixing to kill a gift of God. I felt a sudden strong need to retch. I controlled it, but only with an effort. Water from the sponge was dripping down the sides of John's face.

Dean Stanton ran the strap—let out to its maximum length on this occasion—across John's chest and gave it to me. We had taken such pains to try and protect Dean on the night of our trip, because of his kids, never knowing that he had less than four months to live. After John Coffey, he requested and received a transfer away from Old Sparky, over to C Block, and there a prisoner stabbed him in the throat with a shank and let out his life's blood on the dirty board floor. I never knew why. I don't think anyone ever knew why. Old Sparky seems such a thing of perversity when I look back on those days, such a deadly bit of folly. Fragile as blown glass, we are, even under the best of conditions.

To kill each other with gas and electricity, and in cold blood? The folly. The *horror*.

Brutal checked the strap, then stood back. I waited for him to speak, but he didn't. As he crossed his hands behind his back and stood at parade rest, I knew that he wouldn't. Perhaps couldn't. I didn't think I could, either, but then I looked at John's terrified, weeping eyes and knew I had to. Even if it damned me forever, I had to.

"Roll on two," I said in a dusty, cracking voice I hardly recognized as my own.

The cap hummed. Eight large fingers and two large thumbs rose from the ends of the chair's broad oak arms and splayed tensely in ten different directions, their tips jittering. His big knees made caged pistoning motions, but the clamps on his ankles held. Overhead, three of the hanging lights blew out—*Pow! Pow! Pow!* Marjorie Detterick screamed at the sound and fainted in her husband's arms. She died in Memphis, eighteen years later. Harry sent me the obit. It was a trolley-car accident.

John surged forward against the chest-strap. For a moment his eyes met mine. They were aware; I was the last thing he saw as we tilted him off the edge of the world. Then he fell against the seatback, the cap coming askew on his head a little, smoke—a sort of charry mist—drifting out from beneath it. But on the whole, you know, it was quick. I doubt if it was painless, the way the chair's supporters always claim (it's not an idea even the most rabid of them ever seems to want to investigate personally), but it was quick. The hands were limp again, the formerly bluish-white moons at the base of the fingernails now a deep eggplant hue, a tendril of smoke rising off cheeks still wet with salt water from the sponge . . . and his tears.

John Coffey's last tears.

11

I WAS ALL RIGHT until I got home. It was dawn by then, and birds singing. I parked my flivver, I got out, I walked up the back steps, and then the second greatest grief I have ever known washed over me. It was thinking of how he'd been afraid of the dark that did it. I remembered the first time we'd met, how he'd asked if we left a light on at night, and my legs gave out on me. I sat on my steps and hung my head over my knees and cried. It didn't feel like that weeping was just for John, either, but for all of us.

Janice came out and sat down beside me. She put an arm over my shoulders.

"You didn't hurt him any more than you could help, did you?"

I shook my head no.

"And he wanted to go."

I nodded.

"Come in the house," she said, helping me up. It made me think of the way John had helped me up after we'd prayed together. "Come in and have coffee."

I did. The first morning passed, and the first afternoon, then the first shift back at work. Time takes it all, whether you want it to or not. Time takes it all, time bears it away, and in the end there is only darkness. Sometimes we find others in that darkness, and sometimes we lose them there again. That's all I know, except that this happened in 1932, when the state penitentiary was still at Cold Mountain.

And the electric chair, of course.

12

AROUND QUARTER PAST TWO in the afternoon, my friend Elaine Connelly came to me where I sat in the sunroom, with the last pages of my story squared up neatly in front of me. Her face was very pale, and there were shiny places under her eyes. I think she had been crying.

Me, I'd been looking. Just that. Looking out the window and over the hills to the east, my right hand throbbing at the end of its wrist. But it was a peaceful throb, somehow. I felt empty, husked out. A feeling that was terrible and wonderful at the same time.

It was hard to meet Elaine's eyes—I was afraid of the hate and contempt I might see there—but they were all right. Sad and wondering, but all right. No hate, no contempt, and no disbelief.

"Do you want the rest of the story?" I asked. I tapped the little pile of script with my aching hand. "It's here, but I'll understand if you'd just as soon not—"

"It isn't a question of what I *want*," she said. "I have to know how it came out, although I guess there is no doubt that you executed him. The intervention of Providence-with-a-capital-*P* is greatly overrated in the lives of ordinary humans, I think. But before I take those pages . . . Paul . . ."

She stopped, as if unsure how to go on. I waited. Sometimes you can't help people. Sometimes it's better not even to try.

"Paul, you speak in here as though you had two grown children in 1932—not just one, but *two*. If you didn't get married to your Janice when you were twelve and she was eleven, something like that—"

I smiled a little. "We were young when we married—a lot of hill-people are, my own mother was—but not *that* young."

"Then how old *are* you? I've always assumed you were in your early eighties, my age, possibly even a little younger, but according to this . . ."

"I was forty the year John walked the Green Mile," I said. "I was born in 1892. That makes me a hundred and four, unless my reckoning's out."

She stared at me, speechless.

I held out the rest of the manuscript, remembering again how John had touched me, there in his cell. *You won't 'splode*, he'd said, smiling a bit at the very idea, and I hadn't . . . but something had happened to me, all the same. Something lasting.

"Read the rest of it," I said. "What answers I have are in there."

"All right," she almost whispered. "I'm a little afraid to, I can't lie about that, but . . . all right. Where will you be?"

I stood up, stretched, listened to my spine crackle in my back. One thing that I knew for sure was that I was sick to death of the sunroom. "Out on the croquet course. There's still something I want to show you, and it's in that direction."

"Is it . . . scary?" In her timid look I saw the little girl she had been back when men wore straw boaters in the summer and raccoon coats in the winter.

"No," I said, smiling. "Not scary."

"All right." She took the pages. "I'm going to take these down to my room. I'll see you out on the croquet course around . . ." She riffled the manuscript, estimating. "Four? Is that all right?"

"Perfect," I said, thinking of the too-curious Brad Dolan. He would be gone by then.

She reached out, gave my arm a little squeeze, and left the room. I stood where I was for a moment, looking down at the table, taking in the fact that it was bare again except for the breakfast tray Elaine had brought me that morning, my scattered papers at last gone. I somehow couldn't believe I was done . . . and as you can see, since all this was written after I recorded John Coffey's execution and gave the last batch of pages to Elaine, I was not. And even then, part of me knew why.

Alabama.

I filched the last piece of cold toast off the tray, went downstairs, and out onto the croquet course. There I sat in the sun, watching half a dozen pairs and one slow but cheerful foursome pass by waving their mallets, thinking my old man's thoughts and letting the sun warm my old man's bones.

Around two-forty-five, the three-to-eleven shift started to trickle in from the parking lot, and at three, the day-shift folks left. Most were in groups, but Brad Dolan, I saw, was walking alone. That was sort of a happy sight; maybe the world hasn't gone entirely to hell, after all. One of his joke-books was sticking out of his back pocket. The path to the parking lot goes by the croquet course, so he saw me there, but he didn't give me either a wave or a scowl. That was fine by me. He got into his old Chevrolet with the bumper sticker reading I HAVE SEEN GOD AND HIS NAME IS NEWT. Then he was gone to wherever he goes when he isn't here, laying a thin trail of discount motor oil behind.

Around four o'clock, Elaine joined me, just as she had promised. From the look of her eyes, she'd done a little more crying. She put her arms around me and hugged me tight. "Poor John Coffey," she said. "And poor Paul Edgecombe, too."

Poor Paul, I heard Jan saying. *Poor old guy.*

Elaine began to cry again. I held her, there on the croquet course in the late sunshine. Our shadows looked as if they were dancing. Perhaps in the Make-Believe Ballroom we used to listen to on the radio back in those days.

At last she got herself under control and drew back from me. She found a Kleenex in her blouse pocket and wiped her streaming eyes with it. "What happened to the Warden's wife, Paul? What happened with Melly?"

"She was considered the marvel of the age, at least by the doctors at Indianola Hospital," I said. I took her arm and we began to walk toward the path which led away from the employees' parking lot and into the woods. Toward the shed down by the wall between Georgia Pines and the world of younger people. "She died—of a heart attack, not a brain tumor—ten or eleven years later. In forty-three, I think.

Hal died of a stroke right around Pearl Harbor Day—could have been *on* Pearl Harbor Day, for all I remember, so she outlived him by two years. Sort of ironic."

"And Janice?"

"I'm not quite prepared for that today," I said. "I'll tell you another time."

"Promise?"

"Promise." But that was one I never kept. Three months after the day we walked down into the woods together (I would have held her hand, if I hadn't been afraid of hurting her bunched and swollen fingers), Elaine Connelly died quietly in her bed. As with Melinda Moores, death came as the result of a heart attack. The orderly who found her said she looked peaceful, as if it had come suddenly and without much pain. I hope he was right about that. I loved Elaine. And I miss her. Her and Janice and Brutal and just all of them.

We reached the second shed on the path, the one down by the wall. It stood back in a bower of scrub pines, its sagging roof and boarded-over windows laced and dappled with shadows. I started toward it. Elaine hung back a moment, looking fearful.

"It's all right," I said. "Really. Come on."

There was no latch on the door—there had been once, but it had been torn away—and so I used a folded-over square of cardboard to wedge it shut. I pulled it free now, and stepped into the shed. I left the door as wide open as it would go, because it was dark inside.

"Paul, what? . . . Oh. *Oh!*" That second "oh" was just shy of a scream.

There was a table pushed off to one side. On it was a flashlight and a brown paper bag. On the dirty floor was a Hav-A-Tampa cigar box I'd gotten from the concession man who refills the home's soft-drink and candy machines. I'd asked him for it special, and since his company also sells tobacco products, it was easy for him to get. I offered to pay him for it—they were valuable commodities when I worked at Cold Mountain, as I may have told you—but he just laughed me off.

Peering over the edge of it were a pair of bright little oilspot eyes.

"Mr. Jingles," I said in a low voice. "Come over here. Come on over here, old boy, and see this lady."

I squatted down—it hurt, but I managed—and held out my hand. At first I didn't think he was going to be able to get over the side of the box this time, but he made it with one final lunge. He landed on his side, then regained his feet, and came over to me. He ran with a hitching limp in one of his back legs; the injury that Percy had inflicted had come back in Mr. Jingles's old age. His old, *old* age. Except for the top of his head and the tip of his tail, his fur had gone entirely gray.

He hopped onto the palm of my hand. I raised him up and he stretched his neck out, sniffing at my breath with his ears laid back and his tiny dark eyes avid. I held my hand out toward Elaine, who looked at the mouse with wide-eyed wonder, her lips parted.

"It *can't* be," she said, and raised her eyes to me. "Oh Paul, it isn't . . . it *can't* be!"

"Watch," I said, "and then tell me that."

From the bag on the table I took a spool which I had colored myself—not with Crayolas but with Magic Markers, an invention undreamed of in 1932. It came to the same, though. It was as bright as Del's had been, maybe brighter. *Messieurs et mesdames,* I thought. *Bienvenue au cirque du mousie!*

I squatted again, and Mr. Jingles ran off my palm. He was old, but as obsessed as ever. From the moment I had taken the spool out of the bag, he'd had eyes for nothing else. I rolled it across the shed's uneven, splintery floor, and he was after it at once. He didn't run with his old speed, and his limp was painful to watch, but why should he have been either fast or surefooted? As I've said, he was old, a Methuselah of a mouse. Sixty-four, at least.

He reached the spool, which struck the far wall and bounced back. He went around it, then lay down on his side. Elaine started forward and I held her back. After a moment, Mr. Jingles found his feet again. Slowly, so slowly, he nosed the spool back to me. When he'd first come—I'd found him lying on the steps leading to the kitchen in just that same way, as if he'd travelled a long distance and was exhausted—he had still been able to guide the spool with his paws, as he had done all those years ago on the Green Mile. That was beyond him, now; his hindquarters would no longer support him. Yet his nose was as educated as ever. He just had to go from one end of the spool to the other to keep it on course. When he reached me, I picked him up in one hand—no more than a feather, he weighed—and the spool in the other. His bright dark eyes never left it.

"Don't do it again, Paul," Elaine said in a broken voice. "I can't bear to watch him."

I understood how she felt, but thought she was wrong to ask it. He loved chasing and fetching the spool; after all the years, he still loved it just as much. We should all be so fortunate in our passions.

"There are peppermint candies in the bag, too," I said. "Canada Mints. I think he still likes them—he won't stop sniffing, if I hold one out to him—but his digestion has gotten too bad to eat them. I bring him toast, instead."

I squatted again, broke a small fragment off the piece I'd brought with me from the sunroom, and put it on the floor. Mr. Jingles sniffed at it, then picked it up in his paws and began to eat. His tail was coiled neatly around him. He finished, then looked expectantly up.

"Sometimes us old fellas can surprise you with our appetites," I said to Elaine, and handed her the toast. "You try."

She broke off another fragment and dropped it on the floor. Mr. Jingles approached it, sniffed, looked at Elaine . . . then picked it up and began to eat.

"You see?" I said. "He knows you're not a floater."

"Where did he come from, Paul?"

"Haven't a clue. One day when I went out for my early-morning walk, he was just here, lying on the kitchen steps. I knew who he was right away, but I got a spool out of the laundry room occasional basket just to be sure. And I got him a cigar box. Lined it with the softest stuff I could find. He's like us, Ellie, I think—most days just one big sore place. Still, he hasn't lost all his zest for living. He still likes his spool, and he still likes a visit from his old blockmate. Sixty years I held the story of John Coffey inside me, sixty and more, and now I've told it. I kind of had the idea that's why he came back. To let me know I should hurry up and do it while there was still time. Because I'm like him—getting there."

"Getting where?"

"Oh, you know," I said, and we watched Mr. Jingles for awhile in silence. Then, for no reason I could tell you, I tossed the spool again, even though Elaine had asked me not to. Maybe only because, in a way, him chasing a spool was like old people having their slow and careful version of sex—*you* might not want to watch it, you who are young and convinced that, when it comes to old age, an exception will be made in your case, but *they* still want to do it.

Mr. Jingles set off after the rolling spool again, clearly with pain, and just as clearly (to me, at least) with all his old, obsessive enjoyment.

"Ivy-glass windows," she whispered, watching him go.

"Ivy-glass windows," I agreed, smiling.

"John Coffey touched the mouse the way he touched you. He didn't just make you better of what was wrong with you then, he made you . . . what, resistant?"

"That's as good a word as any, I think."

"Resistant to the things that eventually bring the rest of us down like trees with termites in them. You . . . and him. Mr. Jingles. When he cupped Mr. Jingles in his hands."

"That's right. Whatever power worked through John did that—that's what I think, anyway—and now it's finally wearing off. The termites have chewed their way through our bark. It took a little longer than it does ordinarily, but they got there. I may have a few more years, men still live longer than mice, I guess, but Mr. Jingles's time is just about up."

He reached the spool, limped around it, fell over on his side, breathing rapidly (we could see his respiration moving through his gray fur like ripples), then got up and began to push it gamely back with his nose. His fur was gray, his gait was unsteady, but the oilspots that were his eyes gleamed as brightly as ever.

"You think he wanted you to write what you have written," she said. "Is that so, Paul?"

"Not Mr. Jingles," I said. "Not him but the force that—"

"Why, Paulie! And Elaine Connelly, too!" a voice cried from the open door. It was loaded with a kind of satiric horror. "As I live and breathe! What in the goodness can you two be doing here?"

I turned, not at all surprised to see Brad Dolan there in the doorway.

He was grinning as a man only does when he feels he's fooled you right good and proper. How far down the road had he driven after his shift was over? Maybe only as far as The Wrangler, for a beer or two and maybe a lap-dance before coming back.

"Get out," Elaine said coldly. "Get out right now."

"Don't you tell *me* to get out, you wrinkledy old bitch," he said, still smiling. "Maybe you can tell me that up the hill, but you ain't up the hill now. This ain't where you're supposed to be. This is off-limits. Little love-nest, Paulie? Is that what you got here? Kind of a *Playboy* pad for the geriatric . . ." His eyes widened as he at last saw the shed's tenant. "What the *fuck?*"

I didn't turn to look. I knew what was there, for one thing; for another, the past had suddenly doubled over the present, making one terrible image, three-dimensional in its reality. It wasn't Brad Dolan standing there in the doorway but Percy Wetmore. In another moment he would rush into the shed and crush Mr. Jingles (who no longer had a hope of outrunning him) under his shoe. And this time there was no John Coffey to bring him back from the edge of death. Any more than there had been a John Coffey when I needed him on that rainy day in Alabama.

I got to my feet, not feeling any ache in my joints or muscles this time, and rushed toward Dolan. "Leave him alone!" I yelled. "You leave him alone, Percy, or by God I'll—"

"Who you callin Percy?" he asked, and pushed me back so hard I almost fell over. Elaine grabbed me, although it must have hurt her to do so, and steadied me. "Ain't the first time you done it, either. And stop peein in your pants. I ain't gonna touch im. Don't need to. That's one dead rodent."

I turned, thinking that Mr. Jingles was only lying on his side to catch his breath, the way he sometimes did. He was on his side, all right, but that rippling motion through his fur had stopped. I tried to convince myself that I could still see it, and then Elaine burst into loud sobs. She bent painfully, and picked up the mouse I had first seen on the Green Mile, coming up to the duty desk as fearlessly as a man approaching his peers . . . or his friends. He lay limp on her hand. His eyes were dull and still. He was dead.

Dolan grinned unpleasantly, revealing teeth which had had very little acquaintance with a dentist. "Aw, *sakes*, now!" he said. "Did we just
lose the family pet? Should we have a little funeral, with paper flowers
and—"

"*SHUT UP!*" Elaine screamed at him, so loudly and so powerfully that
he backed away a step, the smile slipping off his face. "*GET OUT OF HERE!
GET OUT OR YOU'LL NEVER WORK ANOTHER DAY HERE! NOT ANOTHER HOUR!
I SWEAR IT!*"

"You won't be able to get so much as a slice of bread on a breadline,"
I said, but so low neither of them heard me. I couldn't take my eyes off
Mr. Jingles, lying on Elaine's palm like the world's smallest bearskin rug.

Brad thought about coming back at her, calling her bluff—he was
right, the shed wasn't exactly approved territory for the Georgia Pines
inmates, even I knew that much—and then didn't. He was, at heart, a
coward, just like Percy. And he might have checked on her claim that
her grandson was Somebody Important and had discovered it was a true
claim. Most of all, perhaps, his curiosity had been satisfied, his thirst to
know slaked. And after all his wondering, the mystery had turned out
not to be such of a much. An old man's pet mouse had apparently been
living in the shed. Now it had croaked, had a heart attack or something
while pushing a colored spool.

"Don't know why you're getting so het up," he said. "Either of you.
You act like it was a *dog*, or something."

"Get out," she spat. "Get out, you ignorant man. What little mind
you have is ugly and misdirected."

He flushed dully, the spots where his high school pimples had been
filling in a darker red. There had been a lot of them, by the look. "I'll
go," he said, "but when you come down here tomorrow . . . *Paulie* . . .
you're going to find a new lock on this door. This place is off-limits to
the residents, no matter what bad-tempered things old Mrs. My Shit
Don't Stink has to say about me. Look at the floor! Boards all warped
and rotted! If you was to go through, your scrawny old leg'd be apt to
snap like a piece of kindling. So just take that dead mouse, if you want
it, and get gone. The Love Shack is hereby closed."

He turned and strode away, looking like a man who believes he's earned at least a draw. I waited until he was gone, and then gently took Mr. Jingles from Elaine. My eyes happened on the bag with the peppermint candies in it, and that did it—the tears began to come. I don't know, I just cry easier somehow these days.

"Would you help me to bury an old friend?" I asked Elaine when Brad Dolan's heavy footsteps had faded away.

"Yes, Paul." She put her arm around my waist and laid her head against my shoulder. With one old and twisted finger, she stroked Mr. Jingles's moveless side. "I would be happy to do that."

And so we borrowed a trowel from the gardening shed and we buried Del's pet mouse as the afternoon shadows drew long through the trees, and then we walked back to get our supper and take up what remained of our lives. And it was Del I found myself thinking of, Del kneeling on the green carpet of my office with his hands folded and his bald pate gleaming in the lamplight, Del who had asked us to take care of Mr. Jingles, to make sure the bad 'un wouldn't hurt him anymore. Except the bad 'un hurts us all in the end, doesn't he?

"Paul?" Elaine asked. Her voice was both kind and exhausted. Even digging a grave with a trowel and laying a mouse to rest in it is a lot of excitement for old sweeties like us, I guess. "Are you all right?"

My arm was around her waist. I squeezed it. "I'm fine," I said.

"Look," she said. "It's going to be a beautiful sunset. Shall we stay out and watch it?"

"All right," I said, and we stayed there on the lawn for quite awhile, arms around each other's waists, first watching the bright colors come up in the sky, then watching them fade to ashes of gray.

Sainte Marie, Mère de Dieu, priez pour nous, pauvres pécheurs, maintenant et à l'heure de nôtre mort.

Amen.

13

1956.

Alabama in the rain.

Our third grandchild, a beautiful girl named Tessa, was graduating from the University of Florida. We went down on a Greyhound. Sixty-four, I was then, a mere stripling. Jan was fifty-nine, and as beautiful as ever. To me, at least. We were sitting in the seat all the way at the back, and she was fussing at me for not buying her a new camera to record the blessed event. I opened my mouth to tell her we had a day to shop in after we got down there, and she could have a new camera if she wanted one, it would fit the budget all right, and furthermore I thought she was just fussing because she was bored with the ride and didn't like the book she'd brought. A Perry Mason, it was. That's when everything in my memory goes white for a bit, like film that's been left out in the sun.

Do you remember that accident? I suppose a few folks reading this might, but mostly not. Yet it made front-page headlines from coast to coast when it happened. We were outside Birmingham in a driving rain, Janice complaining about her old camera, and a tire blew. The bus waltzed sideways on the wet pavement and was hit broadside by a truck hauling fertilizer. The truck slammed the bus into a bridge abutment at better than sixty miles an hour, crushed it against the concrete, and broke it in half. Two shiny, rain-streaked pieces spun in two opposite directions, the one with the diesel tank in it exploding and sending a red-black fireball up into the rainy-gray sky. At one moment Janice was complaining about her old Kodak, and at the very next I found myself lying on the far side of the underpass in the rain and staring at a pair of blue nylon panties that had spilled out of someone's suitcase. WEDNESDAY was stitched on them in black thread. There were burst-open suitcases everywhere. And bodies. And parts of bodies. There were seventy-three people on that bus, and only four survived the crash. I was one of them, the only one not seriously hurt.

I got up and staggered among the burst-open suitcases and shattered people, crying out my wife's name. I kicked aside an alarm clock, I remember that, and I remember seeing a dead boy of about thirteen lying in a strew of glass with P.F. Flyers on his feet and half his face gone. I felt the rain beating on my own face, then I went through the underpass and it was gone for awhile. When I came out on the other side it was there again, hammering my cheeks and forehead. Lying by the shattered cab of the overturned fertilizer truck, I saw Jan. I recognized her by her red dress—it was her second-best. The best she had been saving for the actual graduation, of course.

She wasn't quite dead. I have often thought it would have been better—for me, if not for her—if she had been killed instantly. It might have made it possible for me to let her go a little sooner, a little more naturally. Or perhaps I'm only kidding myself about that. All I know for sure is that I have *never* let her go, not really.

She was trembling all over. One of her shoes had come off and I could see her foot jittering. Her eyes were open but blank, the left one full of blood, and as I fell on my knees next to her in the smoky-smelling rain, all I could think of was that jitter meant she was being electrocuted; she was being electrocuted and I had to hold the roll before it was too late.

"Help me!" I screamed. "Help me, someone help me!"

No one helped, no one even came. The rain pounded down—a hard, soaking rain that flattened my still-black hair against my skull—and I held her in my arms and no one came. Her blank eyes looked up at me with a kind of dazed intensity, and blood poured from the back of her crushed head in a freshet. Beside one trembling, mindlessly spasming hand was a piece of chromed steel with the letters GREY on it. Next to that was roughly one quarter of what had once been a businessman in a brown wool suit.

"Help me!" I screamed again, and turned toward the underpass, and there I saw John Coffey standing in the shadows, only a shadow himself, a big man with long, dangling arms and a bald head. *"John!"* I screamed. *"Oh John, please help me! Please help Janice!"*

Rain ran into my eyes. I blinked it away, and he was gone. I could see the shadows I had mistaken for John . . . but it hadn't been *only* shadows. I'm sure of that. He was there. Maybe only as a ghost, but he was there, the rain on his face mixing with the endless flow of his tears.

She died in my arms, there in the rain beside that fertilizer truck with the smell of burning diesel fuel in my nose. There was no moment of awareness—the eyes clearing, the lips moving in some whispered final declaration of love. There was a kind of shivery clench in the flesh beneath my hands, and then she was gone. I thought of Melinda Moores for the first time in years, then, Melinda sitting up in the bed where all the doctors at Indianola General Hospital had believed she would die; Melinda Moores looking fresh and rested and peering at John Coffey with bright, wondering eyes. Melinda saying *I dreamed you were wandering in the dark, and so was I. We found each other.*

I put my wife's poor, mangled head down on the wet pavement of the interstate highway, got to my feet (it was easy; I had a little cut on the side of my left hand, but that was all), and screamed his name into the shadows of the underpass.

"John! JOHN COFFEY! WHERE ARE YOU, BIG BOY?"

I walked toward those shadows, kicking aside a teddy-bear with blood on its fur, a pair of steel-rimmed eyeglasses with one shattered lens, a severed hand with a garnet ring on the pinky finger. *"You saved Hal's wife, why not my wife? Why not Janice? WHY NOT MY JANICE?"*

No answer; only the smell of burning diesel and burning bodies, only the rain falling ceaselessly out of the gray sky and drumming on the cement while my wife lay dead on the road behind me. No answer then and no answer now. But of course it wasn't only Melly Moores that John Coffey saved in 1932, or Del's mouse, the one that could do that cute trick with the spool and seemed to be looking for Del long before Del showed up . . . long before John Coffey showed up, either.

John saved me, too, and years later, standing in the pouring Alabama rain and looking for a man who wasn't there in the shadows of an underpass, standing amid the spilled luggage and the ruined dead, I learned a terrible thing: sometimes there is absolutely no difference at all between salvation and damnation.

I felt one or the other pouring through me as we sat together on his bunk—November the eighteenth, nineteen and thirty-two. Pouring out of him and into me, whatever strange force he had in him coming through our joined hands in a way our love and hope and good intentions somehow never can, a feeling that began as a tingle and then turned into something tidal and enormous, a force beyond anything I had ever experienced before or have ever experienced since. Since that day I have never had pneumonia, or the flu, or even a strep throat. I have never had another urinary infection, or so much as an infected cut. I have had colds, but they have been infrequent—six or seven years apart, and although people who don't have colds often are supposed to suffer more serious ones, that has never been the case with me. Once, earlier on in that awful year of 1956, I passed a gallstone. And although I suppose it will sound strange to some reading this in spite of all I have said, part of me relished the pain that came when that gallstone went. It was the only serious pain I'd had since that problem with my water-works, twenty-four years before. The ills that have taken my friends and same-generation loved ones until there are none of them left—the strokes, the cancers, the heart attacks, the liver diseases, the blood diseases—have all left me untouched, have swerved to avoid me the way a man driving a car swerves to avoid a deer or a raccoon in the road. The one serious accident I was in left me untouched save for a scratch on the hand. In 1932, John Coffey inoculated me with life. *Electrocuted* me with life, you might say. I will pass on eventually—of course I will, any illusions of immortality I might have had died with Mr. Jingles—but I will have wished for death long before death finds me. Truth to tell, I wish for it already and have ever since Elaine Connelly died. Need I tell you?

I look back over these pages, leafing through them with my trembling, spotted hands, and I wonder if there is some meaning here, as in those books which are supposed to be uplifting and ennobling. I think back to the sermons of my childhood, booming affirmations in the church of Praise Jesus, The Lord Is Mighty, and I recall how the preachers used to say that God's eye is on the sparrow, that He sees and marks even the least of His creations. When I think of Mr. Jingles, and the tiny scraps of wood we found in that hole in the beam, I think that is so. Yet this same God sacrificed John Coffey, who tried only to do good in his blind way, as savagely as any Old Testament prophet ever sacrificed a defenseless lamb . . . as Abraham would have sacrificed his own son if actually called upon to do so. I think of John saying that Wharton killed the Detterick twins with their love for each other, and that it happens every day, all over the world. If it happens, God *lets* it happen, and when we say "I don't understand," God replies, "I don't care."

I think of Mr. Jingles dying while my back was turned and my attention usurped by an unkind man whose finest emotion seemed to be a species of vindictive curiosity. I think of Janice, jittering away her last mindless seconds as I knelt with her in the rain.

Stop it, I tried to tell John that day in his cell. *Let go of my hands, I'm going to drown if you don't. Drown or explode.*

"You won't 'splode," he answered, hearing my thought and smiling at the idea. And the horrible thing is that I didn't. I haven't.

I have at least one old man's ill: I suffer from insomnia. Late at night I lie in my bed, listening to the dank and hopeless sound of infirm men and women coughing their courses deeper into old age. Sometimes I hear a call-bell, or the squeak of a shoe in the corridor, or Mrs. Javits's little TV tuned to the late news. I lie here, and if the moon is in my window, I watch it. I lie here and think about Brutal, and Dean, and sometimes William Wharton saying *That's right, nigger, bad as you'd want.* I think of Delacroix saying *Watch this, Boss Edgecombe, I teach Mr. Jingles a new trick.* I think of Elaine, standing in the door of the sunroom and telling Brad Dolan to leave me alone. Sometimes I doze and see that underpass in the rain, with John Coffey standing beneath it in the shadows. It's never just a trick of the eye, in these little dreams; it's always him for sure, my big boy, just standing there and watching. I lie here and wait. I think about Janice, how I lost her, how she ran away red through my fingers in the rain, and I wait. We each owe a death, there are no exceptions, I know that, but sometimes, oh God, the Green Mile is so long.